THE PEKING INCIDENT

⚜⚜ ⚜⚜ ⚜⚜

THE PEKING

GEORGE ATCHESON

INCIDENT

Prentice-Hall, Inc., Englewood Cliffs, N.J.

The Peking Incident by George Atcheson
Copyright © 1973 by George Atcheson
All rights reserved. No part of this book may be
reproduced in any form or by any means, except
for the inclusion of brief quotations in a review,
without permission in writing from the publisher.
Printed in the United States of America
Prentice-Hall International, Inc., London
Prentice-Hall of Australia, Pty. Ltd., North Sydney
Prentice-Hall of Canada, Ltd., Toronto
Prentice-Hall of India Private Ltd., New Delhi
Prentice-Hall of Japan, Inc., Tokyo

10 9 8 7 6 5 4 3 2 1

Library of Congress Cataloging in Publication Data
Atcheson, George
The Peking incident.
I. Title.
PZ4.A848Pe [PS3551.T35]   813'.5'4   72–10992
ISBN 0–13–655647–7

For
CLAIRE

THE PEKING INCIDENT

SUNDAY

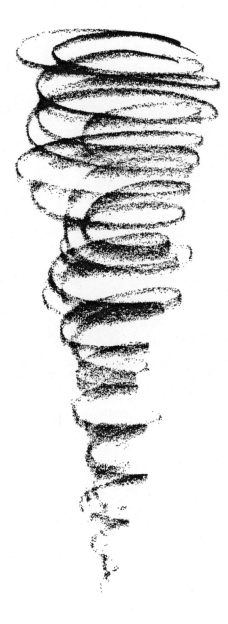

As John Edgerton leaned back against the devil screen, he felt the spongy plaster give under the weight of his shoulders. Old Yang, the innkeeper, squatted beside him, sharing the still gentle heat of the newly risen sun.

A contented sigh escaped the old man, and he fumbled for his tobacco pouch. Edgerton offered cigarettes and, wryly amused, watched as the paper was split and the precious grains transferred into the pouch. Only then was a pinch tamped into the small brass bowl of his pipe and Edgerton's match accepted.

Although the day promised to be another August scorcher, the air was light and fresh, still touched with a bit of the night's coolness. Squinting past the smoke of his own cigarette, Edgerton's gaze wandered idly down the hillside and across the broad plain below.

Checkered in a variety of greens and yellows, its newly gilded surface was laced with long slanting shadows. From the scattered hamlets wisps of smoke rose into the still air.

And eight miles to the east, the city was awakening, too. Boxed within its rectangular walls, it seemed to float on the land like an enormous raft, while above it the smokes of innumerable morning fires spread outward in a dingy canopy. Long rays of slanting sunlight penetrated the thickening pall at random, touching the city here and there as though with a pointer. First the faded tiles of the Forbidden City gleamed like newly burnished gold; then the blue concentric cones that roofed the Temple of Heaven flashed briefly with an electric fire. Only the emperors had worshiped there, on the great marble dais nearby which marked the precise center of the universe. The blue roofs of the Winter Palace, strewn among their gardens and artificial lakes, took their turn in the sun's eye, while on the hill behind the palace the squat stupa of the White Dagoba shone like old ivory. And all around these shifting spots of color the gray tiles of the city glinted dully, hammered out of tarnished pewter. Peking was waking up.

Far away on the eastern horizon, as though just liberated by the risen sun, a thick bank of low clouds rolled inland from the distant sea. Edgerton watched it contently, hardly thinking, aware only of a soft lassitude, the aftermath of lovemaking before dawn. Behind him, beyond the devil screen, beyond the inn gate standing open on massive rusty hinges, beyond the kitchen where a resentful mutter testified to Auntie Yang's annoyance at being left to prepare breakfast by herself, and beyond a musty parlor and an inner courtyard, Tamara lay sleeping in the darkened bedroom.

Old Yang gave a hesitant cough. "Will the *lao-yeh* and *mei-mei* stay here tonight?" the old man whispered in his rural dialect.

[3]

Edgerton suppressed an urge to grin. "No, uncle. We will drive back late this afternoon," he replied in Mandarin.

Nodding sagely the old man sighed, relieved at having disposed of an awkward question with finesse.

Edgerton was reminded of the first time that Yang had referred to Tamara as "Little Sister." He had been puzzled until it dawned on him why Yang had seized upon the diminutive. Only such a euphemism made it possible for him to refer to this wifelike creature who was so plainly not a wife . . . it was a device of delicacy. Thinking that it would amuse her, he had told Tamara about her new name. She had blushed at first, then frowned thoughtfully to herself before giving him a peculiarly inquisitive smile. It had made him wonder if he really knew her after all. But her shyness with the old couple soon diminished, and although she continued to treat them with an almost filial politeness, the relationship grew warm and relaxed. It was all the more remarkable because Tamara was only half Chinese, the mark of her Russian father unmistakable.

"It will be a nice day," Edgerton said absently. "But hot."

Yang nodded. "Too hot. And too much sun for the land." He pointed a gnarled finger. "Bad for the farmers and bad for us who must buy our food from them. If the harvest is bad they will keep it all for themselves."

"I thought it was dry, but not so bad as that. When you live in the city, water comes out of a pipe, not out of the sky."

"Yes. Only small rains this month, and the water quickly lost into the ground. And none last month at all. The gods give us very little water here; we need it all."

"The fields look rich now," Edgerton said, gesturing toward the land below them. It was hard to believe that the lush variety spread out down there was in any danger, or that all the labor it represented could come to nothing. "The harvest should be excellent."

"And it will be," Yang replied patiently. "But only if the rains come before it is too late."

Edgerton nodded, wondering what it must be like to be so at the mercy of the elements. If he ever acquired the insight to know, it would be because of a few incongruous friendships like this one with Old Yang. During his eighteen years in China, the officials he'd come to know and the sophisticated, Western-educated Chinese friends he'd made had taught him much about Chinese history and culture, while entertaining him with the details of innumerable government intrigues and business deals and scandals, but nothing that was really fundamental about the country.

[4]

Sometimes he had the feeling that he was floating in a tiny boat on the surface of a great ocean. He was kept so busy rowing, or trimming his sails, or making repairs, that there was no time left to do more than speculate on what was going on beneath him in the depths.

"We city foreigners are ignorant of such matters," he said.

"Yes," Yang replied, taking him at his word. Then, as though to soften any implied rebuke, he added, "But there is much in the city which I do not understand." Yang had consumed his morsel of tobacco when a clamor of rattling pots arose theatrically from the kitchen, and a muted wail of protest. Edgerton laughed silently.

Spreading his hands in a gesture of helplessness, Yang struggled stiffly to his feet. Another clang of ironware prodded him.

"Be still, old woman! I am coming as fast as I can," he called, shooting Edgerton an embarrassed glance. He placed the palms of his hands together and made a formal bow before ambling off to his chores, defiantly dilatory to the end.

The companionable interlude had been pleasing, but now Edgerton was glad to be alone and have to himself this view of the city where he lived and worked. As he watched, the wave of cloud surged slowly across the plain and flowed up and over the farther walls of the city, drowning the great watch towers and the temples and the palaces as surely as it drowned the meanest hovels.

As Edgerton's face relaxed, it grew strangely stern, as though reflecting old preoccupations. The frown between his brows and the lines bracketing his wide, ironic mouth seemed to deepen. His skull, thatched with gray-streaked brown hair, sat stubbornly forward on a sturdy neck. Because of his breadth, people were sometimes inclined to think him short. That is, until they stood close, and had to look up in order to meet the often skeptical gaze of those brown eyes. At forty, an aura of considerable physical power still clung to him.

He would have been surprised at how forbidding he looked. If asked, he would have described his imagined expression as affable. He felt affable. He enjoyed these weekend excursions in the Western Hills, with their quietness and comfortable, if spurious, air of domesticity. He didn't want much domesticity these days, not as a regular thing. Marriage, he had discovered to his bitter regret, was not for him. And the divorce which ended it had been painful; he never spoke of it now and thought of it only seldom. He had plunged into marriage like a channel swimmer . . . and had got cramps before he was a mile out. He smiled grimly at the ridiculous comparison. The relationship was entirely too close; he was not likely to be that trusting ever again. He looked up and saw only masses of swarming clouds. The city was gone,

[5]

sunk like Atlantis, erased as though its three thousand years of life had never been. Edgerton stared across a sea of white.

His first post had been Peking. There had been others later, but none approached the ancient capital in charm or had the ineffable sense of adventure which clung so tenaciously to Peking. And now it looked as if it might be his last post. Franklin Procter, not longer ago than the day before yesterday, had alluded to the probability that Edgerton would be ordered back to Washington before another year had passed, offering this opinion in the manner of a bearer of glad tidings. Edgerton wanted to protest, to argue . . . but that would have been senseless; he knew he was overdue for transfer.

He didn't want to go back to Washington. He'd served there and knew what it was like: dull and pretentious, and far too theoretical. Besides, he couldn't afford the time. China was changing too quickly for him to go away; he'd miss too much. He had a premonition that if he went back to Washington, he'd never see China again. Certainly not this China: his and Tamara's China.

An attenuated rumble drifted to him faintly. He searched the sky before he saw them: five winged dots, banking and glinting as they circled upward out of the overcast, like flies climbing a sunbeam in a hot room.

Edgerton watched them morosely.

High above the city they wheeled, rising over him in a ragged vee, the roaring of their engines throbbing with the deeper pulse of some harmonic. Twin-engined bombers. The Japanese were off to harry the guerrillas in the mountains far behind him, or perhaps they were headed farther to the southwest to bomb the home base of the Communists in the caves of Yenan.

There was small comfort in the thought that either mission was probably a waste. The mere sight of them recalled the tremendous military power Japan had brought to bear on China. And now, as the war went into its second year, the mass of it was still increasing.

Edgerton wished he hadn't seen the bombers. To hell with them, he decided abruptly, pushing them from his mind. This was Sunday, and the Japanese, like the papers and problems of the Chancery, would simply have to wait their turn on Monday. All he intended to do for the present was to bask like a lizard in the sunlight, and savor his contentment.

He nodded drowsily, then yawned. He hadn't slept very well . . . in the city, discretion kept them from sleeping the whole night together, and he simply wasn't used to sharing a bed. On previous excursions with Tamara, he'd grown used to merely dozing happily

[6]

until long after midnight. Then a deep sleep would usually come and hold him until Old Yang arrived with coffee.

But this morning he'd begun to awaken at the beginnings of first light, to find himself lying close against Tamara's back, the warm crevice between her buttocks sandwiching his half-hardness neatly. Still more asleep than otherwise, he'd been caught by the whimsy of trying to arouse her without waking her. . . .

Smiling to himself, he'd pressed even closer to her, sliding a wary hand around to cover her navel. His hips moved in reflex, and a pulsing, hardening throb went through his loins that very nearly made him groan aloud. Tamara didn't stir, nor did the rhythm of her breathing alter. Emboldened, he sent the hand slowly upward to cup the marvelous soft firmness of a breast, the nipple barely felt at the tip of his finger. Happily his thumb and fingertip caressed it, feeling it swell. Wanting to kiss it, he'd had to content himself with kissing the soft hair at the nape of her neck. Unbidden, his hand shifted to her breasts, repeating its fondling, then wandered southward, palm flat against her skin as though groping blindly toward some mysterious goal of its own that was too magnetic to be resisted. His hips had begun moving with a slow, automatic regularity, the silken friction of her flesh bringing him visions of mounting her from behind like a stallion. Then came a strange mixing of emotions, as the pure hunger of his body became interwoven with a sudden, heart-bursting acknowledgment of love for this slumbering girl, this woman who so delighted and amused him, whose company was so comforting.

He wanted to wake her then, and stop this foolish, sneaky game. As passionate as was her own nature, she should be enjoying the loveplay. It wasn't fair to let sleep hide it from her. But his errant hand had continued its explorations. When his mind located it, it was smoothing the soft swatch of fur she wore between her legs like a black g-string, and he, poor well meaning, selfish man, was too far along to stop. Combing deeper, his finger found her secret place. Gently he touched her, probing cautiously, expecting it to be sleeping, too, and unready for him, but a warm, moist little mouth opened and took hold of his finger, seeming to pull it inward.

Tamara exploded into giggles. Turning in his arms, bright-eyed with laughter, she gave him her mouth to kiss and slanted her leg to offer his fingers free play.

"Sly minx!" he whispered hoarsely, delighted with the trick she'd played on him. Slowly, savoring it, he drew her tongue into his mouth.

"Mmmmm," she murmured, sending fingers that were like tufts of feathers to find and stroke him, enmeshing him ever more deeply in

[7]

these familiar mysteries of love, compelling him to perform the caressing rituals of worship which never seemed to change yet were always new and indescribably exciting. Thus captive, he left her lips to mouth her nipples, swollen now to the size of berries, softer and sweeter. Cupping her breasts in his hands, he tongued first one and then the other, and felt her chest heave and her breathing deepen.

Slowly her pelvis began to gyrate, rustling the tangled sheet, beckoning him. Almost with regret, his mouth left her breasts and began to rove across her undulating belly, working its inexorable way to what had been the playground of his fingers.

Tamara's back arched; dimly, as though from a great distance, he heard her groan, then wild fingers began tugging at his ears and hair, and stroking his temples.

For a space of time forever immeasurable he was a lost man. Finally some still sane part of himself told him he had to stop, had to enter her soon—now—while he still had anything left to give her. After a parting touch of the tongue, he pushed himself to his knees, shaking his head to clear it. Dazed with heat and happiness, he looked down at her as she lay beneath him, open and inviting, waiting to receive him. Then he entered her and taking her into his arms, drove deeply into her, feeling her arms and her legs embrace him. Gasping his name repeatedly, she locked herself to the cadence of his plunging hips as he strove to carry her to the paradise where she was already taking him, lost in a throbbing storm of mutual possession.

Edgerton sighed happily and shifted his shoulders, sending a rattle of loose plaster into the dry grass. She was an incredible woman, ever lovely and desirable, and the mere thought of her filled his heart with a marvelous contentment. Riddled as it still was with vestiges of his old puritanism, his soul knew delight in the presence of her innocent sensuality. She could be so sweetly wanton in her own strange, pure way. From the very start of their love affair, she'd disarm him, dissolving his dour skepticism and habitual wariness with her insistence that great chunks of life could be experienced if one only reached out for them.

Blind to his surroundings, he saw only the dawn-lighted bedroom and relived his joy in her and his boyish pride in the durability of that early morning erection. He had to smile and shake his head at the memory: Hey, everybody! Look at me! And the memory of his sweet Tamara . . . the secret taste of her remained fresh in his mouth, like some mythic honey . . . lovely, incredibly lovely.

He yawned, thinking of Tamara's childlike fall back into sleep,

[8]

while he, relaxed and happy, and as drained of tension as he was of passion, had lain there pondering the changes her love had made in what seemed, now that he looked back on it, a lonely and somewhat barren life. It struck him as odd that only in the past year had he become conscious of the blinders he'd put on after Elizabeth's sordid and commonplace betrayal. Head down and plodding, he'd tramped a rut into his life without even knowing it. But now Tamara was teaching him to know it. Lying there and thinking thus, he'd become restless. A wedge of pale sky seemed to beckon him through the window. Carefully he had slipped out of bed.

Tamara's breathing faltered and her arm reached out to the empty place beside her, then she sighed and went on sleeping. Touched by that instinctive gesture, he found himself watching her as he dressed, wondering if she were becoming too dependent on him. She must not do that . . . not with him so close to leaving. To his dismay, an unfamiliar tightness had taken him by the throat. It wasn't until he was out in the courtyard and had his first cigarette going that he began to feel his old self again.

Recalling the moment, Edgerton lost some of his earlier delight with himself. Tamara needed to be protected from herself, from her own unreasoning optimism. He'd been like that once, but Elizabeth had cured him. Well, no . . . that was neither fair nor accurate, though why he should worry about being fair to that bitch, he couldn't imagine. "Life" had cured him, with Elizabeth being merely the instrument. But it had been a sordid and unpleasant experience to be treated that way, replaced without warning, without a chance to throw up some sort of defense. It was something he'd not wish on anyone.

Well, a year was a long time, he thought, yawning widely. The sun's warmth had been growing steadily, and the weight of his eyelids with it. He stubbed out his cigarette, and let his chin sink onto his chest.

Very gradually he became aware of a noise intruding from somewhere on his right. He considered it sluggishly, but could not name it: murmur and clank and shuffle. He opened his eyes.

Approaching along the road way below him was a small detachment of Japanese soldiers marching in single file, their rifles slung across their backs. The narrow road was steep just there, and they leaned into it, their faces sweating heavily and their eyes seeing no farther than a yard or two in front of their feet.

Although Western men, if they had no women with them, were seldom bothered by Japanese troops, Edgerton was tempted to retire quickly into the inn and avoid all contact with them.

[9]

But it was too late. The soldier in charge had seen him, and had growled an order to his men that straightened them up and brought them into step. He was a short, thick-shouldered man, with long arms and an incongruous dark red beard that gave a saturnine cast to his weathered face.

Sitting there, Edgerton felt conspicuous, uncomfortably aware of being the focus of unfriendly eyes. He wondered what they were doing there.

During their year-long occupation of North China, the Japanese had shown little interest in the countryside. Except for foraging expeditions and occasional punitive strikes against the guerrillas, they left security in the hands of the Chinese rural police—feeble hands, but adequate most of the time. It was only since spring that Edgerton had begun hearing stories about the difficulties the Japanese were having keeping the railroads open, particularly the lines running southward. The guerrillas were becoming more numerous and bolder. From time to time, they tore up whole sections of track, and threw the rails onto bonfires made of the wooden ties. In a country virtually without highways, the rail system was vital to Japanese operations, and replacement rails had to be shipped all the way from Japan.

But the nearest railway was miles from here, and it had been weeks since any guerrilla foray of note. Except for the period immediately following the fighting at the Marco Polo Bridge, Edgerton had not heard of Japanese soldiers coming into these out-of-the-way hills. Seeing them now made him apprehensive that some new antiguerrilla campaign was beginning, and that he'd brought Tamara into the middle of it.

The leader—Edgerton saw that he was a sergeant from the frayed chevrons pinned to his sleeve—brought his men to a halt and dismissed them. Some of them sat down at once and lighted cigarettes. Edgerton's car, an old Willys-Knight, was parked just off the road beside the north wall of the inn, and several of them wandered over to inspect it.

But the sergeant was all business. His bearded chin jutting, he sauntered over. Scowling fiercely, he barked a guttural question.

"I cannot speak Japanese," Edgerton told him in Mandarin.

"Who are you?" the sergeant demanded, shifting easily into the unmusical Chinese that was spoken in Manchuria.

"I am an American official from the Legation in Peking."

"Let me see your papers." The sergeant was plainly determined to demonstrate a tough, no-nonsense-from-the-white-man attitude.

Edgerton shrugged and patted his empty pockets. "They are inside," he said thoughtlessly, immediately regretting the words. The last thing he wanted was for this lout to see Tamara. With his men at his back, in this remote place he might be tempted to get nasty.

Edgerton pointed to the Diplomatic Corps emblem on the rear bumper of his car. "I need no papers when I have that on my car," he bluffed evenly, trying to sound both positive and polite at the same time.

The sergeant stamped over to inspect the emblem, then peered in through the dusty windows. Evidently not much impressed he spat pointedly into the dust. Nevertheless, he was grinning when he got back to Edgerton, his duty performed.

"I speak English," he announced, tapping his chest with pride.

"You speak very well," Edgerton replied, somewhat relieved.

The Japanese squatted down next to him. "You have cigarette?"

Edgerton handed him the pack, gesturing for him to keep it.

Bowing with a polite hiss, the sergeant took out a cigarette and handed it ceremoniously to Edgerton before selecting one for himself and pocketing the package. Edgerton provided matches. When both cigarettes were lighted the sergeant stowed the matches away as well, then gave vent to a loud sigh of satisfaction.

Sitting there smoking—a charade of sociability—Edgerton was keenly aware of the unknowableness of his companion.

Had he come from another planet, the sergeant could not have been more alien, his real nature more obscure. A few things could be guessed about him; he probably was a good husband and devoted father to his children. He respected his ancestors and revered his Emperor. He had the look of being tough and resourceful, someone who had risen to a position of authority in a mean and iron-disciplined army. Living the squalid life of the Asian soldier, he would be familiar with both great risk and danger, the brutalizing mistreatment of his superiors . . . and the soldiers' diversions of drinking and whoring . . . and in the field, carte blanche to loot and rape.

Certainly Edgerton could mean nothing to him, beyond being the provider of a few moments' diversion. As human beings—and he thought again of Tamara with a gripping renewal of apprehension—the Chinese would mean even less. The atrocities of Japanese troops had been so well documented and so widely published as to become clichés already. Edgerton, like so many others, had seen the stacks of photographs: beheading contests among the officers; bayonet practice on live prisoners; prisoners tied together to be doused with gasoline and set afire; rape contests . . . Edgerton saw again a soldier's bespectacled face grinning—proudly and rather foolishly—into the camera

[11]

while he mounted a gray-haired peasant woman from behind, having propped her limp body against a convenient wheelbarrow. The Japanese were addicted to photography and left their film to be developed in Chinese shops everywhere they went. Apparently they never expected copies to be made. Or perhaps they didn't care, assuming that their almost casual brutality conformed to some sort of military norm. Well, maybe it did.

The sergeant pinched out the coal of his cigarette and put the stub in his pocket. As he got to his feet Edgerton instinctively rose with him. The sergeant barked an order, and while his men assembled he turned to Edgerton.

"America Japan friend!" he proclaimed, holding out his hand.

Edgerton shook it, impressed with his calluses. "Japan America friend!" seemed an appropriate rejoinder, so he made it.

The Japanese beamed at his successful diplomatic exchange and saluted.

Feeling slightly foolish, Edgerton saluted.

The soldiers observed these amenities in goggle-eyed silence.

The sergeant rattled off a series of commands and the detachment marched away in the direction they had come, backs rigid and stamping their feet as though on parade. In a few seconds they had dropped down and out of sight in the encroaching mist. Edgerton looked after them curiously.

Old Yang peered apprehensively around the devil screen. Edgerton gave him an encouraging wave of the hand, and the bald head disappeared.

Edgerton glanced at his watch: it was almost time for breakfast. He stretched, knuckled his eyes, and looked around. He felt disoriented by the episode with the soldiers, but everything was as usual.

Inside, the smell of coffee and of bacon frying came to him from the small dark kitchen to his left, and the sound of the Yangs at one of their interminable wrangles. Edgerton was suddenly very hungry.

As he entered the small inner courtyard the bedroom door opened and Tamara appeared. Her blue cotton robe revealed an un-Chinese fullness of breast and hip. Her warm brown eyes regarded him thoughtfully, the delicate oval of her face framed in her thick hair.

Stopping in the middle of the courtyard, Edgerton stared, counting the items of her beauty; wide cheekbones faintly splashed with freckles, a straight nose only slightly flared at the nostrils, eyes barely slanted by the hereditary fold in the eyelids, round and sometimes stubborn chin under full and generous lips that looked always ready to smile. She was dazzling.

A discreet and apologetic cough sounded behind him. He turned

[12]

and saw Old Yang maneuvering his tray through the door. Wryly amused, he could only stand and watch as the old man bustled self-consciously about the business of setting the wicker table for breakfast.

The old graveyard lay hot and still in its grove of pines. A few doves cooed half-heartedly in the high branches, and the dry chirp of crickets sounded in the pine needles. Although the treetops stirred occasionally, no breath of air reached the ground.

A rock was digging into his hip and Edgerton shifted sleepily, Tamara's thigh pleasantly firm under the nape of his neck.

They had spent a quiet morning together, reading in the courtyard until it became too hot, then returned to the cool dimness of the bedroom to make love and then to doze until it was time for lunch.

Wrapping their sandwiches and a bottle of wine in newspaper, they had strolled down to the Summer Palace. Edgerton was apprehensive at first, thinking of the Japanese patrol, but he saw no sign of them.

Edgerton didn't tell Tamara about the Japanese. For one thing, he didn't want to worry her; for another, there was something about the idea of her vulnerability in the face of their unbridled power that disturbed him deeply. He didn't want to talk about it.

As usual, they inspected the arrogant beauty of the dead Empress's marble boat, and drank tea in one of the pavilions, enjoying the light breeze that riffled the surface of the lake. They had planned to picnic in the grotto where the Jade Fountain flowed out of the hillside, but the arrival of a gaggle of schoolchildren on an outing had sent them retreating up the hill to this refuge.

"Your Mr. Procter spoke to me Friday," Tamara said, breaking the silence.

Edgerton was instantly awake. "Not my Mr. Procter," he objected with pretended casualness. "What did he have to say?"

"Oh, nothing really; what you would call passing the time of day."

Edgerton snorted noncommittally.

"This was the first time," Tamara went on thoughtfully. "Usually he just nods politely and mutters."

Edgerton was uneasy. "And this time?"

"It is nothing, I suppose, but I had the feeling he was inspecting me."

"Damn!" Edgerton sat up restlessly. "Did that bother you?"

She smiled slightly and nodded, her eyes focused somewhere in the distance. "A little. He is rather overwhelming; so aristocratic."

"Yes, he's that all right," he said, and then without quite knowing why, he asked, "Did you pass inspection?"

[13]

"No, I don't think I did," she said, raising her eyes and looking into his with an indefinable expression.

"I'm sorry," Edgerton said, feeling terribly inadequate. Damn Procter for a meddling old woman! Only just arrived and already shoving his well-bred nose into matters which did not concern him. "I'm so sorry."

She tried to smile, and reached for his hand. Her fingers were cold. "Don't worry about it, John, about any of it. It was bound to come and we have both known it."

"I don't see why . . ."

"But of course you do, my dear. You lead a very public life. We have tried to be discreet, but in your small foreign community, how many secrets can there be, after all?"

Edgerton fidgeted, the aftertaste of the wine suddenly bitter in his mouth. He fumbled with cigarettes and matches: horse manure rolled in newspaper could not have tasted worse. People never gave up trying to impose their rules on you. And of all the busybodies, Americans were the most sanctimonious and determined. "Bunch of meddlers!"

Tamara smiled faintly, then shrugged. "Even my poor mother is becoming one of them. It is hard for old people to accept the fact that the times are changing."

Edgerton flushed uncomfortably, remembering that her mother was not more than three or four years older than he was. Tamara didn't notice.

". . . and of course she is anxious for me to avoid her own mistakes." She gave a short sarcastic laugh. "It is strange to think of oneself as someone else's mistake, but unavoidable." Her face broke then, like a piece of fragile porcelain, and the tears burst from her eyes.

A nameless pain clutched at Edgerton's heart and he took her in his arms and held her tightly, feeling the rack of her sobs and the wetness of her tears through his shirt. Kissing the top of her bent head, he tasted the clean fragrance of her hair and the bitterness of his own impotence.

Gradually her sobbing subsided. She sniffled and felt in her pocket for a handkerchief, drawing a little away from him. She wiped her eyes and blew her nose, and at last she smiled at him shakily.

Edgerton leaned forward and kissed her. Her soft lips tasted of salt and he felt an indescribable hunger for her, and the desire to possess her and protect her ached in him. A momentary glimpse of life without her taunted him cruelly. He wanted to tell her, but he couldn't speak.

She took a cigarette, holding it awkwardly, waiting for him to strike a match, then puffed inexpertly. The moment passed, and Edgerton sensed that some mysterious opportunity, a time for saying something of importance, had been lost . . . now he would never know what.

While Tamara gathered up the picnic remnants, he found a stick and scratched a shallow hole to bury them. The tiny effort seemed to exhaust them and they lay down on the pine needles, side by side and hand in hand, and let the weighted atmosphere press down on them.

Tamara slept, her lips parted slightly.

Through half-closed eyes, Edgerton watched the tops of the pines blur and waver against the hot blue sky. Under the sedating heat his eyelids drooped, and Edgerton slept.

As he woke an hour later his eyes wandered idly through the grove and out onto the plain below them where the mist had long since burned away. Long feathers of dust marked the passage of distant and unseen vehicles. Minute figures dotted the farmland, toiling at their interminable business. The cloud of suspended dust and smoke over the city had thickened throughout the day, and seemed now almost to throb with the life beneath it.

Edgerton's unhappy gaze settled on a little clump of shacks near the bottom of the hill. In a small square of green a tiny man scattered fertilizer with a long-handled ladle, while from the open *k'ang* buried in the ground beside his house another tiny figure, a woman with a kerchief on her head, kept him supplied with buckets of the precious liquid. This was their Sunday in the country. It was a brutal, exhausting life that broke the people who were born to it.

Moodily, Edgerton found himself thinking of his own life. His concern with visas and protocol, of formal calls and notes and *aides-memoires*, of reports and estimates of the situation, had the look of an esoteric ritual, the examining of chicken guts for portents of the future. What was it all worth? He grinned wryly; in either case it was crap, pure and simple. He and that farmer were destined to go on ladling it out, each up to his ankles in his own peculiar variety. And, in the end, whose were the more useful acts? It was a question he would not care to have to argue. It reminded him of the futility which seemed to haunt even the smallest step forward in this wretched country.

Only the year before, a reconciliation of sorts had occurred between China's two major factions, and it had seemed that Chiang's Nationalists and Mao's Communists might postpone their differences and come to grips with the age-old cruelties afflicting the people.

It was Chiang Kai-shek, after all, who had inherited the revolutionary mantle of Sun Yat-sen, along with control of the Kuomintang, or

[15]

Nationalist Party. But fear of his Communist rivals had kept him from pursuing the reforms promised by Sun. Feeling threatened he had sought to bolster his rural authority by supporting the feudal hierarchy of landlords and money-lenders, and to deal with the Communists by undertaking over the years a series of costly and unsuccessful "bandit suppression campaigns." To accomplish this, he bought time with concessions to the Japanese, primarily the removal of anti-Japanese elements from the northern provinces bordering their puppet state of Manchukuo.

But the Communists considered Japanese ambitions as a threat of pressing urgency. In one of history's more bizarre episodes, they prevailed upon a progressive Kuomintang general to kidnap Chiang Kai-shek and coerce him into meeting with them and agreeing to a new priority for resisting Japan. Thus, after a decade of the bitterest civil war, a viable coalition had again seemed possible.

Since that was precisely what the Japanese didn't want, they watched developments apprehensively. Just the same, they might not have acted had not a series of seemingly minor events occurred near Peking. Although the precise sequence of these events was still unclear, what Edgerton did know was that an apparently accidental encounter took place in July of 1937 between the Chinese garrison and a Japanese force on maneuvers near the Marco Polo Bridge. A truce was arranged, but then a Japanese officer was found to be missing. When his comrades went looking for him in a nearby town, the Chinese commander refused them entry. There was more shooting, another truce was called, then it, too, was broken. Finally a local agreement to prevent further incidents was signed by the two contending generals. Acting on insufficient information reaching him in far-off Nanking, Chiang Kai-shek repudiated the agreement. In Tokyo, there were rumors—false ones—that Kuomintang troops were being rushed into the neutralized zone, violating the understanding between the two governments. In two weeks, Japanese reinforcements were pouring south from Manchuria, reluctantly authorized by the conservative civilian government of Japan who claimed that, under such provocation, they could not do otherwise. By the time Peking fell bloodlessly on August 8, a full-scale though undeclared war was underway against China. The prevailing belief was that what became known as the Marco Polo Bridge Incident had been contrived by the Japanese as a pretext for war before the new coalition of Chinese factions could alter the status quo in North China.

Bitterly opposed to them as Edgerton was, he could understand their feeling of frustration, of being unfairly blocked. Latecomers to

[16]

the competition for Chinese markets and resources, Japan had arrived to find "spheres of influence" already staked out, and "most favored nation" treaties in effect between the Western powers and an apparently docile and corrupt Chinese government. No provision had been made for the admission of new members to the club.

So they set out to take what they wanted, and by now North China had become virtually a Japanese colony, the fiction of a "provisional" Chinese government notwithstanding. China's long coastline and all her ports were in Japanese hands, and all her major cities except Hankow and Chungking. Hankow would fall to them before winter. It was inevitable. Edgerton hated to think of what would happen to China then. At least, the Western traders, though greedy, had been moderately benign. The Japanese couldn't seem to grasp the illogic of killing off their potential customers. Sometimes there seemed no end to their blindness, their intractability.

"What are you thinking?"

Tamara's question made him start, and he turned to her blankly. Awake now, her face was calm and clear, and her eyes full of gentle affection.

When he told her, she laughed, then became quickly serious. "You like it though, don't you? Your work, I mean," she asked, surprising him a little.

He looked at her thoughtfully. "It is the only work I know anything about. I do it well enough, I suppose. There are ups and downs, of course, but on the whole . . . well, yes, I like it." He had to laugh at himself. "How is that for a grudging answer?"

"What do you like about it?" she persisted.

He shifted around so as to sit cross-legged, facing her. "You would have made a good policeman," he said.

"Never mind me." She turned to lean on her elbow. Her breasts shifted softly under the thin cotton, and Edgerton's mind wandered. "Answer my question."

"Yes. Well . . . , " Edgerton said and harrumphed importantly. "I am glad you asked that question. What do I like about it? Well, the pay is not too bad. . . ."

Tamara poked him with a sharp fingernail.

"That's not an easy question," he protested. I haven't asked it myself in years. I suppose it is the idea of being in the middle of things, although that's often an illusion. But even here there is enough reality to make it all worth while, although some of it gets to be routine. You know the sort of thing: trying to keep Americans out of trouble, trying to find out what is really happening in order to inform Washington,

[17]

trying to get the Provisional Government to govern, trying to persuade the Japanese not to behave like a horde of savages, and to abide by their own solemn promises of fair treatment for foreign business. And to get Washington to listen to you when you do learn something, and—once and for all—to realize that while the Japanese may respect firmness and strength, they have only contempt for nagging moralizers." He threw back his head and laughed. "How's that for a job description?"

"Very interesting," Tamara said.

Unexpectedly, two bombers grumbled into view and flew slowly overhead. He turned to watch them, wondering if they were part of the flight he had seen that morning. Three more straggled into the sky from behind the mountain, the last one trailing far behind and smoking heavily from one engine. He thought of the predictable headlines in Monday's puppet Chinese press: great boasts of camps and supply dumps destroyed and "bandits" killed. The Japanese were persuaded, apparently, that air power used against an agrarian and scattered enemy did more than merely terrorize civilians and blow great holes in the countryside.

The lead bomber dipped a wing and began a cumbersome descending turn. One by one the others followed, disappearing behind the city's smoky mantle.

"There is a good job," he said, indicating the vanishing bombers with his chin. "Watching the Japanese. Peking is a good place for that."

"Really? But they are at their worst here."

"So much the better, perhaps. That sounds callous, since they have destroyed so much and killed so many people. But if we can learn enough about them, maybe we can outsmart them instead of merely killing them and having them kill us. As it is, we don't know much and even that is mostly wrong."

Edgerton realized that he had never talked to her about his work before. He had always supposed that she was not interested. "So perhaps seeing them at their worst is the best way: victorious and arrogant, and as impatient as children when they don't get what they want. Japan's a great power; we've been very slow to admit it."

"Very interesting indeed. I understand you better now." Her eyes fell. "It's strange; I've known you for more than a year, known you so well . . ." She hesitated, blushing. ". . . and now I have learned something new—something important."

Edgerton wanted to ask her what it was, but an eddy of air passed through the grove just then, and Tamara shivered and hugged herself.

[18]

The instant slipped away and so did the question. He looked at his watch.

"I guess we'd better be getting back to the inn," he said. "It's almost four, and the Japanese will be closing the city gates at six."

They got to their feet, and Tamara brushed at her skirt and tucked in her blouse. The smile she gave him was an easy one. Edgerton drew her to him and kissed her, and felt the long touch of her body and her legs. He was happy and content, he told himself—why shouldn't he be? Everything would work out . . . somehow or other.

🐜🐜

Lurching and clanging, the dusty streetcar worked its slow way northward, hot blue flashes arcing into the night air from its overhead trolley. Not far ahead the tandem watch towers of the Ch'ien Men squatted on the Tartar Wall, their tiers of dark and empty windows eyeing the boulevard as it approached, pierced the wall, and passed under them into the Tartar city.

The broad avenue teemed. Rickshaws, trucks, carts, taxis, barrows, bicycles, and laden coolies vied with swarms of strollers taking the evening air. Brightly lighted stores, neon flashing and radios blaring stridently, beckoned for attention, and the sidewalks were lined with stalls. Just to the east of the gate, in the shadow of the wall itself, lay the Main Railroad Station. The evening train from Tientsin had just arrived, and its disembarking passengers fought their way across the cobbled surface of the Ch'ien Men Chieh as though they owned it, thrusting their bundles and suitcases ahead of them, shoving, shouting, cursing, laughing.

The motorman tramped more impatiently than ever on his footbell, his hopes of meeting his schedule dwindling.

From a seat near the middle of the car, Serge Puhalski looked out upon the tumult, an expression of aloof contempt twisting his thin mouth. A shock of yellow hair jutted over his narrow forehead, shading it from the flickering ceiling lights. His long angular face was etched with bitter lines and his eyes suggested wet blue stones. One might have thought him frail, he looked so tall and thin in his shabby suit. One might have, until one saw his huge hands, long-fingered and backed by webs of veins, and the thick wrists which poked out of his frayed cuffs like hairy two-by-fours.

Puhalski was annoyed. He had planned rather carefully to miss all this Sunday-night confusion. But plans meant nothing in this back-

[19]

ward country. The only certainty was that the less important the transaction, the more time it took to conclude. The sale of the opium —a deal between professionals—had gone smoothly: no haggling and no formalities. The sale of Nevensky's second-rate diamond had involved one tenth the money and taken twice as long.

Puhalski told himself to be patient. Someday he'd give up the role of go-between for other Russians, and let the fools fend for themselves. But not yet; it was a nuisance, but a profitable one. And his position in the opium trade was still too insecure for anything but sporadic profits. Just the same . . . his fingers brushed lightly over the bulky envelope pinned into the lining of his jacket, and he smiled tightly. Serge Puhalski would teach them a thing or two before he was through.

The streetcar ground to an uneven halt, brake shoes squealing. The standing passengers swayed and stumbled and clutched at one another for support, and good-natured rebukes were shouted at the motorman. Puhalski groaned irritably and stuck his head out the window. Two automobiles had locked bumpers on the tracks ahead. The drivers had dismounted and were already jumping up and down on the bumpers and loudly disputing the question of fault for the benefit of the inevitable crowd growing around them. Puhalski cursed under his breath.

He got to his feet and began to push rudely toward the rear of the car, favoring his game leg and heedless of protests against his roughness. As he shouldered his way down the steps a line of honking cars began to creep past. He retreated a step and a gust of garlic-laden breath doused him from behind.

A gap opened between two cars, then widened invitingly. Puhalski jumped, but as his foot hit the pavement his knee began to give way. Experience told him to fall loosely and let his momentum roll him forward out of the way of the cars. Torn clothes were preferable to the pain of a dislocation. As he went down, the bright white and red of a Diplomatic Corps emblem gleamed at him from the bumper of the car, and he heard the screech of brakes.

He picked himself up and glared angrily at the driver of the car. To his astonishment, he recognized the man . . . and the woman with him. Even as he struggled to hold his face in an expression of simple outrage, his mind began to race ahead, weighing possibilities, considering precautions. He worked his shoulder gingerly and began to dust himself off. Pretending to look down at his clothing, he gave the woman a quick glance. It had been almost a year since he had heard that she'd taken up with a foreigner. He had never bothered to check the story, nor would he have ever guessed that it was *this* foreigner.

[20]

"Are you all right?" the American asked him in Chinese, thrusting his big head out of the window.

Scowling, Puhalski silently checked the contents of his pockets. The condescension of the driver's assumption that he spoke no English infuriated him. "I'm okay," he said shortly.

"You took me by surprise," the American said. "Did the car hit you?"

"No, no thanks to you. You should learn to be more careful," Puhalski told him. "Or hire someone to drive for you." The retort pleased him.

"I'm very sorry," the American replied, unruffled. "May I give you a lift?"

Puhalski almost laughed in his face. No wonder the Americans were fooled and cheated everywhere they went. They had neither the wit to know when they were being insulted, nor the spine to do anything about it. At the mention of a lift the woman averted her face. Puhalski could guess what she was thinking, and was tempted to accept the offer if only to provoke her. He hadn't forgotten what she'd said to him once when he spoke to her on the street. Nor had she, apparently . . . the snotty bitch. And now this stupid American had her. Edgerton: that was his name.

The cars behind had begun to honk impatiently. To hell with them he thought. He finished dusting his trousers.

The American got out of the car. Puhalski was surprised at the size of him. Well-fed bastard! The American fumbled in his pockets, and it dawned on Puhalski that he was about to be offered money.

"I never ride with Americans," Puhalski snarled. Edgerton might be big, but he looked soft and Puhalski knew he could take him in a fight. It would be especially easy since the American would insist on boxing like a bloody gentleman, and especially pleasant since the woman would be watching.

Edgerton seemed unperturbed. "Everyone to his own choice," he said mildly. "At least, let me pay to have your suit cleaned." He handed over several Chinese dollar bills, more than enough.

Puhalski threw it at Edgerton's feet. "Keep your shitty money," he said.

A groan went up from the watchers in the streetcar at this fiscal sacrilege.

The American looked at him in amazement. "You must be out of your head," he said calmly, stooping to retrieve the banknotes.

Had his knee felt stronger, Puhalski would have kicked him. The insufferable self-confidence of the wealthy: dispense some money and

[21]

everything will be all right. The universal cure-all. He had more money in the envelope in his coat than the American saw in a month. And it was half his; that was his arrangement with Colonel Tanaka.

Colonel Tanaka: the name drew him up short. What was the matter with him tonight? he wondered. He just wasn't thinking clearly, wasn't thinking at all.

A skinny, dirty hand was thrust out of one of the streetcar windows, backed by the wizened, bright-eyed face of an old woman grinning toothlessly. "I won't throw it away; give it to me, *go-yeh*," she squawked, making the watchers laugh. "I will wish you a long life and many grandchildren."

The American grinned easily and put a bill in her hand. "Thank you, Old Auntie," he said, reverting to Chinese. "I am grateful for your blessing." He turned to Puhalski and his face sobered. "If you're not hurt, and want only to be insulting," he said, loud enough for all to hear, "perhaps you'll be good enough to get the hell out of my way."

"Well said," someone commented from the streetcar. "The Russians are without manners."

The remark enraged Puhalski. If you were white and poorly dressed, the damned Chinks knew you were a Russian and treated you with contempt. He was tempted to retort—but didn't. It was not the time to indulge himself. Colonel Tanaka didn't like this American, and Puhalski could now understand why.

From behind the dirty windshield, the woman now watched him with worried eyes. "Your turn will come," Puhalski said loudly, looking at the woman and meaning them both. With as much dignity as he could muster, he limped away. The onlookers parted docilely before him.

He gained the center of the sidewalk and sighed with relief, glad to leave the scene of his humiliation by the American.

The meeting had been a strange occurrence, more than a coincidence. More than once events had combined to goad him in a direction he had previously shunned. And every time he'd profited. For the first time, he felt he now had a personal, an intimate, stake in Colonel Tanaka's scheme. Anything Tanaka wanted to do that would embarrass this American was all right with him . . . within reason, of course.

That was the trouble. There was always a stumbling block, in this case Andrei Sobolov. Sobolov! he muttered disgustedly. The fat old fart. He'd not thought of Sobolov all day: a deliberate avoidance. Sobolov was a gutless eunuch, oozing morality from every pore, and good for nothing. And he was also the interpreter at the American

Legation. It galled Puhalski to have to depend on him, but fate had given him the man, and Colonel Tanaka was demanding that he be used.

He smiled thinly, thinking of the look on John Edgerton's face when he would discover that his Legation's faithful translator had been feeding information to the Japanese. Others would learn of it eventually. He'd not look so smug when his superiors in Washington demanded explanations, nor would that half-caste bitch think so much of him either. Puhalski's smile broadened; this meeting on the street had been an omen. Things were going to work out all right, provided . . .

Well, it wasn't the first time he'd been required to make the best of poor material, Puhalski reminded himself. And there was the American. Just the thought of the man buoyed his spirits. Tanaka would have been gratified, having more than once questioned Puhalski's enthusiasm. But Tanaka would never learn that he gave a damn about the American, just as he would not be told about the connection between the American and the half-caste woman. That morsel of information would be reserved for Puhalski's personal use. Being Provost Marshal gave Tanaka more than his share of advantages as it was.

The night air was hot and still and, in spite of the long drought, weighed heavily as though a storm were coming. Puhalski squeegeed the sweat of his forehead with a finger and cursed the weather for making him jumpy and careless. Perhaps he was trying to juggle too many plates at once: one slip, and he stood to break them all. Puhalski shook his head; to hell with that! This was no time for self-doubt, and Sobolov no fit obstacle to an old campaigner like himself.

Ahead of him, the crowd parted suddenly, and Puhalski found himself confronting an oncoming trio of Japanese soldiers. Red-faced with drink, they swaggered along, as contemptuous of the crowd as he had been, but with a difference. They were the conquerors, and from the look of them, they were anxious to demonstrate the fact. Puhalski ducked into a doorway and began a careful study of a display of ornamental clocks.

The Japanese had nothing on him, but in their drunken arrogance they could be as unpredictable as sharks. They too would know him instantly for a Russian, without status or protectors, and they might be tempted into baiting him. His breathing shallow with nervousness, Puhalski waited until they had passed before venturing forth again, all the more anxious to be home. In the plaza before the gate towers, the crowd had thinned and Puhalski was able to lengthen his stiff-

[23]

legged stride. Far to the rear he could still hear the fitful clanging of the stranded streetcar; it made him wonder if the American was still there, too. Puhalski hoped so.

Off to one side, in the deep shadows along the base of the wall, scores of tattered bundles huddled. If it rained these people might be allowed to shelter in the gateway arches . . . and then again, they might not. And maybe in the morning there would be a few coppers worth of work in the railway yards. All over the city there sprawled similar coagulations of paupers, exhausted from begging and foraging in the dumps and alleys, and nursing the coat of life for the next day's struggle. Puhalski refused to look at them.

Nearly gagging from the stinks of the crowd that pressed through the narrow tunnel with him, Puhalski felt himself being swept along, and he fought against a feral urge to strike out with his fists at the beasts who jostled him as indifferently as they did each other. They were reminders, all too specific, of the penalties for failure in North China.

A deep spasm wrenched at him; suddenly, as in a dream, he saw again the frozen surface of the lake, and felt the screaming Siberian wind tearing at his ragged uniform with icy needles. Almost blown away were the crackling of the distant rifles and the bee-whine of the bullets that probed for him in the falling dusk. Again, for a brief instant, he was crawling eastward on bleeding elbows, trying to keep his shattered kneecap off the ice. . . .

Blinking and confused, Puhalski looked around and saw that he was through the tunnel. With shaking hands, he searched his pockets for a cigarette.

He remembered that his rebellious troopers had wanted very badly to kill him then, and had nearly succeeded. But the point was, they had failed. Not only had he outwitted them and escaped, he had given more than one of them something to think about besides the new Bolshevism. Old nightmares to the contrary, he had kept moving always forward from the frozen lake, and in that direction he would continue.

Under a nearby street lamp, a coolie huddled dozing on the footboards of his rickshaw. Nudging the man awake with his toe, Puhalski climbed in and gave him Sobolov's address.

The jogging of the rickshaw was restful, and Puhalski was content to relax; to think about Sobolov and his greedy wife, about Tanaka waiting for news that his scheme was moving forward, and about the American, stalled in traffic and anxious to get his half-caste whore home and into bed. Puhalski smiled and stroked his bristled chin. One

[24]

thing at a time, he thought; he could handle the lot of them if he went about it carefully.

Gazing blandly across the wooden table at Sobolov, Puhalski found himself wondering: what was the use? It was ridiculous to think of depending on such a timid, sweaty, shifty-eyed milksop of a man.

Sobolov fluttered his fat hands. "Would I be doing anything illegal?" he quavered.

Puhalski shrugged candidly. Candor was in order. "Illegal? Well, possibly; but not enough to bother about. Your conscience is over-developed, Andrei. Laws are made by the rich in order to preserve their own precious hides. They have no connection with concepts like justice and fairness, no matter what they like to tell us. If we obeyed all laws to the letter, we'd rot forever at the bottom of the pile . . . deservedly."

"I couldn't do anything illegal," Sobolov mumbled, squirming.

Puhalski wanted to hit him.

As though to explain, Sobolov added, "There is so much at stake." His gesture included the dingy kitchen with its blackened ceiling and scabby walls.

Puhalski looked away. A sink full of dirty dishes, a sooty stove, a table and three chairs, and in the other room another chair and a battered trunk. And, as he knew only too well, a bed. So much at stake! It was ludicrous.

Rolling her eyes upward, Maya Sobolov groaned impatiently and gave her sewing an angry shake. In her dumb way she was trying to help, as she had promised. After he left, she'd give her husband hell. All to the good!

Puhalski let his cold eyes linger on Maya. He had spent two sweaty hours with her on Friday afternoon. Her face, now made paler by the harsh light, was unlined, the flesh of her big body firm and smooth. The whites of her brown eyes were as clear as a girl's. No one would guess her for thirty-five.

Just sitting there and sewing, and being angry with her husband, she radiated a musky vitality which pulled him like a magnet. Puhalski hated her. Hated the hold her hungry body had over him, hated her clinging mawkishness and all her endless gabble about love, and very nearly hated himself. But he needed her.

Sobolov took his glasses off to polish them, his half-blind eyes peering at Puhalski apologetically. He turned to his wife. "Maya dear, I'm sure Serge would like some tea."

The woman shrugged and laid aside her sewing. Puhalski watched her slouch to the stove in her run-over slippers. Her dress was short and tight, and seemed designed to offer him the sight of her buttocks. A deep spasm of desire stirred in his groin, mocking him. The bitch!

Puhalski examined his fingernails. Once Sobolov took the bait, there'd be no further use for her. If only he could touch some vein of cupidity—or of ambition—in Sobolov, the woman would become superfluous. But if he broke with her now, God knows what damage she could do. He had always avoided entanglements with women. . . .

Puhalski forced his attention back to Sobolov. "But my dear fellow, I insist that nothing will be risked. It is merely a question of staying glued in one place or of moving ahead. It's that simple."

"It's all so vague," Sobolov complained. "You know how the Americans are about any sort of scandal. They like my work, but if I got into trouble with the police . . ."

"God damn the Americans!" Puhalski interrupted harshly, wanting to upset the table into Sobolov's lap. "They are fat and rich, and they care nothing about us. We'd starve if we worried about them. This business is foolproof, I tell you; there'll be no trouble with the police. I'm a cautious man and not about to risk all I've gained by any foolishness." As he spoke them, Puhalski wished fervently that the words were true.

Maya returned to the table. Blocking her husband's view, she served Puhalski, giving him a hot and conspiratorial glance. He leered back cautiously. As she settled into her chair, he turned back to her husband.

"The point is, Andrei, I need your help. Ever since the old days in Harbin, I've known you to be a man of honor, scrupulous in matters of money. It's a sad fact, but there aren't many of our compatriots I can say that of. And you're discreet and sober. In short, I could turn my back on you and never worry about being cheated."

Sobolov blushed. "But I know nothing about business. Why, Maya even has to do the household accounts." He laughed idiotically, and mopped his face with a soiled handkerchief.

"Don't worry, I do my own accounts," Puhalski said. "You would be my helper, my emissary. If there is money owed me but I am busy elsewhere, I could tell my debtor: 'My associate, Mr. Sobolov, will call on you.' And then you call on him and get the money. Period. Nothing could be simpler."

"If only you could be a little more specific," Sobolov pleaded.

Puhalski gave a worldly chuckle. "Ah, but that's a problem. I trust you, but I must be cautious. Come in with me and we'll be like brothers, without secrets. Do not, and we'll be friends regardless. But I need

[26]

help, and I need it now. If you refuse, I'll have to ask someone else. Whoever he is, he will be lucky. There is money to be made, Andrei Georgivitch. Money! I am going to get my share. Yours is waiting, but that is up to you."

"Well . . ." Sobolov began dubiously.

Maya whirled on him angrily. "Bah! Show some guts for once, for the love of God. Think of me and Anya instead of only yourself. After all, we are the ones who must live in this hovel while you worry about your wretched scruples."

"Please, my dear, not in front of company," Sobolov whispered, mortified.

Puhalski made placating gestures with his hands. "Do not quarrel, please. I am sorry to have caused dissension. Just think it over, Andrei; that's all I ask." He slapped his hands gently on the table and got to his feet. "So! I must be going. Thank you, Andrei, for your hospitality. And you, my dear Maya. I will call again, if I may, in a day or two, to hear your decision."

As Puhalski got his coat off the hook, he hefted the envelope. It would be but the first of many if Sobolov would only make up his frightened mind. Once Sobolov had involved himself, he would be easy to push on to other things, and soon Tanaka would be getting what he wanted. And then Puhalski could begin to extricate himself gradually . . . from all of them.

As if on cue, Maya turned to gaze up at him avidly, her thoughts all too plain. He would have to speak to her about that; even so great a dunce as her husband could have read the meaning of that look. Puhalski sighed wearily; he was surrounded by fools.

MONDAY

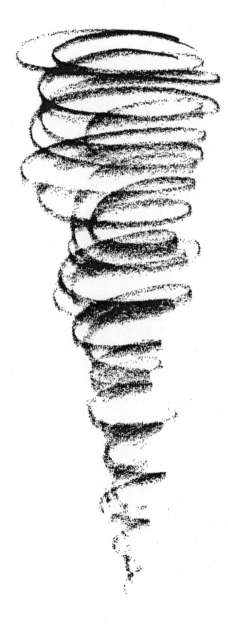

The afternoon sky changed with a terrible suddenness. The little wood grew dark and a cold wind blew. In Tamara's dream, as though in some sort of trance, deaf to her pleas, and blind to everything around him, John wandered off down the hill, becoming smaller and more indistinct with every step. The rising wind shook the pines until they rattled like the old dry bones in the graveyard. . . .

Eyes closed against the early morning light, Tamara reached under the mosquito net and turned off the insistent alarm clock. She did not want to wake up, but she didn't want to dream again. She wanted to hang suspended in some safe place, in some calm and quiet place, where she could work things out in her own way.

There had been a time, not so long ago, when she would have been out of bed at once, ready and even eager for the day. She was more a stoic then, and behind the armor of her sense of independence, she could be as indifferent to her surroundings as she chose. No longer. Now it was a struggle, and every day she seemed to lose a little ground and become more vulnerable. More and more the nightmares haunted her, and she would awaken heart-tired and discouraged.

Lying quietly under the musty tent of mosquito netting, she could see the whole weekend for what it was: an interlude, a holiday from reality, sweet perhaps, but no more substantial than the nightmare. But the nightmare held a hint of prophecy. . . .

As a child, wanting desperately to be inconspicuous and to belong, she had tried to pretend that she was simply a Chinese like any other. But her mixed blood was a barrier that would not disappear. She lived with the Chinese, but to them she was a foreigner. And a tainted one at that, the shameful reminder of the taking of a Chinese woman by the hated stranger, a tribal disgrace. To the foreigners for whom she now worked, she was likewise tainted, evidence of a strayed white man's lust for a "native woman." Compared to these stigmata, she often wondered if her illegitimacy really mattered.

With acceptance from neither side, she had made her own place and lived in her own shell. Having to choose, she had chosen China. She lived as a Chinese with her Chinese mother, and she called herself by the surname of her mother's family. Even had there been shelter behind the name of Brevanov, she would have disdained it. It was characteristic of her to balance, almost to flaunt, the Russian part of her with the given name she had chosen to share with that dead and almost mythical lady, her paternal grandmother. But she could not *feel* Chinese, any more than she could feel Russian.

From the kitchen came the sounds of her mother's stirring. Tamara knew she must get up and help with breakfast. She swept aside the mosquito netting and stood up, stretching and enjoying the coolness of the waxed boards beneath her feet. She ran her fingers through her hair and slipped a cotton robe over her nightdress. Barefooted, she hurried to the door.

The long narrow building had two stories, with a balcony running its length along the back and overlooking a small courtyard. On the ground floor the landlord, who was a tailor, had his shop. On the second floor were two small apartments of two rooms each. She and her mother occupied one, the tailor and his wife the other. Almost as an afterthought, a small square room on stilts had been added to the middle of the balcony and served both families as a communal kitchen. Steep as a ladder, a narrow flight of stairs climbed up beside the kitchen.

Tamara stood for a moment in her bedroom doorway, looking out over the courtyard and the gray corrugations of the tiled roofs beyond, hazy and indistinct in the morning smoke. It was not much, she told herself, but there were an infinity of places a great deal worse. If she was neither Chinese nor Russian, she was nevertheless an Asian, and at home among those gently curving roof-lines. She was Tamara Liu, and it all belonged to her, as much as to anyone.

She hurried along the balcony, past her mother's bedroom and toward the impatient sounds that were coming from the kitchen.

Tamara's mother permitted her cheek to be kissed.

"Are you well, Mother?"

"How can anyone my age be well?" Her mother bent to fan the coals vigorously, raising a small cloud of ashes which drifted out into the room.

Tamara laughed and went to the sink. When she had brushed her teeth, she dashed cold water into her face and combed her hair. "When will you stop complaining of your age? You are barely forty, but you pretend to be a baldheaded old *t'ai t'ai*." Tamara took the fan from her. The older woman put the kettle on the stove and got teacups, bowls, and chopsticks from a cupboard.

"I am almost fifty, and sometimes I feel like an old *t'ai t'ai*. The nights are so hot and dry this summer, and the noise from the street gets louder and lasts longer every night. I hardly sleep at all anymore." She delivered herself of a long and self-pitying sigh.

Tamara shook her head and said nothing. Quite often she sat up late sewing or ironing or reading one of the books that John had lent her, and almost always she had the placid snoring of her mother for com-

[32]

pany. She measured water over the rice in the bottom of the iron pot and put it on the hottest part of the now crackling stove.

Her mother was setting the table. She was shorter than Tamara and still slender. The years of her struggle had given her a lean and wiry look, but her even, handsome features were unlined and offered few clues to her age. Her hair was thick and glossy, untouched by gray, and drawn back severely into a bun lying low on the nape of her neck. She wore the full black trousers and long, high-necked jacket of white cotton that were traditional. A frown creased her forehead and her lips were pressed into a thin line. Anything but fragile, she looked like what she was: an indomitable woman who resisted the inevitable deterioration of the older and better world, but still capable of a fatalistic humor. Tamara could not help grinning. "Poor old *t'ai t'ai*," she teased.

Her mother gave a grunt that was only half-amused, and chose to retain a dignified silence. But not for long. "Where are your shoes?" she demanded to know.

Tamara feigned innocence. "Why, in my room, of course."

"Your feet will get filthy."

"Not on any floor of yours," she replied, peering under the lid of the rice pot.

"Perhaps not, but that woman . . ." Her mother clamped her lips.

Tamara had to laugh. If anything, the tailor's wife was even more fastidious than her mother. Sometimes she thought they would wear the building out with their scrubbing and polishing. She greased a pan with a piece of pork fat and broke two eggs into it.

A stool scraped across the floor and her mother sat down. Tamara could hear fingernails tapping and knew what the sound meant. She sighed loudly. "Am I never to get my rice? I am cursed with an unfilial daughter . . . am I to be starved in my old age as well?"

Tamara waited silently, resigned.

"I suppose a mother shouldn't ask where you have been for two days."

"You know where I have been. I told you we were going out to the Western Hills," she said, her voice expressionless, hoping the quarrel would not develop.

"And I suppose you will be with him again tonight, this aged playboy?"

"Perhaps," Tamara said defiantly, not knowing when she would see him again. "Besides, he is not a playboy. He is an official and does hard work, good work."

[33]

"Good for him, perhaps. They do nothing for anyone else, those foreigners."

"He helped us last year," Tamara said, feeling the tears rise. "He found us a safe place to stay."

"Bah! There was no danger."

Tamara wanted to argue. John Edgerton had arranged for them to stay in the staff quarters of the Wagons-Lits Hotel during those first uncertain weeks of the Japanese occupation. No one had known how the Japanese Army would behave, for all that they had agreed to consider Peking an open city. Nevertheless, the gesture had hardened her mother's attitude against John. She had steadfastly refused his invitations to eat in his quarters in the San Kwan Miao, and when they had returned home it had taken much urging before she consented to have him for supper . . . once. Since then she had grown steadily more bitter and more critical.

"All right, Mother. We have been over all that a hundred times," she said wearily. "Please, let us not do it again."

"We will go over it a thousand times if necessary. You must be made to see your folly: chasing after this, this *foreigner* who . . ."

"Really, Mother," Tamara interrupted, turning on her in exasperation. "Do *you* scold me for loving a foreigner?"

"Don't be insolent. That was different, as you very well know. And your father courted me openly, even if it was at first against my parents' wishes. And in those days that took courage."

"Did they never call you unfilial and disobedient?"

"Sarcasm won't change anything. But they could not accuse me of chasing after him, of throwing myself at him like a street woman."

Tamara refused to look at her mother as she heaped rice into the two bowls and put a fried egg on top of each. She put the bowls and the teapot on the table and sat down. "I am surprised at your lofty attitude. Some of the old-fashioned rules of decorum must have been overlooked. After all, I am here."

Her mother seemed to wither, and tears spilled down her cheeks. Although stricken with a terrible remorse, Tamara found she could not speak.

Her mother took a deep, unsteady breath. "I only want to protect you, to guard you from my errors. You must not live your life as I have lived mine."

"I know, Mother. But you see, that is just it. It *is* my life and I must live it in my own way." She reached across to touch her hand. "Come now and finish your breakfast."

[34]

But Tamara could only pick at her food. All she knew of her mother's life came from scattered bits and pieces.

The middle daughter of a respected Mandarin, a magistrate of some prominence, she had been betrothed routinely to a suitable young man who had died of typhus before the wedding could take place. Tamara's mother had been left in mournful limbo, half-spinster, half-widow. By the time she was twenty, she had resigned herself to the status of dutiful daughter and permanent old maid. At this point her father incautiously invited to his home a young Russian cavalry officer, the military attaché of the Czar's Legation in the capital. The unforeseen proceeded to take place and the young couple fell in love. After much protest and argument, Igor Brevanov was approved as a suitor. Priding himself on his modernity, her father consoled himself with the thought that as the times changed, the old ways must change with them. Then, as the final plans for the wedding were being made, Brevanov was suddenly recalled to Russia to fight the Bolsheviks. Since everyone knew the revolution would be put down quickly, he departed midst assurances of a speedy return.

Just how much the times had changed, the magistrate soon discovered. In a cruel spasm of self-righteousness he banished his pregnant daughter from the house. Too bound in tradition and too concerned with face to be merciful, he gave her only enough money to see her through her confinement. Thereafter, she was to fend for herself and her child, and her name was forbidden to be spoken in his household.

Tamara could only imagine her mother's despair and anguish, for to her father's cruelty was added the heartbreak of total silence. Brevanov vanished as finally as a stone dropped into the sea . . . lost without trace.

And in Tamara's heart sat the small cold stone of despair; her mother was right. Sooner or later, some lunar miscalculation or a flaw in a membrane of rubber would leave her with her own "mistake." Coldly she considered the prospect of one day taking her mother's place: the Liu matriarchy, a dynasty of seamstresses, each a little whiter than the last. She tried to laugh, but it was a stupid joke . . . in very bad taste.

Letting her tea grow cold, she surrendered to dejection. The hot and hopeless tears blurred her surroundings, so that even the sounds of the wakened neighborhood faded away.

"Here, daughter, have some hot tea." Her mother's hand squeezed her shoulder gently as she put down the steaming cup.

"Thank you, Chu-hsing," Tamara said, using her mother's given name. More than mother and daughter, they were at that moment

[35]

simply two lonely women, allies in a world never designed for lonely women.

Brushing at her eyes with her fingers, Tamara felt her determination come surging back, stiffening her spirit. The tea was strong, and she welcomed its bitter heat. She passed cigarettes to her mother and fetched matches from above the stove. Each shrouded in her own thoughts, the two women smoked in companionable silence, watching the early sunlight spread a leaden gloss across the sea of roof tiles, a sea on which they seemed to float like castaways.

It had been nearly nine o'clock when they reached her house the night before, and John had been withdrawn and silent, as he often was when they had been together for any length of time.

They had stopped to eat in the Chinese City, at a small place where foreigners almost never went. Driving on from there, he had seemed to become more despondent by the moment. The near mishap with the Russian had apparently made little impression on him. Except to wonder aloud who the man was, John hadn't mentioned the event again. But something was obviously chafing at his nerves and Tamara could remember hoping that she had not offended him in some way, and that his taciturn mood was due to some pending annoyance at the office, perhaps, or some other outside matter.

Her own preoccupations had been clear enough. She regretted asking him about his work. She had never done that before, and his brief expression of enthusiasm for it, so typically understated, had rung in her ears. As long as it was the only work for him, there would be no place for her in his life that was not sly and hidden.

And then there was the Russian. That he remembered her was obvious. Neither of them was likely to forget their single prior meeting.

The moral ambiguity which her mixed blood seemed to suggest to men of any race was a familiar nuisance. But the approaches which it prompted were usually guarded, almost timid, and a contemptuous look was often enough to turn them aside. Not so with the Russian. Confident and smiling, he had grabbed her by the arm and pulled her into a crowded shop, and whispered crudely and explicitly what it was he had in mind for her. His plain contempt for her had been infuriating. In a voice that carried into every corner of the room, she had told him that he was a Russian pig, a turtle's egg, a contemptible clown, a mockery of manhood, whom she would not permit to touch her if he were the last man on earth. Something about the scene must have been perfect, for the customers and clerks had burst into a roar of laughter, and the proprietor had told the Russian to be off or he would send for a policeman. Pale with fury and humiliation, the Russian had retreated. Now, as she thought of him, she could feel the danger in the grudge he so obviously bore her.

Tamara blew across the surface of her tea and took a cautious sip. Of course she hadn't told John any of that. He was upset enough. . . .

After parking in the silent *hu-tung* and walking with her to her stairs, John had taken her in his arms. But instead of his usual rather perfunctory kiss, it had turned into something else. With an anguished groan he had hugged her to him, kissing her lips and her eyes over and over. Then, with a mumble about phoning, he had released her abruptly and hurried to his car.

She knew him in fragments, from bits of knowledge scattered like islands in an unknown ocean. The twenty years that separated them were a blank to her. She could only guess that they had not been particularly eventful, or even happy. But John was the sort of man who could be lonely and not mind it. And if they were as dull, as routine as he suggested, they had nevertheless conditioned him to obey the restrictions and taboos of his Service. There had been other women in his life, many of them, she was sure. But they did not interest or concern her. All except one. She guessed that he had once been married, although he never said anything about it. She would have liked to know something about *that* woman.

And, she asked herself, who was she? She was a half-caste, beautiful perhaps, but in her rebellion and by her love for John already soiled, the cashier and bookkeeper of the Peking Club, a place where no Chinese and certainly no half-castes were admitted to membership. She was a girl who lived above a tailor's shop with her Chinese mother. Suddenly impatient with the whole introspective puzzle, she declared to herself that, whoever she was, she was a better woman than *that* one.

Tamara and her mother finished their cigarettes and tidied up the kitchen. Back in her room, Tamara stowed the mosquito netting in its overhead frame and made her bed. She selected a Chinese summer dress of pale green silk from the small closet. She slipped her feet into white, high-heeled shoes and inspected herself candidly in the mirror. The dress, designed for figures less full than hers, seemed to flaunt the mixture of East and West in her . . . that was the way she felt this morning.

She checked the contents of her bag, making sure she had fresh underclothes for after her shower in the ladies' dressing room at the Club—"Positively Members Only"—and went into her mother's room to say goodbye.

Her mother was already at her table by the window, well started on her day's sewing. She peered severely at her daughter over the tops of her spectacles, seemed to hesitate, then nodded a firm approval. "You are beautiful," she announced matter-of-factly. "That American must be the champion of fools. Go along now or you'll be late." She returned to her work with a sniff.

Tamara nodded, feeling the determination well up in her. Whatever her inner doubts, none must be allowed to show. Her heels made a brave sound on the stairs, and when she reached the crowded *hu-tung*, her head was high and her face was proud and haughty.

☆☆

Long planes of dusty light slanted across the room from half-closed venetian blinds, and lay in blurred bars of gray and gold against the opposite wall. Overhead, the blades of the ceiling fan flogged ineffectually at the thick oppressive air.

Edgerton's shirt clung to him, and his hands were clammy. Smoking too much, he concluded, and reached automatically for a cigarette. With aversion he inspected the pile of papers centered so neatly on his blotter. The topmost item was from the Japanese Legation. Without looking at it he knew it was but another mite in what had become an endless exchange of notes and protests, pointless dickerings over who should express regret to whom and for what; the exercise of diplomacy at its most futile.

He got to his feet and went to stand under the fan. After a few moments his skin began to dry. A vague depression clung to him. Although their time together had been idyllic, and Tamara warm and natural, something had gone wrong. He just couldn't put his finger on it. But something had caught him firmly in those last moments by her stairs . . . caught him and shaken him and made him run for home like a rabbit.

Frowning unhappily, Edgerton looked around the familiar dreariness of his office: heavy wooden furniture, a scum-colored carpet, a glass-front bookcase filled with useful and boring official tomes. From the wall behind the desk, a portrait of Franklin Roosevelt smiled confidently. The place must have been identical to five thousand other government offices.

Feeling like a convict returning to the rock pile, Edgerton went back to work. He was impatient with himself, with the papers, with the weather, and with the flailing of the fan. They were both about as useless, he and that fan: Western creatures churning away with futile diligence.

He focused his eyes on Mr. Yamaguchi's *aide-memoire* and doggedly

[38]

began to read. It was soon apparent that a counter *aide-memoire* would have to be composed, adding to the pile of international rubbish. Memory tickled and made him laugh. So he wanted to study the Japanese, did he? How pompous he must sound at times! It made him think of Tamara. But he didn't want to think of Tamara. Frowning against the faint ache in his temples, Edgerton reached for pen and paper. Soon he had submerged himself in the familiar diplomatic phrases. His surroundings faded from his consciousness, and his personal dilemma also.

Across the hall, muted voices murmured in the General Office, papers rustled, and a typewriter clacked away, all unnoticed. His ashtray slowly filled and the bars of light and shadow moved inexorably down the wall.

A quick movement outside his window caught his eye. He glanced up in time to see the tall and immaculate figure of the Counselor and First Secretary stride purposefully up the Chancery steps: creamy Panama hat, beige Palm Beach suit, and white shoes gleaming with Blanco. Edgerton looked down at his own wrinkled seersucker.

Out in the hallway, the Legation clock whirred asthmatically and began to strike. A ten-bong salute, he thought. Well, Charles Franklin Procter, it's about time. Remembering Procter's presumptuous "inspection" of Tamara, he frowned, hesitating, then gathered up the papers he wanted Procter to see and headed down the hall.

Procter was just hanging up his coat as he entered the office. An inexhaustible aplomb seemed to radiate from the Counselor. Gold links glittered in his cuffs and his silver-rimmed spectacles flashed. The pocket of his shirt bore a small blue monogram like a discreet medal. "Good morning, old fellow," he cried cheerily, gesturing toward a chair.

Feeling humid and wrinkled, Edgerton did as invited, setting his papers on a corner of Procter's large, empty desk. He watched Procter center the creases of his trousers with a practiced tweak and settle into his chair.

"How was your trip to Tientsin?"

Procter's eyes rolled upward. "Beastly!"

Edgerton grinned.

Procter looked at him crossly. "Your lack of sympathy is hard to forgive . . . that wretched city and its smelly river. . . ." He groaned.

"You forget I was stationed there for seven years," Edgerton pointed out affably.

"I had forgotten; my condolences."

"How did the visiting congressman impress you?"

[39]

"Quite well, actually; a rather dreary lawyer from the Middle West, but well informed and worldly. I expected the usual provincial, embalmed in isolationism." Procter paused to light his pipe, bathing Edgerton in a cloud of aromatic smoke.

Fanning at the smoke with the palm of his hand and wondering at Procter's ability to saturate his acts with boredom, Edgerton observed, "Nothing very beastly about that."

"The train back from Tientsin was an hour late," Procter said crossly.

"Not bad for a three-hour run. No trouble with guerrillas?"

Procter shook his head. "By the way, you haven't forgotten Pamela's party tonight, have you?"

"Certainly not," Edgerton said, having forgotten it completely. Bleakly he canceled the vague notion of asking Tamara to his quarters for dinner. "I'm looking forward to it."

"Good, good. Pamela enjoined me to remind you." Procter swiveled his chair with relief, busying himself with his pipe. "Well, enough of me; how was your weekend?"

"You know me: the stodgy old bachelor," he said nonchalantly. "Went out to the Western Hills and stayed at that little inn I told you about."

"Sounds very placid."

"It was. I read, took a few walks," Edgerton made a gesture of dismissal. "Contemplated my navel."

"Well, so long as it was your own navel . . ." Procter left the words to hang on an avuncular chuckle.

Edgerton flushed uncomfortably, and was furious with himself for doing so.

Procter's expression grew solemn. "I suppose you were with Miss, uh, Liu?" he asked, with the stubborn reluctance of a man performing an unpleasant duty.

Edgerton frowned. "Hardly a threat to American foreign policy," he said in as mild a tone as he could manage.

Procter made a judicious steeple with his fingers. "Perhaps not," he said blandly. "On the other hand . . ."

"On the other hand, Franklin, it's my own business."

Procter's face turned pink. "Now, John, give me a chance. I don't want to meddle . . ."

"Then don't." Edgerton's hand shook and a long cigarette ash fell onto his knee. He brushed at it, leaving a gray smudge.

". . . but I have certain responsibilities . . ."

"I suggest you tend to them," Edgerton blurted.

[40]

Procter swiveled around to glare directly at him. "Don't be insubordinate," he said tensely.

The moment was a long one. Then Procter sighed and gave him a faintly superior smile. It made Edgerton want to hit him. "Please allow me to continue," Procter said. "I have certain responsibilities as *chargé d'affaires*, none of them of my own choosing. One of them, without question, is to caution staff members who, however inadvertently, appear to be headed for trouble." His pause invited agreement. Edgerton was silent. Frowning, Procter continued, "If a staff member makes a spectacle of himself . . ."

"Oh, for Christ's sake! A spectacle! What are you implying, anyway—disorderly conduct, public lewdness?"

Procter gestured patiently. "Please control this urge, this unnecessary urge, to spring to your own defense." He elevated a long forefinger. "In the first place, your liaison with Miss, uh, Liu . . ."

"Look, Franklin, get it straight. Her name is just Miss Liu, not 'Miss, uh, Liu.' It's surely not so bizarre you can't pronounce it."

Scowling stubbornly, Procter pressed on. ". . . is beginning to excite comment, comment which may reflect upon the Legation. Whether or not you choose to concur, whatever concerns the Legation concerns me. Even were this not the case, I would feel constrained as an old, and I hope, valued friend to point out to you that this relationship is bound to damage your career, and might actually destroy it."

Edgerton inspected his shoes gloomily. Procter was right, which made his admonition even harder to take. The plain fact was that the Service was devoted to such vaporous concepts as propriety and suitability and discretion . . . above all, discretion. His career hadn't been so distinguished that his accumulated laurels would protect him. Besides, the Service was concerned with future performance, not past glories . . . and rightly so. "Liaisons," as Procter called them, with women who were considered unsuitable raised doubts about a man and marked him as indelibly as chronic drunkenness. And once marked, you were likely to end up in some backwoods vice-consulate or in a broomcloset office in the basement of the State Department, waiting to be retired. Well, he wasn't ready for that yet. He still had some things to say and needed a platform from which to say them. But it rankled to be scrutinized this way. And how humiliated Tamara would be to know she'd been the subject of such a conversation. . . .

"Okay, Franklin," he said in a defeated voice. "Let's leave it at that. I apologize for losing my temper." He raised his eyes and met a look of sympathy. "I promise not to involve the Legation in an imbroglio; you'll just have to trust me."

[41]

"All right, John. Leave it at that, we shall. We are old friends after all. There has been a long hiatus since we labored together in the Language School, but I want very badly to pick up all those threads. Also, I rely heavily on your experience and judgment. Theoretically, I have the benefit of the Department's current thinking, but you are, um, . . ."

"Not 'Johnny-on-the-spot,' please," Edgerton said, attempting a smile.

Procter grinned. "I must watch that." He cleared his throat and glanced significantly at Edgerton's papers. "Now, what is on the agenda?"

"First off, a note from the Japanese Legation, from Yamaguchi. It's about that search of the Baptist Mission in Tungchow by the Military Police. We discussed it all Friday, Yamaguchi and I, but now he seems to have forgotten what was said." Edgerton picked a thin sheaf of papers off the top of the pile.

Procter gave the papers a distasteful frown. "Brief me, please. I don't seem to remember all the details."

Annoyed, Edgerton found himself wishing Procter's memory were better developed. "Simply stated, it is this," he said. "Three Japanese soldiers from the local Military Police detachment, apparently full of saki and feeling their conquerors' oats, forced their way into the mission compound—plainly marked as American property and where they had no business to be—looking for women. At least that is what they did while they were there. They raised general hell and molested several of the mission's female employees, including one old *amah* in her seventies. Japanese tastes seem to be indiscriminate in these matters. Old Dr. Lewis, a godly man of whom Moses would have approved, drove them off with an umbrella and an unsuspected command of vernacular Japanese. On hearing of it all from him, I protested in 'the strongest terms' since it was a clear case of trespass. The Japanese interpretation is that the soldiers were looking for Chiang Kaishek's spies, suffered grievous bodily assault, and that Dr. Lewis insulted the Emperor." Edgerton sighed and shook his head. "Yamaguchi agreed unofficially on Friday that this was the purest nonsense, that the local commander should apologize to Dr. Lewis, and that the Japanese Legation could get off the hook by an expression of 'regret.' Since then, Yamaguchi's superiors have convinced him otherwise. My answer reiterates the whole business, with the usual pious references to the sanctity of American property in China, and so forth."

Procter took the papers reluctantly. "I'll look them over later. What next?"

"Then there's the chronic problem of Mr. Taylor, the curio exporter."

"Oh, yes," Procter said, obviously at a loss. "What's he done now?"

"Rather typically, he's been operating two automobiles on one set of license plates."

"But that's absurd!"

"Exactly. And a damned nuisance. Major Wu, the Deputy Chief of the Municipal Police, called me about him and was very unpleasant. Gave me a lot of the usual claptrap about Americans abusing Chinese hospitality, the unfairness of extraterritorial immunity, and the fact that anywhere else, Taylor would land in jail. Since I would like to see him there myself, the last point is a difficult one to counter. Furthermore, Wu claims—and I am inclined to believe it—that Taylor has never finished paying for one of the cars. The Chinese owner is about to sue to get his money . . . Taylor has no immunity from that."

"This Wu sounds quite unpleasant."

"He is. He's one of the old-time Japanophiles who crawled out of the woodwork when the Provisional Government was set up . . . they're all in cahoots . . ." Edgerton paused, angry with himself for the generality. ". . . well, not all of them. There are some good men over there."

Procter sniffed. "I'm surprised to hear it."

"There aren't many, but a few stayed on in a genuine effort to ameliorate the occupation rather than merely to line their own pockets. I know one or two . . . you might be interested in meeting them."

Procter cleared his throat. "Well, I don't know . . ."

But Edgerton was determined. "Chang Sun-cheh of the Interior Ministry, for example. He moves unobtrusively in the background and never seems to say very much, but he's done a lot to keep the lid on."

Procter gave him a peculiar look, then his face brightened. "Oh yes, I remember him," he said. "Went to Yale, didn't he?"

"No, Berkeley."

"Oh," said Procter, disappointed.

"In spite of that, he's a good man and well worth cultivating."

"Yes, I suppose so. But it's very difficult . . . collaborators and traitors, and all that."

Edgerton gestured impatiently. It was so like Procter to be finicky about "collaborators and all that" and to miss the point. "Well, even though we don't recognize it, we do have to deal with the Provisional Government. I see Chang occasionally, and he's been very helpful. It would be a good thing to be as pleasant as possible to him, to encourage him . . ." Procter's upraised hand stopped him.

[43]

"Forgive me, old chap; I was teasing you, I'm afraid. Couldn't resist. Chang Sun-cheh and his wife are invited to our little get-together tonight, and . . ." Procter paused, looking contrite.

Edgerton could only laugh at himself. "I deserved that," he said.

Procter held a match to his pipe, his face serious again. "Just the same, I feel a certain uneasiness about that fellow. One instinct tells me to trust him as a patriot who has sacrificed his future in order to stay behind in ignominy. Another tells me that he is just what he appears to be, a man of ability but little principle who is backing what he believes to be the winning horse. Well, we shall see."

Edgerton felt a sudden affectionate respect for Procter and he reminded himself not to be so prone to make snap judgments about him. "There is room for doubt," he said. "But I think your first instinct is the correct one. Anyway, it is something of a triumph to have them accept your invitation. The Changs don't go out among foreigners much anymore, not even among quasi-allies like the Germans and Italians."

Procter affected a look of alarm. "Do you think he means to take my measure?"

"I don't think you need worry."

"Very gratifying." Procter eyed the remaining papers. "Have we disposed of Mr. Taylor?"

"Not quite. I thought you should admonish him; I have a letter here for your signature. I'd like to send it today by special messenger."

"Well, if you insist . . ." Nevertheless, Procter drew away from the proffered letter. "Just the same, couldn't you . . . ?"

"Not this time. Taylor's not much impressed with me, I'm afraid."

"Whatever you think best." Frowning unhappily, Procter scrawled his name at the bottom of the letter and handed it back. "The man sounds like a disgusting oaf, but still and all, we're here to protect legitimate American commercial interests."

"The key word is 'legitimate,'" Edgerton said. "Businessmen are like missionaries sometimes. They seem to presume that a certain sanctity attaches to their activities: the inalienable right to save souls and to make a few fast bucks at someone else's expense. The trouble is, they exert considerable influence on the U.S. government and the next thing you know, protecting *all* their interests has become national policy."

"And quite rightly so," Procter snapped.

"Why should Marines and gunboats be sent over here to protect a shit like Taylor?"

"John!"

[44]

"The word is precise, believe me. Just because he has an American passport . . ."

"You sound a mite socialistic," Procter interrupted with a frosty smile.

Edgerton realized suddenly that he was being a bore. He turned to his pile of papers. "You might be interested in these: Mr. Sobolov's translations from the recent Chinese press."

"Anything special?" Procter's tone denied any real interest.

"If one reads between the lines. Sobolov tells me it's a sort of game: figuring out what's happening from what's not said. He's quite perceptive. Lately, he's been collecting items about the opium traffic."

"Whatever for?" Procter covered a small yawn politely.

"Well, everyone knows the Japanese have been behind most of the opium traffic since 1931. Now, much larger supplies are suddenly available, and the Japanese are denying everything in advance, over-compensating in their usual thick-headed way. The Army actually fosters the sale of opium, as a matter of policy."

"Isn't that a bit farfetched?"

"I don't think so. . . . Anything to undermine Chinese morale."

Procter eyed him skeptically. "How can your Mr. Sobolov know all this?"

"He doesn't need to *know* it, Franklin. It is his informed opinion. He lives among the Chinese. White Russians survive by nosing out what's going on."

Procter shook his head dubiously. "Well, I don't know about that. Anyway, I'm not sure I would put much faith in his editorializing. And that reminds me: how is it that we have Mr. Sobolov in the first place? I thought Department policy encouraged the employment of Chinese in these nonsensitive jobs."

"Yes. But it also encourages the employment of the most qualified applicant. Sobolov was head and shoulders above the others."

"Well, it does seem to be a bit unusual," Procter grumbled. "And as for closeting yourself with this *Russian* . . ."

Edgerton couldn't control an urge to laugh. "Please trust me. I promise not to let Mr. Sobolov acquire an evil influence over me."

Procter shrugged, only partly reassured. "Very well, but remember this is only his opinion. The Russian imagination tends to discover sinister conspiracies under every bush."

"Even his opinions are worth reading."

Procter's nod was weary. "Yes. Well, I will then. But I must say, old chap, it all sounds very devious and Machiavellian." He sat up suddenly and looked pointedly at his watch. "And now I must be off.

[45]

Count Gambini is arriving at eleven-thirty, as you know, and I must be at the station with the other diplomats to show the flag."

"Oh, yes," Edgerton said. The new Italian Minister had to be met with suitable formality, in spite of revolting news from Ethiopia.

Procter shrugged into his jacket; it settled on to his shoulders without a wrinkle. He put on his hat and turned in the doorway. "It's my duty to warn you," he said, eyes twinkling, man to man. "We have a house guest . . . Pamela's old school chum."

"Pamela's determination to bring me and the right woman together is touching."

"You'll like Valerie."

"I'm sure of it." Edgerton grinned. "See you later."

Walking back along the hall, Edgerton glanced over the counter into the General Office. Sobolov was there, all right, slouching fatly among his newspapers, his back to Edgerton. Dark stains of sweat marked his faded gray suit and his wispy hair was untidy. Poor sloppy bastard, Edgerton thought. What a life he must have to lead!

It reminded him of the near disaster the night before. That man had looked vaguely familiar. He wondered, barely interested, if Sobolov might know him.

He was about to sit down at his desk when Procter's car went by, a Packard phaeton with a chauffeur at the wheel. The top was up and in its shade Procter sat serenely, almost royally.

Edgerton dropped the sheaf of papers in his HOLD tray and sank into his chair. "Devious and Machiavellian, my ass," he said to the empty room. He leaned back and put his feet up on the desk. He *liked* Procter, but he was a pain sometimes.

When news of Procter's pending return to Peking had first come in, Edgerton had been pleased. He recalled him clearly from the time when they were both Student Interpreters. Procter was a tall, awkward-looking young man, fresh out of Harvard, with an accent that was almost a caricature. To the remains of the accent he had now added an annoying vocabulary of Briticisms acquired while serving a tour at the Embassy in London. In the two months since his return, Edgerton had grown increasingly impatient with his elusiveness. Edgerton wanted to brief him, to get him aside so as to review the whole setup in North China. But, like today, Procter was always on the verge of going somewhere, or Edgerton was . . . the Legation was shorthanded with people away at the beach, and Anderson home with a broken hip, and the Minister attending a series of conferences in Nanking. . . .

The review would have been as much for his benefit as for Procter's

[46]

. . . Franklin was no dummy, and he was fresh from his briefings in Washington. It would be very useful to get a glimpse of Washington's thinking firsthand, instead of through the pages of cables and position papers . . . sterile and unrealistic. He would like to ask Procter just what they were thinking back there. So much of what emanated from the State Department seemed quite remote from the facts of life that Edgerton saw. However cruel and conscienceless their behavior, the Japanese had some valid aspirations in the Far East which could only be dealt with pragmatically . . . channeled perhaps, or softened, but neither reformed nor denied.

And there were latent forces in China which American policymakers seemed to prefer not to face up to for the present. When Edgar Snow returned to Peking from his enterprising and daring trek to Yenan, Edgerton had talked to him, and had been deeply impressed with what he had to say about the vitality of the Communist movement, and the quality of its leaders.

After Snow got back to the States, there were disturbing stories of an unwillingness there even to listen to him, as though to acknowledge the vitality of the Communists was somehow to endorse them. American officials were to be protected from talk of Communism the way nuns might be from sex.

What the hell! Edgerton was suddenly annoyed with himself. Was he becoming another one of those cranky provincials? Was some of his annoyance really resentment because Procter had been promoted ahead of him? Well, the State Department was leery of provincialism, and took periodic precautions. That was why they were ordering him home.

But he didn't want to go back without a clearer idea of what was really happening in the Orient. The notion of being at the center of events really was an illusion. Even though the accelerating deterioration in relations with Japan appeared to be unstoppable, Edgerton refused to believe it. Although mobilization had been ordered in March, the militarist clique wasn't yet in total control in Tokyo; the Prime Minister, Prince Konoye, possessed great prestige and enjoyed the confidence of the Emperor. The impending disaster might still be warded off if both sides behaved rationally.

The thought of Washington brought him back to Tamara, and he felt a deep visceral chill. He couldn't really bring himself to think about life without her, of not being able to call her at the Club and take her out to dinner, or over to his place, or out to the Western Hills . . . the next time everything would be perfect for them . . . he'd see to it.

[47]

Edgerton got out a cigarette and held it in his hand, unlit. A futile sense of shame and helplessness came over him. There was fakery being practiced, and he was as guilty of it as Procter, and all those nameless others who expressed vicarious dismay over his involvement with Tamara. If he had any guts, he'd fight them on the real issue, starting with Procter himself. Procter might pretend to be bothered by having the Number Three in the Legation where he was Number Two, and temporarily in charge, consorting more or less openly with a woman from the wrong social class. Neither Procter nor the rest had the guts to come right out and say it: The trouble with that girl, Edgerton old buddy, is that she's Chinese.

They couldn't say it. For one thing, they were too fond of talking about how it was 1938, after all, and not the Dark Ages, and how modern and liberal and sophisticated they were. For another, they had too many Chinese friends—business friends, government friends, and "real" friends—before whom they'd be ashamed to reveal such a degree of bias. For a third, if a third was needed, there was their own lingering, ambiguous love affair with Chinese art and culture: the bronzes, the lacquer, the porcelain, the paintings, the translations of Confucius, and Lao-tze, and Mencius, and Sun Yat-sen, and Dr. Hu Hsih.

To speak that truth of theirs to him would reveal all of it as just so much claptrap, and would expose for all to see the kernel of their bigotry: that the Chinese were inferior. That was their belief; no matter how talented and charming and brilliant the Chinese might seem or how old their culture, they were inferior. And why? Silly question! Because they weren't *white!*

It sickened Edgerton to be a party to such blind hypocrisy and prejudice, but he couldn't avoid the admission, at least not to himself. *He* didn't think the Chinese were inferior—in fact he knew damn well they weren't—and he was willing to tell anyone who'd listen, but he wasn't Horatius at the Bridge. It was too much to expect him to be the only one standing up for right and freedom.

The whole subject made him feel tired and cowardly. He had almost twenty years invested in the Foreign Service. He was senior enough now to begin moving in toward that center of action he was always talking about. Once there, he'd be able to influence events, instead of merely watching them parade past him, having already been botched somewhere up the line. He couldn't throw all that away . . . he was forty. A man can't be expected to begin again at forty.

He was too old to begin a lot of things again . . . and much too wise, he thought. He'd been burned too badly to put his hand in the fire twice. He knew how it felt to be disarmed, to wake up naked on a crowded street, where strangers laughed, and your friends had to turn away, embarrassed for you. Sure, falling in love had its good moments, all those sweet preliminaries and secret discoveries, and then that romantic moment to end all romantic moments when you felt the exaltation of "giving" yourself. Not Edgerton; he would never let his guard down like that again.

He lighted the cigarette at last, and dragged in the hot acrid smoke. That intensely disturbing moment of their parting returned to twist his heart. When the time came for him to go, was it going to feel like that? And for how long?

He'd promised to telephone . . . maybe after lunch.

♨♨

Colonel Hideki Tanaka scowled. He didn't like being left to cool his heels in some civilian's anteroom. Nor did he like arriving on time for an unwanted appointment only to have some nonentity in striped pants tell him that the man who had sent for him was now too busy to see him, and would he please wait. Colonel Tanaka didn't like being summoned by civilians; the fact that the summoner was the personal representative of the Emperor did no more to make the the situation palatable than did the obsequious manner of his underling. No matter what they pretended, these damned diplomats imagined themselves superior to soldiers, laughing up their sleeves.

Growing angrier by the minute, Tanaka shifted his booted feet. He fiddled absently with the tassle on his sword, and felt vaguely reassured. The sword meant a lot to him. He was fond of telling strangers that the blade was very ancient and was of the finest steel, and that it had been in his family for three hundred years. Though there was some truth in the former claim, there was none in the latter. If there were a few *samurai* scattered among his peasant forebears, Colonel Tanaka had never heard of them.

He twisted his head and tugged at the high collar of his tunic. He felt permanently wedged into the uncomfortable leather chair, and he began to worry lest he perspire through the seat of his worsted riding britches and make himself look ridiculous. On cue, a rivulet of sweat ran down between his breasts and across his paunch to lodge in his navel. It tickled.

A demure young woman, some sort of secretary, minced by, carrying a folder of papers. Tanaka's face brightened as he watched her retreating bottom with interest— a juicy little piece. . . . Lost for some

[49]

moments in the ensuing fantasy, Colonel Tanaka relaxed, and his face became almost content.

A door opened and the underling reappeared, hissing politely.

Tanaka heaved himself out of the chair with a grunt and pulled his tunic into place. His britches felt quite damp. The underling held the door for him and bowed in a faultlessly insolent manner. How pleasant it would be to have that young fop under his command for a few months: teach him a thing or two about respect for his betters.

The door clicked shut behind him, leaving Tanaka to traverse alone the expanse of carpeting lying between him and Minister Saito's desk. Minister Saito chose to ignore his approach until the last possible moment; even then he raised his eyes and stood up with evident reluctance.

"Ah, Colonel . . . um . . . Tanaka," Saito said, waving a perfunctory invitation toward a chair. "Please sit down."

"Good morning, Your Excellency," Tanaka said, positioning his posterior on the narrow chair and lining up his sword. He looked at Saito expectantly. The Minister was wearing the morning coat, wing collar, and striped trousers considered fashionable in the Foreign Ministry. Aping the British seemed to be one of their principal functions.

Minister Saito sat down and began fussing womanishly among his papers. "Now, Colonel Tanaka, the reason I sent for you is this . . ." Saito was from Hokkaido and his harsh accent grated on Tanaka's ears. Suspiciously he eyed the paper which Saito brandished. When Colonel Itaki, the Chief of Staff, had telephoned that Saito wished to see him, he'd been his usual vague and uninformative self. Tanaka was willing to bet Itaki had known more than he let on and merely wanted him kept in suspense.

". . . His Imperial Majesty's Government has been profoundly embarrassed by the behavior of your men." Saito concluded, pursing his lips and regarding Tanaka severely over the tops of his round spectacles.

Tanaka shook his head, wishing he'd been paying closer attention. "Embarrassed by my men?" he repeated, disappointed by the timid sound of his voice. He was furiously certain now that Itaki *had* known all about it.

"An American missionary doctor in Tungchow has filed a very unpleasant complaint."

Tungchow. Tanaka cursed silently. It was all the fault of that incompetent idiot, Okani. Outpost duty permitted too much independence and had a bad effect on discipline. He'd been meaning to drive down there and make a surprise inspection, but he had been so busy. . . .

[50]

He cleared his throat and inquired cautiously, "What are they alleged to have done?" and then added, "These missionaries . . ." He gave Saito a knowing shrug.

"Dr. Lewis has made a complete and specific report." Saito shook his head with gloomy satisfaction. "He even has the names of the three men involved."

"Their names? How could he have their names?" Military Policemen weren't in the habit of identifying themselves, particularly not to foreign civilians. Tanaka began to feel off balance; it was all very confusing.

"Apparently Dr. Lewis had only to demand them. A determined man, it seems." Saito smiled thinly. "Your men were drunk and barely able to supply that information," he added with distaste.

"Well really, Your Excellency—a little drunkenness . . . hardly unusual in the Army." Tanaka laughed with uneasy joviality, spreading his hands expressively. Saito regarded him coldly. Tanaka put his hands back on his sword hilt, hating the Minister.

"Your men also intimidated several of the mission women. They were lewd and abusive in their language, and made obscene gestures, according to Dr. Lewis."

"The humor of the men is a little coarse, perhaps."

"Dr. Lewis further reports that only his timely intervention prevented at least one rape."

"Well, Your Excellency, everything is rape to these missionaries. A soldier can't take a willing peasant woman out into the fields without some American eunuch screaming about rape."

Saito's smile seemed frozen into place. "In this case the woman was apparently not so willing. Her nose was bloodied and two of her teeth knocked loose."

Tanaka shuffled his feet miserably. There seemed no getting around Saito's unreasonableness. "Were any of these women Americans?" he asked.

"Fortunately for you, no. There would be the devil to pay then."

A great sigh escaped Tanaka. "Well then, Your Excellency, the men are young and full of sap. . . ."

"Colonel Tanaka, you just don't seem to understand," Saito said, his voice becoming heavily patient. "These events took place on mission property, on American property. Every single soldier in North China knows that he is to stay away from American property. How can it be that your men do not know it?"

"A policeman on duty . . ."

"Come, come, Colonel Tanaka. You haven't been listening. These men of yours were drunk, one of them so drunk he urinated in his

[51]

pants." Saito's look was eloquent. "Am I to understand that your men, alone among all the others of the Imperial Japanese Army, are permitted to drink on duty?"

Tanaka squirmed. "No, of course not. But I object to Your Excellency referring to these men as mine. Major Okani is in command down there."

Minister Saito rapped his desk loudly with his knuckles. "Colonel Tanaka, you are the Provost Marshal for the Military District of Peking, are you not?"

"Yes, sir," Tanaka said, vowing that he would break Okani and send him to the front for this humiliation.

"Well then," Saito said and threw the paper down as though all points at issue had now been cleared up.

"I can assure Your Excellency of a most thorough investigation," Tanaka said.

"And I can assure you that won't be necessary. His Majesty's Legation considers this . . . ," Saito flicked the paper with his finger, ". . . as investigation enough. Dr. Lewis has been known all over North China for more than twenty years as a wise and honest man. I think we can accept his account of the incident. He speaks Japanese, by the way; your men managed to insult him deeply."

"High spirited combat troopers . . ."

"Please, Colonel, two of the men are clerks, the third is the detachment cook . . . hardly commandos."

Tanaka shrugged helplessly. It was impossible to reason with a man like Saito. "What do you want me to do?"

"Disciplinary measures must be taken. I'll want a full report of the punishments awarded."

"Perhaps, under the circumstances, severe reprimands . . ."

"No. Reprimands are not enough. They must be punished by hard labor and confinement. They have disgraced their uniforms and their Emperor, and caused me no end of embarrassment and annoyance. And wasted my time with twaddle." Saito's glare invited no objection.

"As Your Excellency wishes," Tanaka said stiffly. "But, if I may say so, satisfying American demands . . ."

"American demands?" Saito's voice rose shrilly, and his face reddened. "Who said anything about satisfying the Americans? I spit on the Americans!"

Taken aback, Tanaka could only stare.

"Get it straight, Colonel Tanaka: It is *I* who demand that these men be punished. Satisfy the Americans, indeed!"

The Minister produced a large silk handkerchief and mopped his face. Then, as he polished his glasses, his face became calmer, but his voice remained edged with anger. "What you military types can't seem to get into your thick skulls is that His Imperial Majesty's Government insists on avoiding any and all incidents with the Americans. Whether or not you know it, the sinking of the American gunboat *Panay* last year upset everyone in Tokyo, from the Emperor and the Prime Minister on down. No one believed all those excuses of the Air Force about mistaken identity and bad weather, and so forth. The military's enthusiasm for that crude and stupid blunder was not shared, and nothing even remotely resembling a repetition of that incident is to be tolerated. The Foreign Minister so informed me personally." Saito put on his glasses and gave Tanaka an owlish stare. "Commanders who are unable to control their men are likely to find themselves assigned to other, less congenial duties. Do I make myself clear?"

Tanaka felt sick. A year of work and planning, and success so near . . . almost ruined by the laxness of an oaf like Okani. He pondered the injustice of it all. The Chief of Staff had never liked him. Colonel Itaki was jealous of anyone with initiative and ability. Tanaka considered the problem morosely. Major Okani he could handle easily; Colonel Itaki would be another matter. The humbling of an officer so close to the General could be undertaken only with the greatest care and subtlety. For the moment he was in a pickle.

"Perfectly clear, Your Excellency," he said submissively.

Saito's face broke into a smile, revealing some intricate gold work. "Very good, Colonel; I knew I could count on you." He punched one of an array of buttons on his desk. "You must join me in a cup of tea. It'll refresh us both on such a hot day."

Eased by this gesture, Tanaka let himself relax. He watched with cautious appreciation as the pretty secretary carried in a tray. Blushing and avoiding his eye, she put it down on the corner of Saito's desk, bowed, and hurried out. Tanaka smiled. Shy women intrigued him . . . the more so since he didn't know any. In fact, all women intrigued him, even the whores who staffed the officers' brothels—generally a sorry lot. Unfortunately, as a Colonel he couldn't properly visit them, and he was much too shy himself to have one sent around to his quarters except on rare occasions, when the urges of the flesh had become irresistible. It had been a long time. . . .

The Minister became expansive over his teacup. "It might be useful for you, Colonel Tanaka, to reflect that wars cannot be fought and won on military lines alone. The diplomatic front is very important, now more than ever. America is near the end of the road in Asia, the Americans and all the foreigners. But they are here now, and it is up

[53]

to the Diplomatic Service to keep them from making trouble. They have frustrated Japan and delayed the realization of our destiny for many years. They look down on us because we are Asians; they laugh at us and ridicule our accomplishments. I loathe them, but my duty requires me to avoid frictions. That is why every incident of this sort must be dealt with ruthlessly." Saito looked grim and polished his pate with the palm of his hand. "They can be very persistent; this man Edgerton . . ."

"Edgerton?" The name broke from Tanaka's lips involuntarily, and he felt the hot rush of blood to his face. "Is he behind all this?"

Minister Saito looked surprised. "Why, yes, you might say so."

Tanaka shook his head. Edgerton. Everytime he turned around the man popped up like some diabolical jack-in-the-box. It was becoming unbearable.

"Edgerton is a stubborn man," Saito continued conversationally. He leaned back in his swivel chair and crossed his legs. Tanaka noticed he was wearing spats. "Our Yamaguchi has been trying to deal with him on a number of matters, but without notable success. In this particular case, we may have to make a formal expression of regret, much as it galls me. We have been left with nothing to say by those men of yours." Saito scowled briefly at Tanaka. "Edgerton insists on treating the matter as one of aggravated assault and trespass. Yamaguchi—he's the young man who let you in—says that . . ."

Tanaka's mind wandered. That pipsqueak! No wonder the American had gotten the upper hand.

". . . but then, Edgerton has always been something of a problem. He has no subtlety. Do you remember the traffic bumps?"

Tanaka would never forget the traffic bumps. He wondered if the Minister could be baiting him, and shot him a suspicious glance. Saito was contemplating the ceiling contentedly. "Yes, I remember," Tanaka muttered.

Saito shook his head in grudging admiration. "He waited until the Japanese member on the Administrative Council of the Legation Quarter was absent, you know. They, the French and British members urged on by Edgerton—the Italian was away for some reason or other—they voted on it and had it all done in one night." The Minister grinned, not above enjoying an event that made the Army look inept. That, Tanaka thought, was one of the troubles with diplomats: They derived a perverse pride from being outwitted by an opponent. They were not realists; they did not understand power and the use of force. And Saito was unfortunately an example of the breed. Unpatriotic attitudes infected even the Army at times, where small men were

[54]

jealous of accomplishment. It seemed to Tanaka that he would never stop hearing the sound of Colonel Itaki's shrill laughter. It had been a joke to him that the Americans could put speed bumps across Legation Street without the Provost Marshal being any the wiser. Army vehicles were supposed to stay out of the Legation Quarter, but Legation Street was a good short cut and the Chinese police were too timid to interfere. Early on the morning following the construction of the speed bumps several trucks had started through at their usual smart clip . . . Colonel Tanaka didn't like to think about it. He heard later that even General Baron Kawasaki had laughed at his expense. Being made ridiculous could ruin a man in the Army.

Yes, he remembered the traffic bumps and the broken axles. And the worst of the humiliation was that Edgerton probably didn't even know his name. Ever since that mortifying moment at the Italian reception when Edgerton had snubbed him, the image of the man had swelled in Tanaka's mind. There was now added to that indifferent rudeness, and to the mortification of the speed bumps, this thinly veiled threat of reassignment, and all because of Edgerton's pernicious meddling. Some day, he would have reason to remember Colonel Tanaka very well. . . .

Saito had pushed back his chair and was standing up. "So, my dear Colonel, I am confident that you will act efficiently." Saito punched another button and the door opened almost immediately. "Yamaguchi-san, please show Colonel Tanaka out."

Tanaka shook Saito's limp hand, gave Yamaguchi a ferocious glare and went through into the anteroom. He was willing to bet that Yamaguchi was the council member who had been absent from that crucial meeting. Tanaka's britches felt very moist, and he was sure that his worst fears for them had been realized. As the front door of the Legation swung shut behind him, he heard the pretty young secretary giggle to Yamaguchi.

A delicious vision of running Yamaguchi through with his sword crossed his mind . . . and then he would skewer Edgerton. And next his stupid driver, who was only then rousing himself and getting the car started.

"Next time be ready when I come out, you piece of pig's dung," he growled as he climbed into the car. "Take me back to the office."

It had been a wretched morning. Tanaka sighed sadly and tried to divert himself with the thought of how well his big American car was running. It was almost new and had been in his possession for exactly two days, but even that failed to cheer him.

Thoroughly downcast, he fumbled in his tunic pockets for ciga-

[55]

rettes. The car slowed unexpectedly, then lurched jarringly over a traffic bump. With a grunt of rage, he fetched the driver a box on the ear with his fist. "Do that once more, you shit-kicker, and you'll be an infantryman again!"

Relieved by the brief spasm, Tanaka drew the smoke in deeply and felt calm returning. Calm, and the recollection of recent news. He was an old campaigner and used to the vicissitudes of Army life. He would survive.

Colonel Tanaka's eyes closed against the glare. Recalling Saito's patronizing little homily on the diplomatic "front," Tanaka had to smile. He really shouldn't let those stuffed shirts get under his skin. Like everyone else, they thought he was merely the Provost Marshal of General Kawasaki's command, a sort of glorified policeman, in charge of deserters and soldiers who got drunk and made nuisances of themselves on the streets. Well, he wasn't only that, not anymore. Before leaving Japan he'd been promised an additional assignment; only the day before the orders had arrived by special pouch, "eyes only" to the General himself. It was unfortunate that Colonel Itaki would naturally be privy to the new situation, but that couldn't be helped. Tanaka intended to build his organization with the greatest care. Soon he would be one of the most powerful men in North China, the rival even of General Kawasaki. No mere Itaki could get in his way then. Already in progress was the plan which would ruin Edgerton while it enhanced his own prestige immeasurably. He could take care of Itaki at his leisure. There would be no contemptuous laughter then, not from anyone.

Puhalski, he said to himself, the key was Puhalski. The time for excuses and delays was over. He must contrive to see Puhalski and prod him sharply into action.

☖☖

The damp floor of the Café Volga steamed in the hot afternoon sunlight that fell on it from the open doorway. The rest of the long room was dim, still comparatively cool from the mopping the coolie had given it before going home.

A small fan oscillated jerkily behind the bar, sweeping Puhalski's back as he polished glasses. He had opened early, to get the place ready and go over some accounts. He paused in his work for a moment and looked about him.

Chairs were piled on all the tables but one. There two garishly dressed young women sat, sharing a beer and clucking monotonously like a couple of bored hens, two among the scores of Russian wanderers who floated back and forth across North China. When in Peking, the Café Volga was their headquarters. No more than a dozen or so of his regulars ever seemed to be in town at the same time. Every week, two or three of them would strike out for somewhere—for Harbin or Tientsin or Shanghai—but then another two or three would presently drift in from somewhere else. Almost without exception they shared a prime ambition: to inveigle a foreign soldier into marriage and thus escape from China. For most of them there was no other way.

Foreign soldiers from the Legation guard detachments came to the Café Volga for the girls, and the girls came for the soldiers. It was an arrangement which suited Puhalski admirably, as he had a commission on the profits as well as a small salary from the old Czarist aristocrat who owned the place.

Of all the troops, the Americans were the most sought after by the women. They were the most emotional and had the most money. Puhalski saw to it that the Americans found the atmosphere congenial at the Café Volga, in spite of his contempt for them. Still, they were no sillier than the others: the French or the English or the Italians. Tin soldiers, the lot of them. Not one in ten could have survived a week's winter campaigning on the Mongolian border.

Puhalski put away the last glass but one, and this he filled with Japanese beer and went to sit on his stool at the end of the bar. It was almost three, and in a few minutes he would have to leave. He yawned hugely; Maya Sobolov was waiting for him. He was bored to death with her, but she might still be useful.

The two women pushed their chairs back noisily, and one of them came over to pay him.

"You'll be open tonight, Serge Alexivitch?"

"Yes, Sonya; until twelve," he said, watching her dig into a shabby patent leather purse.

She laughed without humor. "Tanya," she said.

"Tanya, of course. My humble apologies."

She grinned at him as though they shared a joke. Her teeth needed tending to. The diet, he supposed idly. He had slept with her a few times the year before; she was prettier then. "It's on the house," he said, surprising himself.

It surprised her, too. "Well, thank you, Serge," she said.

"Old times."

She laughed again, her voice hoarse from cheap Chinese cigarettes.

"You'll be in?" he asked, only half interested.

"Every night, rain or shine. Though it will be dead; Mondays are

[57]

always dead. Still, there might be an Americanski or two to console."

"Babies wanting their mothers."

"Not entirely. Half and half . . . and a stiff cock makes a man generous." She rubbed thumb and forefinger together and grinned knowingly at him.

"It does, eh?" Puhalski asked sarcastically.

"Are you coming or not, Tanya?" the other asked from the doorway, her voice edged with impatience.

"Yes, dead Olga," Tanya said, and winked at Puhalski. "Yours never did . . . until today."

"No, and it probably never will again. But I am generous on account of other things. Remember what I told you: keep your ears open. You'd be surprised at the little bits and pieces that are valuable."

"I never forget a thing you tell me, Serge Alexivitch. See you later," Tanya replied, making a kiss with her lips.

Puhalski ignored it, his sardonic grin remaining fixed.

Tanya shrugged, an experienced campaigner used to reverses, and went to join her friend. Disinterestedly Puhalski watched them disappear into the glaring *hu-tung*. Natasha, the new waitress, chose that moment to arrive, her young body fairly bursting from a short-skirted Chinese summer gown. Puhalski's spirits rose as he acknowledged her waved greeting. One of these days, baby, he thought.

"I'll be back in an hour or so," he said.

"Okay," Natasha replied cheerily, already busy setting chairs around the tables.

Puhalski smiled to himself.

Limping rapidly along the *hu-tung* toward the Sobolov apartment, Puhalski remained cheerful. Things were coming along slowly but steadily. Tanaka was a fanatic, but with a little luck and his wits about him, Puhalski was confident of his ability to duck if Tanaka's madness threatened some disaster. Meanwhile he had profited considerably from their association. Not so much as Tanaka himself, of course, but that was the way of the world. The Japanese Army managed the opium business ineptly, indifferent to any sort of accounting or inventorying. If he managed the Café Volga the way they did their supplies, he'd be bankrupt in a week. Tanaka, for example, seemed to have no trouble getting his hands on fairly large amounts of opium. No one seemed to notice that the stuff was missing. All that remained was for Puhalski to feed it to his contacts in small enough amounts so that the Army wouldn't suspect private enterprise. The biggest problem so far had been to keep some sort of brake on Tanaka's greed. He was like a spoiled child senselessly stuffing himself with jam merely because no one happened to be looking.

[58]

In many ways, Tanaka was typical of the Japs. They had neither restraint nor overall plan. They were winning by the sheer weight of men and metal, but the effort was costing them dearly in gold and other resources. And prestige; their senseless cruelties had disgusted the world. Puhalski's objection was not that they were cruel but that they were senseless. The whole war was senseless. The Chinese could never beat Japan, but they could fade back into the mountains and outwait them; China had the stamina. But that was futile, for even if they eventually wore the Japanese out, the Russian bear was waiting his turn, licking his chops. The Georgian butcher would make Manchuria and most of China a Russian Colony.

Although the idea still made him nervous, Puhalski was fairly certain his Cossack background would be forgiven him. Stalin would need Russians like himself. Twenty years in China and Manchuria, ingenuity, the mastery of three languages besides his own—well, too, really; though improving, his Japanese was still weak—and a half dozen Chinese dialects, a finger on the weaknesses of scores of officials, paths into the underworlds of politics and crime . . . no, he could write his own ticket. No more bowing and scraping to Tanaka then, and no more wasted hours with a cow like Maya. *He* would be in the driver's seat, with money and power and all the young girls he could ever want. Power: that was the thing. He was tired of being shit on by every Chink policeman or Jap soldier who wanted to relieve his own boredom. And looked down upon by every clerk in every Yamen in the city and by the fucking Americans.

Suddenly furious, Puhalski paused in the thin shade of a young locust tree and let the crowd flow on without him for several moments. Finally he took out a handkerchief and wiped his face carefully, then lighted a cigarette, inhaling the smoke slowly and deeply. Patience, and self-control, he told himself and his turn would come.

He had to wait at Hata Men Chieh for a break in a string of plodding ox-carts loaded with coal. Then, halfway across the street, he was almost run down by a convoy of Army trucks, loaded with rice, racing northward on the crowded street as though the outcome of the war depended upon them. He had to jump to get out of the way, and he twisted his knee. He was cursing when he gained the sidewalk. Limping even more painfully, he turned down the next *hu-tung* to the east. Up ahead, the Northern Peace Apartments gleamed with deceptive purity in the afternoon sunlight, the building's scrofulous exterior masked by the dazzle.

In the half light of the entrance hallway cockroaches as big as mice scurried away from him, their feet whispering on the bare boards. There were no mice; the rats had eaten them.

[59]

All around him the building seemed to pulse with torpid life. A door would slam, a radio blare out for an instance and then fall to muttering, a child cry and be hushed, or be scolded and cry louder. On the stairs, the hot stench of the place made him gag. In spite of a faint breeze in the upper hallway, the atmosphere hung solidly in place, massive with rancid odors.

Maya must have been listening for his footsteps, for the door opened just as he was about to knock. She was holding a bright and rather dirty kimono around herself and a cloud of her heavy scent floated out to him, making his loins churn.

She smiled softly and stepped back into the dark kitchen. As he turned to face her, her arms lifted and her kimono gaped, caught on her swollen nipples.

Puhalski's eyes slid over the bulges of her heavy breasts, white-skinned and faintly veined, dropped past the firm roundness of her belly with its single staring eye, and stopped at her dark thick bush.

Moaning faintly, Maya moved forward and Puhalski reached a hand for her. As she straddled his probing fingers, he felt himself swell like a bull and wanted to laugh aloud. He was the master, and let no one forget it.

Puhalski awoke slowly, reluctantly, clinging stubbornly to the dream he wanted very much to continue. He'd waited too long to bring the half-caste to heel for her to escape him now, to avoid the complete submission he'd planned for her, but already her crouching form was growing hazy, drifting into nowhere. She'd be gone before he could finish the rape of her mouth. . . .

Confused, Puhalski squinted against the incandescent patch of sunlight papering the far wall, and remembered where he was. Those were Maya's breasts he was feeling against his thigh and it was her breathing, slow and heavy, that he was hearing. Suddenly the raw end of every nerve in his body seemed to terminate in her mouth but still he was disappointed. She was displacing the other one, the one who really deserved what she was getting, reward and punishment combined. But then the urgency of Maya's tongue began to overwhelm him. Drown, you bitch, he thought, his two hands cupping her head. His back arched, and he buried himself in her.

The soft sough of her breathing came to him as he stood by the open window. She was asleep, or maybe only dozing. He didn't know which, and didn't care. He only knew that if he turned to look at her, he'd want to smash her in the face—that devoted, placid, hungry face.

The hand carrying the cigarette to his mouth trembled slightly; the sight annoyed him. She had no hold on him, he insisted. He could amuse himself with her for as long as he damn well pleased, and then she could go to hell, and take her mawkish drivel about love with her. The sooner he no longer had to listen to her, the better.

Puhalski spat out the window, then leaned on the sill to stare down at the slum which festered in the sun behind the tenement. At this remove, Puhalski found he could inspect its filthy denizens with detachment, free of those violent spasms of loathing which came when he was crowded together with them on the street, as though their filth and poverty and failure were contagious. Now they were like animals in a zoo, at this distance only faintly smelly. Losing interest quickly, he flipped away the stub of his cigarette and sat down to tie his shoelaces.

Maya stirred, murmuring, and her half-opened eyes caught his. Watching him coyly, she yawned, stretching her copious nakedness like some great, almost hairless cat. The soles of her feet were dirty. Pig, he thought, reminding himself that he was free of her.

He stood up abruptly. "Come, Maya. I must be going," he said. "Get up and fix me a glass of tea; I want to talk to you." He went into the kitchen and switched on the light.

Yesterday's Russian newspaper lay scattered on the kitchen table. He buried his nose in it until Maya had served him and was settled opposite him at the table, her own tea in front of her.

"What did he say after I left?" Puhalski wanted to know.

Maya shrugged. "Say? What he always says: he is worried, he is frightened, he doesn't want to get into trouble. It is always the same and I am sick of it. He will never change."

"That is not good enough. He *must* change. You must be more persuasive."

"But what can I do? I complain, I argue with him, reason with him. He just sits there like a lump."

What a pair! Puhalski thought wearily. Was he going to have to do everything himself? He had hardly known them until a few months before. They were a pair of poor nobodies, with only the prospect of becoming poorer. Years ago in Mukden he had sold some jewelry for Sobolov, but the few pieces of junk the pair had brought from Russia were soon gone and there was no further reason to think about them, except to know that they too had moved south to Peking. It was only when he heard that Sobolov had been hired by the Americans that his instincts had been aroused. Sobolov was the only White Russian work-

[61]

ing inside any of the foreign legations. It had seemed a good investment of his time to go around and renew their lapsed acquaintance. Who could say that Sobolov might not some day come in handy?

It had not been an entertaining task. He pretended that they shared an interest in books and what Sobolov, in his pedantic way, called "things of the mind." Puhalski had dropped in one afternoon to return a book while Sobolov was still at work; Maya was at home, and . . . well, so much for things of the mind. But Maya soon bored him with her possessiveness, and he'd been casting around for a way out when a chance remark of Tanaka's had opened up an entirely new possibility. That was hardly a month ago, and before he knew it he was being swept along in the wake of Tanaka's crazy scheme.

"There must be something," Puhalski said, a sneer on his thin lips. "Have you tried withholding your favors?"

Maya threw back her head and laughed briefly, humorlessly. "Andrei wants no favors; that part of our life was over long ago." She tapped her temple. "He lives only here, inside his head."

"Well, I can't afford any more delay."

"He needs reassurance. Perhaps if you could tell him a little more . . ."

"No!" Puhalski declared with a definite shake of the head. "It is too risky; too much is at stake. I don't trust him that much at this point."

"Well, if you don't trust him, why do you want him to work with you?"

"You do not understand these things. He must make a commitment to me; then I will trust him."

Maya shrugged and seemed to lose interest. Her eyes wandered around the room, then returned to his resentfully. "What about us, for a change?"

"Us?" Puhalski echoed, puzzled.

"You and me."

That again! Puhalski raised his shoulders helplessly. "We have no money, not enough anyway. And unless your husband comes to his senses we won't ever have enough . . . as I have explained to you a hundred times."

"Don't growl at me, Serge. I do my best." Maya looked ready to cry.

"You say it is your best, and perhaps it is. But it is not good enough . . ."

"You don't love me."

"Bah! Don't be an idiot! What good is love if we have no money?"

"You promised we would go away together," she sobbed.

Puhalski wanted to strike her. He reached across the table and gave her hand a reassuring pat. "And we will, my dear; we will. But we have to have money. If Andrei will only use his head, we shall both make a nice sum."

He looked at his watch. "It is late," he said, getting hurriedly to his feet. "I will be over tomorrow afternoon, if I can make it. Tomorrow evening, for sure; I must have another talk with Andrei. Meantime, keep after him, keep pressing."

Maya nodded dumbly, but in her big eyes there seemed to flicker a warning shadow of doubt, and Puhalski tried to put a little extra warmth into his farewell kiss. Her mouth was wet, and she licked at him; he stepped away, forcing a smile onto his face.

"Everything will be all right," he told her.

On the way down the stairs Puhalski wiped his mouth carefully and spat against the wall. He'd squeeze some milk out of the cow yet, he told himself. One way or another he deserved some payment for his time and services. Sobolov couldn't expect him to do his fucking for him for nothing, could he? Hell no! He'd either milk her . . . or sell her for meat. The notion made him laugh aloud.

♟♟

Mopping his face with a sodden handkerchief, Andrei Sobolov counseled himself to be patient. It had been a long hot day in a summer which was one of the worst in years, but it would soon be over, and he could go home. He told himself he ought to lose some weight, thought about that for a moment, then returned to his reading.

The work he'd been doing lately was interesting. He didn't mind the usual routine of letters, invoices, memoranda, and the proliferating variety of forms required by the Provisional Government, but they were essentially routine. Although they bored him, they appealed to a certain fussiness in him. But reporting on the daily Chinese and Japanese press was interesting, and he welcomed the challenge to his mind. Of course, it often meant taking his newspapers and magazines home with him, to be studied and reported on there . . . provided Maya decided to spare him the catalog of her day's complaints.

Poor Maya, poor dear Maya. He couldn't blame her, really. His friends had cautioned him against marrying a woman so much younger than himself. But that had been fifteen years ago. He hadn't felt old then; he'd felt mature and energetic, and his love for her and for the child they had made together, who was even then waiting in her belly to be born, had filled him with self-confidence. He had hoped that the child—his little Anya she turned out to be—would bring the

[63]

two of them together again. But it hadn't worked that way. Although Maya loved the girl, he was certain, she was too much of a child herself not to be jealous. If they had been rich, it might have been different. But they started poor and got only poorer. He was spoiling the child, she would complain. Sobolov smiled ruefully. A hair ribbon, a doll, and afternoon boating among the lily pads of the Pei-Hai . . . this was spoiling?

Of course, he wanted to spoil the child, so in a sense Maya was right. To spoil her, to protect her, and somehow to spirit her out of this wretched, war-torn, disintegrating country, to a place of safety, to America . . . that was what he wanted.

But none of that could be brought about if he daydreamed. As though to punctuate the thought, Mr. Chiang cleared his throat importantly, and Sobolov knew the office manager's disapproving eyes were upon him.

Although relatives of employees were not eligible for employment themselves, Mr. Chiang's nephew had been among the applicants for the job of Legation interpreter that day six months before. Mr. Chiang had apparently anticipated no difficulty in keeping the relationship a secret, but it made no difference. Mr. Edgerton had hired Sobolov. Mr. Chiang's resentment inclined him to find fault, even where there was none.

But he could be no more than an annoyance. As long as his work satisfied Mr. Edgerton's requirements, his job was safe and his family was safe. That was the thing he couldn't seem to get through Puhalski's head. Puhalski thrived on adventure and risk; Sobolov sought only for security. He didn't want an extra job, he just wanted to keep this one.

Sobolov went back to his newspaper. There was an article about the excellent quality of the Japanese imports being offered to the Chinese people now that the restrictive tariffs of the corrupt Nationalists and the greedy Westerners had been removed. Sobolov circled the headline with red pencil; he'd study it further at home.

A door slammed and Mr. Edgerton's firm, slow tread echoed down the hall. On cue the door at the far end, belonging to Mr. Smith, the new vice-consul, opened and his brisker and lighter step followed the Second Secretary's out of the front entrance. Mr. Procter was already gone. He'd returned briefly that afternoon, mainly to take a nap, as far as Sobolov could tell. He'd heard the gentle snores as he went by the closed door of Mr. Procter's office on his way to the bathroom.

Mr. Procter was a nice man, he supposed, but aloof, almost cold.

[64]

Sobolov had the uncomfortable feeling that Mr. Procter disapproved of him.

At last it was time to leave the office and go home.

Miss Kung, the Number One Chinese stenographer, flicked an imaginary mote of dust from her desk, smiled at him with myopic sweetness, and began to polish her thick glasses. Miss Feng, the Number Two, hummed to herself while touching up her lips, a Western art she'd not yet mastered. Loo, the coolie, was stowing his mop and broom and dust cloth in the hall closet.

Mr. Chiang would stay behind for the evening lock-up; it was his most cherished prerogative. He carried his ring of keys like a major domo.

Let him, Sobolov thought absentmindedly folding his unread papers and stuffing them in his briefcase. Turning in the entry he called goodnight to Mr. Chiang. Mr. Chiang didn't answer.

Pulling the heavy door closed behind him, Sobolov turned to face a sky like a brass mirror; it seemed to focus the power of the lowering sun directly on him. In spite of the frail shade of the Chancery building, waves of an almost liquid heat washed over him. Then, as he started down the steps, the green lawn across the road began to undulate mysteriously, then tilted slowly toward him. Dropping his briefcase, Sobolov groped uncertainly for the iron handrail and held on to it for dear life. He was beginning a sigh of relief when his heart leaped galvanically and a great pain filled his chest. Blind with fear and agony, he clung there not daring to think. After several interminable seconds the spasm faded, and he lowered himself until he was sitting on the top step. There he waited, wondering if death had just looked him in the eye.

It was not a new experience. Several times in the past few years much the same thing had happened, each time a little worse than the last. For a while he had preferred to think the trouble was with his liver. Things were steadier now, but still out of focus . . . with a twinge of annoyance he realized he still had on his reading glasses.

By the time he had fumbled through his pockets for the other pair, he was ready to descend carefully to the pavement, five steps below.

But he was glad to be going home. He had a steady job and was doing well at it; after all these years in China, he could face the future with guarded optimism. With hard work and a little luck he need never return to that demeaning life of random clerking, translating, tutoring, borrowing and begging . . . anything to grub up a few dollars for his family.

Sudden fortune was a storybook notion, like expecting to find money in the street. Maya would come to understand that in time, and her voice would become less harsh. Puhalski never would. Puhalski meant well and was a good friend, but he didn't realize that all his talk of extra money only made Maya more discontented than ever. The only thing to do was to turn Puhalski down once and for all, bear Maya's anger until the storm blew over, and then settle back into a life of some serenity.

Sobolov showed his identity card to the Marine sentry and let him peer into his briefcase. Seemingly satisfied, the sentry crashed through the remainder of the ritual of his rifle. The sentries had frightened him in the early days of his employment. Now they were a comfortable part of the routine . . . and called him "Andy."

Beyond the Gothic gateway to Legation Street the usual line of rickshaws waited at the curb. Eyes squarely ahead, Sobolov determined to ignore the contemptuous whispers of their pullers. Because they paid an extra fee to solicit passengers in the Legation Quarter, their rates were higher, and they knew he was too poor.

The terrible discouragement which had filled him the day he came to apply for the job would never fade. The hard glances of the Chinese applicants, resenting him as a foreign interloper, and his awareness of his age and threadbare appearance had combined to smother him in a feeling of impotence and impending defeat. Miraculously he had been hired, and his life had changed. And symbolic of that change was his new identity card. In English and Chinese, it described him as an employee of the American Legation. His photograph was on it, and it bore the signature and personal chop of the Second Secretary. And into its expensive paper was impressed the seal of the United States. Its addition to his papers raised him a notch above those other stateless Russians whose refuge in China depended so precariously on a Nansen passport from the League of Nations and a municipal identity booklet in good order. Now, when called upon to identify himself, he showed the Legation card first . . . it was always treated with respect. The thought of it made the contempt of the rickshaw coolies more bearable. Sobolov gave his wallet a protective pat.

Tree-lined and shady, Legation Street stretched ahead of him. He was looking forward to a quiet evening at home. His face brightened: there might even be a letter from Anya, his little Anyitchka. She had been away at the seashore since the beginning of the summer with the American family for whom she worked. That, too, had come about on account of his job. Somehow it had never occurred to him that she could get a job looking after someone's children for a summer. It had been so easy with Mr. Edgerton's help. She was safely out of the city and it was even possible—Mr. Edgerton had been encouraging—that she could go with the family to America when they went home in the fall. The prospect was so wonderful he hardly dared think about it. The shadow of her growing into womanhood as a refugee in China had haunted him for years. Now, with the country infested by the Japanese, the thought of it was unbearable. To his nightmare that she would end up like those pitiful painted creatures who hung around the cabarets waiting for the foreign soldiers was added the hazard of drunken Japanese soldiers. More than once she had come home in tears, frightened by rude words and gestures. To get her out of China and safe at least . . . he would give his life for that.

Arriving presently at the East Gate of the Legation Quarter he selected a rickshaw from the eager cluster always waiting there. He bargained briefly and skillfully over the fare, then climbed into the shabby vehicle. As they started off, he leaned back into the lumpy cushions, gave his tie a yank, and settled his hat more firmly on his head.

A horn blared raucously, brakes screeched, and there was a rending of wood and metal. Sobolov clutched at the arm rests in sudden panic. Just ahead, the brown mass of a Japanese Army truck was entangled with an ox-cart. As the rickshaw coolie slowed, there was a clash of gears, and the truck surged backward, wrenching its bent bumper clear of the wreckage.

Sobolov felt the terrible tightening deep in his chest, and his pulse drummed in his ears. Pressing his fists against his solar plexus, he waited for the great pain. Hemmed in by traffic, balanced on the edge of terror, Sobolov could only sit there and watch.

The cart was on its side and the ox lay kicking in the tangled traces, bellowing with fright. One wheel had collapsed and several bags of grain had spilled into the street. Stunned by the catastrophe, the bare-foot carter stood to one side and stared at the shambles.

Sobolov watched petrified as the truck driver, a short broad man in the sweat-stained uniform of a corporal, climbed down from the cab. He elbowed his way through the crowd, drew his bayonet, and began to beat the carter methodically with the flat of it. Wailing plaintively, the carter collapsed slowly to his knees, trying to cover his head with his arms. Long gashes opened up across his shirtless back welling with blood. Soon thin strips of flesh hung from him here and there like pieces of bloody bacon. The top of one ear came away and hung upside down for a moment from a thread of tissue, then fell into the dust. By now numbering better than a hundred persons, the crowd strained and shifted, careful not to get too close but too fascinated to move

[67]

away. A thin hum came from them, as though deep within each one some spirit moaned vicariously.

At last the corporal was satisfied and stepped back. Panting heavily, he looked down on the body of the whimpering carter, then bent forward and wiped his bayonet on the man's trousers. As he pushed his way back to the truck, the crowd parted like so many cows. From the running board he turned and gave them all a glance of absolute indifference.

Sobolov heard only the roaring of an exhaust and the peremptory blast of a horn as the truck moved away. Although his heart called out to him to go and help his wounded brother, he was vomiting between the rickshaw poles, and could do nothing. He wiped his mouth on his sleeve and looked around, suddenly embarrassed, but no one was paying any attention to him. The crowd had melted away, intent on continuing with their business as though none of them had ever seen what they had seen. At last other carters in the caravan helped their wounded partner to his feet; no one else was interested.

His rickshaw coolie backed into the clear, swung smartly around the remains of the cart, and was soon jogging along as before. Sobolov sagged in his seat, his head bouncing feebly like a baby's. Slowly the hard congestion in his chest ebbed away. Although the big pain had never come, the threat of two spasms within an hour terrified him. What would become of Anya and Maya? He couldn't bear to think about it.

His suit was soaked, and the acrid sourness of his fear surrounded him like a mist. He yearned with an inexpressible longing to be home, to be out of the jarring discomfort of the rickshaw, off this dangerous street, and away from these alien people who thronged its sidewalks. Gone was his small momentary contentment. He was alone, a foreigner surrounded by millions of these people who cared nothing for each other, much less for him, and whom he despaired of understanding. Legation identity card or not, he was as helpless as that cart driver, as likely a target of casual brutality, and of no more consequence to his fellow humans. Theirs was the apathy of centuries of struggle for a bare existence; there was no energy left over for compassion. In their numbers, they could have trampled that Japanese into dusty bits of cloth and skin and passed on anonymously, but it had never occurred to them to interfere. A crowd in Russia would have obliterated that soldier, he told himself. It would have mattered nothing that they were defeated and that he was the conqueror.

But such thoughts were idle. For him, as for the other refugees, there was no Russia. The only way to survive was to orientalize oneself, be

[68]

selfish, mind one's own business, stifle all Samaritan impulses. His only hope was that, with the help of God and the Americans, Anya might soon be out of it.

The rickshaw drew to a stop at last, and Sobolov climbed down unsteadily. As he felt for his coin purse, he inventoried the contents of his pockets with a series of precautionary pats, reassuring himself in particular that his precious wallet was safe. Then, he began laboriously to climb the steps into the Northern Peace Apartments.

恭恭

Candlelight diffused through the rice paper lanterns and flowed delicately over the flagstone patio. In one corner a Victrola mourned nostalgically, in another a table covered with a white cloth gleamed with bottles and glasses. Under the wicker chairs and sofas spirals of incense smoldered, spicy and exotic, keeping the mosquitoes at bay and masking the pervasive odors of nearby farms. Edgerton had to restrain the impulse to lean back in the sofa and compliment his hosts with an Oriental belch.

A rooflike extension of the straw p'eng, built over the house to shade it for the summer, jutted across the patio. Several mats were rolled back and through the opening he could see the stars pointing down the deep black sky.

The dinner had been expectably excellent, and accompanied by quantities of a chilled white wine which had mixed well with the martinis of the cocktail hour. Now, savoring the first swallow of his whiskey soda, he felt himself emanating a warm and beatific glow. He let his gaze wander among the company, and he gave them his slightly groggy blessing.

In a nearby corner, somewhat out of the lantern light, Hal Mac-Donough danced slowly with Marie Bardinet. Benignly objective, Edgerton allowed that Hal cut an impressive figure in his high-collared white uniform. The light gleamed on his captain's bars, and when he turned it caught the bright colors of two campaign ribbons. He wondered if Hal suspected the complications which might lie ahead with the warm Marie, and felt perversely envious. He'd had his chances with Marie, but had shied away from a love affair he couldn't manage. Yet there he was with Tamara, and things were as cluttered and complicated as ever any intrigue could have been, even with Marie.

Uncomfortable at the thought, he shifted his eyes to the blocky profile of Chang Sun-cheh, whose head was cocked intently toward

[69]

Franklin Procter. Recalling their conversation, he was impressed by Procter's relaxed manner. He wondered what they were talking about.

Edgerton had known Chang ever since his own first years in China —they'd been at Berkeley at the same time but had never met there —and he thought he knew him well. He liked him and wanted to trust him. He insisted that he *did* trust him, but nagging doubts remained, perturbing him and leaving him with a rueful sense of loss. Chang caught his glance and nodded. He'd find an opportunity to talk to him later.

"Isn't she being a little obvious?"

Valerie Warner's whispered question startled him. For a moment he'd quite forgotten she was there. Turning to look at her, he thought how oddly attractive she was with her frank rather homely face: wide-set blue eyes and a thin straight nose over a broad and mobile mouth. Her hair was honey-colored. It came to just below her ears and looked very clean and soft. He composed his face into an expression of exaggerated blankness.

"The great stone face," she laughed. "How do you do it?"

"Years of diplomatic training."

"I can see they haven't been wasted . . . but answer my question."

"Question?"

"Don't be dense." She nodded toward the dancers. "Aren't they being a bit *intimate?*"

Edgerton pretended to study them. "The flagstones are a bit uneven; perhaps it's merely a question of providing mutual support."

Valerie laughed softly.

Marie Bardinet was smiling up at her partner, her teeth sparkling between wet red lips. She seemed literally to flow into him. Edgerton knew what that could be like.

It had been after a Bastille Day reception. Full of champagne and loneliness—he didn't know Tamara then and had just broken off with a stenographer from the British Legation—he had been asked by the Bardinets to stay on and have supper with them. Even more champagne later the aged Rene had excused himself and gone off to bed, and he and Marie had danced. In minutes what had seemed mere flirtation became an invitation too explicit to ignore. Her touch working quickly at his buttons and the taste of her mouth had robbed him of what little sense he might have had left. She had held his prick in her hand like the tiller of a rowboat and steered him into the darkest corner of the panelled room, a grinning, bumbling, drunken boob. And there on the floor behind a long couch they'd coupled . . . feverish, frantic, quick as rabbits, both of them. For a while she'd been angry with him for never going back.

[70]

"Do you suppose Hal is really interested in her?"

"He's near death if he isn't."

She laughed again, and shifted to face him directly. "I must stop staring at them so much." Her eyes fell. "Won't there be an awful scandal?"

"Who can say? We'll just have to await developments."

Through some subtlety of Pamela's, he'd been seated next to Marie at dinner, with Hal happily monopolizing Valerie across the table . . . in sight but out of reach, he supposed was the idea. He hadn't really minded; it was no hardship to give his attention to the vivacious Frenchwoman. He had rather enjoyed being reminded of their brief intimacy and was somewhat surprised to discover that they had become good friends. When she recalled old times, he directed his gaze pointedly, into the front of her low-cut dress, making her squirm with delight. Silly, perhaps, but it was fun. Their only awkwardness came when Marie inquired coquettishly after *"votre-petite Chinoise"* and Edgerton had pointedly changed the subject. Reminded of her question now, he swore silently. Procter knew what he was talking about. If Marie knew about Tamara, who could there be who did not?

The record ended. MacDonough dipped, and Marie followed, fully astride his leg.

"My word!" Valerie giggled. "What will her husband think?"

"Oh, he's a Gallic gentleman of the old school: *savoir faire,* and all that. Besides, she's only flirting; he must be used to it."

She regarded him curiously over the top of her smile. "Well, tell me this: with all the diplomatic taboos, how do *you* divert yourself?"

"Me?" Edgerton looked shocked. "I live only for my work."

She shook her head impatiently. "You're impossible! Here I am trying to pry some information out of you, and you're being positively dim."

"Ask me anything." Edgerton made an expansive gesture with his hands. Her interest flattered him, and he liked watching the play of expression on her face. Beyond the mobility of her mouth and eyes he thought he saw passion and sensuality, and was intrigued. "My life is practically an open book."

"Do you know many interesting girls?"

He brightened. "Thousands of them. There are American girls, English girls, Japanese girls, Chinese girls, Russian girls . . . The place is literally infested with them. The mind boggles . . ."

"You're a wretch!"

He gave her a hard look, wanting her to know that he was stubborn and not to press him. Pamela would have told her about Tamara, and he could imagine in what terms. He was abruptly and intensely angry.

[71]

It was as though Tamara were standing there watching him, waiting to see what he would do. It was all so unfair to her, so demeaning. "I said 'practically' an open book."

"I understand," she said quickly, diffidently. "I guess I'm too curious."

"Don't worry," Edgerton said, wondering if he'd hurt her. He liked the look of her. When they were introduced, her eyes had acknowledged what they both knew: Pamela had "plans." Her strong fingers had seemed to signal an alliance. There had been a brief exchange of preliminaries before Pamela took her off to meet Captain Harold MacDonough, United States Marine Corps.

Some shift of light revealed a trace of sadness among those few signs of age which she seemed to take no pains to hide. Feeling strangely moved, he wanted to reach out and touch her. Over the incense, her perfume came to him, and an aroma all her own, feminine and exciting. He felt a deep stirring in his groin, and his face grew hot.

"Pamela's incredible," Valerie said suddenly. "She never changes. We were certified young ladies together at Smith, an unmentionable number of years ago." Her mouth turned down in a wry smile. "Time's remorseless fingers have been a little more gentle with her, I think."

"Hmmm," Edgerton said, leaning forward and inspecting her with medical concern. "I think you can expect to survive the evening . . . provided you're very careful."

She looked pleased and went on to talk about Washington. Edgerton's mind drifted, and he let it, mellowed by Procter's excellent Scotch.

"They were very nice to me," Valerie was saying. "I was coming out of a rather bad time and Pamela took me under her wing."

Edgerton found himself wondering about it, that "bad time," hoping both that she would confide in him and, on the contrary, that she would not. He wanted them to pursue this incipient relationship unfettered by either of their pasts. But he wondered how to do that.

He felt suddenly completely incongruous, sitting there in a pretty garden talking to this sophisticated woman. Just beyond the garden wall there seethed a strange and hidden country being dismembered in a war. It was a country that he understood hardly better than she, the newcomer, for all of his time there and his fumbling attempts to make comprehensible the obscurities of China. God damn China! He was sick of it and would be glad when he was out of it.

Tamara appeared in his mind, as though asking him what he was

[72]

doing here among all these people, making small talk and getting drunk, when he could be there with her? There, somewhere. But that was just it: there was no somewhere for them.

Moments later, standing at the edge of the patio with a fresh drink in his hand, he watched MacDonough lead Valerie away to dance. He had no wish to monopolize her, nor did he need to. A soothing sense of having plenty of time came over him. They were interested in one another; the future could decide the rest. She was a very feminine creature. She had a good walk, too, and a nice ass.

Turning away, he found the amused eyes of Chang Sun-cheh fixed inquiringly on his from the opposite side of the patio. He grinned and began to thread his way across.

"How are you, Jimmy?" he said, hesitating over the incongruous nickname, recalling that Chang preferred it for some reason.

"Hello, John. Long time no see," Chang replied with an ironic grimace at his own corniness. Although his manner was easy, he looked worried, and his eyes were shadowed with fatigue.

"Too long. I have been wondering how you and Madeline were."

Chang gestured clumsily with the hand that held his drink, and a little of it spilled over. He seemed not to notice. "We are both as well as the complicated circumstances permit," he said, pretending lightness. "I have my chores at the Ministry, and Madeline is up to her neck in women's committees for this and that." He laughed shortly, shaking his head. "Civic-minded women are an enigma to me. Really, all women are."

Edgerton sipped his drink. "There is no arguing with that."

Chang's eyebrows went up quizzically. "But you are a confirmed bachelor. When can you find the time to observe the riddle of womankind?"

"I have my moments."

Chang grinned broadly. "Yeah, I noticed." He laughed then, suddenly and easily, reminding Edgerton of the old days. Sobering, Chang went on, "I was just hoping for a chance to talk to you. We have wanted to have you over. Pot luck, or something, but . . ." His voice trailed off and he shifted his feet uncomfortably.

Those good old days were not always very good for Chang, Edgerton reminded himself, recalling that the Chinese was sometimes criticized for being too Western and for having too many American friends. Now his position would be particularly awkward. The Japanese needed him partly for the stability and reason which his Westernness lent their regime and, perversely, would distrust him for it. It was identical to the xenophobia the Foreign Service encountered in its

[73]

dealings with the Congress. Its expertise, derived from associating with foreigners, was distrusted. No wonder the Changs did little entertaining; tightrope walking must consume most of their energies. He smiled understandingly.

"This is our first outing among the foreign devils in a long time," he said, and leaned a little closer. "Frankly, the invitation put us on the spot. The Japanese haven't quite decided what they want me to do about my foreign friends, so we took a chance. I'm glad we did . . . for now." His grin tried to make light of his uncertainty.

"I saw you deep in conversation with my boss a few minutes ago," Edgerton said. "What was that all about . . . or shouldn't I ask?"

Chang's face went deliberately blank. "From somewhere he'd gotten the notion that the Japanese are importing opium. He asked if I'd heard of it."

Chang's gaze was impenetrable; Edgerton groaned silently. Where was Procter's vaunted diplomatic tact? "What did you tell him?"

"Why, I denied it, of course." Chang stared down into his glass as though expecting to find something he'd lost hidden among the ice cubes. "He's very direct."

Edgerton thought Chang was blushing but, in the flickering candlelight, could not be sure. He waited.

"I don't know him well enough to be candid," Chang said at last. "And frankly, I'm too ashamed. Of course, the Army manages all that business. They don't confide in us civilians . . . not that we could do much to block them in any case."

Chang was silent for several seconds. "And then he wanted my opinion on the nature of Chinese Communism. He spoke of it as 'godless' and expressed surprise that the traditional religious attitudes of the Chinese would bend so far. I was at a loss. All I could say was that the movement seemed peasant-oriented, with tax and land reforms as its main concern. I told him the peasants of China, as elsewhere, aren't deep thinkers and that for many, their religion consists of propitiating various gods of nature in a timely fashion, and commands them to venerate their ancestors." He took a sip of his drink. "I went on to suggest to your boss that when the peasant achieves more control over his own destiny, he'll put less reliance on the good offices of the God of Rain and the others. I must have sounded flippant, disappointing as well as offending him." He shrugged. "He didn't know quite what to make of me. Not surprising; I wonder at myself sometimes."

"One does what is necessary," was all that Edgerton could think of to say.

[74]

Chang's expression was grateful. "Exactly; but it's a continuing puzzle. Every now and then you do something that appears necessary at the time but proves otherwise later, and you realize you've lost ground . . . and pride. You can't get them back, you know." He shook his head, then brightened suddenly. "By the way, I've a bone to pick with you."

"With me?"

"Yes. My agents—who are everywhere—report unanimously that you were solely responsible for the speed bumps on Legation Street."

Edgerton laughed a bit uneasily. "I hope that business didn't cause you any embarrassment."

Chang waved the thought away. "Nothing I couldn't handle. But it caused a furor at the Municipal Yamen, I can assure you. The Japanese were apoplectic and turned on me in a rage, apparently reasoning that as I had been to school in California, some sort of Yankee telepathy should have warned me."

In spite of Chang's light tone, he could see that there was real difficulty, even danger, in his situation. "I didn't think; I'm sorry. We felt the time had come for strong measures . . ."

Chang stopped him with a tap on the arm. "I understand." He looked around conspiratorially. "You did the only thing possible, though if you quote me, I'll deny it. The Japanese are humorless, you know, particularly about themselves. You made the Military Police look foolish. I thought Colonel Tanaka would have a stroke."

"Ah, yes . . . Tanaka," Edgerton said, vaguely remembering a fat Japanese officer who spoke a strangely accented American slang which he seemed to want desperately to show off. They had met at some reception or other, probably Italian. He couldn't recall what they had said to each other.

"Tanaka's rivals at Headquarters were quick to make it hot for him. At first he wanted to bring in tanks and root out the bumps with brute force . . . he has a nasty temper. I finally convinced him that the Legation Quarter was still sacred ground and would remain so for as long as the Western boot rested so firmly on our Asian necks. We became almost fraternal over it." Chang laughed quietly, reminding Edgerton of the times they had argued this very point, and not always in good humor, Berkeley notwithstanding, Chang had always been a patriot, openly impatient for the time when China would be strong enough to deal with the great powers on equal terms. "He predicted, rather ominously, that the sanctity of the Legation Quarter was only temporary."

A time was coming when there would be no room for Legation

[75]

Quarters and similar anachronisms; Edgerton's own conclusion was that it was overdue. He nodded soberly. "He's probably right. Unfortunately, the abolition of the Quarter and the other Concessions, when it comes, will work to their benefit and not to yours."

"Yes. But even a limping step in the right direction is still a step. If they are going to occupy the country, why not the foreign enclaves as well?"

"So that when they are finally beaten, China will get the country back intact, minus any nasty foreign residue?"

Chang grinned. "Something like that."

"I am inclined to agree . . . though if you quote me, I'll deny it." They both laughed. Edgerton turned serious at once. "Can China win, do you think, the way things are going?"

"Not the way things are going, no. But eventually, yes. Things, as you call them, will change."

"I wish I could be so optimistic."

"It's not merely optimism on my part; it's necessity. What could I believe, if I didn't believe that?"

"I see your point. It's going to take some doing. We'll end up helping you do it, I guess. Unofficially, of course."

"Help unofficially, or guess unofficially?"

"Guess."

Chang chuckled softly. "I agree . . . unofficially. But expect no thanks."

"Some will."

"They'll be disappointed, I'm afraid. Gratitude is an unnatural emotion for nations. I would distrust expressions of gratitude, if I were you."

"Self-interest is more trustworthy, then?"

"Up to a point, yes."

"But isn't it on account of our self-interest that we're already distrusted?"

"No. You're disliked for it, but not distrusted. You're distrusted for your generosity."

"That sounds discouraging. You mean the missionaries?"

"Precisely." His grin flashed briefly. "And there is another thing which you should think about, you in particular, John. Where are all these roving, ambitious businessmen and missionaries leading you?"

"It's a good point and I do think about it. But we're individualists; we cling to the notion that an American has the innate right to go anywhere he chooses. Frankly, I find the notion an attractive one."

"Yes, but at what risk, what involvement? More Marines and more gunboats? That won't work here when China begins to wake up. And you risk becoming deeply involved where you have only a commercial interest. And perhaps a spiritual one, if you count the missionaries." His broadening smile showed how ridiculous he thought the latter interest was.

Edgerton took a swallow of his drink and fished a cigarette out of his pocket. Chang handed his empty glass to a passing houseboy and produced matches. An interesting man, Edgerton was thinking. If only he were not so retiring. He missed the long arguments they used to have, and told Chang so.

Chang smiled warmly. "Me, too," he said. "Sometimes I think the two of us could have made a better job of things than all these cabinet ministers and ambassadors and generals . . . and generalissimos."

"An intriguingly immodest thought," Edgerton said. "Perhaps someday we'll get our chance, though I must admit the thought of exercising political power leaves me aghast. One problem is finding competent and honest helpers."

"Ah! That's good! As long as you feel that way, you can be trusted. I flatter myself that I'm equally modest, and, therefore, equally noble. As a matter of fact, there are a few good ones available. Which reminds me: I was talking to one of them just the other day . . . an admirer of yours."

Edgerton raised his eyebrows.

"Yes. A police officer with whom I have something to do from time to time: Li Ching-wei."

Edgerton grinned; he hadn't seen Li in several months. "He's a remarkable man in many ways. How is he?"

"As well as can be expected. We're in the same leaky boat, he and I." Chang's voice dropped. "Being a nominal traitor is an uncomfortable business. It's not as easy as it looks and there are many frustrations. Anyway, Li asked if I knew you and was surprised to learn of our long acquaintance, just as I was to discover that you knew each other. Quite extraordinary, an American diplomat and a Chinese cop becoming friends! But I keep forgetting, John: you're an extraordinary fellow."

"We met some years ago, in Tientsin."

"So Li said. What was that business all about?" Chang's grin broadened. "Sounded like some sort of cops and robbers stunt. And you're so dignified . . . I was amazed!"

Edgerton laughed, then shook his head, remembering. "It was the Martin kidnapping in, let's see, 1930, I think it was. The family was having trouble getting the ransom money together and were expecting to begin receiving severed fingers and toes any day. . . ."

"Chinese kidnappers mean business," Chang interrupted. "No stalling or bargaining. Those were lawless days up here."

"I know, and so did Martin's wife. Anyway, we got a tip at the Consulate that indicated a rescue was possible, and I was told to set up what I could. The municipal police weren't much impressed with our tip and assigned Police Corporal Li to the case. But we fooled them, and pulled it off."

"Just the two of you?"

"There wasn't anyone else."

"Li seems to think you saved his life."

"As I remember it, I was concentrating on saving my own," Edgerton said, grateful for Li's good opinion.

"Mmmm, such commendable modesty," Chang said dryly. He looked at Edgerton for a moment. "What would the Secretary of State have said about such goings on?"

"I tremble to think. Fortunately, he never found out. No one did."

"Well, it's a good story, and illustrates my point. With enough Lis to help us, even our dreams become practical." He snorted. "But it would take an army of them to overcome the nincompoops."

"We must sound like we're plotting a *coup d'état.*"

Chang gave him a rather sour grin. "Don't think I haven't thought about it. I'm not so reticent as I pretend. Power frightens me, but I hunger for it."

"You can have it. I'll stick to my reporting and advising."

"And being ignored?"

"Not always. And to do my superiors justice, I haven't had much advice to give lately. Things seem already beyond control . . . I have no feasible remedies."

"Yes, 'feasible,'" Chang repeated soberly. "That cautious word. How many good schemes have run afoul of the concept of feasibility?"

"What good's a plan that won't work?"

"Ah, but unfeasible doesn't mean that. It merely means the authorities are afraid to try it. And the more it's proved that what *they* are already doing is what's unfeasible, the more frightened and rigid they become." All of a sudden Chang looked very angry. "Let's face it: One thing we have in common is that we are governed by frightened idiots. If I had my way . . ."

Madeline seemed to materialize at her husband's elbow, startling him into silence. The smile that she had for Edgerton seemed affable enough, but although it showed her handsome white teeth, it stopped well short of her dark almond eyes. "What are you two conspiring about?" she asked lightly.

[78]

Madeline Chang had been educated in Hong Kong, where her father had been a banker, and her speech still retained the accent she'd learned in her English missionary school. Once Edgerton had found it quaintly attractive, almost a brogue. Now it seemed merely aloof, almost snooty, as though she might reserve it for complex insults. She made the right social motions but her animosity was palpable.

Chang looked uncomfortable, almost sheepish, and his muscular body seemed suddenly stiff and awkward. It was obvious that Madeline wanted to talk to Jimmy alone, so Edgerton stayed with them only long enough to exchange a few of the usual banalities. Conscious of having been dismissed, and not much liking it, he drifted toward the bar table. Madeline's sibilant whisper began even as he turned away. The encounter left him depressed; they had been good friends once, the three of them. What had happened?

Hal was keeping Valerie for another dance and Edgerton felt an odd sense of relief, glad for a moment by himself. The music and the murmured voices came to him attenuated, as though a thick pane of glass intervened. The scene was decorous and tastefully elegant in that modest and cozy way that only the rich could manage. It looked so easy and so comfortable, but he told himself that he had no yearning for that sort of thing. It was nice for a visit, but. . . . He thought of his own small courtyard and tidy quarters . . . the picture should have reassured him, but it didn't. The privacy looked merely lonely, and he saw himself petrifying there in the San Kwan Miao, he and his venerable valet doddering into senility together. But he was leaving China . . . how could he have forgotten that? He felt more than ever the outsider, the observer. It was time to go home.

Inevitably, his move to leave precipitated a general exodus. Pamela gave him a mock accusing glance for breaking up her party and whispered for him to stay for a nightcap. He was briefly tempted, then shook his head. Things had reached a perfect balance between himself and Valerie, and he wanted to leave them that way for now. Besides, he'd chatted enough.

As he took Valerie's hand, he felt her fingers give him back something extra, and there was invitation in her candid glance. I accept, he wanted to tell her. But later. Next time. Soon. Don't worry.

Walking out to his car, he felt a little unsteady, but devilish and horny and very much his own master. He could see himself with Valerie and knew what it was going to be like . . . different, rawer than what he and Tamara knew together, closer to depravity, wilder. . . .

But he would have to be circumspect. He mustn't risk hurting

[79]

Tamara or taking the even more dreadful chance of losing her. It could be managed.

Suddenly a wave of shame broke over him, and he asked himself if he really knew what he was doing. Valerie seemed well able to take care of herself, but what about Tamara? Demanding nothing, that was precisely what she got. He was free to amuse himself in a world from which she was excluded, leaving her free to do nothing. She was supposed to be waiting when he needed to lose himself in her lips and honeyed body, and then to be left, empty-handed and empty-hearted, when he was through with her. Was not that the way he had arranged matters? "You son of a bitch!" he muttered and rammed the car into gear.

愛愛

It was hot and close in the apothecary shop, and reeking with the conglomerate odors of the "doctor's" stock. Liu Chu-hsing wrinkled her nose.

Like her daughter, she had no particular faith in either Chinese or Western medicine, *Han yao* and *Yang yao* were merely contending myths. It was an indifference that comes naturally only to those who are never ill.

But that evening Tamara had come home complaining of a headache. After supper, when it seemed only to be getting worse, Chu-hsing had insisted on coming to the apothecary for a remedy. It was not far—not more than three squares . . . and it gave her time to think, and get a welcome breath of air. Although it was after ten, their rooms were still furnacelike.

Chu-hsing was certain that the American was the cause of her headache. It had taken all Chu-hsing's willpower to resist another attempt at making her daughter see the truth about that man, but she had managed it. After Tamara had left for work that morning, Chu-hsing had vowed never again to provoke another angry scene, no matter how justified, and she was determined to keep her word.

Chu-hsing knew what the trouble was. Tamara was dazzled by the man. Oh, he was charming enough, and attractive in that strange way those Western men had, with his American good looks and courteous language—Liu *t'ai t'ai*, he had called her: "Madame Liu." It had a nice sound. Then there was his obvious virility. She was not so old as to be unable to recognize it, for all that she had thrust that part of life behind her as completely as if she had become a nun. She was barely older than the American, for that matter, although she had never mentioned that fact to her blind and stubborn child.

[80]

But by now she knew that argument was worse than useless. She needed other tactics, other methods, if Tamara was to be spared the life she'd led.

Chu-hsing stared around the dimly lit shop impatiently. Long and narrow, with a high dark ceiling, it was a place of gloom and dust. Barely visible above her, hanging like growing roots might hang from the roof of a cave, were clusters of herbs and tubers. Shelves of dusty jars displayed an unnameable variety of pale and wrinkled things floating in colorless preservative. Chu-hsing gave them only a quick, disgusted glance. At least the foreigners had the wisdom to reduce their medicines into the form of pills and liquids. This was too explicit.

There was a stir behind a beaded curtain, and the wizened old proprietor shuffled out of the murk at the back of the shop and gave her a tiny paper package. She thanked him, paid him, and tucked the medicine into an inner pocket.

Though it was early—the darkness not yet two hours old—Hata Men Chieh was nearly deserted. The neighborhood to the east of the boulevard, toward her own house and beyond, was almost rural, with several small farms scattered between there and the city wall. Like country people elsewhere its residents tended to go to bed early.

Chu-hsing turned to the right, toward the entrance of her own *hu-tung* only a third of a block away. Beyond that, farther up the street and on the opposite side, red neon glared down onto the sidewalk, and some nasal Japanese lament rent the still air. It was a place for soldiers; they could get beer and saki, and there were women there and cubicles upstairs: Japanese and Korean women and a few Chinese. Little was seen of any of them in the daytime, especially the Chinese women. They seldom came out, and when they did no one would look directly at them. No one except the children, and they would only look for a moment before running away and giggling to one another.

The soldiers were truck drivers, and were quartered in a *hu-tung* to the west of the bar. They were a small group and didn't cause much trouble. Being drivers and mechanics made the difference, she supposed. With regular soldiers, riflemen, it might have been a different story. Just the same, there had been a few mean incidents: rickshaw men beaten up and pedestrians molested, and some drunken brawling and shouting among the soldiers themselves. It was rumored that one of the women had been thrown from an upstairs window earlier that summer, but with what result nobody knew. No one saw it, and in any case it was Army business and the wise were careful to show no curiosity.

Behind her, a mile to the south, things were not so quiet. There was

[81]

some sort of headquarters down there, with a large barracks and a rash of little beer and saki parlors that were filled with roistering soldiers every night. That was an area to be avoided, especially after dark. Fortunately, the soldiers there were content with their local amenities, and seldom strayed in search of amusement. Only once had a contingent from the headquarters come up to try the wares until then reserved for the truck drivers. A battle royal had ensued, spilling out into the middle of the street in a great turmoil. A large crowd had gathered, watching with impassive rapture while thirty or forty Japanese beat one another senseless. It was a rare spectacle for the Chinese. Finally a platoon of Military Police was called in to break up the melee and cart off the bodies. It was too bad it could not have gone on longer, everyone agreed, but while it lasted the sight of the helmeted police swinging their clubs at all those Japanese heads had indeed been a grand spectacle.

Chu-hsing smiled to herself and turned into her *hu-tung*. Suddenly one arm like iron took her around the neck from behind, while another completely encircled her waist, pinning her arms like a straitjacket. A breath that stank of beer and turnips blasted hotly past her face, and a bristled jaw dug into the soft hollow of her neck. She tried to scream but the arm held her jaws clamped shut, and only a sort of whinny escaped from her nose.

The man's arms were long and powerful, and the straining arch of his body kept lifting her off her feet. She tried futilely to twist and turn, but could get no leverage. A narrow curving path led away between two buildings, and inexorably she was carried down it and away from the *hu-tung*. Her first thought was that she was to be robbed . . . but that was ridiculous. She had only a few coppers, the change from her purchase. Besides, Chinese women who were dressed as she was never had any money, and everyone knew it. She tried desperately to break away, but the arms only tightened their grip on her, limiting sensation to the searing pain across her throat, the aching effort of her lungs to breathe . . . and the intruding presence of some hard, insistent thing which was thrusting rhythmically into the cleavage of her buttocks. She was several seconds figuring out what it was.

With the coming of the Japanese and their large unruly Army, the threat of rape had become a constant fact of life—a commonplace—and women of all ages were eligible. She had thought of it, of course, but primarily in fear for Tamara. That she might become a victim herself had not occurred to her.

Again she wrenched around, more violently than before, and all of a sudden she was free, and face to face with a squat hulking shadow.

[82]

Panting like a horse, the man staggered drunkenly for a moment, then began to inch warily toward her. She could make out his putteed legs and baggy military britches, and the white singlet he wore instead of a jacket. Shadowed by the visor of his pointed *kepi*, his bearded face was a dark smear in which the eyes were only darker holes.

Backing away, Chu-hsing was brought to a stop by a brick wall. A panicked glance showed her that the wall and the high fence next to it formed a cul-de-sac in which she was trapped.

Now that she was free to scream, she didn't. It would have been futile. It would have wasted her precious breath and provoked her adversary. Besides, screams in the night went unheeded in much of Peking nowadays.

The man was weaving and seemed about to fall. Seizing the moment, Chu-hsing tried to rush past him. For a moment she thought she'd made it. Caught unawares, he grabbed for her clumsily, his fingers clawing down her arm and raking her back as she went by him. But then his hand closed on the hem of her jacket, jerking her to a halt. She struck backward at his arm with her fist, trying to break his grip, and then again, and his fingers closed around her wrist like steel clamps. Grunting with the effort, he slammed her back into the niche so powerfully her head cracked against the brick wall, stunning her even through the cushion of her hair. Chu-hsing felt herself collapsing slowly to the ground. She heard the man laugh then, triumphantly, and saw him tearing eagerly at the buttons of his fly. Muttering to himself, he lunged toward her.

On her knees now, she tried to dodge, but only lost her balance, taking his blow high on the temple. For a moment she sagged groggily against the wall, unable to resist the hands fumbling at her sash. She stirred, however, when the sound of her trousers being ripped down the front came to her, and she clawed at his eyes. But the effort was feeble, and he merely butted her in the face for it, almost breaking her nose and blinding her with a gush of tears.

Even though she still struggled weakly, she could feel herself being driven steadily backward under his onslaught, and she knew in her heart that he was unstoppable. His body had become a machine with the single function of plunging its protrusion into her.

Stunned and seared with pain, she knew she was sinking into unconsciousness. She fought back desperately, sensing that it would be the end of her if she fainted, that he would kill her or leave her so hurt that she would die before morning. Blindly, as though groping for some fingerhold on life, her hand moved crablike across the ground, was stopped, explored momentarily, then closed upon a piece of brick.

[83]

The man was intent about his business now, pumping away in her, panting heavily, his hands kneading her breasts. Common sense told her that it was almost over, told her to wait, to seek her advantage when he was done and exhausted, but rage and defiance took control of her mind, and a terrible sense of humiliation. She struck him fiercely in the face, seeing even in the starlight the instant welling of blood on his cheekbone. He grunted with pain and surprise, and his hands stopped their work. A strange silence settled over them.

Then the man roared with fury, and the sound caught in his throat, choking him, sending him into a convulsion of great racking coughs. Gathering her strength, Chu-hsing thrust her hips upward like an acrobat, heaving him off of her, out of her. For an instant he loomed unsteadily above, gasping, blotting out the starlight, and almost upright on his knees.

It was her instant, and she knew it would be the only one she'd get. As he lifted his fist to strike her, she grasped his erect penis as though it were a handle, then punched upward with the brick, driving it into his unprotected crotch. It was clumsy, but her arm had the strength of desperation in it. It was enough.

The soldier bellowed like a wounded animal, the cry pitching up into a scream, only to die in his windpipe as though pinched off by a pair of fingers. He fell away from her, slowly and heavily, to lie on his side, his hands comforting and protecting his damaged parts, his feet in their hobnailed boots kicking at the ground like a dog running in a dream.

Dazed and terrified, Chu-hsing got unsteadily to her feet. She leaned against the wall for a moment, panting heavily and stared down at him, her piece of brick still clutched in her hand. Her throat was dry, and her shoulder ached from the twisting he had given her arm. Her breasts felt bruised and tender. Along with the burning pain between her legs, she could feel a moistness which she was sure was blood.

All around was silence, that special waiting silence of the held breath and the stilled tongue. She could sense the surrounding listeners, the hearers of that feral cry, waiting quietly for the tumult to pass on and leave them out of any nighttime mysteries.

It was as though she and the soldier were isolated together in that tight space, they and their small noises held in by the willful indifference of the ordinary world beyond.

Coldly she considered hitting him on the head with the brick, just to make sure, but she couldn't bring herself to do it. Almost daintily, she stepped over him and tiptoed the few feet to the *hu-tung*. There

[84]

she looked back, seeing only a dark bundle on the ground, nondescript and half hidden by the shadows. She turned quickly for home.

A streetcar went by on Hata Men Chieh, and as she walked along she heard several motor cars. She met a rickshaw in the *hu-tung* —empty, its poles high in the air, the tired coolie walking slowly—and then an old man on a squeaky bicycle, and perhaps a handful of pedestrians. She asked herself if they were keeping their faces blank even in the darkness, and their eyes turned inward? Did they recognize her as someone in trouble, someone to be avoided? Or was their manner merely nighttime caution?

But then she began to tire, and her mind went blank, refusing to think of anything but the business of putting one foot in front of the other. The *hu-tung* was beginning to seem endless, and there were moments when she wanted nothing so much as to stop and rest, but she dared not.

Then she saw her house up ahead, and a moan of relief escaped her. Smoothing her hair back from her forehead and trying to hold her clothing together, she wondered what Tamara was going to think.

☖☖

Somewhere in the distant reaches of the house, the doorbell jangled faintly. Toothbrush in hand, Edgerton frowned at his watch. It was after midnight.

What in Christ's name now? he wondered crossly. He'd only just returned from the Procters' and was minutes away from bed. His self-disgust had dimmed somewhat, leaving mere depression, but he was very tired. His head ached dully; he'd have a hangover in the morning.

The bell rang again.

"Come on, Ch'en, answer it," he muttered impatiently. Then he remembered: It was Ch'en's night off. Edgerton was tempted to ignore the summons . . . if it was important, let them come back in the daytime.

Another ring sounded, longer and more demanding, reverberating with staying power.

"Damn!" he shouted aloud, tossing the toothbrush into the basin. He quickly rinsed his mouth and ran wet fingers through his hair. Fists in his pockets and his mind a weary blank, he strode through the darkened rooms and courtyards. Tomorrow loomed over him drearily . . . his alarm would sound all too soon.

He slid back the iron bolt and pulled open one of the heavy doors.

[85]

Framed in the narrow gateway, looking drawn and anxious in the weak light hanging from the lintel, was Tamara.

Edgerton stared at her, his tired mind groping clumsily. "Tamara," he heard himself say. "How did you get here?" Stupid question! What did that matter?

"By taxi. I tried to telephone."

"I was out . . . at the Procters'," Edgerton explained, feeling like an amateur actor in a stilted, vapid play.

"Oh," said Tamara vaguely. "Well, there's been some trouble." Her hand reached out uncertainly.

What was the matter with him? Edgerton wondered remorsefully. "Come in, please," he said quickly, taking her hand and drawing her over the high threshold. "Come in and sit down." Her fingers were like ice.

The trouble, whatever it was, must have been serious to have brought her to him in such a state. He'd never seen her so tense, so stiffly controlled, nor so near exhaustion. For a transient moment of near panic he wondered if she'd finally taken the suggestion he'd once made, had left her mother's house and her nagging, and had come to live with him. As he led her across the courtyard, he had a premonition of inexorable forces gathering to harry him. The portents were certainly ominous enough.

As they neared the kitchen, he remembered gratefully that there was a bottle of whiskey in the pantry. "Let's go in here," he said. "I'll fix you some tea." He was about to be involved in something he wasn't going to like, and the need to bolster his spirits was becoming imperative.

The stove was cold, and he didn't know how to get it going. But Tamara accepted the whiskey he offered her, somewhat to his surprise. He got a bottle of boiled water from the ice box and sat opposite her at the well-scrubbed table. "Now, then, what's this all about?" he asked, trying to mask with heartiness the extent of his misgivings. He was touched that she had come to him, he really was, and he wanted with all his heart to help her. But please God, let it not be some complicated, troublesome mess!

Tamara's answering look was briefly hesitant, dubious. There was no fooling her, he saw, and he felt himself flush.

"It's about my mother," she said slowly, her eyes never leaving his. "She was attacked by a soldier . . . he raped her."

Edgerton was stunned. As he sat there staring, his mind flooded with the images inevitably triggered by this news, hardly able to imagine such gross violence being inflicted on that dignified, unbending lady. "How did it happen?" he asked. "And where?" He had the sudden vision of Tamara's mother stubbornly going where she didn't belong.

"In our *hu-tung*, down by Hata Men Chieh. She'd gone to the druggist." The rest of Tamara's story was brief enough, but it carried with it a sense of the mundane and commonplace which Edgerton found chilling. It was as though a blindfold were being removed from his eyes. Blinking dumbly, unwillingly, he was glimpsing something of the life Tamara and her mother were forced to lead these days.

He recalled vividly how worried he'd been in the first weeks of the occupation; things were no better now, it seemed. In their fighting, the Japanese were reportedly as disciplined as Germans, but their off-duty behavior would have surprised Genghis Khan. Because Peking had been spared the wild rape which later befell Nanking, Edgerton, like all the rest of them, had allowed himself to become complacent, to be lulled into taking casually the daily brutalities of the soldiery. They were taken to be mere matters of course, as inseparable a part of the Japanese presence as the Army trucks caroming heedlessly through the crowded streets. There was no excuse for it, not for the behavior, nor for the spineless docility of the foreign community in the face of it.

"Has that ever happened to you . . . something you never told me?" he heard himself asking in a hoarse voice.

Solemnly Tamara shook her head.

"But almost?"

She shrugged, and for the first time her eyes shifted away from his.

Edgerton felt a sense of grievous outrage rising in him like a fever. Although prompted by Tamara's predicament, it was at the same time entirely his own. Her story and its implications were injuring him as personally as if he'd been struck in the face. And yet, angry as he was, he felt the restraint of a profound reluctance. He simply didn't want to be drawn into Madame Liu's difficulties, no matter how sorry he was for her. There was literally nothing to be done. Besides, he couldn't help but ask himself what that critical, unsympathetic woman had ever cared about *his* problems.

"Is she hurt?" he asked belatedly, wondering if he was going to have to get Jim Ramsey out of bed.

Tamara shook her head. "Only her spirit . . . otherwise she's all right. She's very tough, you know."

"Yes, I know," Edgerton said, relieved. Adding some water to his whiskey, he took a large swallow. He was still smarting from Procter's

[87]

gratuitous lecture of that morning, and didn't much feel like adding the Navy doctor's name to the list of people who seemed to feel themselves entitled to inquire into his and Tamara's affairs.

Mind wandering, he recalled the soldier in the Western Hills, the Japanese sergeant, recalled him all too clearly. He'd certainly seemed capable of this sort of act, had probably indulged himself with unwilling women so often he'd lost count. There must be a thousand equally callous, equally unrestrained men scattered through the city's garrison. He realized with a start that he'd been on the verge of asking Tamara if the police had been notified! How ridiculous! Except for a few cops directing traffic, the Japanese Army was the police.

A spasm of annoyance swept over him. Damn that cranky, pigheaded woman anyway! Why couldn't she have stayed home where she belonged, instead of wandering the streets at all hours?

"Does she need anything?"

"No, thanks. There's an old friend with her, a neighbor who is a midwife. I would never have left her alone otherwise." Tamara's fingers began moving her glass back and forth across the smooth, worn surface of the table. "But there's a problem . . . the reason I'm bothering you like this. It seems silly now, but I was worried for a time, afraid they might send someone to investigate tomorrow, or the next day." Her gaze held his briefly, imploring his understanding. "You see, the soldier was drunk. Mother thinks she may have hurt him rather badly."

"Oh, Christ!" Edgerton said softly, shaking his head. Trust Madame Liu to pile on the complications. He should have known there'd be more.

"She hit him with a brick . . . in the eggs!" Tamara said, her voice faintly tinged with pride. The Chinese idiom sounded strange in English, adding an exotic twist to Edgerton's reflexive twinge of pain. He opened the drawer of the table and discovered some cigarettes of Ch'en's. The smoke was harsh and bitter, more like burning weed stalks than tobacco. He was beginning to feel half-anesthetized, with his mind fairly alert, but his extremities numb and tingling.

As he stared into his whiskey glass, Edgerton acknowledged that his impending transfer was beginning to exert a strong appeal. The Japanese would only grow increasingly disorderly as the Chinese became more abject. Before much longer, it would be the foreigners who were being abused and beaten on the streets, and that would be the end of the road. Washington, on the contrary, would be clean and tidy and organized. And at the State Department, what had once been simply paper shuffling in Foggy Bottom could now be seen as sound administrative practice, indispensable to efficient government. And Valerie

[88]

would be there, willing, attractive, uncomplicated, and, most especially, unencumbered by an obstreperous mother.

It wasn't his fault there was a war on, and the Chinese were losing it . . . had already lost it. These were cruel times for China, for the women most of all, but he was only one man, with neither influence nor power, the minor functionary of a foreign government. He was tired of being in the middle—tired, tired. It wasn't fair. . . .

And it wasn't true either, he told himself, ashamed. He was reacting like a baby, and could only hope the petulance he felt didn't show in his face. He raised his eyes. Though still worried, Tamara's expression was one of total trust. It said quite plainly that she knew he was going to take care of everything. And Edgerton, grudgingly, acknowledged that somehow he was going to have to try. And, even though it rankled, he felt a perverse satisfaction in the confident way she had passed the responsibility to him.

Looking at her now, it dawned on him what it was that made her seem so different. She was wearing the everyday clothing of a lower middle-class Chinese woman: the long-sleeved white jacket, buttoned to the neck; the loose black trousers held at the waist with a sash. She even had conventional black cloth shoes on her feet. He'd never seen her in these unstylish, "native" clothes, never imagined her in them. Her thick hair was pinned back carelessly. In the hard artificial light, it looked nearly black, and her face was without its usual touch of makeup. Never had he seen her look more Chinese, or more beautiful.

"I'm feeling better now—and braver," Tamara said, raising her glass and smiling slightly. "It's a nuisance, I know, but I should be getting back . . . if you don't mind."

Edgerton nodded easily, wanting her to think his burdens were resting lightly. "Sure," he said. Recalling his soul-searching moment in the Procters' driveway, he searched her face quickly, needing to see evidence of the things which made her so necessary to him. They were all there: her youth, her vitality, the special light in her eyes which seemed to shine directly into his most inner heart. A great affection warmed him, enhanced—oddly, it seemed to him—by the inevitability of his losing her. He supposed the feeling could be called love, although he was still shy of that entangling, emasculating word. Love was the domain of the young and the optimistic. But there was no doubt that she loved him. She'd made it plain to him in too many ways. And now, when she was most alone, she had come to him.

"I'll get the car out," he said.

Once settled beside him on the front seat, she sank back with a sigh and rested her cheek against the worn mohair. Her face was turned

[89]

toward him, and in the faint light of the instruments, he could see that her eyes were closed. Her forehead was marred by a small frown. Edgerton felt well up in him an overwhelming urge to protect her.

The Hotel des Wagon-Lits was dark and silent as they went by, with only a single light burning in the deserted lobby. Canal Street was empty, the wide old trees leaning heavily overhead. The wrought iron gates of the Peking Club were padlocked across the driveway, guarding those exclusive, pristine premises. As they passed through the Legation Quarter wall onto the glacis, the police sentry came out of his tiny guard house to give Edgerton a sleepy salute. Instead of reassuring him, as the sight of this tiny symbolic force usually did, the solitary man with his old Springfield seemed to epitomize the futility of all the foreigners' works.

This glum assessment was quickly confirmed. As they started east on Ch'ang An Chieh, a convoy of Army trucks turned out of Hata Men and began to approach them at high speed, engines roaring, headlight beams quivering with the vibration. One by one they pounded by, massive, impersonal, invincible, their cargoes of sleepy soldiers like so many dozing robots, ready for anything, anytime.

Edgerton could feel Tamara's eyes follow them, and her body stiffen with apprehension. It occurred to him that she was not the only vulnerable one. The character of these familiar-seeming streets had changed profoundly without his realizing it, making this city he'd known for so many years suddenly an alien place, a Japanese garrison. Even his diplomat's papers and the ostentatious emblem on his car had value only by the Army's sufferance.

"I don't like your staying there by yourselves," he announced abruptly. "You're right, you know: The Japanese are bound to make a stink. Wouldn't it be better for you both to come back to my place until this blows over?" The invitation had come spontaneously, taking Edgerton himself rather by surprise.

"Thanks, but I don't think so," Tamara said softly, her voice apologetic. There was a pause while the car rattled along. Except for a single streetcar far to the north of them, swaying and sparking its way toward the car barn, they were alone on that long river of crumbling macadam. "You understand?"

Yes, I understand, Edgerton thought wearily. Madame Liu was too proud to sleep in the same house with the despoiler of her daughter. Suddenly he was very angry. He was being pushed and harried into a situation where he was only minimally concerned, enticed into trying to protect that uncompromising scold of a woman from the consequences of her own recklessness, and being balked by the woman herself. He felt in his pockets for another of Ch'en's cigarettes and found that he had forgotten them. In the completeness of his frustration, he almost laughed, and the rage drained away from him as abruptly as it had arisen, leaving only a bitter patience in its wake. "Well, maybe I can work out something with LaGarde at the hotel, something like last summer." He sighed aloud. "Would she approve of *that*, do you suppose?"

Tamara's hand reached out to touch him on the arm. "Don't be angry, John. She can't help the way she is. Yes, I'm sure she'd approve . . . and gratefully."

Edgerton was relieved. "I'll call in the morning and set it up for you both."

"Not for me. It's better if I stay where I am."

"But if they send someone around investigating . . . "

"That's not really likely," Tamara interrupted. "But even if they do, I can say Mother's gone to visit relatives in another part of the city. It would only look suspicious if we were both away at the same time."

"Well, I don't like it," Edgerton said. There was a flaw in her logic, but he was too tired to search it out at the moment. The city was too dangerous a place for her to be out in it alone, but he knew it would be useless to argue. Prompted by his new sense of wariness, he turned down the *hu-tung* of the American School, so as to approach Tamara's flat discreetly from the east. When they were near, he pulled over and parked. A profound silence descended upon them, broken only by the sounds of his engine cooling.

Tamara yawned deeply, then gave him a smile which was visible even in the dark interior of the car. "Everything will be all right now. Oh, John . . ." Pausing, she took his hand in her strong fingers and leaned forward to kiss him. "I knew you'd help us," she whispered.

Her lips were soft and yielding, and the touch of her breath like a feather on his cheek. In spite of his fatigue, he felt a demanding surge of lust . . . one more thing which made her indispensable.

At her stairway, he took her in his arms. "I'll call you at the Club," he said. "And if you need me tonight, don't hesitate." She nodded. Except for the transitory sound of her feet on the stairs, the silence of the *hu-tung* was as thick as if the houses on all sides had long been deserted.

Driving away, Edgerton realized with a start that the back way he had chosen led very near the Procters' house. He hadn't really considered the fact that they and the Liu women were, in a sense, practically neighbors. He thought of Valerie, sleeping in her room so close at

[91]

hand. In his imagination it was as though she had already surrendered to him, and lay dozing, resting, the glow of her tanned, knowing body heightened by the white outline of her bathing suit. Someday, he thought, turning onto Hata Men Chieh and accelerating toward the Legation Quarter.

茎茎

The long narrow slot between the warehouses was ominously dark. A rectangle of starlight at the far end outlined the shapes of old crates and other refuse. A thin ribbon of sky separated the overhanging roofs overhead. Li wondered how long he would have to wait for another shadow to appear and move against the rectangle. Ling was being very quiet. "Tiger" Ling he liked to call himself. Well, it was wise of him to be quiet; he was in serious trouble. Two other policemen were posted at the far end of the slot, and they were tired, too. Ling had blundered; stupid man, but desperate: bad combination.

"Come out, Ling. You are wasting my time!" Li's hoarse voice echoed between the brick walls. There was no answer. "You cannot get away from me this time . . . you are a tiger, not an eagle. Actually, you are a mouse and I am laughing at you."

A loose board scraped in the darkness and Li peered cautiously around the corner. Ling's pistol fired with an eardrum-tearing roar that seemed to compress the air. A piece of brick next to Li's head disintegrated, peppering his face with its fragments.

No longer sleepy, Li squatted down behind the corner of the building, squeezing himself close to the ground. His own pistol was still buckled into its holster. He patted it, regretting that he had never learned to shoot well. There was something ludicrous about a police lieutenant who could not shoot, and ludicrous policemen generally failed. He promised himself to begin a serious course of practice.

"Your shooting is very bad, Ling. I suggest you give up."

"I fuck your mother," Ling growled back at him.

Li chuckled. "You are more trouble than you are worth." He raised his voice and called down the corridor, "Sung! Corporal Sung! When your men are in position on the roof, have them commence firing."

"Very well!" Sung called, his high voice brimming with confidence.

"When they are finished shooting, we shall go in and get the body."

Ling cleared his throat nervously. "Li *p'eng-yu*, do not be hasty," he called, the edge of desperation just audible in his voice.

Li grinned to himself. "I am no *p'eng-yu* of yours, you scoundrel. I choose my friends very carefully."

"But we have known each other for years," Ling wheedled plaintively.

"Too many years."

"What can I do to convince you that I am your ally?"

"Surrender at once, and stop talking."

There was a long and uneasy silence. In a beaten voice, Ling mumbled, "How long will I be kept in prison?"

Li cupped his hands to his mouth. "Corporal Sung, hold your fire and stay in position." Then, in a lower and more confidential tone, he answered Ling, "That would depend."

"Depend on what?"

"On me. I want a lot of information."

"Will they beat me at the Police Yamen?"

"I do not believe in beatings."

"But Captain Wang . . ."

"I am in charge of this case, not Captain Wang."

"What happens if I surrender to you?"

"It will be easier for you."

"How much easier?" Ling was beginning to sound as though he thought he was dickering for eggs in the market.

"Easier than being dead; you are in no position to bargain."

"I know all about the opium business," Ling offered cajolingly.

"So do I," Li said flatly. "What do you think you can tell me that I don't already know?"

"The names of the peddlers and where they go to hide from the police."

"You must think I am an amateur; I know all that. Do you know the Japanese who are involved?"

"I know some names."

"Name one."

"Tanaka."

"Everyone knows Tanaka. Do you know Puhalski?"

"He came to the Chinese City last night, just to see me," Ling said, unable to keep the pride out of his voice at this evidence of his importance.

Li thought a moment, smiling slightly to himself. He had been waiting for a long time to get his hands on that Russian. "If you try and cheat me, I will put you at the bottom of the Pei Hai for the Imperial carp to eat. Do you believe that?"

"Yes, I believe it." Ling said, sounding as if he wanted to cry.

"Then surrender."

There was a long silence. He could hear Ling's heavy breathing. "I surrender."

"Throw your pistol out where I can see it."

As the pistol clattered onto the hard dry earth, Li stood up, wincing at the stiffness in his knees. "Put your hands on top of your head, and come out slowly."

Li followed him out into the loading yard. "Stop right there," he said. "Lower your hands to your sides . . . slowly." Li took a short leather strap out of his pocket and belted Ling's elbows together behind his back.

Panting loudly, Corporal Sung stumbled out from between the warehouses, followed by a wide-eyed young patrolman with a rifle. Sung's round shaven head gleamed with sweat, and his grinning mouth with silver teeth.

Ling looked at them suspiciously. "Where are the men on the roof?" he asked.

"I have caused them to vanish," Li told him.

"You tricked me!" Ling accused.

"Never mind, I won't tell." He turned to Sung. "Tell that fellow to go and watch the gate. I don't want anyone barging in here and catching us together like old comrades. My reputation would be ruined."

When the rookie hurried off, Li turned his attention back to his prisoner. "Now tell me this," he said, "just how deeply is Puhalski mixed into this opium business?"

"Deeply enough, but he is a newcomer. All that he has to sell is what Tanaka steals from the Army."

"Does Tanaka have other agents to sell his opium?"

"I don't know of any. You see, the opium comes from the Political Education Section, not from the Military Police."

"Does Puhalski still trade in women?"

"No." Ling hesitated. "Well, perhaps he has a few Russians, but no more Chinese women." Ling grinned briefly. "The Brothel Keepers Guild scared him out of that last winter."

"What about stolen goods?"

Ling shrugged. "Who has anything worth stealing anymore? Maybe cigarettes and whiskey; he can sell those things in his café and make a big profit."

"He's doing very well, then?"

"Well enough, I guess. With a friend like Tanaka, how can he go wrong? If Tanaka were my friend . . ."

"You are in enough trouble without friends like Tanaka."

Li had never felt so weary. It was the letdown from being frightened. He hated crawling into dark places after people, and Ling's near

[94]

miss had shaken him. Ling was a shifty scoundrel and ordinarily Li would not have bothered with him. But Ling's connection with Puhalski made him worth troubling with, plus the fact that he might know more than he realized about Tanaka.

"My arms are sore," Ling complained.

"Unstrap him," Li told Sung.

Sung hesitated, then removed the strap. Ling flexed his arms and emitted a series of exaggerated groans.

Li stared at his prisoner for several seconds, causing him to shuffle his feet.

"Ling, do you know how we caught you tonight?"

"No."

"Three separate people told me where you would be."

"Who were they?" Ling asked, outraged.

"Never mind. You have enemies; there are a surprising number of people who want to build up a little credit with the police these days. Next time there will be men on the roof, and your luck will have run out. Come and see me tomorrow evening."

"You want me to come to the Police Yamen?"

"No, you idiot! You come around the Yamen asking for me and I will personally turn you over to Captain Wang. Come to my house."

"To the house where the lady lives?"

Li cursed under his breath. He had not thought his relationship with Mei-ling was so well-known, and that was foolish of him. He should have expected it. He wondered if he had put her into danger by his stupidity. "No, not that house. To my own house in the Feng Sha *hu-tung*. Do you know it?"

"Yes."

"At eight o'clock tomorrow."

"I will be there." Ling spread his arms emotionally. "You must believe me, Lieutenant. You will never regret . . ."

"I am beginning to regret it already. Go now before I change my mind."

The two policemen watched in silence as Ling scuttled off into the darkness.

"Do you really think he'll obey you?" Sung asked.

"It's worth the risk. He has no choice, and I'm counting on his realizing it."

They turned and started to walk across the empty yard. At the far corner there was a small pedestrian gate where the three of them had left their bicycles.

"What is all this business about Tanaka and that Russian crook?"

"I wish I knew. Their names keep popping up together." Li was briefly tempted to confide in him, but resisted. Sung was loyal, but it was too soon. Only the other day, Chang Sun-cheh had told him a rumor which had surfaced at the Interior Ministry. Someone from the Commanding General's staff had leaked the story that Colonel Hideki Tanaka, the Provost Marshal, had been ordered to set up the first unit of the Kempeitari—the dreaded Thought Police—in Peking. Men from the underworld were natural recruits for the first cadres, and Ling might have heard of something. Li intended to squeeze him like a lemon.

"What difference does it make what Ling tells you?" Sung argued. "We might be able to get the Russian, but the Japanese can do what he wants; we can't touch him."

"For now, that is so. But someday, a cleverly planted account of his private actions might disgrace Tanaka. Then his superiors would punish him for us."

"They all belong back in Japan, the apes."

"Yes, but that will bring new trouble . . . for me, at least."

"Me, too."

"Maybe not. Be thankful you are not an officer. Besides, if either the Nationalists or the Communists ever make trouble for you, you need only to grin and shrug and look stupid. You are good at that."

Sung laughed quietly. They had worked together for years, but never so closely as since the city was surrendered to the Japanese. The corporal had many attributes, not the least of which was his unprepossessing appearance. He had wide cheekbones and a square jaw and very close-set eyes. His skull sloped down to a low forehead which was perpetually wrinkled in bewilderment. With only minor changes in dress he could pass as a Mongolian camel driver or a river bargeman from Tientsin.

They came to the gate and wheeled their bicycles through it. Li snapped the ancient padlock and turned to the young patrolman. "How long have you been on the force?"

"One year," the man answered proudly.

"Corporal Sung tells me that you did well tonight. Keep it up and you will have an interesting career. If you stick with me, you will never be fired, but you will never be Chief of Police either. My advice is: Do what the Japanese tell you only when you have to, and ignore politics. We have our hands full, without worrying about whether Chiang Kai-shek or Mao Tse-tung is correct. Our job is to protect the people of this city, nothing else. Keep your mouth shut about tonight and listen to Corporal Sung. You can go home now."

[96]

The patrolman saluted. Li watched speculatively as he pedaled off, his chain protesting dryly on the sprockets.

"What about your report?"

He turned back to Sung. "What about it?"

"How will you explain Ling's escape?"

Li shrugged. "Our information was faulty and we arrived too late."

"You will look foolish to Captain Wang."

"Excellent. As long as that turtle's egg thinks that I am foolish, my job is safe and so is my life."

"I'll see you tomorrow."

Long after Sung had gone, Li still stood there. Although drenched with weariness, he was unwilling to break the spell of well-being which the night's business had left in him.

Slowly but stubbornly, the honest policemen were reorganizing. It had been a long slow pull uphill since the beginning of the occupation. Many good men had fled, some to join the guerrillas or the Chinese Army, some merely to disappear to save themselves and their families, fed up at last with the bungling of the politicians. Left behind was a high proportion of dimwits and crooks whose only interests were the squeezing of cumshaw out of the tradesmen in their precincts and kissing the Japanese diligently on the *p'i kou*. In his own precinct there were himself and Sung, and a few others who could be relied on . . . and now, perhaps, the young patrolman also. What was his name? T'ang? T'ien? He'd ask Sung in the morning.

All around him the night hummed and mumbled sleepily, giving Li the strange feeling that the whole great city was depending upon him alone for its protection. Although it made him all the wearier, the thought was pleasing.

Li struck a match and lit the wick of his bicycle lamp, then clipped the cuffs of his trousers to his ankles. For the first time in over a year, he had the sense of the future brightening perceptibly, and felt well pleased with his lot.

He yawned loudly. It was late, but he didn't want to go home, to be alone. He'd go to Mei-ling's house. She'd be asleep, but glad to see him, even though she'd scold him for being out so late and taking chances. She always seemed to know when he'd been in any sort of danger. She was depending on him, too . . . he'd have to remember that.

Li straddled the bicycle and, wobbling slightly at first, pedaled away, his thoughts divided between sleep and the cool fragrance of Mei-ling's skin.

[97]

The snap of the padlock was loud in the quiet *hu-tung*, loud and very final. Puhalski gave a tired sigh of relief. He wished it were really final. The damned place was taking up too much of his time. It was becoming a bloody bore besides.

It had been a dull Monday night, with no more than twenty paying customers. Once, around ten o'clock, there were no customers at all. Puhalski never considered the women to be customers although they all bought drinks of one kind or another.

He felt limp and bedraggled. There had been no proper rain for weeks. An electric tension in the air drew out his nerves like piano wires. His knee was sore and swollen and felt hot to the touch. He would rub some liniment into it when he got home. His room would be like an oven—and probably covered with the sawdust that sifted through the floor from the cabinet shop below. He ought to move, to get a better place with more room and more privacy. He could afford it now, but at the moment it would require an enormous expense of energy.

Hata Men Chieh appeared deserted. Puhalski yawned widely and stepped off the curb. From somewhere behind him an engine roared throatily and a pair of headlights came on, bright as the searchlights of a battleship, pinning him to the macadam like some rare bug on a display board. Tires whining softly, the black limousine slowed to a gravelly stop in front of him. Puhalski was surprised to see the gold five-petaled cherry blossom it carried as a bumper emblem, since it didn't look like an Army car. "Good evening, my dear Puhalski. May I offer you a lift?" Colonel Tanaka said in his oily and strangely accented English.

You tricky bastard, Puhalski thought angrily. Made awkward by his stiff knee, he climbed in slowly. Tanaka's round face beamed at him with spurious friendship. Puhalski promised himself that someday he would destroy Tanaka.

"Good evening, Colonel," he said calmly, refusing to show surprise.

Tanaka chose to be coy. "I hope I didn't startle you . . . my driver isn't used to the car; he's a little quick with the clutch." He growled an order to his soldier driver, and the car pulled smoothly away. Beaming, Tanaka cranked up the glass partition. Puhalski was reminded of an enormous baby playing with his toys. Tanaka offered cigarettes. When both men were smoking, Tanaka settled back into the soft upholstery and waved a chubby hand around the interior of the car. "Not bad, eh?" he prompted.

"Very nice," Puhalski said.

"Yes, I'm in the mood to congratulate myself this evening. For the son of an indentured pineapple picker, I have not done at all badly."

Puhalski could not conceal his surprise. Tanaka was obviously pleased.

"You didn't know that, did you? No, of course not; how could you?" Tanaka sighed reminiscently. "It was all so long ago . . . I saw the last of Hawaii when I was seventeen. We were a very poor family, and old-fashioned; there was an educational fund for the eldest son. It took many economies in those days to send me to a Japanese university." He gave a soft laugh. "Who would have guessed that I was very nearly an American? An American subject, of course, not a citizen. There is a great difference. The Japanese of Hawaii are not quite good enough for citizenship in that illustrious democracy." Tanaka mused, pulling at his underlip, then he brightened. "I am the first in my family to own a car," he said proudly.

Puhalski muttered something appropriate. It had never occurred to him that the colonel could have come from any such background, and now he didn't know what to make of it. At least Tanaka's strange pronunciation was accounted for, as well as his hatred for the Americans.

"A man in my position is expected to be self-sufficient. The Provost Marshall confiscates a motor car from a Nationalist sympathizer and spy, and consigns it to the service of the Provost Marshal. What could be more practical?" The colonel smirked, then cleared his throat importantly. "But that is beside the point. You and I must have a talk."

Puhalski knew what was coming: Fatigue and apprehension seemed to stifle him, dulling his mind.

Tanaka leered at him. "I'm not keeping you from an appointment with a young lady?"

"Not tonight."

"Good! You are a reliable comrade."

"I try to be, Colonel."

"Tell me then, my dear Serge: Is your friend Sobolov ready to cooperate?"

"I am making encouraging progress."

"What you mean is that Sobolov is not ready to cooperate."

"I thought I had made it plain that it would be necessary to move very cautiously, to persuade . . ."

Tanaka chopped at the air with the edge of his hand. "You, my esteemed Puhalski, made it plain to me that you would have this man eating out of your hand in a matter of days."

[99]

"Sobolov is a meek, cautious man, not an adventurer. He's a typical intellectual . . . timid."

Tanaka turned cold eyes on him. "A former squadron leader of Cossacks should be a match for such a one."

"I have to persuade him, not merely give orders. If I press too heavily, he's likely to panic and blow the whole scheme to the Americans."

"Evidently you have no confidence in my 'scheme,' as you call it," Tanaka observed severely.

"It isn't that at all," Puhalski said, denying the truth. He cursed the day he had ever mentioned Sobolov and his job with the Americans. The Colonel had been instantly agog, imagining himself pulling off some great coup of espionage: Tanaka, the man of destiny, delivering into the very hands of the Emperor himself the American diplomatic codes. Minutes after first hearing his name, Tanaka had Sobolov stealing code books and safe combinations. It was frightening. The inevitable fiasco would be Tanaka disgraced and transferred, and himself ruined after all those years of working and saving and planning. And his nice little opium business down the chute before it was even properly begun.

Puhalski had to struggle to keep his tone reasonable. "Ordinarily, one appeals to greed or ambition, but Sobolov has neither. He imagines his future to be secure, provided he takes no chances. For now, I'm trying to create dissatisfaction, to make him compare the poverty in which he lives to what life might be like if he cooperates with me." It sounded weak.

Tanaka thought so, too. "A lengthy process," he said harshly. "Will any of us survive to see it through? Time is very short."

"I know, but I have to build up his confidence, get him committed." Puhalski could feel the sweat gathering on his palms. Why was it always so difficult to explain even the simplest thing to this man? "I can't simply walk in, throw a hundred Chinese dollars on the table, and say: do thus and so. And Sobolov has loyalties; even though they are stupid ones. This man Edgerton . . ."

Tanaka lapsed into a fit of coughing. Puhalski waited until it passed. "Well, that's about it. I cajole and I argue, and his wife does likewise."

"His wife?" Tanaka frowned disapprovingly.

"Don't worry, I've told her nothing. In fact, neither of them knows a thing. They think I have been proposing something merely mildly illegal: black market, foreign exchange, a little dope—nothing political. She doesn't care what he does so long as he brings home more money. In short, a good ally."

"An ally, eh? You *are* persuasive if you can make his wife your ally in front of his very eyes."

"Well, circumstances were in my favor. The woman is bored and lonely . . ." Puhalski spread his hands modestly. "I've been able to . . . well, entertain her."

Tanaka cleared his throat. "You're a lucky rascal, Puhalski. Combining business with pleasure, eh?" he said, his voice strangely thick.

"Yes, I suppose I am," Puhalski agreed. A tiny intriguing bud of an idea was growing in his mind. "She's in love with me." He chuckled, man to man. "Quite a woman, the best Ukranian type: big breasts, big hips, a very voluptuous nature." Puhalski sighed, listening.

A faint noise strangled somewhere deep in Tanaka's throat, and he began to twirl the tassel of his sword.

As though oblivious, Puhalski went on, "But she's very demanding." He passed a weary hand across his brow. "She's insatiable, and her tastes are a bit rich for my simple peasant blood. Besides, such a woman should be enjoyed at leisure and in the proper surroundings. I have neither the time nor the place."

"Hmmm," Tanaka muttered, suggesting that while some men might have no taste for richness, he, Tanaka, was not one of them. Puhalski grinned out of the window.

Tanaka loosed his collar. "Ah, yes, my dear Serge, you're very fortunate. When I was on duty in Dairen, there was a woman—a famous geisha—a splendid creature, splendid! We were very close. Since then . . ." Tanaka gave a nostalgic sigh. "Of course, there are many opportunities here for a man in my position, but . . . well, we're almost in the front lines and the women are of mediocre quality . . ." His voice faded morosely.

Puhalski could hardly contain himself. It was *the* solution. While freeing himself of Maya, he would ingratiate himself with Tanaka and, best of all, distract him from those damn code books and all that other nonsense. Properly managed, Maya might give him considerable advantage over the Colonel. He needed it badly. She swore she loved him; well, then. . . .

"I hope you won't think me forward, Colonel," he began with cautious servility, "if I say that I'd be happy to introduce you to Madame Sobolov. You're a man of the world, of discrimination, and would appreciate her charms—providing, of course, that my prior acquaintance with the lady wouldn't offend you."

Tanaka bridled, rubbing his hands together. "My dear Serge; you're most generous. After all, we're comrades-in-arms, so to speak; soldiers sharing equally . . ." He interrupted himself with a nervous cackle.

[101]

"However, these delightful prospects must not interfere with our main program."

"Well, Colonel, there'll be no problem about that," Puhalski argued, fighting disappointment. "Once Sobolov has begun to work with me, he'll be hooked. As long as you and the lady are careful, he'll be too absorbed in his work to become suspicious; I'll see to that."

"Yes, yes; I suppose so," Tanaka said, only partly persuaded.

Puhalski looked out the window, wondering vaguely where they were. Damn Tanaka! The man was an eel, and had left him uncertain whether anything had been accomplished. He peered at his wristwatch in the light of a passing street lamp.

"What time do you have, my dear fellow?" Tanaka asked.

"Nearly two." Puhalski was tired and needed sleep. And above all, he wanted time to think.

"I have some Army business to check on . . ." The Colonel looked quickly out of both sides of the car. "It's quite nearby."

Puhalski tensed. Instinct told him Tanaka was pretending.

Tanaka muttered directions into the speaking tube. The driver reversed direction in a wide turn, throwing the beams of the headlights across a string of dark, poor shops and an empty sidewalk with weeds growing through cracks in the pavement. Presently they slowed, and the car turned into a bumpy *hu-tung*, which soon narrowed, barely permitting passage of the car. To the left rose the blank windowless walls of warehouses, to the right a mixed group of buildings which appeared to be a closed-down factory of some sort—long rows of broken windows and two tall tapered chimneys.

Tanaka explained offhandedly. "Smuggled rifles and ammunition for the Communist bandits in the hills. They are collected here and then smuggled out of the city in nightsoil carts, submerged in the excrement." He laughed harshly. "Ingeniously appropriate. But fortunately for them, there are always men whose idealism is for sale." Tanaka grinned at him confidently. "These Reds are so stupid. . . . I'm surprised that Chiang Kai-shek could never wipe them out."

The car turned into a narrow cul-de-sac, and a group of helmeted soldiers materialized suddenly in the headlights . . . a dozen men armed with machine pistols, clustered between two high-wheeled Army command cars. They eyed the approaching lights nervously. One of them ran forward waving for the car to stop, but when he saw the bumper emblem he jumped aside. Puhalski didn't like the look of things.

Tanaka tapped on the glass partition and the car braked to a stop. "Stay in the car, Puhalski," he said curtly, getting out with surprising agility. Short and fat, with his shiny boots and huge samurai sword, he should have been ridiculous. He wasn't. On the contrary, he radiated force and power. This was a man Puhalski had not seen before.

One of the soldiers stepped forward and saluted, and he and Tanaka spoke at length together. The group milled for a moment, then broke apart, and a tall thin Chinese was thrust forward out of the shadows. His long blue gown was patched and faded, and looked almost gray in the bright light. His arms were tightly bound behind his back.

Tanaka waved an arm and the Chinese was shoved to one side. On the ground were several long bundles, wrapped in some shiny waterproof material. The shadows in the background shifted, and Puhalski made out a mule harnessed into the shafts of a cart. At Tanaka's command, the bundles were heaved into one of the cars. All but three of the soldiers climbed in and drove away, following the *hu-tung* deeper into the maze of buildings.

With a show of interest, Tanaka turned to the Chinese prisoner, and proceeded to inspect him, circling him slowly as though contemplating buying him. Puhalski could not escape the growing certainty that he was watching a charade, a dumbshow staged primarily for his benefit.

One of the soldiers gave the Chinese a push in the chest, slamming him hard against the wall. They all stepped back then, and Tanaka's arms flailed angrily. Through it all, the Chinese had stood as though dazed, his head back, his eyes closed. Abruptly, one of the soldiers stepped forward. He worked the bolt of his weapon, raised it to his shoulder, and shot the Chinese in the face from a distance of about five feet.

Puhalski sat petrified while the shots crashed and echoed among the high brick walls. Slowly the noise receded, rolling like distant thunder. The Chinese pitched forward, raising a small cloud of dust. An asthmatic bray erupted from the terrified mule, and one of the soldiers laughed nervously.

Tanaka gave a negligent gesture. The body was lugged over to the remaining command car and tumbled into the back seat. Then, impassively, the three soldiers stood and listened while their Colonel addressed them. When he was done they climbed in and drove away after the others. Watching Tanaka tuck his sword under his arm and dust his palms together, Puhalski found himself wondering if the cart and now driverless mule were to be abandoned there, or whether somebody would be sent to fetch them. The question existed for a fraction of a second. Puhalski licked his lips, but his tongue was dry as the dust of the *hu-tung*. His body, aching from muscular tension, was drenched

[103]

with sweat, and smelled as though he hadn't bathed in weeks. Dumbly he watched Tanaka stalk back to the car. The door was pulled open and the Colonel climbed in.

"Shot while trying to escape," Tanaka announced with satisfaction. Puhalski had the feeling that somewhere back at Tanaka's office there was a form to be filled out, with a blank space precisely the right size for that particular explanatory phrase. Tanaka would be a stickler for properly kept records. He watched, fascinated, as Tanaka calmly fitted a cigarette into his holder and pushed in the button of the electric lighter. The Colonel grunted an order to his driver, and the car began backing and filling to reverse direction. Puhalski had to clutch the hand strap to steady himself.

"Excuse me, by dear Serge! How rude of me," Tanaka said, offering his cigarettes with elaborate courtesy. Puhalski's hand shook as he took one, and he wondered if Tanaka noticed.

But Tanaka only sighed. "A regrettable business. The men I wanted, the leaders, must have been warned by someone. But I'll get them sooner or later." He puffed contentedly for several seconds, rolling slightly from side to side as the car threaded its way among the potholes. "There's always a next time. Some Chinese still refuse to believe that we're in charge here . . . isn't that incredible? But Japan is very much in earnest, and no treachery will be tolerated . . . no one plays tricks on us." Tanaka grinned wolfishly and rubbed his hands together. "I'm a very good policeman. And now, my dear fellow, I'll drive you home. I apologize for involving you in this unpleasant affair." He cleared his throat. "What were we talking about?"

Puhalski took a breath, but before he could speak, Tanaka was continuing. "Sobolov, of course. I realize you're doing your best, but please try to understand my impatience," he said affably. "Perhaps I spoke too harshly to you, but we must press ahead, get things moving. I'll leave the pace to your judgment. About the lady, I'm intrigued, of course; she sounds charming, and your offer is very generous. However, it might be best to wait until Sobolov is, as you say, hooked. Then we shall see. Yes, yes." Tanaka smacked his lips.

Puhalski could only nod. Tanaka was telling him to make no more explanations and complain of no more difficulties. Action was wanted, and wanted soon. Tanaka was not to be trifled with—as he had just demonstrated so pointedly.

"Here, my friend," Tanaka said, interrupting his reverie. He held out an envelope. "I almost forgot."

Pulaski could feel the banknotes inside, but there was no pleasure in them. They were symbols of Tanaka's power, and they mocked his earlier ambition to destroy this man . . . delusions of grandeur. The plain fact was that Tanaka was invulnerable. On the other hand, should he cease to be useful, he'd matter to Tanaka no more than that wretched, nameless Chinese. God damn Sobolov! Like it or not, squeamish or not, the fat old fool was going to have to get to work.

TUESDAY

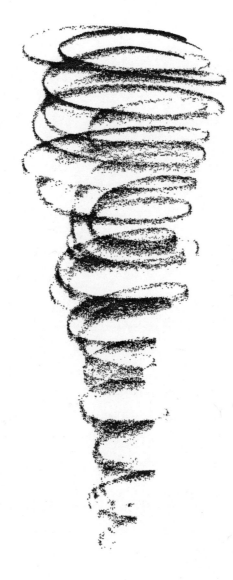

The slashing bayonet whirled faster and faster until it became a solid disc of light in the sun's glare. Unaccountably it began coming toward him, flying at him like some glowing bullet. Paralyzed with terror, he could only await the inevitable impact. At the last possible instant he rolled out of the way and opened his eyes. A solitary lance of sunlight thrust through a hole in the window shade and stabbed harmlessly into the middle of the soiled empty pillow. Sobolov wiped a clammy hand across his forehead.

Although it was not quite six-thirty, the airless room was already stifling. He must have slept for eight hours, but he was exhausted.

As Sobolov looked over his shoulder to see if Maya were awake, the clang of a pot and the sound of running water came from beyond the closed kitchen door. Slowly untangling himself from the sweaty sheet, he sat on the edge of the bed, rubbing his eyes. His stomach churned queasily. Sobolov pushed in the button of the alarm clock and got unsteadily to his feet.

The kitchen was even hotter than the bedroom, and Maya was silent and sullen; she did not even acknowledge his greeting. Paying him back for his silence of the night before, he supposed. Well, that couldn't be helped. He had been no sooner in the door than she had started in on him about Puhalski's offer, combining that topic with several lesser peeves more exclusively her own. Still shaken by what he'd seen on the street, Sobolov had simply walked on through the kitchen and into the bedroom, leaving her muttering crossly over her ironing board.

At supper—some sort of fish soup with cabbage leaves floating in it like bits of colorless paper—she resumed the attack. She never gave up; his refusal to respond only goaded her further.

Now she shoved a plate of stale buns at him and a saucer with a blob of half-melted butter. Then, with his glass of tea, she handed him a folded slip of paper.

"A boy brought it at six; he woke me up with his hammering," she told him petulantly.

Sobolov patted his pockets for his glasses, feeling confused. They never received messages. He peered at the note, deciphering the scrawl with difficulty. It was from Puhalski. Christ deliver me, he thought.

"Well, what does it say?" Maya demanded from across the table, as though she had not already read it.

Sobolov eyed her sharply, tempted to challenge this bit of subterfuge, then shrugged. "Puhalski," he said. "He wants, he *insists* I come by the Café Volga on my way to work." Blast Puhalski! he thought with unusual vehemence. The man was becoming a nuisance: popping

[109]

up at odd hours, dropping in on them whenever he felt like it.

"Well?"

"Well what?" he evaded, eyes lowered.

"You'll go, of course?"

"What good will that do?"

She stared at him in disbelief. "Why, he may have news of this other work."

"I'm sure he does."

"Ah, you're impossible! You sit there like a toad and won't even find out what he is offering. You are so stupid."

"I know what he is offering," Sobolov said, feeling the hurt of her words. "Trouble with the police. What good is a little extra money if I'm in jail?"

"Serge is not in jail."

"And I'm not Serge."

"That much is evident. With your education, you could be a rich man. But what are you? A nobody sitting on every opportunity like you sit on your fat bottom. You bring home the wages of a coolie while your wife sits in rags in this . . ." Her outflung arm almost upset her tea. ". . . this hovel."

Sobolov felt his patience ebbing. "You can sew," he told her, surprising himself. "Make a dress."

"For what? So I can wear it to go haggling in the market with the other coolie women?"

Maya crossed her arms stubbornly, squeezing her breasts together. He dropped his eyes, reminded for a painful instant of his passion when they were first married. My God, he thought, had it really been fifteen years? Somehow, time and her remorseless carping had quenched it all.

". . . and have to put your fifteen-year-old daughter out to support herself as a white *amah*," she was saying. Her full lips clamped shut and she glared at him with bitter rebuke.

Sobolov felt the shame rise in him with the blood that suffused his face. He could not counter the charge, nor could he forgive himself. That was what it boiled down to, he admitted miserably, watching his fingers crumble a bun. No matter how he tried to rationalize it, he had failed to provide for his Anya.

The dim interior of the Café Volga was cool, but the stink of stale tobacco smoke and spilled beer still laced the air, making his stomach turn.

Puhalski greeted him pleasantly enough, although he seemed preoccupied. His bony face looked tight and drawn, and the skin under his eyes was stained with shadows. He got two chairs off one of the tables and they sat down.

"Well, Andrei, have you made up your mind?" Puhalski asked, showing his long yellow teeth.

Sobolov couldn't keep his eyes from shifting. "To what?" he asked weakly.

Ignoring the question, Puhalski simply fixed him with those cold blue eyes. When at last he spoke, his voice was empty of emotion. "Listen to me, Sobolov. I don't have time for any foolishness; events are moving too rapidly. Even the plans I spoke of Sunday night will now have to wait their turn. I'm still going to need your help with them, and the rewards can be considerable for both of us. But now even greater rewards are suddenly possible, and I intend to get my share."

Sobolov felt dizzy. Changes, changes! He couldn't keep up with them. He just wanted to be left alone, to do his work and care for his family. Was that too much to ask?

Starting to protest, he'd barely opened his mouth when Puhalski's hand went up sharply. "Don't interrupt!" he snapped. "Listen instead. I'm tired of screwing around with you; so let me explain a few of the facts of life. And remember: this is in the strictest confidence. Not a word to anyone, not even Maya. Understand?"

Sobolov could only nod, numbed by this icily angry Puhalski whom he'd not seen before.

". . . have many contacts," Puhalski was explaining. Sobolov forced himself to concentrate. "I've gotten to know a number of Japanese officials. They need things done sometimes, complicated things, but they're too busy or too unfamiliar with the set-up so they come to me. They pay well. I've every reason to want them to remain satisfied with me. Now then, this is the part that concerns you; one of my clients wants some special cooperation from the American Legation."

Puhalski paused, eyeing him expectantly.

Obviously Sobolov was expected to make some response, but what it could be he had no idea. Sobolov cleared his throat, wishing he had a glass of water. "Well, a considerable correspondence goes back and forth between their Legations," he observed hesitantly. "Perhaps if they wrote the Americans a letter about it, made a polite approach . . ."

"Ha, ha. Very funny," Puhalski interrupted coldly. "Don't be a fool. They want cooperation from the inside, from an employee. To be explicit, from you."

[111]

"But . . ."

"No buts, please. My meaning must be perfectly clear."

Sobolov's chair seemed to sway under him like a hammock. "How much cooperation?" he whispered, terrified.

This time Puhalski's laugh was real. He leaned forward confidentially, beaming at Sobolov. "That's the beauty of it: nothing, really. It's so easy, so simple, I can't believe it."

"But *what?*" Sobolov insisted.

"All they want is a simple floor plan of the offices, a list of personnel, and a summary of Chancery routine." Puhalski spread his hands. "Nothing could be easier."

"But that is ridiculous."

Puhalski nodded delightedly. "Exactly. And for that they will pay you one hundred Chinese dollars."

"But they must know all of that sort of thing already."

Puhalski shrugged, giving him a peculiar look. "Maybe so; who cares? If they want to pay for something they already own, let them. They also want to know about routine reports: the subject matter, how often they are sent, and whether by cable, post, the Marine radio station, and so forth. And naturally they are interested in what the Americans talk about among themselves."

"I know nothing about that sort of thing."

"Then find it out."

"But Serge, don't you understand? I don't do reports, or share conversations with the Americans."

"Make it your business to listen, then."

"That is spying."

"Shit!" Puhalski's fist crashed down onto the table. "So what? Are you the Pope that you should be so righteous? What do you care?"

"But I have loyalties . . ."

"I piss on your asinine loyalties! Loyalty to whom? To Roosevelt perhaps? Or to that thick-headed ox of an Edgerton, living like a bishop there in the San Kwan Miao with servants and a swimming pool? Bah!"

Prompted by Puhalski's outburst, there popped into Sobolov's agitated mind a picture of Edgerton on the day that he had been hired. Then, for the first time in years, Sobolov had felt that he was being seen as a human being. And then, still later, the talks they had had about the press reports, and the local situation, and what the Russians thought, what *he* thought . . . how long had it been since anyone gave a damn about what he thought? "Yes," he said with surprising firmness. "To Mr. Edgerton."

[112]

"*Mister* Edgerton," Puhalski simpered. He seemed to make an enormous effort at self-control. "Well, let me tell you something about the birds and the bees, Andrei, the Japanese birds and bees. Point number one is: when the Japanese want something, they get it." Puhalski slashed the air with the edge of his hand. "Without exception. Point number two is: the Japanese have me by the balls. When they send me for something, they expect me to return with it. If I disappoint them, they will squeeze me." Puhalski clenched his fist slowly under Sobolov's nose.

Sobolov felt the sweat running into his eyes. He fumbled for his handkerchief. "I would like to help you out, but I must, with great regret, refuse. You see . . ."

"With great regret, eh?" Puhalski interrupted, giving him his rodent's grin. "And after you refuse, then what?"

Sobolov shrugged; it seemed a strange question . . .

"What about Anya?"

Sobolov staggered. "What has Anya to do with this?"

"How safe will she be if you refuse to cooperate? What about her exit visa? What about that, eh?"

Heartsick, Sobolov sagged back in his chair. "But how would they know about her?" he whispered, knowing the answer.

Puhalski's face hardened like concrete, his meaning plain.

"But we are friends; you come to my house . . ."

Puhalski grinned coldly.

"I don't understand." Sobolov said, his voice breaking.

Puhalski shook his head. "Andrei, where have you been living? In fairyland?" he asked softly.

Sobolov felt dizzy with wretchedness and confusion. He was tottering on the brink of some bottomless abyss; if he so much as breathed, he could lose his balance and drop from sight.

"Andrei, I am sorry; truly, I am. We have been, we are friends. But this is war, and, as someone said, war is hell. The Japs have my testicles in a vise. It is simply a question of self-preservation." Puhalski leaned far across the table and pointed a long finger directly in Sobolov's face. "If you let me down in this thing, I will be finished, but so will you be, and Maya, and the girl. I promise you. I am a vindictive man."

"But, Puhalski, she's a child . . ."

"Don't waste your breath appealing to my better nature; I don't have one." He inspected his cigarette for a moment, then looked up. "Andrei, let me give you some free advice: we Russians are nobodies, singly and collectively. We have no power and no influence, and no one gives a shit for us one way or the other. But being nobodies has

[113]

one advantage; we owe nothing; no allegiance, no obligation, no loyalty, except to ourselves and our families. If you give a beggar a copper, he owes you nothing for it. If Edgerton gives you a job, you owe him nothing but a day's work for a day's pay."

"But Serge . . ."

"Don't argue about it, my friend. Think about it instead; ponder it. You are responsible for your wife and your child. Not for Edgerton or Stalin or the Hague Conventions, nor for the fact that tomorrow will probably be hotter than today. Keep that fact always in the front of your mind."

Puhalski glanced at a gold wrist watch. "You must go, or you will be late," he said, sounding like a weary schoolmaster. He pulled an envelope from his pocket, and counted out fifty dollars onto the table. If I don't see you tonight, come here tomorrow morning with your report. You will get the other fifty dollars then."

Puhalski's chair scraped shrilly, and his footsteps faded away. Sobolov never looked up. Not in twenty years had he so dreaded making a decision. Then, remembering, he had to admit that on that dismal day in St. Petersburg he'd been alone and the alternatives before him were simple and clear-cut. He could stay, in which case the minor, empty title Czar Nicholas had bestowed upon his father would mark him for the mob. Or he could leave for the East, for Manchuria. Chances were that he would perish somewhere along the way, but death would be postponed . . . infinitely preferable.

Now he had Anya's innocent life in his hands. What did his paltry scruples amount to when compared to that? Sobolov got slowly, wearily to his feet. He stood for a moment with the money in his hand, then stuffed it into his pocket.

♟♟

Laughing quietly to himself, Colonel Hideki Tanaka hung up the phone. He had every reason to be pleased. Puhalski had apparently been impressed by his little demonstration. That wily Russian rogue liked too much to play his own game and set his own pace. Tanaka could understand the temptations: a tidy income from opium and other enterprises, afternoons free for dalliance with the Sobolov woman . . . and any number of other women as well. Tanaka sighed enviously and his mind wandered. With an effort he wrenched his thoughts back to Puhalski, who was now beginning to hurry because Tanaka wanted him to hurry, and to Sobolov who even now should be entering the American Chancery to begin work for his new master.

Tanaka stared into the distance as he swiveled meditatively in his chair. According to Puhalski, Sobolov was loyal to Edgerton. How childish, Tanaka thought, picking up his field telephone and giving the crank a brisk twist.

Captain Okamura's nasal voice came on the line with commendable dispatch. "Yes, Colonel?" he inquired breathlessly.

"Okamura, get me the file on the American, Edgerton," Tanaka told him.

"Now, Colonel?"

Tanaka gave a sigh that quavered with resignation. "Yes, Okamura; now, please." Tanaka hung up and buzzed for his orderly.

Sipping tea, Tanaka leafed through Edgerton's dossier, recollection nagging at him vaguely . . . something that had caught his eye the day he had read through it after the episode of the traffic bumps. Something about . . . ah, there it was! Congratulating himself on having a memory like an elephant, Tanaka read the pencilled memo, and his smile broadened. Edgerton, the lofty and condescending diplomat, would be amazed at what was in that file. Smiling happily, Tanaka made a note on his pad.

The orderly entered with a pile of disciplinary reports for him to approve. They reminded him of Major Okani and that troublesome detachment of his in Tungchow, and the skies seemed to cloud momentarily. Those drunken wretches . . . when the report of their court-martial crossed his desk, his endorsement would be severe. They would regret having embarrassed the Provost Marshal.

When he was finished with the paperwork, he rang for more tea and put his booted feet up on the desk. As though he had been saving her for last, for dessert, his mind fastened on the Russian woman. Madame Sobolov, Puhalski called her. Tanaka laughed gently. Ah, Puhalski, you sly devil, trying to take advantage of a lonely soldier far from home. So you would be delighted to arrange an introduction, eh?

A speculative expression came over Tanaka's round face. He had never had a Caucasian woman. The white whores who frequented the soldiers' cafés revolted him with their painted faces and brassy voices. The Sobolov woman sounded rather special . . . Puhalski had seen to that with his hints about her "tastes." Tanaka permitted his thoughts to wander among the delights which the word evoked for him.

After several moments his mind obediently returned to the subject of Puhalski. The Russian's mental processes were as clear as if his brain were some sort of rudimentary machine in a glass box: turn the handle so many times, watch the cogs and levers, then see the idea pop out. Puhalski wanted to provide Tanaka with a woman. The advantages he expected were not difficult to imagine. Tanaka folded his hands complacently; allowing a scheming subordinate appear to have his own way was often a useful device. People were never more revealing of themselves than when they thought they had the upper hand. Let Puhalski think him hoodwinked.

But he intended to be cautious. Puhalski was apt to be less fastidious than he. He couldn't afford to encumber himself with some slut. Just the same, he hoped the woman would prove suitable. There was something tantalizing about playing one game with the woman and another with her husband and yet another with her lover.

But another thought occurred to him, and he frowned. Puhalski was frightened; he was not above trying to lie his way out of an uncomfortable corner. What if Sobolov hadn't swallowed the hook? The Russians were a deceitful people, and Sobolov sounded like a man of unstable temperament. He might take the money, and then get cold feet, try to give it back, stall . . . and more days would go by with nothing accomplished. It was intolerable! The master plan must go forward without further delay! Things were beginning to get ticklish at Headquarters. Only that morning Colonel Itaki had been indulging in one of his periodic snoops around the stockade. He claimed to be merely making an inspection of the prisoners' living conditions. It had not been lost upon Tanaka that these "inspections" occasionally resulted in a soldier under discipline being assigned to Itaki's residence as a gardener or some such. They tended to be young, handsome fellows, and none too bright. Tanaka snorted, revolted by the obvious possibilities.

But Itaki was the Chief of Staff, and powerful. That morning, chatting emptily about the weather and the intransigence of the Chinese, Itaki had eyed his new Buick rather pointedly. He was jealous, obviously, and his mind was full of transparent schemes. A few more episodes like the traffic bumps and the Tungchow fiasco to put Tanaka in a bad light and Itaki would be ready . . . or so he thought. Even knowing that he'd soon have the upper hand failed to moderate Tanaka's loathing for the man. It was disgusting—the lengths some men would go out of jealousy and spite. How a corsetted old pervert like Itaki had ever become Chief of Staff . . . disgraceful!

Tanaka cranked his telephone and told Okamura to come into his office at once.

Okamura was not an impressive figure. By some genetic misfortune he resembled more than anything one of those insulting American cartoons of a Japanese soldier. He was also a Reserve Officer.

Tanaka inspected him with a pretense of·benignity. "Captain

Okamura, I have a confidential task for you, something requiring subtlety and discretion."

Okamura stiffened alertly and whipped out a notebook.

"No notes, please." Tanaka sighed; Okamura was always writing things down, a bad habit for an Intelligence Officer. "There is a Russian woman, Sobolov—we have a file on her husband—who may be involved in matters relating to the security of the Provisional Government. I tell you so you will understand the importance of all this. It's imperative for me to get a look at her. She may be involved in other matters, and I have the feeling that I may recognize her. As an experienced Intelligence Officer, you'll appreciate the possibilities."

Okamura nodded eagerly.

"Call that idiot, Major Wu. He's to send a plainclothesman to locate the woman and devise some way for me to observe her from my car. She mustn't suspect she's under observation. This will tax Wu's ingenuity to the utmost, but that can't be helped. The matter is urgent."

"Where does the woman live, sir?"

"I don't know, Captain," Tanaka said patiently. "It's in the file."

"Oh."

Wearily, Tanaka closed his eyes; Okamura was a trial at times. "Now, you must impress Wu with the urgency of the matter. He'll complain that he's shorthanded and all that, but I don't care. Tell him it's a top secret matter . . . you know how talkative these damned Chinese are. As soon as the woman's located, I'm to be notified. Got that?"

"Yes, Colonel!"

Tanaka thought for a moment, tapping the desk lightly with a pencil. "One other thing," he began again, "when you've explained my wishes to that nitwit Wu, tell him that I want the woman's husband . . ." Tanaka paused. "No, I'll tell him myself. Have the call transferred in here when you've finished. Got that?"

Okamura nodded solemnly and brought his hand up in a clumsy salute.

"Carry on, then," Tanaka said, forcing a smile.

At the door, Okamura turned and started back toward the desk, fishing a folded paper from a pocket as he came. "I almost forgot . . . this just came in from the emergency ward at the hospital."

"Wait!" Tanaka barked, eyeing him crossly. Quickly Tanaka raced through the brief report, then containing his mounting fury with difficulty, he read it again. "What are you waiting for? Get out!" he shouted at Okamura.

Tanaka stared out of the window, oblivious to the swarming activity

[117]

of the large compound. The situation was intolerable, with un-provoked attacks on Japanese soldiers occurring with ever increasing frequency, of late. In a cowardly manner typical of the Chinese, the attacks were invariably on lone men, late at night, often when they were returning to barracks from an evening's relaxation. In not one single instance had an attacker been apprehended, in spite of repeated memos from Tanaka to his own Military Police and to the Municipal Police. Tanaka had begun to get memos from Headquarters on the subject. The Japanese MP's were often helpless, since possible wit-nesses invariably refused to cooperate, but not even the monumental incompetence of Wu could account for his people's lack of success. It was a blatant conspiracy of inaction, and Tanaka intended to see it stopped. He would have a few words with Wu on the subject, words which would make that imbecile wish he'd gone into another line of work.

Tanaka twisted in his chair in an agony of rage and frustration. What was particularly infuriating in the present case was that Seiko, the injured man, was a sergeant of Military Police and one of Tanaka's most faithful informers from among the enlisted ranks. An attack on him was almost an attack on Tanaka himself, making him wonder if Seiko might have been punished by disloyal elements within the Mili-tary Police. The notion made Tanaka yearn for the day when his Kempeitai organization would be operational. In that happy time, the perpetrators of this sort of outrage would be exposed at once. In the meantime, the MPs would redouble their efforts, and the Municipal Police would turn themselves inside out. One thing he was certain of was that the guilty party would be discovered and appropriately dealt with.

Poor Seiko, Tanaka thought . . . so brutal an attack, his testicles nearly crushed. Tanaka shuddered at the thought, automatically shift-ing his own precious glands into a more secure position.

Outside, a large company of Army prisoners marched across the dusty compound, heading for some work detail.

And some miles to the south, a whistle sounded faintly: four long, mournful blasts. It was eight-thirty and the morning train for Tientsin was pulling out.

☆☆

As the door clicked shut behind Bob Smith's departing figure, the room sank into its accustomed silence. Edgerton stared at the door, thinking of the things he might have said and had not. A vice-consul,

[118]

Smith was new to the Service and newer still to China. Edgerton liked him, and found his still untarnished idealism quite appealing. In Peking barely a month, Smith had left an odd sort of composite impression on him. Physically he was reminiscent of the young Procter of eighteen years before, but in Smith's somewhat naïve enthusiasms Edgerton saw a reflection of his own youthful self. At the moment the reminder was depressing . . . so much had happened since those days.

Edgerton had become interested in the Foreign Service while taking a diplomatic history course in college. Until then he'd had no real idea of what he wanted to do. He'd thought of teaching, and had given it up in favor of the law. Then the Army interrupted for a year. Although he wasn't sent overseas, the experience convinced him there had to be a better way for governments to manage their relations with each other. When regional Foreign Service exams were scheduled in San Francisco he took them, hoping that this was work he could get his teeth into. In due course he was appointed, and he was delighted to be sent to Peking for training and language study.

It had been a fascinating and tumultuous time to come to China. The political turmoil following the collapse of Manchu rule in 1911 had been aggravated by the Great War and by the Russian revolution. When he arrived in 1920, the futile and ill-conceived allied occupation of Siberia had only just wobbled to a halt, leaving a large force of Japanese in the Manchurian-Siberian borderlands. A White Russian Army had ended Chinese suzerainity in Mongolia, only to be replaced in its turn by a Bolshevik-sponsored Mongolian Peoples Republic. In the south, Sun Yat-sen's reformist Kuomintang was slowly rebuilding its strength after a disastrously premature bid for power, while a young colonel named Chiang Kai-shek devoted himself to training and reorganizing the Kuomintang Army.

But the capital remained in Peking, in the old imperial quarters within the Forbidden City, with power passing through the hands of a series of warlord-presidents as coalitions were formed and then dissolved.

Edgerton had been impatient for his student days to end so he could get on with his real work. Everything was new then, or so it seemed, and one made up the rules as he went along. Bandits roamed the countryside, threatening the more remote missions, and the Chinese authorities had continually to be cajoled or threatened into taking a hand. Military garrisons of several nations had been established after the Boxer Rebellion. From America there were the Marines in Peking and the Fifteenth Infantry in Tientsin, and they could be called on in emergencies. Adventurers and soldiers of fortune, leftovers from

[119]

the Great War, came and went, scheming and cheating, and getting caught at it. Many—all too many—were Americans and had to be tried in Consular Courts and fined or sent home to serve their sentences. American companies—oil and construction and shipping and trading —had continual contractual difficulties with their Chinese customers, and intervention by consular officers was often the only way to straighten things out.

China was breaking out of the old cast iron Imperial-Confucian mold; young men and women were reaching out for new ideas and new freedoms and filling the universities. Although perhaps not as free and as wild as their sisters in America, some of the young women were pretty free. And there were plenty of those same sisters around, both from America and England. They'd come out as tourists, and then stayed on, working for Standard Oil, or Texaco, or the British and American Tobacco Company, or the Rockefeller Foundation, or Butterfield and Swire, or any one of a score of other enterprises. There were great parties and great times, and everyone was young and excited and full of hope . . . hadn't the world just been made safe for democracy? And behind it all was the feeling that your job really mattered, that the challenges arising almost every day could be met and overcome. You could actually *do* something.

Yes, the reminder was depressing. And his mood was not improved by his predicted hangover. Whatever had possessed him to drink more whiskey when he got home? Well, he knew the answer to that: concern and worry for Tamara and her grouch of a mother, and the childish feeling that the world wasn't treating him fairly. Idiot! And now he couldn't remember what he'd told Smith. He hoped it wasn't a lot of soggy, chewed-over pap.

Edgerton picked up a sheaf of cables, then put them down unread. He glanced through a week-old copy of the Shanghai *Evening News,* then thumbed the May issue of the *National Geographic.* Also into the wastebasket. A news magazine of the month before quoted a group of economic pundits to the effect that Japan's gold reserves were nearly exhausted, and their prediction that once the last ingot was spent, her huge war machine would inexorably grind to a halt, and the war would be over without America or anyone else having to lift a hand.

Blind wishful thinking. Japan was in difficulties, no question. But the deeper her trouble, the more desperate she would become, leading to wilder and more extravagant adventures—not the opposite. Procter would not have agreed; Procter would side with the experts, being something of one himself.

It was one of those mornings when any reasonable man would vow to give up drinking altogether. His head throbbed and his mouth was lined with ashes. What *can* you tell a man like Smith? Repeat high sounding vagaries like the "Open Door" and the "Territorial and administrative integrity of China," and pretend they represented policies? They had once sounded grand perhaps, but they had become theological quibbles now, like how many angels could dance on the head of a pin. They had been the cornerstones of policy, whatever he might think of them. Smith, somewhat shocked, had asked if he then thought American policy had been a failure. Evading, Edgerton could only point out that all policies failed sooner or later . . . history saw to that. The other man had been unconvinced.

Smith's appearance had come just as he finished speaking to Tamara. La Garde, at the hotel, good fellow that he was, had agreed without a murmur to make the same arrangement for Madame Liu as he had the previous summer.

Tamara had sounded quite light-hearted and seemed free of the worry which had so oppressed her the night before. Her mother was better, too. Her only concession to events had been to stay in bed an hour past her usual time. And she had decided against moving to the hotel for the time being.

Hearing this, Edgerton had groaned aloud, making Tamara laugh. On the spur of the moment, he'd asked her to come for dinner at the San Kwan Miao. She accepted gladly, planning to send a message to her mother by rickshaw.

The brief conversation left Edgerton confused. Nothing was changed, it seemed to say. He found that difficult to believe. Was the attack on Madame Liu to be forgotten as though it were just another minor eruption in the nighttime life of the city? Did it no longer merit the indignation which he had expended upon it at the time?

These speculations made him impatient, almost angry. If Madame Liu wasn't outraged, if even Tamara was no longer particularly upset, why should he bother? Although it sounded much too easy, Edgerton was honest enough to admit to himself that he hoped it would stay that way.

It was in this mood that Smith's diffident knock had come. The interruption had been brief, returning him too soon to his own devices.

Their conversation evoked doubts about the efficacy of his own "policies." An ancient vision returned fleetingly, and he saw himself surrounded by a large family of assorted children, with dogs and cats snoozing in the background, and a faceless woman clucking over them all. She hadn't always been faceless. He'd tried to pin Elizabeth's face

[121]

on her, but like a badly made mask, it had not fitted. No other face had ever suggested itself until . . . but that was out of the question, Edgerton insisted, one fantasy superimposed upon another.

His phone buzzed and Miss Kung's shy whisper told him that Captain Madun was there to see him. Reprieved once again from either working or thinking, Edgerton grinned into the instrument. "Send Captain Madun in, please."

MacDonough looked young and efficient in a fresh khaki uniform. "Morning, John," he said, as he strode across the room.

Edgerton inspected him with mock solemnity. "You seem none the worse for wear. How do you do it?"

"A clean mind in a healthy body," Hal said, pulling the visitor's chair out of a patch of sunlight and sitting down.

"Whew, that's a relief! I was afraid I might be in for some embarrassing confessions."

"Certainly not!" Hal said, his freckled face reddening.

"Well, anyway, it's good to see you. What's on your mind?"

"Nothing much; had some free time and thought I'd drop in. You busy?"

"I should be but I'm fighting it."

"Well then, come on over to the PX for a cup of coffee."

Edgerton got to his feet thankfully. "Just let me check with Miss Kung."

Outside, although it was not yet ten o'clock, the heat was already oppressive, radiating from a sun which seemed to throb in a pale, metallic sky.

As they turned through the gate which connected the Chancery with the compound of the Marine Legation Guard, a squad of men approached, swinging along with the easy rhythm of veterans. The noncom in charge broke his chanting of the cadence long enough to give MacDonough a relaxed salute. The red, wet faces of the men looked blank to Edgerton, military masks which concealed their thoughts. When the squad was past, they crossed the street and entered the welcome shade of two rows of massive oaks.

It can't last, Edgerton thought, looking around at the neat, substantial buildings and the well-tended gardens of the officers' houses, and heard the distant, mixing cadences, and all the military martial bustle that filled the air of the place. It was indeed an anachronism, and a very temporary one, it seemed to him, in spite of all the brick and pavement and old trees.

Suddenly curious, he turned to MacDonough. "What's going to become of all this, do you suppose?"

[122]

"When the war starts, you mean?"

"Well, no," Edgerton said, surprised. "I was thinking of a simpler future . . . more evolutionary."

"Forget it . . . the war's inevitable."

"All right: when, if you're so positive?"

"A few years," Hal said, shrugging. "We can't screw around like this forever."

Genuinely puzzled, Edgerton looked at the other man, so young, so certain, so efficient, full of neat, military precision. "Are we screwing around, really?"

MacDonough gave him a patient glance as they started up the broad steps of the headquarters building. "Well, we're not doing anything to stop the Japs. Sooner or later . . ." He let it hang.

"Well, provided we have to stop them, war may be the only way. But who told us to stop them? Why us?"

"Who else is there? Besides, we can't just let them take over the whole of China!"

MacDonough's vehemence evoked for Edgerton a picture of decades of blundering and policies gone wrong, and he wanted to shout: "It isn't that simple!"

Instead, he asked, "But how many American lives is the saving of China worth . . . provided of course, that it really can be saved that way?"

"How the hell should I know?" MacDonough retorted, suddenly exasperated.

"Precisely. I don't know either. War is a difficult enterprise to budget for. Sometimes the things at stake end up costing more than they're worth. Our experience in the Great War should have taught us that."

MacDonough shook his head, but didn't respond.

Turning off the wide lobby into the PX cafeteria, Edgerton was relieved to find the place dim and empty, pleasantly cooled by an electric fan the size of a small airplane propeller.

When they were seated and the Chinese waiter had taken their order, Edgerton said, "You won't agree, I guess, but it seems to me that we Americans are refusing to face the facts as they exist out here. The Japanese are one of those facts. How long will we go on trying to avoid the business of working out a way to live with them, of making the necessary accommodations?" Edgerton was dissatisfied. it wasn't his day to be lucid. "Of course, they must make accommodations too. We can't both expect to kill the other off merely for being inconvenient."

[123]

"That sounds like appeasement," Hal said, shaking his head. "It's the same with people. If you don't like being pushed around, sooner or later you have to fight."

"Well, there's something to that," Edgerton conceded, moving to another tack. "But it's useful to remember that the right doesn't exist solely on one side. The Japanese have some reason for claiming it is we who have been pushing them around."

"For instance," Hal said, looking skeptical.

"Oh, you know the lot: protective tariffs, immigration restrictions, congressional rantings about the Yellow Peril, a feeling that we helped cheat them out of their victory over Russia, that we forced them to accept unfair and humiliating limitations to their Navy . . . and on and on. All these things add up. Whether or not they're true doesn't really matter, so long as the Japanese think they're true. And I gather from the Japanese I've known that one of the most galling things to them is our discrimination against Japanese living in the States, many of them citizens. They were badly treated when they were contract laborers, and they're still mistreated. The Japanese are proud. And they know that European immigrants—white people—get a better deal."

"The only trouble with that argument is that all those things have happened to the Chinese, and they don't feel that way."

"Don't they?"

MacDonough looked surprised for a moment. "Well, they're not giving us a lot of crap."

"That's because they have hold of the short end of the stick. One day they may get things into better balance. Four hundred million people with their industry and endurance and hard-headed guts could really give us a lot of crap."

Hal looked somewhat relieved. "I'm beginning to get you. At first I thought you were just apologizing for the Japs."

"Merely looking for causes. Repeating the same mistakes could become fatal."

Jim Ramsey stuck his head in the door, waved to them, then continued in the direction of the front steps. The sight of the doctor reminded Edgerton of Madame Liu. Although he'd put her out of his thoughts as a troublesome meddler, he had to give her credit for hard-headed guts of her own. How many women were there who could have fought and apparently beaten a Japanese soldier, even a drunk one? But she was stubborn. He'd expected her to move to the hotel as soon as he'd made the arrangements, not scurrying, but at least

[124]

with some dispatch. Well, Tamara seemed satisfied, he reminded him-self. It was up to the two of them, after all.

He looked across at MacDonough. "Well, getting back to that other question. What will happen to all this, to you, when the war does come?"

MacDonough made a thumbs down gesture, like a Roman emperor, and smiled slightly. "*I* probably won't be here."

"Do you plan for it, you Marines? Train for it?"

"Nothing very practical," Hal said, shrugging. "It would only be a delaying action, anyway . . . a token defense. But there's talk we might get pulled out, if war began to look imminent."

"Getting caught here would be a gloomy business. I suppose you'd be prisoners of war."

"I wouldn't want to be a prisoner of the Japs," Hal said, taking a cigarette from Edgerton's pack. "The guys at the beginning of a war always have it the worst. They're the fewest and the farthest from home, and all the worst mistakes are made in the beginning."

"Mistakes by the politicians and diplomats, you mean?"

MacDonough laughed. "No, those mistakes are made all the way through: beginning, middle, and end. I meant the generals' mistakes—but they probably don't stop either."

"I never heard that they did," Edgerton said. "Well, it's good to know you're a philosopher. It's the only thing to be these days." A sudden recollection made him grin. "And you're a man of action, too, unless my eyes deceived me last night."

"You weren't exactly moping in the corner. When I danced with Valerie, all she could talk about was how interesting and amusing you were, and how well-informed, and blah, blah. Marie said the same. It was disgusting."

So Valerie had liked him; he hadn't mistaken the meaning in her eyes and the pressure of her fingers. The thought left Edgerton both pleased and vaguely excited.

"That could go either way for you," Hal said, as though reading his mind. "Nice to play with, but pretty nice to be serious about, too." He hesitated a moment. "You need a good steady woman."

Edgerton heard himself laugh uneasily, and wondered at this uni-versal desire to get him married off. "I don't know that I'm ready for the fireside and slippers . . . I tried that once, you know."

Hal nodded soberly, suddenly looking very young. "Can I ask you something personal?" he asked.

That again? Edgerton was at a loss. Hal was his friend, he knew,

[125]

and he only wanted to be helpful. "Do you have to?" he asked gently.

Hal looked surprised. "No, I guess not." He thought for a moment, his eyes fixed seriously on Edgerton's. "But let me tell you about a bind I was in last year. I met this Chinese girl, see . . . all I was looking for was a nice *kun-yang* to do my laundry and, you know, teach me Chinese. At first I thought: Wow! This is great . . . no responsibility, no obligation. But I surprised myself, and fell for her." Edgerton sensed an ambivalent regret, as though Hal might miss the young lover as much as he missed the girl herself.

"But no matter how I twisted and argued with myself, the answer always came out the same way," Hal went on, his face and voice coldly serious. "It was either her or the Marine Corps."

Edgerton realized suddenly that his palms were moist. "What did you do?"

"I dropped out of sight. Never called, never sent any messages, never answered any. I hated it, and hated myself, but I knew it had to be that way." MacDonough shook his head at the memory. "It's like a bad tooth, a thing like that. The more you fool with it, the worse it gets and the more it hurts. The only thing to do is yank the fucker out."

Edgerton could only nod. It was strange to have a man who was his junior by at least ten years point out the obvious so succinctly. It was brutal, Hal's way, but perhaps necessary . . . emergency surgery for Tamara's sake as much as for his own. A sense of helpless shame afflicted him.

"I guess I sort of stuck my oar in," MacDonough said, somewhat apologetically.

"No; not at all. You made sense and I thank you for it," Edgerton said, managing a flimsy smile. An idea struck him and he acted on it without further thought. "Look: why don't you come over to the San Kwan Miao tonight for pot luck. We can have a swim and a couple of drinks. Ch'en can always scrape up something to eat."

"Well . . ."

Hal's face suggested that the ingenious Marie had already made plans for them. "You'll be free by nine and can go where the spirit moves you." Edgerton added impassively.

Hal grinned quickly. "I'd like to come."

"Good," Edgerton said. "About six?"

As MacDonough nodded, a group of Marines pushed through the swinging door, all talking at once. He gave his watch a quick glance and stood up. "I've got to go. Have a class to give in five minutes: new wrinkles in bayonet fighting."

[126]

At Edgerton's surprised look, he threw back his head and laughed. "No, it isn't," Hal said. "It's really about field hygiene. Military life isn't as bloodthirsty as many people think."

"See you later, then," Edgerton said, amused. They surprised each other by shaking hands.

Back at his desk, Edgerton felt an odd truculent stubbornness come over him. It was simply not in him to drop from Tamara's sight, nor to let her drop from his. He was insulted by this assumption that he would be a good little boy and not rock the boat. Sometimes he wanted not only to rock it, but to tip it over, to flaunt Tamara in their faces. But that would be unfair to Tamara, and would leave it to her to pick up the pieces of his foolish defiance.

Edgerton lighted a cigarette, then at once stubbed it out.

Everywhere he looked, things were coming apart at the seams. The country where he had spent almost half his life was slowly dying; his beloved city was deteriorating before his eyes, becoming shabbier, dirtier, more disorderly. The people of Peking—to him the most charming and interesting in all China—were defenseless, prey to the whim of any drunken soldier. And no one did anything.

He thought of Yamaguchi at the Japanese Legation. A reasonable, civilized young man, trying to do his best—but he was powerless against the Army. Reams of well-documented complaints against Japanese soldiers had passed into Yamaguchi's hands, never to be heard of again. He was always apologetic, even ashamed, but Edgerton knew he could do nothing. Only rarely did a case like the one involving the Tungchow mission receive a second glance.

An idea, wild and unorthodox, flickered in his brain, hovering on the verge of extinction. Ridiculous! he decided. Not the way to do things at all. He discarded it regretfully. It had both the promise of raising a memorable stink and allowing him to personally show the rule-makers what he thought of them . . . and their supposedly un-rockable boat.

But the idea refused to die. Edgerton sat thinking, swiveling slowly, for about ten minutes, weighing pros and cons. Finally he got out a pad and a couple of freshly sharpened pencils. Here was one memorandum which would be a pleasure to write.

☘☘

Peking's City Hall, or Municipal Yamen, resembled nothing so much as a soldiers' barracks which had unaccountably been built of

[127]

marble, as though the contractor had misread the specifications. There was nothing in it of the grace and tastefulness of Chinese architecture. Lieutenant Li Ch'ing-wei hardly looked at it as he climbed the wide stone steps. Scowling, he returned the police sentry's salute and pushed into the revolving door. Li did not approve of policemen being used as ceremonial mannequins, saluting the comings and goings of a lot of bureaucrats.

The light was bad in the cavernous foyer, and Li had to squint to read the temporary directory chart. His destination, the Police Training Department, was mentioned by name, but there was no room number.

He stood there indecisively, a tall, thin, narrow-faced man whose badly fitting black uniform hung on him as though he were made of sticks. He was tired. He had slept a little at Mei-ling's house, only to awaken before dawn and lie beside her on the straw sleeping mat and mull over the arrest of Ling. If he had made a mistake letting the rascal go, and his negligence were discovered, Captain Wang would find ways to make him pay for it.

"Well, Ch'ing-wei, are you lost?"

Startled, Li turned and found himself looking down into the square, faintly smiling face of Chang Sun-cheh. "Sun-cheh, it's good to see you." They shook hands in the Western manner. "Or should I be properly respectful and address you as the Honorable Assistant Deputy Minister?"

"Please don't; we have entirely too many empty titles as it is." Chang waved a hand at the directory. "Are you searching for someone in particular, or merely planning to blow up the building?"

Li grinned at him. "My face is too easily read. No, I am looking for the Training people, to get a copy of the new police manual. We should have been mailed one weeks ago, and it is not possible to reach anyone on the telephone who will admit to knowing anything about it."

"Maybe you have been forgotten. Don't complain; it is better that way, believe me. Come; I have an extra copy in my office."

They walked side by side down a dingy corridor lined with closed doors. The place hummed with hidden activity, but no one was visible.

"You have an office here?" Li asked. "I thought you spent all your time in the Executive Yuan."

"I used to. Now I race back and forth between the two places—the new efficiency. I am thinking of having a desk built into my rickshaw." Chang made a grand, sweeping gesture. "Over here I am in charge of coordinating municipal and rural police activities."

"What does that mean?"

[128]

"It means," Chang began, lowering his voice and glancing quickly over his shoulder at the empty hallway, "that they are scared shitless of the guerrillas."

Li laughed silently.

They stopped by one of the closed doors, and Chang rummaged awkwardly in his pockets for his keys.

"It also means that they don't quite trust me. There is a rumor that I am a spy for Nanking." They went into a tiny office; Chang gave Li a sour grin. "A Kuomintang spy! If Chiang Kai-shek heard that, he'd have a heart attack from laughing."

Li watched thoughtfully as Chang bolted the door from the inside. Always a prickly customer, Chang had made a nuisance of himself while a member of the Generalissimo's government in Nanking, with his urgings for reforms in the National Police. After exposing a number of cases both of corruption and of trafficking with the Japanese, the reactionaries only hated him all the more. His recommendations had all been blocked. Chang had finally carried his demands directly to the Generalissimo, and that had been the end of him. Chiang Kai-shek, whatever his good points, was not a man of whom subordinates made demands.

Chang moved some books off a chair so Li could sit down. One of them was the police manual, and Li put it on the desk under his hat.

"Speak softly," Chang cautioned him. "These walls are thin as rice paper." He got out cigarettes and matches, and when they were smoking he asked, "Well, how are the protectors of the people's safety?"

Li made a wry face. "These days we spend much of our time protecting ourselves from our leaders. With Captain Wang in charge and Major Wu meddling diligently from above, it is a wonder my precinct is able to function."

"Those two!" Chang said disgustedly. "I find myself continually embarrassed. I would have thought, before I became one, that traitors were sensible men. Instead I find myself surrounded by turtle eggs."

Li frowned at him sadly. "Don't say that, old *p'eng-yu*, you hurt my feelings, since I am as much a traitor as you are."

Chang gave him one of his humorless smiles and threw up his hands. "I get discouraged; and the Japanese are the greatest asses of all."

"What now?" Li was disturbed by the bitter note of defeat in his voice.

Chang shrugged. "I've just spent a trying morning attempting to sort some sense out of a killing up in old Nankow Iron Works."

"I heard about that. Not in my precinct, I'm happy to say."

"You're lucky. I have a witness who saw the Military Police shoot

[129]

a man in there. Actually, 'execute' is a better word for what happened. But I can't get that madman Tanaka to tell me what it is all about."

"Tanaka, eh?" Li said.

"Yes; Tanaka. I am unable to explain the simplest principle of civilian police procedure to that man. He nods and smiles and sucks on his teeth, and all the time I have the feeling he is thinking about something else."

"What really happened?"

"*They* claim they caught someone who was supposed to be a smuggler . . . arms for the communists, or something. Someone tipped off the MPs, and according to Tanaka they caught the fellow red-handed. Okay so far, but then they manage to shoot him 'while trying to escape.' Tanaka claims ignorance, but my witness, who was in the area on, um, other business, puts Tanaka right there giving the orders." Chang sighed and rubbed his eyes with his fingers. "The man probably was a smuggler; how should I know? If it wasn't such hard, dirty work, I'd be one myself and get out of this . . . this lunatic asylum." His voice rose angrily.

Li touched a reminding finger to his lips.

Nodding, Chang grinned, and then went on in a lower voice, "So I ask Tanaka, 'Where are the arms?' Confiscated. 'Where is the body?' Disposed of. 'Who is the man so the municipal police can check into his associates?' Military secret. 'What am I supposed to tell the foreign press and the legations about machine-gun shooting in the night in the middle of this supposedly peaceful city?' Tanaka shrugs and changes the subject to some minor incident of a soldier beaten up in a *hu-tung*. Naturally, Tanaka suspects a plot."

Reminded of a report he'd seen that morning, Li wanted to hear more. "What about the soldier?" he asked.

"Some corporal got his balls kicked. The MPs found him this morning, just off the An-wei Hu-tung near Hata Men Chieh. That's not your precinct either, is it?"

"Not ordinarily, but we're sharing that neighborhood with the Seventh, now that so many men are on assignment to the villages. He was badly hurt, my assistant tells me. Testicles the size of turnips, and a cut face. Major Wu has already called us about the case. The man is actually one of Tanaka's own men, it appears. Tanaka is particularly incensed, wants immediate action, and so forth. Captain Wang is half out of his few wits with worry. Of course, the chances of our catching anyone are very slim, unless we do a house-to-house of the entire area. And even then it's a gamble."

Chang nodded sympathetically, then had to grin. "According to Tanaka it must have taken a gang to do the job; the man is jujitsu

[130]

champion of his regiment, it seems . . . or anyhow, he was. But the MP report said he was full to the gills with saki."

"I don't envy whoever kicked him. They're bound to try and find him."

"Right; even if it's the wrong person. With Tanaka, the soldier's balls are more important than the summar execution of his alleged smugglers. Although, maybe it's just as well . . . only the gods know whom he'd have implicated . . ." Chang fell silent, frowning at this new thought.

"It's a strange business we're in these days. Nowadays we don't mind if smugglers get away . . . anything to torment the Japs."

Chang grinned sourly. "Yes; we're half on one side of the fence and half on the other. Damn these wretched greedy Japs anyway!" He spat furiously into the brass spittoon beside his desk. "It's impossible to reason with any of them, Tanaka in particular. I try to tell him that he can't run this city like a prison, with beatings and shootings, unless he wants to maintain a permanent garrison of five thousand troops here. He only smiles and sucks his teeth. Why should he care?"

"Well, for that matter, why should you? The troops are at least out of action."

"Bah! Listen, Ch'ing-wei, the 'action' is now almost over. In any case, one division more or less of these rascals would make no difference. What I want is to get five thousand loafers off the backs of the people of this city so they can get back to the normal business of living their miserable lives without this army of leeches. Let Chiang Kai-shek worry about the action; that's his business, not mine. If he'd listened to a few of us . . ." Chang inspected the tip of his cigarette moodily.

Li watched him thoughtfully. Chang Sun-cheh remained something of an enigma; sooner or later, a curtain would always drop between them. He wondered, almost academically, if Chang had joined the Communists. Li was indifferent. Politics bored him; it was too much like religion. Li had heard it rumored that Sun-cheh's intellectual wife was a Communist and had been one for years, but intellectual women made him uneasy. Li felt a certain grudging respect for the Communists. They were beginning to give the Japanese a wretched time of it. If the Japanese could be driven out, and if enough Communists remained alive to organize things, and if the Russians . . . if, if, if . . . Stupid speculation. He remembered something else.

"Do you know this Russian crook, Puhalski?"

Chang gave an indifferent shrug. "I have heard of him."

"There is something peculiar going on between Puhalski and Tanaka."

Chang looked skeptical. "One steals opium out of the Army stores

[131]

and the other sells it, and then they divide the money. What is so peculiar about that?"

"About that, nothing. But Puhalski is sleeping with the wife of another Russian, a man named Sobolov, and . . ."

"With several wives probably."

"Well, let me finish and I will tell you."

Chang laughed. "Scratchy as ever. This miserable person begs most humbly for pardon."

"Sobolov works for the Americans."

Chang's eyebrows rose. "He does, eh? For the Marines?"

Li shook his head slowly. "For the Legation as an interpreter. Specifically, for Edgerton."

A deep frown creased Chang's broad forehead. "I am stupid today. What is the connection?"

"Tanaka is now interested in this woman also."

"How interested?"

"He wants her located right away . . . so that he can see her."

"See her?"

"Look at her, identify her; he says she may be involved in matters connected with the Imperial security."

"He says, eh? I am beginning to get your point. Well, Wu will make a botch of that. He couldn't find the Legation Quarter without a map."

"He won't have to. He passed the problem on to Captain Wang, who immediately tossed it to me. I had to take a man out of another investigation for this nonsense."

"At least you seem to know what's going on."

"There is something else which I may not get to know much about. Wang would only tell me that it was a matter much too sensitive for my ears."

"*Ai-ya!* Ch'ing-wei, you are killing me with suspense! Will you be so good as to get to the point?"

"Wu is to have Sobolov called to the Police Yamen on some pretext, so Captain Wang can 'question' him. Wang would tell me no more than that."

"It sounds like they are all crazy." Chang chewed his lip thoughtfully. "What do you think is up?"

"I think Tanaka is preparing Sobolov to be squeezed for information."

"What kind of information would an interpreter have?"

Li spread his hands eloquently. "I used to think Puhalski's interest in the Sobolovs centered solely around the woman—but now that fat pig Tanaka is snuffling in the background. Finally I reminded myself

[132]

that Puhalski can get all the women he wants, and younger ones, from his café."

"How do you keep up with all these people, anyway?"

"I have been watching Puhalski for years," Li said. "He is a hobby of mine. One day he will slip, and then I will get him."

Chang laughed shortly. "You dedicated professionals frighten me."

"I was almost ready to grab him last year but the fighting interfered. The first thing I knew, my witnesses had disappeared and Puhalski was working for Tanaka. But his usefulness is limited. When Tanaka drops him, I'll get him."

Chang gave him a brief look, then his gaze grew distant. "Funny thing. I was talking to Edgerton only last night. Your name came up, as a matter of fact. He spoke of you with considerable warmth."

Feeling absurdly pleased, Li struggled to control his expression. "Didn't you go to school with him in America?" he asked.

"Not exactly. But I have known him for many years."

"He is a good man . . . for a foreigner. For every Edgerton they send over, we get twenty vultures. I am sick of them."

"So am I."

As the two men smoked in silence, Li's mind drifted to that long-ago night in Tientsin, and suddenly, in Chang's cramped untidy office, the wide Hai River seemed to stretch before him, dark and oily under the stars. Summer showers swept the river, drenching them, as he sculled the heavy sampan, and the American with the then unpronounceable name crouched miserably in the bow. They had both been lucky that night, himself in particular. He would have died there in the old Russian Concession in that abandoned house, had it not been for the bullish courage of the big American.

Subsequently, a tenuous friendship had developed almost clandestinely between them. Even the American's name had become pronounceable. Nor was the basis for the friendship simply gratitude. There was something about the American that touched him, despite his self-proclaimed cynicism. Li's world was rigidly stratified into ranks and classes. But when he saw Edgerton occasionally, he would carry away the feeling that the layers which separated them had ceased to matter. What was more—and this made him unhappy with himself—he realized that his own fear of compromising his job created barriers where otherwise there would have been none.

Li got to his feet abruptly. "I'll dig up what I can about Sobolov, and let Edgerton know if the Legation is involved." Li said.

Chang nodded. "Keep me informed, if you will. It's none of my business, but I collect facts like a crow collects sticks."

"Do you make nests with them?" Li asked, half-amused.

"In a way," Chang replied seriously. "I may have to run away some day. I must know when to make my move."

Li nodded at him. "Not a bad idea. "Let me know; I may come, too." "I will."

Outside again, Li stopped for a moment on the steps and looked around. The Municipal Yamen was outside his precinct, but the shabby buildings and the bustle in the street below were much the same. Also the same were the people all around him, struggling, fighting, stealing, fornicating, hating, and providing for their families. Chang Sun-cheh had surprised him with his show of feeling for the city. . . . he'd always pictured him as a man with only regional and national concerns—the inhabitants of a mere city would just be pawns in a more important game.

The thought reminded him of his own obligations. Helping Edgerton had to be balanced against the need to remain useful. The risks and the shame of staying behind and working for the conquerors must not be wasted. The Major Wus and Captain Wangs and a swarm of toadying parasites mustn't be turned loose. This was Li's city, the place of his birth, and his duty was to it. And to Mei-ling. He had a powerful duty to her, too, now. It had grown on him in these past months without his being aware of it. He realized suddenly that it was perhaps the most compelling duty of them all. And standing there on the steps he knew that he was glad that this was so, and that he no longer thought only of himself. That night there was to be an American moving picture showing, something about the cowboys and the Red Indians. Mei-ling would like that.

Soon he was pedaling, apparently aimlessly, through the streets of his own precinct, a barely perceptible stir accompanying his progress. In these uncertain times it did the people good, the honest no less than the dishonest, to be reminded that the police were likely to appear at unexpected moments. And Li knew he had a certain reputation in this regard; he stifled a smile. They didn't call him "that devil Li" for nothing.

❦❦

The big car nudged the thickening crowd aside like a boat threading a reed-choked stream. Colonel Tanaka felt himself tense with anticipation, glad to thrust aside other concerns.

He had just come from the hospital. Sergeant Seiko had indeed been badly hurt, and bemoaned the possibility of never again performing

[134]

his manly functions. Tanaka didn't care about that. What Tanaka cared about was that Seiko had sustained his injuries at the hands of a mere woman, rather than the gang of thugs Tanaka had originally suspected. The plain fact was that the sergeant, the vaunted wrestler, had been too drunk to defend himself against the woman he had attempted to molest. It was ludicrous.

Just the same, no Chinese woman had the right to take such brutal action against a merely amorous soldier. An example would have to be made. Seiko claimed to be able to identify the woman, but it didn't matter. Even if the wrong woman were punished, the example would lose none of its force.

Tanaka wished he'd known in time that the suspect was a woman. Unfortunately, a full-scale investigation was already under way with the MP Special Unit on the job, and Major Wu thoroughly frightened. He'd have to brazen it out now, and let any embarrassment be paid for by the woman.

Pushing Sergeant Seiko from his mind, Tanaka craned his neck, trying to see beyond the heads of his driver and the Chinese plain-clothes policeman sitting next to him on the front seat.

The car nosed up to a makeshift barricade and stopped. Tanaka chided himself for not having engaged a Chinese taxi and worn civilian clothes for this delicate mission. Although no one stared at the car or at him, the crowd's curiosity was discomforting. But gradually his almost childish sense of excitement returned. To keep from squirming, and betraying his inner turmoil to the men in front, Tanaka placed his feet firmly together and gripped the upright pommel of his sword in both hands.

Beyond the barricade, the street market seethed in its customary afternoon stink. It was a jerry-built conglomeration of bamboo stalls and peddlers' carts and barrows, all roofed over with straw mats and bits of mildewed canvas. By now the stalls were half-empty of produce, but throngs of shoppers still shoved and jostled, feeling the bruised vegetables, eyeing the softening fish and the bloody remnants of various nameless meats, and bargaining raucously with the tired proprietors.

Inside the black car, the temperature soared. Tanaka could feel the rivulets of sweat pour down his face and body. He was thinking longingly of the cool bath he would have when he got home, when an eddy in the crowd revealed a Russian woman picking over a mound of turnips. Even before the Chinese detective could nod, Colonel Tanaka knew instinctively that she was the one.

She had a basket on one arm and was wearing a faded cotton dress.

[135]

Thick brown hair, held back by a few pins, framed her pale face. She stood with her weight on one leg so that her haunch strained against the thin fabric of her dress and Tanaka could see the slanting line of her underpants. She leaned over the bin of vegetables and her heavy breasts swayed forward. Tanaka swallowed, nearly choking. The woman turned and moved toward them to the next stall, and an opening in the matting overhead threw a ray of sunlight onto her face. Her full, unpainted lips were red and moist, turned down petulantly at the corners, and an impatient crease divided her dark eyebrows. Her dress was splotched darkly under the arms with sweat. She shifted her basket and showed him the firm swell of her belly with its deep central indentation.

Tanaka's toes curled up inside his boots and his eyes cemented themselves to the shadow of her navel. It was deep as a saki cup, but his mind's eye refused to linger and went down to the thick bush that must be hiding from him just below. Abruptly she turned away, turned back to the other stall, mesmerizing Tanaka with the rolling of her buttocks. His stubby fingers roved to his sword tassel, and began to twirl it gently. She stopped then and hesitated. Tanaka willed her to stay in sight a little longer, and she turned back, nearly collapsing him with relief.

A lock of her hair escaped its pin and fell across her cheek. With a careless gesture she thrust it back, and as her round strong arm went up he got a glimpse of the furry smudge in her armpit. The sword tassel twirled faster. The woman changed her mind again and moved away, and the crowd surged in behind her. Briefly the brown tangle of her hair remained in sight. And then it, too, was gone.

The revolving tassel slowed, then stopped, and Tanaka sighed. Belatedly remembering his dignity, he stuffed his wayward fingers into the tops of his boots.

Following his previous instructions, the Chinese policeman slipped from the car and began to move nonchalantly after the woman. Making use of this distraction, Tanaka surreptitiously adjusted the front of his trousers under the guise of searching his pockets for cigarettes. He smirked: there would be no question of his ability to perform *his* manly functions. Looking up, he met the driver's questioning glance in the rear view mirror, and he gestured peremptorily for the car to be backed into the street and driven away. Soon the faint breezes of motion were bathing his hot face, and helping to calm his muddled thoughts.

How different this had been from his expectations! Seeing the woman had begun as a pleasant truancy, similar to the inspection of

[136]

a vase or a painting he was thinking of buying, but now . . . well . . . Tanaka patted his cheeks and forehead with a folded handkerchief. He was frankly surprised at himself. He who had always been fastidious in his choice and use of women, wanted to rape this woman, wanted to mount her and couple with her grossly like a plundering soldier, to bruise that soft and most un-Oriental flesh with kneading fingers, wanted to . . . Colonel Tanaka groaned quietly, and began puffing furiously on his cigarette.

As the sweat dried on his face and his mind became more serene, Tanaka turned his thoughts to ways and means. He wanted this foreign woman, wanted her badly and at once, and Puhalski was going to have to arrange something without delay. Ah, Puhalski, he thought almost fondly, you cannot imagine the enormous favor you are about to do me. And Puhalski would do it, too, even when he saw that affairs were not developing according to his own scheme, whatever that might have been. Colonel Tanaka was in charge now, and Colonel Tanaka always got what he wanted.

♟♟

All during that long morning as throughout the sleepless remainder of the night before, Puhalski had been racking his brains for ways to extricate himself from Tanaka's messy plottings. Running away had its attractions, but the places left to run were few and, if Tanaka chose to be vindictive, they became even fewer. In any case he could get to none of them without impoverishing himself, and once there he would be nothing but a penniless newcomer with twenty years of work to do over again. Running was out.

Staying kept him involved with Tanaka. It would be a neat trick to avoid being caught and ruined in the inevitable debacle. Under suitable circumstances, he might have managed it. With no one to help him but a spineless blunderer like Sobolov it became an impossibility. So, solely on those terms, staying was out.

But if Maya could divert Tanaka enough so that he was left alone to manage Sobolov in his own way, there was still a chance. Puhalski had only to recall the smuggler's face disintegrating under the impact of those bullets, to be convinced that he had to make it work. He glanced across the littered table. Maya gazed back witlessly over her glass of tea. "We are in trouble," he said.

Worry clouded her eyes. "But I thought everything was settled between you and Andrei."

"That part is settled. Now there are other complications."

[137]

"What is it you want him to do?"

"That's not the problem," he snapped, dismissing her question. "That is only business. This is something else."

Puhalski crossed his legs, and felt the tightness of drying sweat across the small of his back. Now that he was confronting the moment, he found it strangely difficult to continue. The blasted woman was forever upsetting his plans. He had intended this meeting to be short and businesslike.

But the sight of her had made him forget; he had even torn her dress in his eagerness. So much for his intentions. Well, it didn't make any difference. She was there to be plowed, and he was the plowman of the moment. That was all it amounted to.

"You are going to have to help me," he told her. Her eyes melted soulfully, and Puhalski repressed a shudder. "Everything depends on you."

"Serge, my darling!" Her hand reached for his across the dirty plates. "I will do anything for you."

His eyes fell regretfully to the table. "I hate to ask it of you but I must."

"I am so happy to please you, to help you. Just tell me."

"You are wonderful," he said warmly. "But you must do exactly as I say."

"Always, dearest." She gave his limp fingers a squeeze.

"It may be a little distasteful at first, but . . . well, I do distasteful things twenty times a day. The world is seldom exactly to our liking."

Her eyes shifted warily. "I don't understand," she said.

"I would never ask anything that wasn't absolutely necessary. You do believe that, don't you?"

She looked at him for several seconds before giving a small, hesitant nod.

"Good." Puhalski took a deep breath. "You see, there is this very powerful Japanese, a high officer in the Army. I am deeply in his debt, and now he has demanded a great favor. He has seen you at a distance and is very attracted to you. I *must* keep his friendship and, well . . . he is a man like any other, after all." He disposed of the implications of this statement with a gentle shrug, but he kept his eyes locked most sincerely upon hers.

Comprehension dawning slowly, Maya stared back at him. "And you want me . . . ?" Her voice trailed off into silence.

"Oh, come, Maya," he chided her. "Don't play the tender virgin with me."

"But how could you?" she gasped, her face collapsing, her fingers

[138]

playing nervously with the front of her kimono. Tears filled her eyes, spilled over, and began to run down her face, streaking the traces of rouge on her cheeks.

Puhalski was suddenly enraged. He hit the table with the flat of his hand, the noise echoing like a shot in the dim kitchen. "Because I must!" he barked at her. "Because there is no other way!"

"Oh, but I couldn't," Maya moaned. She sagged forward against the table, her sobs sending the plates and glasses rattling.

"Nonsense! What is so terrible about that?" He gave her a grin of encouragement, and a jovial wink. "Just lie down and spread your legs, and think about something else; think about the future." His eyes grew warm. "Our future."

"But I am not a whore!"

You were born to be a whore, Puhalski thought, his face frozen into a picture of patient understanding. "Mayichka, listen: this is no time to be a romantic schoolgirl. You are a woman of experience, of sophistication."

"I am not!" she blubbered. "And you . . . how can you ask such a thing if you care for me at all? And with a Japanese . . . ugh!"

Controlling his temper, Puhalski said cajolingly, "Oh, come now, Maya; you know better than that. The Japanese are no worse than anyone else. Besides this man is a high officer, not some turnip-eating private."

"No worse, perhaps, but different," she sobbed. "And I know their officers. We were in Mukden when they took over in 1932 . . . you were here then. You don't know what it was like."

But he'd heard about it. It had been a hard time for the Russian refugees . . . as usual. The Japanese, suspecting treachery on all sides, had been ruthless.

"But you don't understand, my dearest," Puhalski said, forcing a throb of sorrow into his voice. "Do you think I *like* the idea of another man with you?"

Swaying in her chair, Maya peered at him through swollen eyes. She shook her head at last, and whispered, "I can't do it."

Puhalski heaved a sigh and got noisily to his feet. "Well, then, I suppose I must take the consequences." With a heavy tread he marched across the room and picked up his hat.

"Consequences?" she repeated, her voice shaking.

"Of course! The Jap will be furious." He shook his head, and began to get into his jacket.

"Why not one of those women from the café?"

"He doesn't want a cabaret girl. He is an educated man, cultured, rich . . . he can be very generous. He wants to meet a lady of the upper classes, someone with intelligence, with artistic interests. He is a great admirer of the ballet; he doesn't want a woman of the streets."

"If he is such a gentleman, why can't you explain to him about me?"

"He is very stubborn; besides, as I told you, he has a hold on me."

"But why me? How does he know about me?"

Puhalski spread his hands helplessly. "That is my fault, I suppose. I was boasting about your beauty, and he became infatuated when he saw you on the street. Now he talks of nothing else. I'm in a position where I must pay up or . . ." He let the last word float off ominously.

"What will he do to you?" she whispered.

"I don't know; perhaps nothing. But this is war, and Japanese officers expect to get what they ask for." Another great sigh. "Who knows; perhaps he will merely ruin me. I will have to leave Peking . . ." The room was quiet except for her unsteady breathing and the faint whistle of the kettle.

"Would he . . . would I have to often?"

Puhalski almost laughed aloud. He had won . . . he always did. "Ah, that's my girl! I knew I could count on you." Beaming his gratitude, he spread his arms. Maya stumbled out of her chair and rushed into them, fresh sobs erupting.

Patting her shoulder affectionately, and grinning sardonically over the top of her head, he eased her toward the door. "There, there," he said, his arm enclosing her protectively, his fingers kneading the soft flesh over her hipbone.

"Will you come tonight?" she asked.

"I can't, my dear. I have to catch up on my accounts."

"How about tomorrow afternoon?"

Puhalski winked at her. "If I can possibly make it, I'll be here," he said, squeezing her ardently. "By the way, remind Andrei to complete the work I asked him to do, and drop it off at the café first thing in the morning."

Maya brushed at her eyes with her fingers. "When . . . ?" she whispered.

"Perhaps next week," Puhalski told her sadly, hoping it would be sooner than that. To forestall any further protest, he bent and kissed her quickly on the lips.

"Remember, my dear: this is a time for discipline. You must obey me without question. Everything depends on it."

Finally she nodded. She was dumb and helpless, and he dominated her completely, but in the very reluctance of that nod he sensed evasion. He didn't like it.

Puhalski slid his open hand under the vibrant weight of one big breast. He fondled her nipple through the thin stuff of her kimono, feeling it swell and seeing the look in her eyes as she responded. Her fingertips stroked the back of his wrist.

With clinical detachment, he measured the extent of his own reaction. He had been right; he *was* the master of his own passions, and of hers, as well. She was his to use, to caress, to command, to punish. His thumb and forefinger closed down upon the swollen button of flesh in a brief but powerful pinch.

Maya screeched thinly, and tried to pull away from him, but his arm held her rigidly. Looking down at her with a cold smile, he gauged the pain and panic in her distorted face precisely.

"You must obey me without question . . . always," he said very slowly, as though explaining something to a child. "Do you understand?"

She squirmed feebly, her eyes trapped by his. She nodded.

"Answer me!"

"Yes, I understand," she whispered hoarsely.

"Never forget it, my dear Maya," he said, and kissed her lightly on the forehead. "Until tomorrow."

Smiling, he backed into the corridor and pulled the door closed. Her wounded eyes followed his face until the very last.

∗∗

They were across the threshold of his courtyard, with the gate closed behind them, when Edgerton remembered that he hadn't told Tamara he was expecting another guest.

There hadn't been time. He'd walked up Canal Street toward the Club, hoping to surprise her and walk with her to the San Kwan Miao. But he'd been a few minutes late, and found her already near the corner of Legation Street. His intention had been—in spite of earlier arguments for discretion—to escort her out of the Club, past all the tennis players and poolside loungers. Bravado perhaps, he'd admitted to himself when he'd made the decision, but in a good cause.

Just as well, he said to himself when he saw her. At best, the gesture was empty; at worst, it might earn her a lecture from the Manager.

She had looked beautifully free striding down the sidewalk toward him, her slender legs swirling the tight skirt of her short Chinese dress. Looking at her then, he could hardly recognize the haggard, worried girl who'd rung his bell the night before.

Tamara told him she'd telephoned her mother rather than send a message by rickshaw. There was a phone in the tailor shop below their flat, and she and her mother were grudgingly permitted the use of it. Madame Liu had sounded well enough, Tamara said, and in a better mood than when she had left that morning. She had gossiped discreetly with the neighbors and sent her midwife friend scouting. There was no sign of any police activity in the area, and now her mother was questioning the necessity of ever going to the hotel.

"She just doesn't want the trouble of moving," Edgerton said. "That, and accepting a favor from me."

Tamara had quickly protested that on the contrary her mother had sent him her sincere thanks and had raised no objection to Tamara's dining with him. Skeptical of miracles, Edgerton had let the matter lie there.

Her elbow was warm in his cupped hand and he could feel the brushing of her skirt against his leg as she walked beside him across the empty outer courtyard. She smiled happily up at him, squeezing his hand close to her side.

MacDonough was already there. Drink in hand, he unfolded himself from a wicker armchair as they approached. He looked cool and clean in a freshly pressed linen suit, making Edgerton feel damp and bedraggled. Although he searched his friend's face, he saw only an expression of frank admiration for Tamara and a quick look for him which seemed to contain amusement.

Pleased and self-conscious, Edgerton mumbled the unnecessary introductions, then left them together while he fixed drinks for Tamara and himself. He was surprised at Tamara's easiness with MacDonough and her quick acceptance of his presence. Of course, she would know him as a Club member and had probably spoken to him often enough. Just the same, he had been afraid that she would feel intimidated by the novelty of the situation.

Staring down into the two ice-filled glasses and forgetting what he was there for, Edgerton got a glimpse of the implications of his total preoccupation with himself. They were always alone together, he and Tamara. When they went out, he took her to out-of-the-way places where an inconvenient meeting with anyone from his own group was unlikely. Everything was managed for his benefit. His impulse that afternoon had been unique; the thought shocked him. What must Tamara have been thinking all this time about the secrecy of their relationship? What must that secrecy have said to her about him? And about herself?

Scotch and water, he said to himself, remembering his mission, and proceeded to mix their drinks.

[142]

Ch'en, his house "boy," had rolled back part of the *p'eng* that sheltered the courtyard and had dampened the straw matting; the air around them was cool and pleasant. The bricks had been swept and sprinkled and the geraniums watered so that their leaves and petals were bright with droplets of moisture. Ch'en had arranged wicker chairs, a sofa and a low table next to the courtyard's solitary tree, and on another table had set out bottles and glasses and a bowl of ice.

As if on cue, he bustled in with a tray of toasted *hsiao-chih*, hovered for a moment as though estimating their ability to manage for themselves, and then silently removed himself, looking smug. Ch'en loved a party.

Edgerton smiled after him affectionately. Handing Tamara her drink, he took a seat beside her on the creaky sofa. Tamara and Hal interrupted whatever it was that they were saying to smile at him, and then continued. Edgerton took two good swallows of the cold whiskey and felt much better. Hal was at his relaxed and easy-going best and Tamara was obviously comfortable with him. Edgerton was content to sit and listen with half an ear.

Tamara had never looked more beautiful to him. Her expressive open face, now animated as she spoke, or serene and interested as she listened, glowed like soft ivory under her dark hair. Her short summer gown barely covered her knees, and through the slit in the side he could see a bit of thigh above her stocking. Had they been alone he would have had to touch her.

Almost wrenching his eyes away, he looked past her and saw that the side gate was open. Beyond it there was a small court onto which the three apartments of their small complex opened, and beyond that, through a moon gate overgrown with vines, the still, green water of the pool shimmered invitingly. At a pause in the conversation, he suggested that they all have a swim.

Tamara had left a suit there one day early in the summer, and Edgerton had kept it among a collection of suits left by tenants over the years, a sort of legacy to the guests of the San Kwan Miao pool.

For some reason, it seemed important to pretend she'd never been there before. When he dug out her suit, he brought back several others, as though offering her a choice, and then went through a rather elaborate pretense of showing her where to change, and so forth. For her part, she listened solemnly to his directions as if she were hearing it all for the first time.

Leaving her in his sleeping quarters, he and MacDonough went to change in his study. Tamara was still sequestered when they came out,

[143]

so they busied themselves carrying drinks and chairs out to the pool. With Tom Reynolds and his family away at Pei T'ai Ho, and the third apartment empty while being renovated, they were sure to have the pool to themselves, and Edgerton was glad of that.

On the way MacDonough muttered, "You're full of surprises, aren't you?"

"It seemed a good idea."

He must have appeared sheepish, for Hal laughed shortly, then eyed him soberly. "I'm beginning to understand you," he said at last. "I don't think I ever realized how beautiful she is. I was wrong this afternoon. They're not the same at all, your case and mine . . . not even similar."

They swam a couple of slow laps together, then floated silently. Edgerton luxuriated in the caress of the soft cool water and stared up at the pale sky, thinking only of the evening ahead, and aware of an enormous contentment.

They were sitting at the far end of the pool, smoking and dangling their feet in the water, when Tamara came hesitantly through the moon gate. It was almost seven and dusk had just begun to fall. The gate was in shadow, and Tamara looked small, almost lost, in Edgerton's bathrobe. The white of her bathing cap and the white towelling of the robe brightened the shadows briefly, and Edgerton felt a deep interior brightening within himself at the sight of her.

Eyes down and smiling under their frank gaze, Tamara shed the robe and stood for a moment at the pool's edge, her reflection shifting brokenly on the moving surface of the dark water. Her black wool suit was cut unstylishly high in both front and back, and had a short skirt that clung to her hips. Spellbound, Edgerton felt his eyes travel upward from her feet as though discovering her for the first time . . . long strong legs, full thighs rising into the curve of her hips, small flat waist. Preparing amateurishly to dive, she raised her arms over her head, and her breasts lifted and swelled into the black fabric. A passing twinge of jealousy hit him because Hal was there: he wanted the sight of her all to himself.

She dove awkwardly, making a big splash. Edgerton felt a mysterious catching at his heart, and he took a long involuntary breath as the blur of her slid toward them under the liquid shadows.

"You lucky bastard," Hal said, his voice hoarse.

Ch'en's footsteps faded as he bore away the last of the dinner dishes. Ever prone to embellish, Ch'en had rigged a string of paper lanterns while they were in swimming, and the frail glow of the candles had bathed them in gentle light throughout dinner. Now the candles had

[144]

burned down and only the center of the courtyard caught their yellow flickerings, leaving the corners lost in blackness.

The meal had been a gay one. They had talked a lot, all three of them, and now seemed content for the present to sit quietly and merely enjoy one another's company. The two men had brandy and Tamara, a small coffee.

How fine it all is, Edgerton was thinking. How fine the company, how fine the soft night air, how fine their seclusion. They sat upon a golden island while far away the city rumbled like the sea, and the benign stars looked down on them as though there were no trouble anywhere. He congratulated himself on bringing them all together. It was a stroke of genius. Why hadn't he done this before?

All at once, depressing memories washed over him: the solitary evenings here, wasting time in lonely and all too often drunken introspection, indulging himself alternately in spasms of self-pity and bleary fantasies of success.

Inevitably, he pictured Tamara there with him. Not as she was then, a guest for a swim and dinner, nor as she had been a few times, a clandestine visitor smuggled in like a whore and then whisked away before daylight. No, that vision was too repulsive now, too shameful; he refused it altogether. He wanted to see her as the mistress of the place. She belonged with him here in this courtyard, with him anywhere. With him she would be safe. She was right for him, he told himself. They fitted each other in so many ways, and yet stubbornly he would insist on denying her and himself, telling himself it was only a romantic dream and that it would be too cruel to expose her to the prejudices of all those predatory foreigners. He would be taking her away from the little that she had, in exchange for the promise of something he really couldn't give her . . . something she might not even want.

MacDonough finished his brief study of the refractive qualities of brandy and Tamara put down her cup. No one had noticed his preoccupation.

"I'm afraid I've stuffed myself into a stupor," he said.

"Me, too," MacDonough declared.

"How gallant!" Tamara chided them affectionately.

Rather somnolently the conversation gathered momentum. Edgerton was content to let them carry it forward while he smiled and looked attentive. Relaxing to the pleasant drone of their voices, he found himself thinking of the first time he had seen Tamara.

He had gone to the Club for his noontime swim one day late in the spring of the previous year. Spring had come late in 1937; the pool had

[145]

only just been filled and the water was still cold. When he stopped by the office afterward to pick up his monthly bill, so struck was he by the beauty of the shy young stranger behind the counter he had been able to do no more than burble some idiotic remark about the weather and rush out. Walking back to the Chancery, his mind had struggled with a confused mixture of juvenile schemes to find out who she was, and stern admonitions to himself to act his age.

He found out her name a few days later by a rudimentary expedient: he asked her. At the time it impressed him as an act of considerable daring. It was all a great puzzle to him then; his diffidence, because he was not usually shy with women, and his fascination, because, as he kept telling himself, she was so much younger than he they could not possibly have anything in common. Furthermore, he had the feeling that if he didn't watch out he would make a colossal fool of himself. He even tried telling himself that she was really not all that beautiful anyway. The facts continued to confuse him.

Inch by cautious inch, he found out more about her. An ambition of hers, he soon discovered, was to improve an already good command of English, having had a missionary teacher. By the time he met her, she was reading avidly everything she could get her hands on. Her interests were catholic, and went from Gibbon through Mark Twain to Agatha Christie. It delighted him to lend her books; there were no mind stretchers among them, but the dialog was generally good and her fluency improved. She asked him many questions. Sometimes, when his answers became pedantic, she would pull his leg gently. Her wit surprised him and her teasing did him good.

During all this exploratory time, he agonized about taking her out. If he took her dancing at the Peking Hotel or at the Hotel des Wagons-Lits he might compromise her and risk her job. The Club's Board of Governors would not look kindly on the situation and having no one else, might take it out on her. That he might compromise himself as well was an idea he considered briefly and then dropped. He told himself that it was nonsense, that the idea was beneath him and, damn them, he didn't care what they thought. In any case he clung to the more comfortable fiction that he was protecting her job, which he knew she very badly needed. The quandary remained.

Finally, contriving to be passing by as she was leaving the Club at the end of the day, he offered her a lift. She accepted with quiet dignity, but they hadn't gone a block before their glances met, and Tamara burst out laughing. She had seen through him like glass. They went to the Winter Palace and went walking along the banks of the Pei Hai until dusk fell and the mosquitoes came out, and then went to eat at a small place near the San P'ai Lou. The neighborhood around

[146]

those three old memorial arches was given over to small restaurants, and foreigners seldom went there. Already he was scheming. In any event they had a meal of excellent *chiao-tze*, and talked and laughed and ignored the stares of the other patrons. The memory still glowed.

Tamara's gentle voice intruded; she was chiding MacDonough. "You Americans! You claim to be so progressive, yet how you resist even the idea of change. The changes that will come in the future . . . well, we will have to learn how to live with them when we see what they are. But many important changes have already taken place. China has been changing all along, but I wonder if you have not prevented yourselves from seeing it."

"What makes you think we have?"

"I know it. You refuse to look. You are too insulated by your wealth."

Hal shook his finger at her. "I'm not as insulated as you seem to think. I've seen lots of changes in the two years I've been here."

"You are talking about trains and telephones and motor cars. I am talking about people and their attitudes."

"Those things change people."

"Yes, but we are still not talking about the same thing. Do you mean that having these things changes people?"

"That's about it," Hal said with a quick nod.

"I thought so. I was thinking about something else. Perhaps not having them changes them even more. The more new miracles they see, the more aware they become of how far behind they are, how much they do not have. The Chinese are beginning to look around and to realize how very rich you are. Even your soldiers are richer than most of us."

"What do you suppose that means?"

"It means for one thing that you will be resented more and more. Eventually you will have to pay for that."

"That sounds hardly fair. Americans have done a lot of good things for China and her people."

Tamara's voice became gently amused. "True, it is not fair. But to the Chinese some of these good things are like the charity given by a reformed thief. Since it all comes out of his loot, we see less merit in it than you might think."

"We, eh? Well, maybe you're right." Edgerton had to laugh. Everyone wanted to teach America a lesson, it seemed. How Chang Suncheh would have enjoyed this conversation! "What will happen?" he asked, perversely proud of her for putting him on the spot.

[147]

"Eventually all foreigners will have to leave China. Missionaries, soldiers, businessmen . . . perhaps even diplomats." Her smile returned fleetingly, then she shrugged and stated the old Chinese disclaimer flatly: *"Mei yu fah tze."*

"No help for it at all?" Edgerton attempted an easy smile, "That sounds so drastic."

Tamara regarded him calmly. "Many Chinese are bitter. They know that China has been a thing for you . . . a thing to use and to make money from; when it is broken or used up, you will discard it and move on to another, fresher place."

"You don't really mean that," Edgerton protested, as hurt by the hard accusation as if it had been directed at him personally.

"*I* don't, but that is because I know people like you and Hal and old Russell *t'ai t'ai* who taught me English and who worried more about teaching her orphans how to sew than how to be Christians. But I can understand that point of view. Very few Chinese know any foreigners at all, much less any Americans. Millions of them have never even seen one and will never see one. But many will see that you grow rich from your life in China, while they are still poor. They will be able to make the connection, even if it is not precisely accurate, and certainly not fair." Her voice softened and she smiled on the last word.

Tamara took a cigarette out of the red lacquer box on the table. There was a strange awkward grace in the way she held it, awaiting Edgerton's match. When he leaned across to her, her scent, very faint and almost washed away by her swim and shower, stirred him as it came to him over the acrid smoke of the punk smoldering under the table. She smiled her thanks and then, through the cloud of smoke, gave them both an apologetic look. "I'm talking too much," she said. "My mother would be scandalized. Half-foreign and half-Chinese, I don't even know how to behave." She forced a laugh, then drew deeply on her cigarette.

Embarrassed but sympathetic, MacDonough smoked silently.

Edgerton could only look at her glumly, helplessly. He was dismayed to see her on the point of tears. It stunned him to learn that this failure of identity even bothered her. To him she was, had always been, Chinese. He'd just assumed she was content with that choice too. He ached with the yearning to take her hands and say something reassuring, something comforting. His mind remained numb, blank.

It was Tamara who revived the conversation by asking MacDonough some question about the Marine Corps. Edgerton tried halfheartedly to listen, but his thoughts kept drifting away, thinking of that first evening of theirs in the crowded little restaurant by the San

[148]

P'ai Lou. With great candor and without being asked, she had laid out for him the cold bare skeleton of her life.

There was no drama, no self-pity, no masked appeal for sympathy in the story she had told. There were merely facts. He could only listen, nodding from time to time and making what he hoped were appropriate noises. After that one time, she having made her statement and he having heard it, they did not resurrect the subject. He could see now that he'd been quite content to avoid thinking about many of the more sombre aspects of her situation. It was so much less disturbing to toy with comfortable mental clichés such as how well the races had mixed in her, how delicate was her complexion, how beautiful her hair in the sunlight, how everything was bound to get better because man was growing kinder to his nonconforming fellows. Tamara's story had been finished by the time the waiter brought them a fresh pot of tea and hot scented towels for their hands and faces, and she had gone on to tell him some amusing anecdotes about the Club and its hodgepodge membership. Her eye was sharp, but she was without malice. Typically, as he was to learn, she left the actors in these dubious pecadillos nameless, and Edgerton did not press her.

Her candor applied not only to herself, but to the world around her. She was neither cynic nor romantic, and avoided generalized judgments. Thinking about that evening later, Edgerton regretfully admitted to himself that he must have been something of a prude in those days, and that the glimpses he got of the world through her wise young eyes had helped to keep him from becoming impossibly stuffy. In the year and more that followed he became more and more aware of her subtle, uncritical influence. It made life so much easier to acknowledge that there were a great many things requiring no pronouncements and taking-of-stands from him at all. Why had he been so long in learning that?

When he had taken her home that night she made him stop his car at the entrance to her *hu-tung*, on account of her mother's feelings. She had sent a message by rickshaw that she expected to be late, but her mother was suspicious and sure to be full of questions. Edgerton had heard enough by then to know that Tamara's mother was a formidable and old-fashioned lady, and not to be trifled with. She must have been to have survived. Later, having gotten to know her slightly, he found he liked her in spite of her suspicions of him. But now . . .

Fragmented voices interrupted the thought, and he looked around, blinking.

"No, Hal, I don't think he is," Tamara was saying. "You see: his eyes are open."

[149]

"I beg to differ. It's a clear case of catalepsy . . . right out of the Field Medical Manual." MacDonough peered across at him, nodding professionally.

"What should we do?"

"Perhaps a pail of water . . ."

"What are you two cooking up?" Edgerton said, trying to get his bearings with dignity.

"You seemed to be having some sort of seizure."

Edgerton had to laugh. "All right, so I was daydreaming. You seemed to be amusing yourselves without me, and I was piqued by your indifference. Left to my own devices, I let my mind wander." He stretched comfortably and was overtaken by an enormous yawn.

They both laughed at him, and Tamara asked, "We're not keeping you up?"

"Not a bit. In fact, I was thinking we needed some music." He got up to wind the portable phonograph.

By the time he had the first record going, MacDonough was leading Tamara out to dance. The sight of them dancing, and the frail sound of the tinny music evoked a memory of the first time he'd brought her here. He remembered even the moment of asking her to come for dinner . . . she had given him a brief and unfathomable look before accepting. He was never sure just what that look had meant . . . part speculation, he supposed, and part something else he could not identify. Previously he had taken her on a picnic, several walks, and twice more to dinners much like the first. He had kissed her soft, closed lips twice only, carrying away with him a demanding desire for her that fought with his repeated insistence to himself that she was much too young for him and he was an idiot to pretend otherwise. He scolded himself for being infatuated with her, and argued back that he was not infatuated at all, having only a fatherly (no, no, brotherly) tenderness for her.

On that night a year ago, after Ch'en had cleared away the plates, he had asked her to dance, and had regretted it immediately. He couldn't seem to find the beat of the music, his palms sweated, and the cracks between the bricks of the courtyard became chasms into which he stumbled. All he could think of, as he floundered in elephantine misery, had been the inevitability of stepping on her toes. But he persisted. While he rewound the machine, she would pick over the records and ask him about the titles. He tried to relax, but dancing with her made him desire her, and the desire frightened him. His arms began to ache with the effort of not holding her too closely.

Then at last a record ended, and they drew a little apart. Their eyes

[150]

met and they both started to speak. They both fell silent but their eyes held. The moment balanced precariously, then Edgerton took her into his arms. The phonograph scratched on, its needle trapped in the record's last soundless groove. Presently the spring unwound and the scratching stopped. The silence of the courtyard had been filled with the drumming of his pulse, and his heart with the taste of her lips and tongue, as it had been ever since.

The record ended, and Hal and Tamara were coming toward him before he knew what was happening. Hastily he rewound the phonograph and claimed Tamara for a dance of his own. She was light in his arms, and he could feel the play of the strong muscles in the small of her back under the palm of his hand. He wanted to hold her closely, but Hal's presence inhibited him. Their legs touched from time to time and her hair brushed insistently against his cheek. He looked at her and almost groaned with delight. Aware of what was happening to him, she gave him a smile full of mischief and of love. He yearned to tell her about the things he had just been thinking. It was as though hidden among those recollections was some sort of clue, a secret to be discovered only in the retelling of them. It was very important, that secret; he felt he should have known it anyway, but like a word on the tip of his tongue, it kept eluding him.

MacDonough must have been waiting for the record to end. "No idea it was so late," he muttered, glancing at his watch, amazed by the unmarked flight of time. "I really must be going."

Edgerton coughed significantly. "Don't go yet. Have another drink," he urged, overly hospitable.

"I have some work to finish," he said loudly, his tone daring Edgerton to contradict him.

"Ah, duty!" Edgerton exclaimed, relenting.

MacDonough thanked him, then turned to Tamara. As he took her hand in both of his, he looked directly into her eyes, all of his reserve falling away. "We don't know each other well," he said. "But I want to tell you I think John is a very lucky man."

"Thank you, Hal," she said, obviously touched. "That is a lovely thing to say to me."

The gate's sharp closing click was almost lost in the hurrying crunch of MacDonough's footsteps on the gravel. Edgerton stood there for a moment, half envying the other's haste and the uncomplicated cause of it. The priorities of MacDonough's life were more manageable than his, apparently. He could dally with the compliant Marie and her successors for as long as he chose to do so, meanwhile enjoying his carefully uncluttered military life. It was enough for now, certainly,

[151]

and when it stopped being enough . . . well, MacDonough had said it himself: he still had plenty of time.

He caught himself; what was he doing, grumbling and wasting precious time being envious of MacDonough, while Tamara sat waiting for him? Abruptly the spectre of losing her loomed threateningly. Edgerton shivered and turned back into the house.

"Tamara," he whispered to the silent courtyard, as if her name were magic and could evoke in him the strength to master his indecisiveness. He wanted to make her happy and wanted the empty spaces in his life filled out. She was exactly what he needed. Then why didn't he take all that she was so plainly offering him?

The answer came to him in the midst of his dark and proper living room, among those uncomfortable chairs and inconvenient tables.

He was afraid to.

♟♟

Alone and suddenly restless, Tamara was uncomfortable. She couldn't sit still. The courtyard seemed darker, no longer the pleasant place of only moments before. Several candles had guttered out and the empty shells of the paper lanterns hung like dead cocoons in the cold light of a lumpy moon. She got to her feet and began to pace the rough flagstones, hugging herself against an imaginary chill.

In a way, the evening had been all hers, but the afterglow of the relaxed talk and the frank admiration of both men was already fading. John's face had showed her plainly how proud and happy he was with her. She told herself to be grateful for having been entertained just like any other person. How often she had ached for no more than that! More than once she'd gone to the verge of forcing him to make up his mind about her, to decide once and for all. But only to the verge; every time she'd backed away, telling herself to wait, to be patient and let him discover what she was to him in his own time. Now it was too late. This little party, this small step forward was already superfluous. She had faced the fact that there was no place for her in his life . . . his government would never permit it.

She tried to tell herself it wasn't really his fault. They were too different, she argued; their lives and circumstances diverged too widely. East and West would find no meeting place in them. It wasn't merely a question of race, but of class and culture, as well. He was an official, a man trained in a great university for an American's rich, serene life . . . whatever that mysterious life was. She was a clerk, educated to the mediocre limits of a Chinese middle school, with an icing of dressmaking taught her by a well-meaning missionary lady. Where was there common ground for them to meet and build a life together? Could a meaningful, living edifice be constructed with only a mattress for a foundation? Highly unlikely.

The attack upon her mother not only dramatized the differences between them, it typified them. A foreign woman would have been spared that ordeal, solely by reason of her pale skin. Even the poorest of the White Russian women, except for the whores, had been immune so far, so great was the magic of whiteness.

The attack had brought back to Tamara all the fears of a year ago, fears laid to rest by months of relative quiet and the natural tendency to see calamity as befalling someone else. She knew now that the threat had never really faded. She didn't want to have to face that threat every day; she wasn't brave enough. She wanted to be protected from it.

She could see now that in hurrying to tell John about her mother, she had only wanted to tie him to her, to make him stay with her, or take her with him, to use his fear for her safety where his love alone was not enough . . . love, or whatever it was he felt for her through that strange, tough shell of his.

So this had been her farewell party. The notion hurt her bitterly. A sob rose in her throat, and her eyes burned with tears. Fate was cruel, and wasteful of the womanhood which filled her to overflowing. In her heart's eye she could see the image of the inner John, the shell's true inhabitant, and could glimpse the sort of life that she could give him.

But it was as though John were crippled, literally unable to reach out for what she offered.

Sooner or later, he would be sent back to America. A few months, a year or so . . . the result would be the same. Being the sort of man he was, he'd go on postponing all decisions regarding her until the last possible moment. She wondered if she was supposed to be flattered by this refusal to give her up sooner than was necessary . . . well, she wasn't. He had simply left it to her to do the deciding for both of them. Well then, she would do it, but in her own good time. In any event, this particular night must not be marred.

The screen door slammed. Tamara turned to watch him coming to her across the courtyard, and knew she would do nothing to make him leave her sooner than he had to.

She lay with her head in the hollow of his shoulder, the hair on his chest just tickling her lips. The tangy maleness of his drying sweat was strong and reassuringly intimate. Deep in his chest his heart

[153]

thumped slowly. The weight of his arm across her shoulders seemed to be pressing her downward into the abode of that unfaltering engine.

Sleep pressed its demands on her, but stubbornly she clung to wakefulness, savoring the peaceful lassitude which clung to her now like a warm perfumed steam, reminding her of the strange hunger that had possessed her. Her earlier fatalism in the face of the inevitable had had to struggle against a deeper, more powerful instinct, as though even at that last minute she could draw him into her and lock him there, keeping him forever in that place where his passion had striven so plainly to plunge him deeper and deeper.

Dozing briefly, she dreamed she'd been successful, that he'd entered her totally and lived now in her body, sharing her skin, the cells of his flesh alternating with hers. And, strangely without contradiction, she was also inside him, holding his throbbing heart in her arms as though it were a baby. Awake suddenly, she wondered if she were pregnant, if her own heart could know such a thing so soon. The idea frightened her, but not so much as she would have thought. She smiled.

And John had been different in some indefinable way, both more powerful than usual, and more tender. Although always gentle and considerate of her in his lovemaking, there invariably overtook him a driving urgency which swept him before it like a storm. It always thrilled her even though it sometimes left her behind.

But not tonight. Tonight he was slow and patient, seeming bent on savoring her with the utmost care, lifting her gradually upward through plateaus of delight, each one unsurpassable, each one immediately surpassed. Thus inch by inch he had ignited her, his hands and his mouth setting fires all over her body, his lips working their way down the length of her with countless kisses, drinking symbolically from her swollen nipples and from the cup of her navel until, after a tantalizing time, they had fastened onto her burning cleft . . . she grinned into the darkness, remembering that John always called it her pussy . . . incongruous word! Smiling dreamily, half-amused, ensnared by the memory, she could almost feel his tongue making love to her as though it were the organ of some strange little animal intent on procreating a new species. But then, before, she had not been smiling. Caught in the maelstrom, spinning dizzily downward, she had known only that suddenly he was on her, spreading her, spearing her with infinite thrusting care, and her legs were up and around him, her arms clasping his shoulders, and her mouth was taking the probing rhythm of his tongue in time with the feeding of that other, even greedier mouth. Clamped to him she had surrendered totally to the

[154]

joy of his riding her. Once he stopped for a while and rested in her, panting and whispering unintelligible words to her, and she had felt his hardness as though it were a giant candy whose sweetness she was digesting, yet whose size seemed to grow slowly, as if perhaps it were digesting her. And then he had begun again, taking her with him all the way. At last, near to fainting, she had known, as her body still gulped the sap from him, that once in their lives, they had been inseperably joined, and were indeed one creature. Caught up in sensuous memory, she ground herself against him instinctively, duplicating the motion of love.

"Tamara?" he whispered huskily, surprising her.

"Yes, my darling."

"Did I wake you?"

"No," she said, shaking her head against his chest. "I was lying here dreaming with my eyes open, dreaming and thinking about sex."

Amused, he snorted faintly, then his arm tightened around her and his big hand cupped her shoulder. She could feel him draw in a lungful of air, hold it for several seconds, then expel it in a long sigh that was loud in the quiet room.

"I love you," he said. "Did you know that?"

The never-spoken words made her heart ring like a bell; she pressed closer to him. "Yes, my dearest, I know. And I love you . . . more than anything in life." The words came with difficulty, almost choked off in her full throat.

He turned toward her and stared at her in the dim light, his hand absentmindedly stroking her thigh. "Tamara . . ." he began, and faltered. "Tamara . . ."

Where there had been joy, pain struck her like an arrow, and she felt the whole massive weight of his dilemma in his hesitation. She knew what he wanted to say, what some part of him was trying to tell her, but yearn though she might to hear the words, some wisdom told her they must not be said, not yet and perhaps not ever. In the dreamy, vulnerable world of sated sex it was too easy to talk of love. His guard would be down and the words he could say then would not look true to him tomorrow, sitting in his office under the ponderous mass of official disapproval and disgrace. For him to have to take back the hasty words would only bring shame and agony to them both. Joyous that he had tried to speak, and hurting from the need to silence him, she kissed him, stopping the reluctant words with her mouth. When she felt him relax, she drew her lips away and whispered quickly, "Sssh, my dearest; don't speak. No words are necessary." Gently she shifted position, bringing his head to rest between her breasts. "Believe me,

[155]

John. Don't say anything now . . ." It was her turn to grope for words as all her English seemed to desert her, the unfamiliar language running out of her mind like water from a leaky pot; Chinese was all that was left to her. "You love me and you want me," she said, the somehow alien phrases sounding strange and stilted. "It is enough and I am content. I am happier now, tonight, than I have ever been, ever dreamed of being."

Her arms tightened around him. With a triumphant sadness, she felt him acquiesce. She had won . . . won and lost. It could never have been any other way.

Soft abstract patterns dappled the walls of the gray room as a solitary lantern swung gently in the courtyard. "Kiss me again, my darling," she said softly, her hand sliding over his belly to his groin. "Kiss me and love me again. We're together now . . . that's all that matters."

His lips were soft and gentle with her, not ready yet for the passion which was growing, unwilled by him, in her slowly moving hand. At least he tried, she told herself. Determined to distract them both, she parted his lips with her tongue.

WEDNESDAY

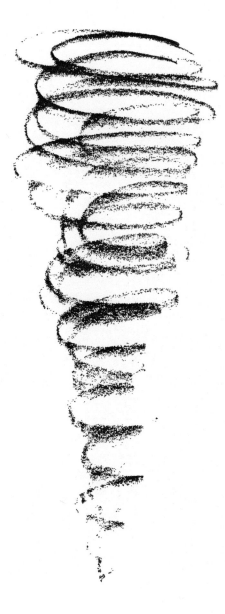

Tanaka sat immobile at his desk, breathing deeply, evenly, mastering his temper. At length, he picked up the memorandum and read it through a second time. As he read, his lips moved, and his mind savored the rudeness of the words. It was almost as though by accepting these heaped-on insults and disparagements, he was enhancing the sweetness of his inevitable revenge.

Edgerton's heavy phrases crashed about his ears like ocean combers: chronic misbehavior of Japanese soldiers . . . depredations against civilian persons and property . . . notorious lack of discipline . . . shocking to civilized nations . . . innumerable protests . . . criminal attacks and vandalism . . . indifference of occupation authorities . . .

Suddenly he could bear no more. With trembling fingers he began to insert a cigarette in the holder. The paper tube broke, cascading tobacco into his lap. Hurling the remnants into the wastebasket, he hurriedly lighted another, this time without the holder. He smoked for a few moments, harnessing his emotions.

When he was calmer, Colonel Tanaka reminded himself that in spite of Edgerton's intentional insolence, the American had done him one great service. Even the American's empty threat to complain to the Imperial Government through the United States Embassy in Tokyo unless "speedy steps are taken to correct these insupportable conditions," could be comfortably brushed aside.

For the bare fact was that, somehow or other, Edgerton knew of the Seiko incident. Elementary deduction showed that he could only have come by that knowledge through the woman. Unlikely, perhaps even incredible, but there it was. All that remained was for Tanaka to devise a way of extracting her identity from him. He was certain his ingenuity would be up to the task. He sighed; as usual the really important tasks came back for him to do himself. Although already a day old, the search for Seiko's assailant was still without results. A few more hours and the officer in charge of the Special Unit as well as Major Wu would begin to feel the weight of Tanaka's impatience.

Tanaka paused, looking out the window. A thought continued to nag at him, something which would provide a key, a lever to be used against the American. He knew the way his mind worked: sooner or later the searched-for fact would surface. It was only a question of time.

Colonel Tanaka turned confidently to the remainder of his morning's work.

He must have been dozing with his eyes open. Sobolov looked up at Miss Kung blankly, feeling disoriented and slightly dizzy.

Miss Kung's eyebrows were raised expectantly.

"What?" he asked.

"Do you have anything for me to type?" she repeated in her precise Mandarin.

"Type?" He shook his head. "No. No, thank you." He could feel his face adjust itself into some sort of vacant smile.

She frowned, concerned for a moment, but then she shrugged and went back to her desk, apparently satisfied. He'd always liked Miss Kung.

No, he didn't have anything to type. In fact, except for a few notes on the morning press and an errand for Mr. Chiang, he had done nothing since hanging up his hat besides moving papers about and rearranging his pencils. And he felt terrible; his head ached and his eyelids burned with fatigue and he hadn't had any breakfast. His stomach grumbled hollowly at the reminder.

Maya had been sad and distracted when he got home the night before. She wouldn't tell him what was wrong, but she had been strangely gentle with him in spite of his questions. Questions usually made her angry. Again there had been no letter from Anya, but he reminded himself that she was young and having a good time, not really thoughtless. Besides, what could happen to her while under the protection of an American family? She would be safe forever—provided only that he did as he was told.

Maya had served his supper in silence, remembering only at the end to give him Puhalski's unnecessary message. What Puhalski had been doing there in the middle of the afternoon, Sobolov didn't understand; Puhalski was such a busy man. And how could he possibly have forgotten? Suddenly the money had become a hot, poisoned lump in his pocket; he was glad to give it to Maya, to be rid of it. She had stared at it in an odd way, then carried it into the bedroom. He had got out pen and paper and set to work on the wretched report for Puhalski, while Maya went to bed.

He had worked until long past midnight, meticulously drawing floor plans, listing names, and outlining what little he knew of Chancery routine. It was so minor, so insignificant, what he had to tell them. They must have had it in their files, if they would only look. It wasn't fair, involving him in their inefficiencies . . . it meant so much to him and so little to them.

When he did finally get to bed, his sleep was disturbed and he tossed restlessly in the heat, awaking to find himself swathed in the sheet as though already in his shroud. Drained hollow by exhaustion, he had shaved and dressed and fixed himself some tea.

Even his meeting with Puhalski had a trancelike quality. Puhalski had been remote, preoccupied with problems of his own. He'd begun one of those half-contemptuous jokes of his but became lost somewhere in the middle of it—and ended by merely taking Sobolov's sheaf of notes and drawings with an absent-minded nod. In his memory it was a scene without reality. It simply was not possible for him to be spying on his employers and giving Puhalski a report on them. The additional fifty dollars had been as so much useless paper.

Timidly, he peered around the office. It was as always: Miss Kung typing, Miss Liang filing, Loo emptying wastebaskets in back, his falsetto humming drifting in through the open window. And Mr. Chiang guarding his hoard of paper clips and rubber bands and reams of paper, and watching them all like a prison guard. It looked the same but it was different. A feeling of despair stabbed him. He was no longer a part of it. He had become Sobolov the spy, the thief, the cheat. From behind his shoddy mask, he worked against the common effort. The sense of mutual endeavor, once so precious, was dead, and his connection with all of them was severed. What would Miss Kung think of him now?

Suddenly the front door opened, letting in a gust of hot air. It was Mr. Edgerton, back from some errand. He stopped and took off his hat.

"Mr. Sobolov, will you come here, please," he said in his deep voice.

As he got to his feet, Sobolov could feel the sweat start. Something must have happened, he thought, sickened.

Heart pounding, he hurried across the office, banging into Miss Kung's table on the way, and knocking some papers off onto the floor. He would have picked them up but Miss Kung wouldn't let him.

"*Please*, Mr. Sobolov!" she hissed at him as he bent over, her eyes flashing with annoyance behind her glasses. "I'll get them."

Blushing unhappily, Sobolov could only blunder on, all too aware that Mr. Edgerton had witnessed his clumsiness.

"Yes, Mr. Edgerton," he panted, attempting a smile.

Mr. Edgerton cleared his throat. "I had a call from the police about your papers," he said. "There seems to be some discrepancy. You're to see a Captain Wang at the Police Yamen at noon."

"Discrepancy?" Sobolov repeated dumbly, knowing there was no discrepancy. If you learned nothing else in China, you learned to keep

[161]

your papers in perfect order, free of discrepancies. He wondered if he would have time to call Puhalski for advice, for help. His eyes strayed to the big clock in the foyer. It was nearly half-past eleven already; there would be no time.

"It's a nuisance," Mr. Edgerton was saying. "But I'm sure it's nothing serious. You know the Chinese police . . . not very efficient."

Yes, Sobolov knew the Chinese police. And it was worse since the Japanese came. The collaborators had swarmed into all the government offices, but particularly into the police because of the opportunities for squeeze. And whatever they lacked in efficiency, they made up for in intimidation. But what could they possibly want him for? Could Puhalski have betrayed him? But why would he do that? And what would it matter to the police in any case? Spying on one's foreign employers was hardly likely to either shock or concern them.

"You don't look well, Mr. Sobolov," Mr. Edgerton said. "Would you like an aspirin, or something?"

"No, no; I'll be all right. The heat . . . a little indigestion . . ."

"Yes. Well, why don't you go on home when you're through at the Yamen; take a nap. No point in coming back here today."

Sobolov managed to nod. "Thank you, sir."

Mr. Edgerton started to turn away, then stopped. "Oh, by the way, I've had a cable from Washington giving us authority to issue your daughter a visa." His big square face broke into a smile.

Sobolov felt himself sway and groped for the edge of the counter. By the way! Oh, by the way, here is a million dollars!

"Naturally, it all depends on whether the Sloanes decide they can accept the responsibility for, ah, Anya and, of course, on whether his company transfers him as expected." Mr. Edgerton's smile blurred and shifted.

"Naturally," Sobolov echoed. "That's wonderful, wonderful." If only there was no trouble with the police, if only he could please Puhalski, if only the Japanese were satisfied with his report, if only no one found out and got him fired . . . if only he could fend them all off until autumn and get Anya safely out of the country. "Wonderful! I am so grateful," he said, crushed by the weight of all the things that could still go wrong.

"I knew you'd be relieved," Mr. Edgerton said. "I'll speak to the Sloanes again, when they get back from Pei T'ai Ho." He cleared his throat. "Well, you had better be getting along." Sobolov could see he was already thinking about something else.

Sobolov's chubby hands kneaded each other nervously. So many things could go wrong, things over which he had no control and

October seemed years away. He could only do his best to keep them all satisfied, but it wasn't his sort of work at all. It shamed him; and when he thought of the danger he became ill.

But he must hurry now. He would take the fastest rickshaw he could find—a new one with a young man pulling, and never mind the expense. Whoever Captain Wang was, he couldn't afford to keep him waiting. A tentative spasm gripped his stomach and his mouth flooded with saliva. Clamping a hand over his mouth and clenching his jaws together, Sobolov ran heavily down the corridor to the washroom.

🌾🌾

Bob Smith must have stopped by while he was out. Centered on his blotter was the rough draft of the economic report. Edgerton eyed it warily, remembering their conversation. He wondered whether Smith had remained loyal to his own views, or whether he had written something he thought Edgerton would like to read. Or, worst of all, tried for a mix of those probably unblendable ingredients.

Edgerton felt hot and tired and somewhat resentful.

Most of the morning had been consumed by pettifogging details of one sort or another. The call about Sobolov's papers was an example. More time had been spent in the arbitration of a dispute between Chiang, the office manager, and Feng, the *t'ai ch'ing*. They were natural enemies, Feng having come to the Legation years before Chiang. Technically, the *t'ai ch'ing* was a subordinate position; in practice it was independent. It was a traditional office, now somewhat obsolete. At one time, the *t'ai ch'ing* had combined the offices of sentry, driver, go-between with local functionaries on minor matters like licenses and permits, supervisor of the grounds crew; he was also the office coolie, general handyman, and anything else that came up. Actually Chiang only managed the Chinese office staff, the regular manager being Miss Henshaw, the senior secretary, now away with the Minister in Nanking. Of the two other American secretaries, one was home on emergency leave and the other was at Pei T'ai Ho, swimming and lying on the beach. Which was where Edgerton wished he was; then he wouldn't have to contend with Chiang and the problems he caused. Someday Chiang would have to go . . . he was getting to be more trouble than he was worth. It was Edgerton's own soft-heartedness —or softheadedness—which prevented him from acting. He just didn't want to be put to the trouble of finding and breaking in a replacement.

Nor had Tamara called. Edgerton cursed Liu *t'ai t'ai* quietly, ima-

[163]

gining quite clearly how she could continue to resist his very sensible advice. The mere fact that he had given it would be enough. For one fervent moment, he wished Tamara had never told him anything about the rape. He couldn't do anything effective . . . his letter to Tanaka had been as futile as his arrangement with LaGarde. Nothing would come of either. It was very likely a tempest in a teapot from the first. Nothing he'd ever heard about the Japanese Army suggested that it was particularly solicitous of its men. If drunks got into fights and were hurt, the Army was probably the last to seek revenge. Whoever the man was, he'd probably ended up with a couple of aspirins and the scorn of his buddies for being bested by a woman. The more he thought of it, the more it seemed to Edgerton that he'd let himself be swayed by Tamara's near hysteria. The simplest solution was for Tamara to call in a few minutes to tell him that her mother refused to go to the hotel at all. Then he could phone LaGarde, thank him, apologize for troubling him, and call the whole thing off. And there was Smith's report.

Edgerton emptied his ashtray, got out a pad of scratch paper, and carefully selected three of his sharpest pencils. The room seemed uncomfortably bright. He got up and adjusted the blinds. There was nothing left to do but pick up the report.

By the end of the first page he was nodding his head. Smith had written a reasoned account of recent developments. His style was clear and direct and had none of the clutter of bureaucratese which was replacing English as the dialect of government. He didn't agree with every one of Smith's conclusions, but his logic was sound. They could dispose of the quibbles later.

Edgerton was just about in the middle when there was a knock. The door opened, and in came Franklin Procter, looking as if he had just stepped out of some aristocratic British magazine.

"Am I intruding?"

"Not at all, Franklin. Come in."

"Another scorcher," Procter announced, pulling a chair around and inspecting it carefully for dust.

"Yes. Doesn't seem to bother you, though," Edgerton said and grinned. "You look very cool and, um, very fit."

Procter gave him a suspicious look. "How kind of you to say so," he said. "As it happens, I don't feel very fit. A belated though fortunately mild case of Tientsin Tummy."

"Oh, oh!"

"Exactly. I stayed home this morning on account of it . . . pondering world affairs from afar, and all that sort of thing."

[164]

"It's sometimes the only way to preserve one's objectivity."

"I thought so. By the way, what's the matter with old Sobolov?"

Edgerton frowned, puzzled. "I didn't know there was anything the matter with old Sobolov."

"He rushed by me as though the place were on fire—almost knocked me down."

Edgerton glanced at his watch; Sobolov had better be hurrying, poor bastard. "There was a call for him to check with the police about his papers. It was one of *your* calls. I handled it myself."

"Only one? You were in luck!"

"Yes. I always enjoy a good long chat with Major Wu."

Procter laughed. "I'll remember that."

"And Mr. Taylor paid you a visit."

"Dear me; sorry to have missed him."

"You should be; he's an experience. He was sorry to have missed you, too."

"Sounds ominous."

"I more or less threw him out."

Procter sobered at once. "Really?" he asked disapprovingly.

"Physical assistance provided by the management," Edgerton said, feeling smug.

"Was that quite necessary?" Procter stiffened into an official posture.

"Perhaps not, but it was a great pleasure. He gives me a pain in the ass."

"Tut, tut, John. Such intemperance hardly seems wise."

"I'll admit it was self-indulgent. It was just too hot this morning to put up with that son of a bitch."

"Well, let's hope there'll be no repercussions. He objected to my letter, I take it?"

Edgerton nodded.

"I was afraid the wording was a bit strong. Oh, well . . ."

"If there are repercussions, let them fall upon my head. But I don't think he'll be a problem."

Procter relaxed a little. "Well, I hope not."

He pointed to the papers on the blotter.

"What's all that?"

"Smith's draft on the economic report."

"How is it?"

"Begins very well."

"Nice young chap. Had a talk with him yesterday."

"Yes. I think he's got a lot of promise."

"He's very impressed with you, I might say."

[165]

"With me?" Edgerton inspected him for signs of irony.

"Yes; said your discussion of the general situation gave him a lot to think about."

"I was sure I'd bored him."

"Not at all." Procter displayed a small frown. "He kept going on about seeing things in a new light."

Edgerton straightened his mouth with his fingers. "You sound dubious, not quite certain that that's a good thing."

Procter had to smile. "I'll admit to a momentary qualm."

"Patriotic, right-thinking youth corrupted by cynical old bastard, is that it?"

"Something of the sort may have crossed my mind; you are a bit unorthodox at times. But I prefer to think of you as skeptical, rather than cynical. Cynicism seems merely defeatist, somehow."

Edgerton paused to light a cigarette. "I must admit I feel defeatist at times," he mused. "So much to do, and no one doing it. We seem to have become a nation of observers, waiting for the dust to settle."

"Sometimes it's best to wait and see."

"Perhaps. Still, there's such a thing as the right time. If we'd been a little tougher with Japan over Manchuria, we might not be faced with the necessity of being a lot tougher now."

"But I thought you were an advocate of Japan's rights."

Edgerton was surprised and must have looked it.

Procter smiled. "I made a point of searching the files in Washington for your reports."

"Well, I'm flattered. As I recall, they weren't exactly hailed with loud cheers. I'd have thought they'd be in the incinerator by now."

"You *are* outspoken, you know. Some people thought you laid about with unnecessary vigor . . . State is still a very conservative place."

"Some people, eh? I bet I know who they were, too. Well, I meant to be outspoken, to stir them off their petrified asses."

Procter laughed. "I don't know that you accomplished that, but you made an impression."

"They probably have me tagged for some kind of crank: poor old Edgerton, out there so long, he's gone Asiatic."

Although Procter smiled, he looked a little uneasy, and Edgerton guessed he'd struck close to the target. He thought for a moment. "Well, I suppose I am Japan's advocate in a sense. Although it's hard . . . my *sentiments* are all with the Chinese. Anything Japan gets can only be at China's expense. Or ours, and we'd never let that happen. Everything that's happened in Asia in recent decades seems to have been at China's expense."

[166]

"I was going to point that out as an inconsistency in your position."

Edgerton shrugged. "What I really advocate is balance. Wouldn't reasonable concessions, even though unpalatable, cost China less than the war is costing?"

"Very nice in theory, but who is to impose these concessions?"

"Ah!" Edgerton said, the very sound an admission. He stubbed out his cigarette and immediately lighted another one. There were all sorts of inconsistencies; chief among his own was an aversion to any one nation's setting itself up as an arbiter of morals. That was what the League of Nations was supposed to be for, but America had retired into xenophobia and refused to join, while predator nations like Italy and Germany and Japan merely stamped out when the heat was turned on them. Censure alone was obviously useless, whether from a group of nations or only one. "Of course, Japan shouldn't be allowed to do anything she wants with complete impunity," he said.

"Quite so. How do you stop her, then?"

"With reason and logic, I would hope." Before he could go on, Procter burst into gentle laughter.

"Tempt them with alternatives is what I mean," Edgerton insisted, feeling his face redden, but determined not to let Procter get his goat. "Except for the idiot fringe, any government would rather achieve its ends without the expense of war. We've never really tried reason with the Japanese. We either do nothing when they misbehave, or we bluster and lecture them. They don't know whether to treat us as a threat or to laugh at us. Our ambiguity only strengthens the diehards in the government at the expense of the people who understand us. Talk about inconsistencies: we moralize against their actions, while selling them unlimited amounts of oil and scrap metals. No wonder they don't take us seriously!"

"But what alternatives are there? My God . . ."

"I don't know, Franklin. The point is we don't seem to be trying to find any. Presuming that they buy oil from us because it's advantageous for them to do so, couldn't we bargain with them, using the oil as a lever? Then, if they decide to go elsewhere, we've only lost their business. As it is, we look like a country whose affairs are managed by greedy pigs, complaining loudly even as they slurp up the profits. If they don't want to bargain with us, then let someone else supply their war materials."

"You mean break relations with them?"

"Oh, no . . . that should always be the last resort. It's an admission of failure, really. No, we must keep talking, by all means."

"Ah, you are a diplomat, after all!"

[167]

Edgerton laughed then, liking Procter. "Of the old school. In any case, Smith will probably survive my blandishments."

"Probably," Procter conceded, refilling his pipe carefully. When he had it drawing properly, he went on, "You know, I think I'm going to like it here."

"Good. I'm glad."

"It's a funny thing; I was afraid at first I'd made a mistake, asking for this post. It was neither what I remembered, nor what I expected."

"It's changed," Edgerton said with a smile. "Like me, you yearn for those older, better times."

"You like it though, don't you?"

Edgerton thought for a moment, recalling the mixed feelings which kept recurring. "I wax hot and cold," he said at last. "I get burned up at the abysmal stupidity of the government. And then the people can be pigheaded beyond belief." He paused, thinking first of Liu *t'ai t'ai* and then of all the stubborn Chinese he had known, remembering how he had praised them for that very quality. Obstinacy in one instance became tenacity in another. "I suppose I'm merely railing at a fate which has kept this country from achieving the greatness it has in it, with all that that would mean for the Chinese people. And this town . . . you know something? In a very real way, this is *my* town."

"It may surprise you, John, but I know what you mean. I remember you in the old days. You learned the language so painlessly, and you seemed to . . . well, make yourself comfortable more quickly than the rest of us. As though you felt that you were home. Is that too far-fetched?"

"Well, given the fact that no foreigner is ever really 'at home' in China, I suppose I came fairly close to it. I knew as soon as I arrived that I wanted to stay." Edgerton laughed, remembering. "It was a lot of fun in those days." He stared at the ceiling. "As a matter of fact, I don't recall your having any trouble acclimating. Speeding about in that exotic motor car—what was it? A Stutz?—and bashing polo balls all over the place with gusto. And wasn't there a young lady from the British Legation? A Scottish girl . . . MacGregor? Marian MacGregor?"

"MacGowan, I think." Procter actually blushed. "Those were the days. Great parties." His glance was a bit apprehensive.

"Don't worry; I won't tell Pamela."

Procter's flush deepened. "Pamela knows all about my lurid past."

"Does she now?" Edgerton asked, intentionally doubtful. "I'd have thought that while confession might ease the soul, it didn't necessarily help the marriage."

"One must edit judiciously," Procter said, looking sly.

"Ah!" Edgerton gave him a sage nod. "And did you tell her about the time you attempted to scale the Tartar Wall?"

"Attempted? I *did* scale it."

"My recollection is that you fell off half way up. You were saved only because Tubby Jackson and I interposed our frail bodies between you and Mother Earth."

"Did I really? Memory has drawn a merciful curtain . . ." Procter pulled at his ear lobe, smiling. "I saw Tubby a few years ago. He hasn't changed; he could have cushioned my fall all by himself." Procter shook his head. "No, I didn't tell Pamela about that."

"Just as well; had you been successful, wasn't your prize to have been that young teacher from the American School?"

"There's a ring of truth to what you say." Procter squinted with nostalgic effort. "Do you suppose the young lady ever knew that?"

"I don't think she did. We staked her favors on the outcome without bothering to tell her."

"It's coming back to me in bits and pieces," Procter said pensively. "I can almost see her. In fact, I *can* see her!" Procter looked triumphant. "*You* got her!"

Edgerton nodded, smiling wryly, half at Procter's expression and half at the memory of a pretty girl. What had ever become of her? She came into his life laughing, made him laugh and went out the same way. That was all before Elizabeth . . . B.E. It was a little sad: he could remember Tubby's name but he couldn't remember the girl's.

Procter sighed. "I think I may have told Pamela about her . . . the part concerning you, that is. Out of envy, I suppose."

"Thanks! I hope she didn't get the wrong idea about me." Edgerton had to stop and laugh.

Procter gave him a speculative look. "What *is* the wrong idea about you, John? No, don't tell me. One thing Pamela did say: you made a *profound* impression on Valerie."

"Did I? Well, that's always pleasant to hear. She's a nice girl," Edgerton said casually.

"You should really think about marrying again," Procter said smoothly.

"Well . . ." Edgerton began, surprised that he felt no annoyance. It wasn't like him. "All right, I will think about it," he said, grinning.

"Seriously."

"With the utmost seriousness."

"Be a great help in your career."

[169]

"Well, I don't know about that. My career is beyond molding at this point, I would imagine."

"Humbug! Your most rewarding and productive years are still ahead of you."

"That's one of the more debatable statements of the year, I'm sure. Thanks anyway. And if I do decide to marry again, I'll come to you for advice and counsel."

For some reason, the notion of remarriage, on Procter's terms, was not as repugnant to him as he would have predicted. It wasn't the institution of marriage which had let him down, he reminded himself, but his partner in it. Or, more honestly, his choice of partner, which put the onus right back on him—where it probably belonged all along. Elizabeth hadn't been that keen, had, in fact, proposed candidly that they merely live together. It had been he, with his own puritanism and dread of State Department censure, who had held out for episcopal sanction.

"You could do a great deal worse," Procter told him confidently. He stood up and carefully shook the wrinkles out of his trousers. "Come over this evening, why don't you? I'd ask you for dinner, but Pamela tends to panic if she doesn't get twenty-four hours' notice. Come around eight-thirty or so; Valerie'll be there and we can have a drink or two."

The invitation came as a reprieve. Edgerton almost sighed aloud with relief. Earlier, he'd toyed with the idea of having the Liu women over, provided Tamara's mother had finally moved to the hotel and was willing. The prospect didn't exactly thrill him, but it seemed like an opportunity to improve relations and perhaps take some of the heat off Tamara. But he didn't want to play host. Even if only Tamara came, they'd end up talking about Madame Liu and her misfortunes and whether she would move or not, and if not, why not. No! he thought, resentment coming to a head. Hell, no! He wanted to go home and have a swim and a drink and a quiet dinner by himself. Then, if he wanted to go out later, he would go; if he didn't, he wouldn't.

"I'd like that very much," he said, vaguely excited by the prospect of seeing Valerie, recalling the signal from her fingers. As Mac-Donough said: she'd be very nice to play with. Still, the thought of Tamara nagged at him.

The phone buzzed. Edgerton picked it up and listened for a moment. "Damn!" he said, hanging up. "What a memory!"

"Is something the matter?"

"No; just a meeting with Benson . . . I forgot all about it. Some days I don't know what I'd do without Miss Kung to keep me on the rails."

[170]

"Benson? Benson?"

"Chief of the Legation Quarter police."

"Oh, Benson!" Procter said, then looked anxious. "No trouble, I hope."

"No, no trouble. Purely administrative . . . a couple of points to settle before next week's Administrative Council meeting, plus the monthly audit of his accounts. Being a delegate to our little League of Nations here is a heavy burden."

"Great decisions pending?"

Edgerton gave an exasperated laugh. "Earthshaking!" he said, making a wide gesture with his arms. "For instance: should patrolmen shift from summer kit into modified winter kit on September first or fifteenth."

"I say!" Procter's lips twitched. "A knotty problem."

"Quite."

"But not insoluble?"

"Certainly not. But there are others not so simple."

"Ah!"

"Should patrolmen wrap their puttees in a clockwise manner on both legs, or clockwise on the right leg and counterclockwise on the left leg, or . . . but you grasp the permutations?"

"Difficult, difficult." Procter pulled at his ear.

"And most important: should the ammunition allotment be increased from five to ten rounds."

"A tricky business, that."

"And complicated by reports from Staff that the ammunition has become useless with age."

"Dear me; how awkward! Still, ten rounds *are* better than five."

"Precisely," Edgerton said, nodding gravely. "I must say you show a flair for these hard decisions. Next time the chairmanship is open to an American, I shall be proud to nominate . . ."

"No, please! All very flattering, I'm sure, but I'm more than content to leave these complex matters in your capable hands." Grinning broadly, Procter walked to the door and pulled it open. "See you tonight . . . eight-thirtyish?"

"I'll be there," Edgerton said, wondering why Procter was making it all so final. It was not yet noon, after all. He settled back in his chair and lighted a fresh cigarette. Reminiscing with Procter had lifted him out of the doldrums.

Taking up Smith's report, he felt himself charged with new energy. But the thought of his memo to Colonel Tanaka interrupted. He wondered when he would hear from the Japanese officer; he was beginning to regret the memo. Futility was always regrettable.

[171]

His phone buzzed. The line crackled noisily in his ear, when Tamara's low, warm voice came over the wire.

"John? Sorry to be so long calling you back, but Mother just called to say she was packed and leaving for the hotel as soon as she could get a taxi. I am so relieved."

"I am too," Edgerton said, meaning it. He saw now that it had been merely pique at Liu *t'ai t'ai* which had made him regret any part in her problems. He could again feel a distant affection for her, on Tamara's account, and concern as well.

"You'll be going home to an empty house," he said, not wanting to say more than necessary, the shifting images of Tamara and Valerie suddenly together in his mind.

"It'll be a relief in a way," Tamara said lightly. "The place is so small . . . we do a balancing act to keep from stepping on each other. I'll be stopping by the hotel first. Mother is friendly with the Housekeeper, you know. I may stay for supper with them."

"Why don't I take you home?" he asked, aware of a strong reluctance, and feeling a twinge of shame on account of it. He was getting ready to do something he wasn't going to be proud of, but he was going to do it anyway. Wasn't he free to go where he pleased? He owed no explanations to anyone.

"Well . . ." said Tamara uncertainly.

Edgerton was disconcerted, thinking she'd divined his thoughts. She was so damn perceptive.

"I don't like to be a nuisance, but thanks, John; that would be wonderful. It will be nearly dark by then, and frankly, I'm still a little nervous. Oh, and I meant to tell you before: Mother says there *is* some kind of investigation going on in our *hu-tung*. She just heard about it this morning; it helped make up her mind, I think. But it's our own police, not the Japanese. They're supposed to be looking for stolen property." Tamara paused. "It may be nothing," she added unconvincingly.

"I don't like the sound of that," Edgerton said. "Or the idea of your being there alone."

"I'll be all right; there are the people downstairs, after all. Besides, it'll be days before the police get to us. They'll have probably given up by then."

"Mmmm," Edgerton muttered, unconvinced, but devoid of arguments or alternatives.

"Well, call me, or just come on over when you're ready to go." He hesitated, then blurted, "I wish you could stay with me."

"Oh, I do too, John," she said quickly, her voice warm. "But don't

[172]

worry; everything'll be all right. Have to go now . . . the Manager's ringing for me. 'Bye."

The click echoed loudly in Edgerton's ear, leaving him wondering whether he was relieved or not.

Before he could hang up, the instrument buzzed. "Yes, yes, Miss Kung, I remember. I'm leaving now," he said.

♟♟

Quaking, Sobolov hesitated on the sidewalk. Above him the dingy gray mass of the Police Yamen loomed. He felt himself shriveling into total insignificance, a mere pinch of dust from the dusty pavement. Government buildings meant clerks and petty functionaries, each with his power to award, to punish, to delay, and to misplace. And he had been decreed by destiny to be their ultimate victim. Yet now, he recalled previous visits to the Yamen almost with nostalgia: applications, validations, reports of changes of address and employment . . . bureaucratic trivia.

The sentry at the top of the steps seemed to be eyeing him suspiciously. Sobolov was tempted to snap his fingers as though suddenly remembering an errand, and melt into the crowd. But they had sent for him; he had no choice but to appear. He took a shaky breath, straightened his tie, resettled his hat, and started reluctantly up the steps.

The stale air of the gloomy foyer hung about him in layers, ammoniac and sweaty: the stink of fear and despair.

A desk sergeant listened indifferently to Sobolov's question, muttered into a telephone and gestured down a cavernous tributary to Sobolov's right. Clutching his hat over his sternum like a shield, Sobolov went in the direction indicated.

The door to Captain Wang's office stood open; Sobolov peered in uncertainly, squinting against the glare from the open window at the far end of the room. There was a desk by the window and at the desk sat a man, indistinct in the brightness. A haze of tobacco smoke surrounded him. Sobolov swallowed. The room was long and narrow, with stacks of ledgers piled untidily along the walls.

Captain Wang, whose soiled uniform hung emptily on his thin frame, ignored him. His attention was fixed upon the paper uppermost among the litter while nicotine-stained fingers pulled at a stringy moustache. Wisps of dandruff-flecked hair partially encircled his scalp, the thin skin revealing the cranial sutures. Sobolov's legs began to tremble.

[173]

Finally Wang tossed aside the paper, letting it flutter unheeded to the floor, and fixed Sobolov with yellow eyes. He extended the hand not preoccupied with his moustache, and said sternly, "Papers."

Hastening to comply, Sobolov made sure his Legation identity card was on top.

Wang examined it dubiously, fingering the impression of the American seal as though suspecting a forgery. The yellow Nansen passport he disdained to look at. Before opening Sobolov's blue refugee's passbook, he gave him a wary glance, cleared his throat, and spat inaccurately at the cuspidor. He read the passbook from cover to cover, shaking his head from time to time as though its endorsements confirmed his worst suspicions. Sobolov was suddenly afflicted with a tormenting need to urinate.

Wang closed the passbook with a snap, rummaged for the other documents and negligently returned them. Swiveling back and forth, Wang stared at Sobolov, his fingers fondling the row of fountain pens which adorned his breast pocket, then returned to the encouragement of his moustache.

"Why have you come here?" he barked.

Sobolov jumped. "Major Wu's orders," he stammered.

"Exactly. Orders must be obeyed, is that not so?"

"Oh yes," Sobolov mumbled.

"Without question, is that no so?"

Sobolov nodded dumbly.

"Are you happy in China?" Wang asked, his face twisting to form a closed and humorless smile.

Sobolov could only give a sickly grin, and nod again, certain he would be unable to control his bladder.

"You are treated fairly?"

"Oh, yes sir!" Sobolov squeaked, too frightened now to wonder where all this was leading.

"You are, of course, grateful?"

"Very grateful."

"You believe it is your duty always to cooperate with the authorities?"

"Yes indeed. I always . . ."

"Good! Come with me." Wang fairly leapt out of his chair and snatched up his hat. He gave his pistol a slap, tugged at the skirts of his tunic, and hurried toward the hall. Sobolov trotted in his wake, his mind grinding with anxiety. They descended a flight of steep and poorly lighted steps, Sobolov steadying himself against the wall with a sweaty hand.

The basement consisted of a long dank corridor lined with doors,

[174]

each one inset with a closed wicket and provided with a light. Only two of the lights were burning. The effluvium of the upper hallway had settled densely into the basement, where it lay about in smelly pockets. Sobolov's urge to urinate was joined by one to vomit.

Wang turned to him, displaying a collection of stained teeth. "Interrogation Rooms," he announced in the proprietary manner of a museum guide. Sobolov felt his stomach lurch with dismay.

Marching to the nearest door, Wang opened the wicket, standing on his toes to do so. A rhythmical thumping, like some slowly idling machine, throbbed out of the wicket and into the fetid air. He stepped aside, waving an invitation for Sobolov to look. A half-step forward let Sobolov hear the grunts that accompanied the thumps. He retreated then, his eyes pleading and his hat making imploring gestures in Wang's direction.

Snorting his contempt for such squeamishness, Wang slammed shut the wicket, chopping off the noise in midpulse.

"Very uncooperative man," he said, with a gesture of his thumb.

Marching to the next lighted door, Wang stared through the wicket for several moments, nodding with satisfaction. He stepped back, and Sobolov knew that this time he would have to look.

What he saw was a windowless concrete cube, lighted by a single bulb. It was occupied by three men. The man to whom Sobolov's eyes automatically went was kneeling tautly in the center of the floor. But for a dirty bandage on one elbow he was naked. His bound wrists were lashed to his ankles, arching him backward. From beneath his bindings blood dribbled, forming pale pink pools on the wet floor.

Two men stood over him, one in front and one behind, inspecting him with apparent boredom. To Sobolov they were alike enough to have been twins. A rubber hose lay on the floor, discharging a stream of water into a corner.

Suddenly the man behind the prisoner grasped him by the hair and wrenched his head back, causing the veins and tendons in his neck to spring into relief. His eyes rolled in their sockets, wide and fearful. The other interrogator picked up the hose, gripped the hinge of the prisoner's jaw in one broad hand and thrust the hose deep into his throat.

At once the prisoner began a labored and spasmodic gagging that racked his entire body; his breathing wheezed and gargled desperately as sprays of water jetted intermittently from his distended nostrils. His belly began to swell, slowly enlarging to the size of a basketball. His veins became huge as every iota of his energy went into the struggle.

Fainting, Sobolov sagged away from the wicket, but Wang rammed

[175]

his head forward, waffling his nose into the mesh with a crunch. Though the pain revived him, his eyes filled with tears, and the blurred and dreadful scene continued . . . medieval, terrifying, inexplicable.

The end came in seconds. From some deep reservoir of life the man summoned his last resource. His body heaved in a massive convulsion and he spewed out a great gout of water onto his tormentor. Cursing, the interrogator yanked out the hose, and kicked the prisoner smartly in the face with his bare foot. The other interrogator laughed harshly and let go of the prisoner's hair. The kneeling figure wavered for a moment, then slowly toppled over, his head striking the concrete with the splashy crack of an overripe melon. Sobolov could almost see the prisoner's soul rise up and the life go out of him. The hose, forgotten, gurgled in the background.

Sick with terror, Sobolov felt his knees turn to jelly. Aware only of the waves of encroaching blackness, his hand implored the Captain's assistance. Wang evaded it nimbly. As Sobolov fell, his head struck the knob. Dazed with pain and illness, he sat on the floor.

Captain Wang grinned sourly, his fingers straying among the hairs of his moustache, plainly a man who knew he had done his duty. "Go!" he barked, pointing.

Sobolov gritted his teeth and struggled slowly to his feet. Steadying himself with one hand against the dank wall, he made his slow way to the stairs.

Somewhere in the distance lay the oasis of the street and the ordinary world.

♟♟

Li's bony body sagged awkwardly in the tilted wooden chair and his bare feet rested on the table. He was in his undershirt, and across his thighs the evening paper lay open. As he idly turned its pages the corded muscles of his thin arm bunched and stretched. A beer bottle perspired at his elbow, and a few flies buzzed aimlessly around the still room.

Mei-ling was in the cooking shed, just outside the back door. She was chopping vegetables for their supper, and the sharp clop of her cleaver had a nice domestic sound to it. She was humming softly. Li listened for a moment, smiling vaguely to himself, then took a long swallow of beer and went back to his paper.

An item in the middle of the page caught his eye, and the corners of his thin mouth turned dubiously downward as he scanned it. With a sudden movement of his big hands he crushed the paper into a ball and hurled it to the floor.

"*Ai-ya*, what stupid nonsense!" he grumbled loudly.

"What is the matter?" Mei-ling asked absentmindedly. She came into the room and got a dipper of water from the sink, giving him an affectionate look as she went by.

"The foolishness of this so-called newspaper is the matter."

"Well, you don't have to throw it on the floor," she said mildly, bending gracefully despite the full dipper, and picking it up. Li felt a qualm for causing her this extra work, and pleasure at the sight of the fluid movement. "What have they done now?" she asked.

Li shrugged his narrow shoulders. "The same old thing. Another story about the good deed of a simple Japanese soldier. This one assisted a farmer in rounding up his scattered flock of ducks. Fortunately for us, a photographer from the New China Press just happened to be passing.

"What's so bad about that? I suppose it happens."

He listened to the paper crackle as she straightened and folded it. It would make a frugal addition to the kindling for her charcoal. "You suppose what happens?" he asked argumentatively.

"Tsk, tsk," she said, chiding either the fire for its stubbornness or him for his bad temper. "I mean there are some simple Japanese soldiers who try to help."

Li gave a cynical laugh. "A new role for the Imperial Army: the farmer's friend. Last week a soldier waded into a pond to retrieve a child's ball. Our correspondent was there too."

"I know it's propaganda . . . I'm not a donkey, after all," she said sharply, giving the rice pot an impatient blow with her spoon. "I am only saying they are not all barbarians. Remember the fellow who bumped into me and then helped me pick up my vegetables?"

"He did that because you are beautiful . . . probably bumped you on purpose. Had you been ugly, he would have kicked you."

Mei-ling's laugh rewarded him. And made him wonder if he ought to tell her. The story had not yet been given to the press. He didn't want her to worry, but neither did he want her to become careless. This "simple soldier" business wasn't a good sign.

"When I'm not here at night, do you go out?"

"Go out? You mean, go out dancing?" Her tone was ironic; then she teased, "And what if I do?"

"I couldn't blame you . . . you must have a score of suitors," Li said. "No, I mean just walking, an errand to a shop, anything."

"Very seldom."

"Don't do it at all anymore."

Mei-ling came and stood in the doorway, her expression serious. "What has happened?"

Li turned and faced her soberly. "There was another rape Monday night. I wasn't going to say anything, but the Japanese are making such a fuss over this one, I thought I ought to."

"I don't understand."

"Well, in this one, it was the soldier who was hurt, not the woman; at least not as far as we know. But it's the sort of thing, as the word gets around, which seems to challenge certain men. Who can explain human nature? Already there have been a rash of minor assaults and one very bad rape and beating. The woman isn't expected to live."

"How awful!"

"Yes," Li said softly, almost gently. Then he struck the table a blow with his fist. "But those men won't even be reprimanded. And the women are simply out of luck, as usual." Li's voice had hardened as he spoke, his anger barely under control. "Meanwhile, we are turning half of Precinct Seven upside down looking for the first soldier's 'assailant.' "

Mei-ling made a face. "What a job!" she said.

Li grimaced. "Don't worry, we won't find her. We won't even try very hard. The soldier claims he can identify the woman, but one of the Japanese MPs told me he was so drunk he didn't even wake up until the following afternoon." Li looked at Mei-ling for several seconds, his expression softening. "Go nowhere after dark . . . not even dancing."

Mei-ling smiled at him. "Tyrant!" she said happily and went back to her cooking.

Li was glad that he had told her. She'd be sensible. Li sighed, weary all of a sudden, and not nearly so confident as he pretended. There had been no point in telling her that the Japanese Special Unit was on the case as well. There was always the possibility that they might stumble onto the right person, or someone might betray the woman. Or, they could simply pick someone at random, fake the identification, and then punish her as an example. They wouldn't care.

"Any news of the war?" Mei-ling asked.

"The war is finished," he said.

She came to the door to look at him.

"Finished?"

"Practically. We have been beaten, I'm afraid."

"*Ai-ya!*" she said sadly, and stood for a moment with her head down, thinking. Her husband had been killed the year before in the futile fighting for Shanghai. Li wondered if she were thinking of him, and felt a twinge of jealousy. She hardly ever mentioned him, and he had guessed that they had not been happy.

"The Japanese have nearly everything they want," he said to break the silence. "There is not much left to fight about."

Mei-ling shook her head and gave him a quick smile. "You are such a pessimist," she scolded.

He returned her smile and felt very content all of a sudden. "A policeman learns to expect the worst."

"That is because you are always looking for it . . . you like it that way," she told him and went back to her cooking.

Li nodded to himself and didn't answer. The war *was* over. By winter, Chungking would be the only major city left unoccupied. And for all the inaccessibility of that redoubt, it was anyone's guess how long the Chinese government could survive there. The hopeful talk about the Communists joining forces with the Kuomintang didn't impress Li. What could one expect from politicians and generals? Politics made no difference. The surrender of Peking had begun a chain of defeats and defections, unrelieved except for a few victories too isolated to affect the course of the war. Often badly led and poorly equipped, the Chinese armies had been crushed under the Japanese avalanche.

At first Li had felt shame and anger, but the shame had turned to bitterness, and then, he told himself, to indifference. And the anger had faded away too. Now his primary concern was to exist, to keep his job and do it as well as he could, to put aside a little money, to look after himself—the rice pot clanged again as though daring him to forget—and to look after Mei-ling . . . most especially Mei-ling.

Li stretched and gave an enormous yawn. This was comfortable, he told himself, pleased by the domestic noises coming from the cookshed. He had been alone too long and ought to marry again. Li felt a twinge of sardonic amusement at himself. How familiar these wistful yearnings for marriage and domesticity! They came predictably at meal times and in the dark comfort after love. But there were other times, the dangerous times and the times when an assignment kept him going day and night, that made him thankful he was solitary, and need not worry about another's concern. And yet he knew Mei-ling worried about him anyway, although it was not her way to say anything. His wife had been like that, hating his being a policeman but holding her tongue about it.

Li felt a deep sadness engulf him. It was always the same when he allowed himself to think about the woman and the little boy, both so

[179]

swiftly gone of fever. But that was past. He was happy with Mei-ling, and she was young enough to give him another son. She felt no great enthusiasm for his work, but she was older than his wife had been and more philosophical.

Marriage to Mei-ling? Yes, it was a very pleasant thought. They had met casually and come together with the haste that is bred by war. They got on well. Mei-ling was both a good cook and a thrifty housekeeper. And the cold and lonely nights of winter lay ahead. Her tongue was sometimes sharp, but there was usually a smile to ease the sharpness. He would think on it.

The front door stood open, ready for any chance current of air from the *hu-tung* as the land cooled and the dusk descended. Li let his mind wander idly, glancing out from time to time and watching the lengthening shadows of the passersby, drinking his beer and smoking.

Mei-ling came in unnoticed, her hands full of bowls and chopsticks. "Ch'ing-wei, remove thy great feet from my table!" she ordered crossly.

Pretending fright and penitence, Li did so, elaborately dusting at the table with his hands.

Mei-ling put down her burden and shoved him back into his chair. Although her mouth was pursed, he could see amusement glint in her eyes, and felt pleased because of it.

"Be so good as to get out of my way," she said, nudging him aside with her hip and wiping the spotless table with a damp cloth. "How many times have I told you not to lean back in my chairs? Am I a rich singsong girl with a wealthy lover that I can afford to buy new chairs?"

"How do I know what you do when I am at work?" He patted her tenderly on the bottom.

"Shameless!" she accused him, striking his hand away. He could hear her laugh softly to herself as she went back to the cookshed.

Li watched her carry in a bowl of vegetables garnished with slivers of pork, and one of steaming rice. Still affecting a demure and dignified expression, she served the rice and began to add meat and vegetables to his bowl. When she handed it to him her face relaxed into a full smile that crinkled her eyes at the corners and showed some of the gold in her teeth. She is so pretty, he thought, and still slender and graceful as a girl. Smiling admiringly at her, he felt an immense and sudden satisfaction with her and with himself and his good fortune. He laughed aloud with delight.

"Well, that's a little better. You looked so grim and forbidding when you came . . . when you arrived." She blushed furiously, and her eyes fell in confusion.

[180]

Li knew she had almost said "home," and he stifled his smile so as not to embarrass her. He *was* home, he realized with some surprise. The notion filled him with happiness.

"I was feeling grim," he said seriously, suddenly reminded of the afternoon. "Some days that Yamen is almost more than I can stand."

"*Ai-ya!* What has gone wrong now?"

"The place just gets under my skin like a splinter. Bah!" he said, dismissing it.

Holding the bowl to his lips, Li began to eat. The food was delicious. And Mei-ling brewed perfect tea and served it at precisely the right temperature. As he glanced at her appreciatively, she transferred two pieces of pork from her bowl to his.

"Are you fasting?" he asked ironically.

"It is stylish to be slender nowadays."

"Ah," he said, savoring one of the morsels. He looked closely at her. "You are too beautiful already."

"You are making fun of me," she said, as a shadow of worry crossed her face.

"Not at all," he said earnestly. He laid his chopsticks across the top of his bowl and reached across the table to take her hand, wanting very much to reassure her, the strange shy girl.

"You think I am too skinny."

"Never!" Li gestured with his two cupped hands. "You are just right . . . round and womanly." He leered grotesquely.

Mei-ling giggled, the worry gone. "You must not say such things at the table. Eat your supper."

Relieved, Li continued with his meal, wondering a little at the sensitivity of women.

"Well, are you going to tell me about the Yamen?"

Li grinned briefly at the sudden shift. "The trouble is that worthless turtle's egg, Captain of Municipal Police Wang."

"That weasel!" she sniffed. "What is he up to now?"

"He had a prisoner killed for no other reason than to intimidate some Russian."

"A Russian?" she interjected, as much as to ask: why bother with a Russian?

"Yes, he made the Russian watch."

Mei-ling shuddered, frowning at him over her rice bowl, her chopsticks motionless in her hand. "He must be crazy," she said. "Why would he do that?"

"That's what I would like to know."   .

Li stirred thoughtfully at his bowl. He picked up a piece of cabbage

[181]

and studied it carefully before putting it in his mouth. "The Japanese are mixed up in it some way," he told her. "Or at least Colonel Tanaka is. Also that swindler Puhalski."

"But what do the Japanese care about a Russian?"

"Well, this particular one works for the American Legation."

"Ah!" she exclaimed knowingly. "A spy."

"So one might think. But this man is only an interpreter; there is nothing for him to spy on. They don't operate that way, the Americans. Besides, I know this man a little; he is too honest and too simple-minded to be a spy."

"How do you know how the Americans operate?"

"Chinese people work there, too, you know." Li gave her a humorless grin.

"You frighten me, you policemen."

Li shrugged. "It is necessary to know what is going on, especially with foreigners. The Americans are very careful with their papers."

"Still, the Japanese must think he can get hold of something."

"You are right, obviously. But it puzzles me." Li picked up his bowl and ate a few mouthfuls. "The Russian's wife is mixed up in it as well. Tanaka wants her."

Mei-ling raised her eyebrows.

"Though I can't imagine why. She is an ox of a woman."

Mei-ling's eyes glittered. "You know her, too, do you?"

"I have seen her," Li said, blandly innocent.

"What does she look like?"

"She is enormous: breasts like melons, legs like trees, a backside like a mare." Li sculptured the air with his hands. "A huge Russian potato of a nose and acres of sickly white skin."

Mei-ling laughed. "You are very poetic. It sounds like she has taken your fancy."

"Bah! I prefer women of more manageable proportions . . . like yourself, if I may say so."

"You think I am manageable, do you?" Mei-ling jabbed the air with her chopsticks. "I have been too docile, I can see that."

"You? Docile? You are a wildcat, a tigress!" Li shook his head as though overwhelmed by the thought of her. "And you are a scold as well," he added in a tone of profound resignation.

Mei-ling laughed happily, and had to wipe her eyes on her sleeve. She forced a serious expression. "But what does the woman have to do with it?"

"I don't know; it's confusing. Puhalski has been bedding her and now Tanaka wants a turn, and wants to frighten her husband who works for the Americans."

[182]

"You express yourself so romantically. They sound like a basket of eels: no way to know which head goes with which tail. And so many Russians . . . what a people!" She shrugged helplessly. Then, as an afterthought, she asked, "How do you know Tanaka is behind that dirty business at the Yamen?"

"Too much is happening to leave any room for coincidence. Besides, Wang won't take a piss without Major Wu's permission, and Wu would never give permission without clearing it with Tanaka."

Mei-ling shook her head at these follies. They ate in silence for a few moments.

Li cleared his throat and looked down into his almost empty bowl. "I should tell the Americans about it."

Mei-ling looked surprised. "What do you care about them?"

"I don't really, but I owe one of them a debt. This way I can pay him back a little."

"Ah, yes, the American from Tientsin."

"The one. I tell him things from time to time. He says it is helpful, and that's enough for me. Most Americans are no better than the other foreign devils, but this one is different."

Mei-ling's sniff was dubious. "How can that be?"

"Who knows about foreigners? Just the same, I feel it. In the first place, he doesn't claim to know everything. The rest of the big noses are like school teachers: they know all about the gods and the weather and the nature of mankind and what is right and what is wrong. They are very tiresome."

"They do know quite a lot," Mei-ling observed sensibly. "Look at their wealth and their machines. We must learn from them."

"Yes, machines." Li ruminated for a moment, probing around his teeth with his tongue. "You are right, but they should try to learn from us. They are like precocious children; and they forget history. Chinese people were living right here in this city, in houses and palaces and wearing silk, before the Americans even existed. And the English, who everyone says are so civilized, were still living in caves and rubbing their bodies with berry juice to keep out the cold." Li had to laugh. He thought for a moment, wanting to make his feelings clear to her. "Maybe that is what I like about this American. He is willing to learn. He can almost think like a Chinese. It is impossible, of course, but at least he tries."

Mei-ling gave him a quizzical look. "You are a strange man," she said wonderingly.

Li shrugged. "It all goes back a long time."

"He really saved your life?"

Li nodded.

[183]

"Maybe there was nothing else for him to do."

"He could have run away."

"What did you do for him?"

"Nothing."

"You mean he asked nothing in return?"

Li shook his head.

"He will," Mei-ling said.

Li made an indifferent gesture with his hand. "I doubt it. What could I do for him? He is rich, a high official."

Mei-ling looked at him for a long time. "I'm glad he didn't run away," she said simply.

Li grinned at her. "So am I." He scooped the last of his rice into his mouth and tossed off the remainder of his tea.

"I am sorry there isn't any more," Mei-ling said.

Li shook his head. "*Wa chih bao-la,*" he said, patting his stomach, then belching politely in confirmation.

Mei-ling smiled at the compliment, and began to clear the table, carrying the bowls and chopsticks to the washstand beside the sink. Li turned and watched her affectionately, aware of his meal radiating comfortably in his stomach. Mei-ling found good things to eat in the market when other women came home with empty baskets.

As she leaned over to wipe the table, her small breasts swayed softly against the thin cotton of her jacket.

"Why don't we get married?" he asked suddenly, feeling his heart accelerate in an unfamiliar manner.

Standing back, she gave him a glance of cool surprise, her eyebrows elevated proudly. The corners of her mouth twitched. "What would one want with you?" she asked him. "A poor policeman with no prospects?"

"One awaits a proposal from the governor of the province, I suppose?"

She leaned toward him defiantly, hands on slender hips, her legs spread in their wide cotton trousers. "And why not?" she demanded, and tossed her head. She wore her hair short, like a schoolgirl's, with the bangs cut square across her brow. Her delicately pointed chin was thrust forward with challenge, and her eyes sparkled proudly.

"Why not, indeed," Li said admiringly, and felt suddenly quite young and clean, as though the cynicism and disgust of his day had been washed away and his life was full of promise.

Mei-ling grinned mischievously and her pose relaxed. "I shall consider your proposal when I have time," she said. "But first I must wash the bowls." As she went by him, her fingertips brushed his cheek.

[184]

Li found mysterious tears in his eyes. He rubbed them impatiently away.

��

As he turned into the Procters' driveway, it seemed to Edgerton that he left responsibility behind him.

The afternoon at the office had passed quickly for him, the burst of energy he'd felt when Procter left staying with him to the end. He'd completed work on the economic report and given it to Miss Kung to type, a task now out of the way a week ahead of time. A number of other chores, already postponed more than once, had been disposed of.

He'd returned home from the office warmed by a sense of accomplishment, regretting only that in the evening ahead he wouldn't be seeing Valerie alone.

But in the pool, and in the courtyard where he mixed himself a strong whiskey, and where Ch'en served his supper, Tamara's aura still clung tenaciously, driving the other woman out of his mind. Thinking of Tamara made him miss her and drew him to the conclusion that he was about to make a fool of himself, but it made him miss her terribly.

At eight o'clock, Tamara walked over from the hotel. If it hadn't been so late, he would have made love to her. He would have had to. The same urge was still with him when they reached her flat, but Tamara seemed very quiet by then, as if depressed by her unwanted solitude. And he was running even farther behind schedule.

Although he hadn't liked leaving her in such a mood, she'd promised to call him in the morning. He wasn't really worried. The atmosphere of the *hu-tung* had seemed better, lighter and more communal, than it had on previous nights. That a routine investigation could be going on a block away was believable; that it posed any direct threat to Tamara or her mother was not. Just the same, he was glad Madame Liu was at the hotel.

The only thing really nagging in Edgerton's mind was Colonel Tanaka's letter. Or at least he was assuming the letter was from Tanaka. The similarity between modern Japanese script and what Chinese he knew had told him only that it was from the Headquarters of the Military Police. He regretted giving Sobolov the afternoon off. He was fluent in both written and spoken Japanese, and could have run up a translation in an hour. Well, now it would have to wait until tomorrow.

[185]

Edgerton consoled himself that even if he'd made a diplomatic blunder, it would quickly blow over. Diplomacy seemed to become a cruder art as the world grew more complex, rather than the other way around. What would have got one banished to the wilds of Canada ten years ago was shrugged at today.

Pausing on the graveled turn-around, Edgerton was struck by the silence and a sense of utter solitude. And confirming his sudden suspicion that things weren't as he had expected, his headlights had just showed him the Procters' garage, open and empty. The chirp of crickets and the faint crackling of his cooling engine seemed the only sounds, the muted roar of the city almost too distant to be noticed.

Except for the living room, the house was dark. There, the French windows stood open and through the screens he could see the softly lighted room, with its comfortable chairs and couches. He could only guess that the servants were somewhere in the back, doing whatever it was they did when the *lao-yeh* and *t'ai t'ai* were away. Gossiping and playing Mah-Jongg, probably.

Edgerton wondered how he could have misunderstood Franklin's invitation. And he was no more than ten minutes late. He cursed quietly under his breath, aware of vague, unformed plans gone glimmering.

The big front door swung open, washing the steps in a fan of light. Valerie stood there, looking uncertainly in his direction.

"Well, hello," she called softly. "I thought I heard a car. I've been waiting demurely for the bell to ring."

Edgerton heard himself laugh with relief as he started toward her. "I was beginning to think I'd perpetrated the classic gaffe and come on the wrong evening," he said as he started up the steps. "I was on the verge of slinking away."

Valerie was wearing a simply cut cotton dress of pale yellow. It enhanced the tanned smoothness of her skin and turned her pale hair almost to silver.

"Where is everybody?"

"A forgotten cocktail party. Franklin was in a dither of remorse and was all for calling you. I told him never mind, that I would be their stand-in. I didn't want to go to another cocktail party anyway." She grinned mischievously over her shoulder as she led him into the living room. "Where is everybody, indeed!"

Edgerton spread his hands in a silent apology. "And Pamela found no fault with your offer?"

Valerie smiled. "Strange to say, no. What will you have to drink?"

A silver tray with filigreed decanters, a syphon, ice, and other paraphernalia stood on a small table. Edgerton watched her admiringly as she went about fixing their drinks.

To keep from being caught staring, he turned and surveyed the familiar, tastefully furnished room. Many of his own Chinese things, collected over the years, were still in boxes, waiting to be moved again. He never seemed to get around to putting them out. He moved on to look more closely at a T'ang horse rearing gracefully on a dark mahogany sideboard.

Valerie chuckled behind his back. "Here," she said. "I've been following you around like a slave girl."

"Nice idea." Edgerton took the cold glass, toasted her in silence and took a deep swallow. She returned the gesture, regarding him with speculative directness for a long, eloquent moment.

"Let's sit down," she said at last, showing only a small secret smile. She indicated a large white couch fronted by a low ebony table. Edgerton settled into it with a sigh. Music flowed seductively from a large electric phonograph in the corner. It was one of the new models that changed records automatically—the only one he'd seen in Peking.

"You look like you've been spending the summer on the Riviera," he said admiringly.

"I'm a sun worshiper," she said. "Every afternoon at the Club."

A cold finger touched Edgerton's heart, leaving a guilty mark. What the hell! he was quick to argue, he was a free agent; he could go where he wished.

". . . luckily I tan easily," Valerie was saying. "Nevertheless, it feels very warm underneath."

As she reached for the cigarette he offered, he noticed the fine hairs on her forearm, bleached almost to invisibility. He told himself that he felt no trace of guilt in the impulse to reach out and touch her bare shoulder, to find out for himself just how warm she was "underneath."

He looked up to find her regarding him gravely. "I have a small confession to make," she said almost in a whisper.

Edgerton waited curiously.

Almost defiantly, she forced her eyes to remain on his. "I made a point today of taking another look at your Miss Liu."

Good Jesus Christ! Shifting his eyes away from hers, Edgerton gritted his teeth, annoyed and disappointed in her.

"Why would you want to do that?" he asked coldly.

"Just feminine curiosity," she faltered, obviously sorry she'd mentioned the subject. "She's lovely; so young and fresh."

Another blunder! Edgerton felt a bitter urge to laugh. Serves her right!

[187]

"I am sorry, John," Valerie said at last, and he could tell she meant it. "I shouldn't have done that, or even mentioned her name. I only did because she's been on my mind a lot, and so have you."

He looked at her quickly. Her blue eyes were guileless.

Edgerton forced a smile, relenting. "Don't worry about it," he told her.

Valerie looked relieved, but before she could speak the record ended. They waited in silence while the Victrola clicked and whirred mysteriously. At last another tune began. "This piece is one of my favorites," Valerie said. "Will you dance with me?"

"I'm not much of a dancer," Edgerton confessed, glad the awkwardness was over.

He needn't have. Valerie was so good, she made him good. She was quite short, he was surprised to discover, her forehead coming barely to his chin. Her fine hair tickled him faintly. At first, he felt constrained to hold her loosely, but the slow movements of the dance kept bringing them into subtle contact. And then not so subtle, as he became increasingly aware of her, and she of him. There developed a sensual suppleness in the way she danced which seemed almost explicit in its simulation of the rhythms of love, and its effect on him became no longer possible to conceal. Nor did he try to, nor she pretend. Neither of them spoke, acknowledging what was happening only with the motions of their bodies, but with still a vestige of reserve, neither one giving way fully.

The next number was a rumba, and Edgerton led her pointedly back to the couch. Their glasses were empty. He carried them to the liquor tray, wanting to calm himself, glad he had kept on the jacket of his Palm Beach suit.

"How long will you be able to stay in Peking?" he asked over his shoulder.

"I don't really know," she said, sounding relaxed and easy. "Not as long as Pamela is urging, certainly. I have to get back to Washington and find myself a job."

"What sort of a job?" he asked, returning to the couch.

"Government secretary, I suppose. I worked for the Interior before I married." She looked at him uncertainly. "You knew I'd been married, didn't you?"

"I guessed," he said, smiling, "I presume you aren't now."

"Didn't Franklin tell you about me?" She sounded mildly incredulous.

He grinned at her and shook his head. "No."

"I'm a widow."

[188]

"I'm sorry."

She smiled strangely. "Don't be. It seems a long time ago. He killed himself. It was a car smash, but suicide just the same. Driving too fast, too drunk. It was a habit of his." Her silence sounded final.

"I'm sorry," Edgerton repeated, at a loss for other words.

"Thanks," Valerie said at last. "I'm glad I told you. I don't say even that much very often, but each time the memory fades some more. It's almost gone now."

Edgerton nodded, distracted. He'd never told anyone his paltry tale of Elizabeth and her strayings. If he had, her memory might almost be gone as well. His friends knew only that he was divorced. He'd been hoarding the whole sordid business. Idiot!

In the hall the telephone jangled stridently.

While Valerie went to answer it, Edgerton asked himself if he had let Elizabeth play a larger role in his life than she deserved.

Valerie's voice startled him. "That was Pamela," she said, standing in the door for a moment. "They'll be home in a quarter of an hour." She made a rueful face. "I was hoping they'd be gone longer."

"So was I," Edgerton said.

It would have only taken a few more dances like that last and they would be making love . . . in bed, on the floor, somewhere. But there would be another time . . . there had to be.

Valerie returned to sit beside him on the couch. "I hear you might be going back to Washington yourself soon."

"Yes, but not exactly soon. Maybe by this time next year."

"I hope I'll see you there."

"You couldn't avoid me if you tried," he told her. She would be just right for him in Washington, and vice versa. Without her, life in that once-again strange city would be too much the monotony of work and a lonely apartment, and the dreary succession of secretaries who deserved better than to be merely his—or anyone's—one-night stands.

The fly in all that ointment was that he would have to leave China, and everything his life in China meant to him. Of course, leaving was inevitable. That was the way the Service worked, sooner or later. But if Tamara were right, and all foreigners *had* to leave . . . well, then, he wanted to stay until the last minute. Tamara . . . Her name blotted out all other thoughts. Cruel and aimless and unstable as their love affair had been, he couldn't turn his back on it. The thought of losing her haunted him, yet it seemed impossible to keep her.

"You seem less than overjoyed at the prospect," Valerie teased him gently.

Edgerton forced a laugh. "I'm an old stick-in-the-mud, I guess. The prospect delights me, but the thought of pulling up my Chinese roots frankly scares hell out of me. I'm one of those cantankerous souls who's never happy anywhere. On closer acquaintance you might not like me much."

"I'd like you under any circumstances," she said firmly. "But you do surprise me. I'd have thought you would have had your fill of all the dust and filth and frustration by now."

Her tone and her words irked him, but he didn't care to argue the point. "God knows, there've been times when I've had all I can take of this place," he conceded. "Just the same . . ." He wanted to tell her, to try and tell her what the totality of China meant to him, but he doubted he could do it. He smiled instead, saying, "You see what a crank I am? Hardly a bargain."

Valerie licked her lips quickly, showing a small pink tongue. "I feel very reckless," she said, an earthy glint appearing in her eyes. "My needs are simple. Other things being equal, I think you're quite a bargain."

"Other things? What other things?" Edgerton teased her. Unbidden, his thumb and forefinger took hold of a lock of her hair at the temple.

She blushed warmly. "You know," she replied, her voice a throaty whisper.

Slowly, as the tug of his fingers increased, her face came toward him and he kissed her. Her half-open lips were moist and hotly alive. She tantalized him with a brief taste of her tongue, then when his followed into her mouth, she sucked it into her as though trying to uproot it. Hardening demandingly, Edgerton let his hand cup her breast, weighing its firm liquid fullness, his tongue probing deeper.

From far down the driveway, headlight beams swept the walls and ceiling. They pulled apart reluctantly.

"Damn!" Valerie swore intensely; then she laughed, her voice strained. "But maybe it's just as well. That was all too nice; you'll do very well, I think."

Getting to her feet, she straightened her skirt, then went to the mirror over the mantle and examined her face critically. Her reflection smiled at him, and the tip of her tongue showed itself, teasing.

As he grinned back at her, Edgerton was promising himself that he'd be in her bed long before either of them met in Washington.

The sound of a powerful engine came to them from the drive, and the crunch of gravel.

THURSDAY

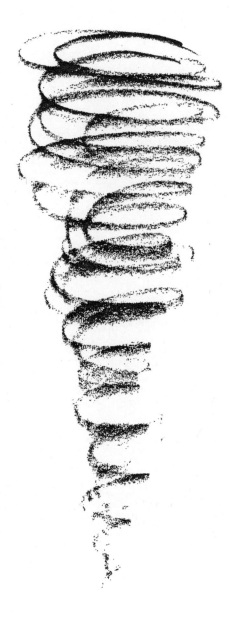

The neatly typed Japanese characters kept sliding out of focus. Although he was nearly finished with the letter, Sobolov retained no coherent sense of its meaning.

He took off his glasses and rubbed his burning eyelids. After polishing the glasses for the tenth time, he began again, determined to work on to the end, to complete the job once and for all. Mr. Edgerton had said that it was important, more important than his other work. And it was to be done by Sobolov alone . . . no typing by Miss Kung. On a better day, Sobolov would have been gratified by this sign of confidence. But too much had happened already, and much more loomed in the precarious future.

Of that terrible hour inside the Yamen only the briefest flashes remained: Captain Wang's predatory eyes, the unknown victim spouting water like some grotesque statue, the feral stink of the dungeon, the callous, casual laughter of the "interrogator." Finally reaching the sidewalk, he had found a lump like an egg on the back of his head.

Now Sobolov fingered it gingerly, as though it were the single shred of evidence proving that the episode hadn't been a bad dream.

One memory about which there was no doubt was the expression on Maya's face when she saw him. Although there had been emotions reflected in it which he even now could not identify, there was no mistaking her deep concern for him.

She had laced his tea with vodka and then run him a hot tub. She stayed with him, too, helping him to bathe and to dry himself. And when she had gotten him to bed, she fed him a bowl of potato soup with onions in it. She sat with him while he finished the soup, listening, her eyes full of worry, while he told her what had happened at the Yamen. She listened and told him not to be concerned. He could remember all that clearly.

Then he had slept for a while, only to awaken slowly long after night had fallen and find himself in her arms. As though still in some fantastic dream, they had made love. She was tender and affectionate with him, and kept whispering indistinctly. It reminded him of those first years in Harbin when they had had so much happiness. Afterward, Maya had cried bitter tears, but she wouldn't tell him why. Women were inexplicable creatures.

But by morning they were back in their real world. Maya was remote and uncommunicative, and her accustomed frown was in its place. Although he felt weak and ill, a strangely stubborn confidence pervaded him. He had eaten his breakfast in thoughtful silence, not even hurt because she had turned away from his good-morning kiss.

Then, when she had told him Puhalski had sent his coolie to tell him to come to the Café Volga on his way to work, Sobolov had flown into a rage.

"God damn Puhalski!" he had shouted at her. "Every time I turn around, it's Puhalski this and Puhalski that. Will the son of a bitch never leave us alone?"

Maya had looked startled, but no surprise could still that tongue of hers once it got going. "He only wants to help us," she insisted, waving a spoon at him.

Sobolov had glared at her. The woman was naïve as a baby. "Listen," he told her, "Puhalski wouldn't throw us a stick if we were drowning. That one helps no one but himself."

Then when he got his hat off the nail in the wall, he'd stared at it morosely, wondering if around every corner for the rest of his life there was to be a Puhalski, cruel, ambitious, greedy, lying, and always pushing at him and arguing. And threatening.

Maya took an argumentative breath. It was a familiar sound, and he silenced her with a hand.

"All right, all right! I know," he said, suddenly deflated. "I'm his puppet now. If he pulls the string, I jump. But you don't realize what all this means. You think that what I do for him is a simple thing, because he says it's simple. Don't believe everything Puhalski says. It's not so simple; it's dangerous and it goes very strongly against my conscience." He stopped, beaten.

But Maya wasn't listening, and her mouth twisted disapprovingly. Following the direction of her gaze, he saw that she was watching his hands unconsciously roll and unroll the brim of his hat. The hat looked worse than ever, dirty and all but ruined. With a cry of revulsion, he wadded it furiously into a ball and threw it into the trash pail by the sink.

"Give me ten dollars of that money," he shouted. "I need a new hat!"

"Ten dollars for a hat?" Maya protested, her voice shrilling automatically with outrage.

"Of course not ten dollars for a hat! The hat is five at the most." Sobolov shook his head, feeling a surge of defiance that threatened to burst him. "Can I not have five dollars in my pocket if I want it? Who is the man of this wretched house, anyway?" He glared at her, wondering if he might be going too far, but unable to stop. "When we were penniless, you carped at me about money; now that we have some, are you going to badger me still? Do as I say, woman, and let me alone."

Maya turned and went meekly into the bedroom. Bewildered by his own temerity, Sobolov stood in the middle of the kitchen, panting.

[194]

"Remember, we aren't rich yet," she said, and handed him a sheaf of soiled bills. In spite of her tone, there was a new and unfamiliar look in her eye. If he hadn't known her so well, he might have thought it was respect.

"Bah!" he barked at her, then stamped angrily out the door. She always had to have the last word, he told himself, aware that he nevertheless felt strangely happy. Maya had started singing before he had gone a dozen steps. Hearing her, he nearly laughed aloud, although he didn't know quite why.

But those pleasant feelings had been short-lived; Puhalski had seen to that. Always Puhalski.

Cold and contemptuous, with no more human feeling than a toad in a mud puddle, Puhalski had listened with half an ear to his experience at the Police Yamen and had brushed it all aside as merely some sort of clerical mistake. That a man had died there meant nothing. Besides, Puhalski hadn't demanded his appearance that morning to listen to tales of woe, Sobolov had been summoned in order to hear Puhalski lay down the rules . . . the new rules. Now the Japanese wanted papers, special secret papers. To be exact, they wanted the plain texts in English of messages that were put into the diplomatic code and sent out by radio. It was terrifying.

He had tried to convince Puhalski that he had never even seen such papers, that it was impossible. Why not have him procure President Roosevelt's autograph? he had demanded in his exasperation. Or perhaps they would prefer to have the code books themselves? Sarcasm proved a mistake.

Puhalski had reached across the table and taken the front of his jacket in one enormous hand, and had shaken him like a rag doll.

"Listen to me, you little shit," Puhalski told him through gritted teeth. "Stop arguing and protesting. They have told me that they want these things, and now I have told you. You get them."

His eyes were shifting wildly. "And believe me, if you fumble this, you can expect no help from me. I'll be too busy looking after my own skin. Do you understand me?"

Sobolov had never seen Puhalski so overwrought. "Yes," he whispered.

"Good. Now, just in case you're tempted to try anything funny, do you know what will happen to you?"

Sobolov shook his head, staring at him like a bird at a snake.

"First, I'll inform *Mister* Edgerton what you have done: the money, the report, the lists, everything. Anonymously, of course." Puhalski gave his shark's grin. "Do you know what'll happen then?"

[195]

Sobolov's head oscillated ambiguously, although he knew perfectly well.

"You'll be fired," Puhalski told him with considerable satisfaction. "Your job will be finished, you and Maya will be finished, and Anya will be finished. But that won't be all. Then I'll see to it the Japs know how clumsy you have been. What you saw at the Police Yamen will seem like children playing in a sandbox compared to what they will do to you . . . to say nothing of what they'll do to Maya and Anya. Think that over!" Puhalski stood up then and glared down at him, seeming taller and more menacing, more implacable than ever. "Now get out of here!" Thus had Sobolov's feeble illusion of manhood been disposed of.

Sobolov blinked and stared cautiously around the Chancery office. Besides himself, only Miss Kung was in the big room. She was busy at her interminable typing, and paying no attention to him.

Sobolov felt like a cricket in a cage. He could look out, but there was no way to escape. If only he'd resisted them in the beginning. If he'd given them nothing, he could go to Mr. Edgerton now and ask for help. But that was nonsense: if only, if only! What could Mr. Edgerton have done, even had he been so inclined? Nothing.

The trouble was—and the knowledge made him tremble—the sort of papers the Japanese wanted could be got. It should have been impossible, but it wasn't. In fact, there was every chance that it could be ridiculously easy. Mr. Edgerton had become very careless lately, and more than once Sobolov had picked up after him. The papers were minor things mostly, and of no concern outside the office, but not all of them. There were days when Mr. Edgerton just didn't seem to be paying much attention to what he was doing, as though he had some personal problem weighing on his mind. Though what a man like him, a well-to-do American with a wonderful profession, could find to worry about so intensely was something Sobolov found difficult to imagine.

Since the Chancery was shorthanded, Mr. Edgerton had been doing the code work himself. Except for the weekly report to Washington, there really wasn't very much of it. But the weekly report was done on Thursday. Sobolov didn't have to look at any calendar to know that today was Thursday.

It had been late in the afternoon of the previous Thursday when he had gone into Mr. Edgerton's office to leave some translations on his desk. Mr. Edgerton had already left for the day. There on the desk, lying half-hidden under a correspondence tray, were several sheets of yellow tablet paper covered with Mr. Edgerton's familiar scrawl. Sobolov's eyes had rested on the topmost sheet, long enough to see that this was something never handled in the General Office, that, in fact, it was the draft of the weekly cable to Washington. Sobolov had muddled over what to do next, but not for very long. He knew the office routine, and so he followed it: he burned the papers in the barrel behind the Chancery, and stirred the ashes into dust with a stick.

That simple act had made him very happy. He felt loyal and responsible; he had preserved his benefactor from embarrassment. That Mr. Edgerton would never know of it only added merit to the act.

And now it was Thursday again, and Mr. Edgerton was vaguer and more preoccupied than ever, and more than ever likely to be careless.

A dim resentment stirred inside Andrei Sobolov. What right had Mr. Edgerton to tempt him in this awful way on the very day when Puhalski was squeezing him so hard? If only it were Wednesday, he would have a day to think of some way out; or Friday: then he would have a whole week. But it was Thursday, and in his heart Sobolov was certain that Mr. Edgerton would be careless again. He'd get his opportunity, but he knew he could never get away with it. Disaster was bound to strike; that was his destiny. They would all be ruined, every one of them, and all his struggle and worry would have been for nothing, and Anya . . . what would become of Anya?

Sobolov didn't know what to do.

♟♟

Mouth dry and head aching dully, Edgerton stirred among his deskful of papers. He had slept badly, and what sleep he'd had was punctured by confusing dreams. In one, some lascivious deity had offered him the willing charms of both Tamara and Valerie together. But when it came time for him to join them in a huge circular bed, he'd been mortified to discover that he was impotent. His tiny, flaccid penis was shrinking. Fortunately he awoke before it disappeared altogether.

He'd gone to bed aroused and restless, annoyed with the Procters both for their untimely arrival and their teasing chitchat thereafter. And annoyed with himself for not taking Valerie on the seat of his car, as she seemed to be asking him to do when she walked out with him. To relax himself, he'd mixed a strong whiskey before turning in and had smoked too many cigarettes while drinking it.

It promised to be a tiresome day. His energy of the day before had vanished. The work that lay ahead of him reeked of futility and he knew he would have to drive himself to attend to it.

[197]

Mr. Sobolov, pale as a ghost, had come in a few minutes late insisting that, yes, everything was arranged with regard to his papers, and no, he was not ill. He looked very ill indeed. He'd been working on Tanaka's letter for over an hour but hadn't yet produced a translation. Edgerton wanted to go to the door and shout to Sobolov to for Christ's sake, get off his fat ass and translate the letter. He hoped that it would never become necessary for him to tell Procter about that letter. Procter was a stickler for protocol, for channels, and for what he liked to call the chain of command. His aristocratic face would purse up like a prune were he to learn that Edgerton had taken it upon himself to correspond directly with an officer of the Japanese Army—and on Legation stationery to boot. Staring down at the disorder of his desk, Edgerton drummed his fingers restlessly.

The telephone intruded insistently.

"A Chinese gentleman on the line," Miss Kung announced apologetically, as though it were somehow her fault.

"Well, who the hell is it?" Edgerton snapped.

"He won't give his name," Miss Kung whispered, abashed.

"Forgive me, Miss Kung. I didn't mean to be rude," Edgerton said, exasperated with himself. "Put him on, please."

The instrument buzzed and crackled as Miss Kung made the connection. Pessimistically Edgerton waited, wondering who it would turn out to be. An irate comprador with an unpaid bill for groceries delivered to a mission? A curio dealer whose tourist customer was not at the hotel at which he had claimed to be staying and who, in fact, had left for Shanghai with his art treasure the week before? A student wanting a visa to study in America? The father of a pregnant girl whose Marine boyfriend was called by the name of Sam? The diplomatic life, Edgerton thought sourly, summing up a few of the possibilities.

"Hello!" Edgerton prompted loudly, determined to deal shortly with whomever it might be.

"A thousand respectful greetings," a hoarse Mandarin voice intoned, oily and obsequious. "This miserable boatman requests an audience with the mighty warrior."

Edgerton's laugh was relieved. "O famous sharpshooter, this unworthy coolie awaits your honor's pleasure," he answered in the same manner.

Li started to ask after his health, then cursed pungently. "Wang is ringing for me; he'll be in here in a minute if I don't go to him. Can you meet me on the wall, down by the wire near the Chien Men tower?"

[198]

"When?"

"Half an hour?"

"Yes."

Li had made him laugh, but Edgerton's face was serious as he hung up the phone. He'd heard nothing from him for several months. Li was a cautious, economical man, not given to wasting time in pointless meetings. Edgerton leaned back in his chair with a frown.

When he'd first returned to Peking about two years before, after a tour of duty in Shanghai, he'd run into Li on the street. They hadn't seen each other for several years and then it had been in Tientsin, where they'd first met. Edgerton had hurried forward, feeling glad and full of questions. To his chagrin, Li had about-faced, as though suddenly remembering an errand elsewhere, and disappeared down a narrow path between two shops. Refusing to be avoided, Edgerton had followed to find Li waiting. Shamefaced, he'd muttered something about times changing and the unwisdom of their being seen together in public. Not wise for Li, obviously; Edgerton could only guess at the internal jealousies and maneuverings in the Police Yamen. In the months that followed Li had called him several times with bits of inside news of Americans with incipient difficulties. It was very helpful, and Edgerton was often able to straighten matters out before official notice had to be taken.

Then, some months before the battle at the Marco Polo Bridge, his car had been stalled by a passing funeral procession. With sad detachment, Edgerton had watched the coffins pass. There were two; one of adult size and, beside it, pitifully small, a child's. The sight had touched him deeply, in spite of his years in a land where death was as commonplace as dust. There was the usual photograph riding with the coffins, a woman with a little boy standing in her lap, both smiling anxiously at the camera. Edgerton's eyes had followed the photograph until, into the corner of his vision, strode a solitary figure. It was Li Ching-wei, tall, thin, and awkward in his white mourner's gown.

The spectacle had hit Edgerton hard and made him regret even more the loss or lapse of that cautiously developed friendship, begun so oddly with what Edgerton always thought of as the cops and robbers episode in Tientsin.

Snapping himself out of his woolgathering, he looked at his watch. He ought to leave the Chancery in ten minutes.

He swiveled in his chair, wondering whether or not to wait for Sobolov. Franklin Procter's figure appeared suddenly in his field of vision, pushing open the Chancery door. His dapper figure quickly disappeared into the foyer. It was barely half-past eight.

[199]

Surprised, Edgerton was just rising to go down to Procter's office when his door opened and Procter appeared, looking wan and peaked. Hoping to cheer him up, Edgerton gave his watch an incredulous inspection. "To what do we owe this visitation?" he asked. "Has war been declared?"

"Spare me your rather heavy humor, if you please. This promises to be a wretched day for me; my patience is already nearing its end." He patted his forehead with a folded handkerchief, pulled up the creases of his trousers, and sat down.

"What seems to be the trouble? You seemed jolly enough last night."

"Please don't mention last night. No sooner had you left than my unspeakable ailment assaulted me with renewed fury."

"You look terrible," Edgerton said. "You ought to be in bed."

"I know. And I intend to be very soon. I wouldn't have come in at all except that the whole East District telephone exchange is on the blink."

"Life in the mysterious East."

"Yes. A day inauspiciously begun. My dunce of a chauffeur couldn't get the car started. He left the lights on, or something, and the battery ran down. There was nothing for it, but to make the journey by rickshaw."

"Well, you see more that way."

"And smell more."

"True," Edgerton said. "But what was all this agony and travail in aid of? Why didn't you send me a note and stay home?"

"I was tempted but I wanted to get something to do. There are a lot of back reports I've been wanting to go over, including, by the way, the file of your Mr. Sobolov's translations from the press."

"My Mr. Sobolov and I are gratified."

A grimace of intense distress crossed Procter's face, and he hurried to the door with a muttered excuse.

Edgerton lighted a cigarette and turned to stare out of the window at the large rectangle of lawn which fronted the Chancery building. Procter's arrival reminded him of Tamara, and he wondered morosely what she was doing. Bills, probably, or typing one of those letters the inexhaustible manager sent after departed members with delinquent accounts. She hadn't phoned yet. He was on the verge of calling her when Procter returned, looking relieved though somewhat paler.

"How much longer must I endure this torture?"

"Several days, I'm afraid."

Procter groaned.

"You should check in at the Marine dispensary, as long as you're here. Dr. Ramsey claims to have invented an excellent specific."

[200]

Procter's face brightened at this ray of hope. "Good idea; I shall." Then he smiled slyly. "And now for some really good news!"

Edgerton waited suspiciously.

"*You* will have to stand in for me at Tungchow."

"At Tungchow?"

"Yes; my speech to the missionary conclave."

"Oh, Christ!" Edgerton sighed. "It's today?"

"This afternoon at three, in the assembly room of the American School."

Edgerton's mind groped futilely for a way out. "I suppose I must lie gracefully and say I'm delighted. What's your topic: Papal infallibility and Santa Claus?"

"Ha, ha," Procter said without amusement.

Glumly Edgerton remembered Procter's possible sensitivity about religion. Jimmy Chang's experience should have warned him.

"As a matter of fact," Procter went on rather frostily, "I intended to inform them of the Department's latest directive to us about discouraging missionaries and other Americans from going to live and work in out-of-the-way places. Tensions in the countryside, bandits, guerrillas, Japanese military operations, undisciplined troops . . . all that sort of thing must be emphasized most strongly. This latest incident involving Dr. Lewis can only help convince them of the wisdom of the Department's advice. They must be made to understand that the practice of sending gunboats and Marines to the rescue is passé; quite out of the question these days."

Producing an envelope from an inside pocket, Procter went on, "Here are some notes I made; you might care to look them over."

"I shall be proud to follow them faithfully."

Procter frowned at him. "Don't kid me, John. Just get the main points across and try not to alienate these people."

"Calm yourself, please," Edgerton said, giving him a bland look. Imagining the cramps and churnings of Procter's poor stomach, it was easy to forgive him for being testy. "Missionaries find me unfailingly charming and persuasive. I've been dealing with them for years."

"Well, I hope they'll find you persuasive in this instance," Procter said, somewhat mollified. "One thing we don't need is a bloody incident in some remote mission." Procter cleared his throat. "And as for dealing with them, I seem to recall an occasion when you were reported as having been somewhat less than charming."

Edgerton's laugh was rueful. "I confess. But remember, that was *force majeure.* I had to be rude to the silly buggers in order to save their fat asses. But today I promise to conduct myself in a way that'll be in every particular above reproach. How's that?"

[201]

Procter gave him a grudging smile. "Please do so. Now, here's another thing: I was going to take the ladies with me, as neither of them has seen anything of the countryside. Unfortunately, poor Pamela is also indisposed, but when I told Valerie you might be going in my stead, she lit up like a bulb. You'll take her, won't you?"

"Now I really am delighted," Edgerton said. He'd bring her by the San Kwan Miao on the way back.

"You're lucky to be having Valerie along as your consort . . ." Procter stopped, reddening. "Um . . . not quite the right word."

Edgerton chuckled gently. "I quite understand. She can help with the driving, read maps, change tires . . . that sort of thing."

"I knew you'd see it in a practical light." Procter got to his feet with a sigh. "Now, I'll get the things from my office and trek home."

"Look here, Franklin, take my car," Edgerton said. "I'll get the *t'ai ch'ing* to drive you. You don't need another rickshaw ride today, I'm sure."

Procter's face flooded with relief. "That's very thoughtful of you."

"Not at all. I'll tell him to take you by the sick bay first. And you might tell Valerie I'll pick her up at . . . let's see: half-past one. It's only fifteen miles, but the road is never in very good shape. That'll allow us an hour's traveling time and a half hour for contingencies."

"Splendid! This is a great load off my mind, John. I knew I could count on you."

Seeing Procter huddled in the back seat, Edgerton blessed his own galvanized innards, tempered into a general immunity by his years in China. But time was racing by, and he was already late for his meeting with Li. Sobolov would have to wait.

He was drenched with sweat by the time he'd hiked up the long ramp to the top of the wall. He took off his jacket and loosened his tie, thankful for the faint breeze that stirred among the weed-grown bricks. He looked around for a minute, breathing deeply.

The five-mile stretch of wall on which he stood not only divided the Tartar and Chinese cities, but in this short segment also formed the southern wall of the Legation Quarter itself. At its eastern and western extremities, concertinas of barbed wire had been laid down, and at night sentries from the Legations patrolled there.

Eighteen years before, Edgerton had taken his first walk in Peking along this bit of wall and it had become a favorite strolling place. He couldn't remember the last time he'd been on it.

To the west of him, the Ch'ien Men tower rose up in shabby and dilapidated dignity, enormous and archaic and useless. Midway between himself and it lay the barbed wire entanglement, but the rest of the broad top of the wall was empty. There was no sign of Li.

He was fifteen minutes late; he realized that Li might have come and gone. That would be a mess. Li wouldn't have suggested meeting were it not important, and it would not do for Edgerton to telephone him. Of course, Li might himself be late. The only thing to do was to go on down to the wire and be patient. Edgerton slung his coat over his shoulder and started off.

Just below him was the Main Railway Station. A muted chug and clatter drifted up to him, accompanied by a whiff of that unforgettable mixture of steam and coal dust indispensable to the ambience of trains. A whistle tooted peremptorily, two short blasts, ordering someone out of the way.

He had almost reached the rusty barbed wire before he saw Li sitting in one of the crenels of the parapet with only his black clad legs and large policeman's boots protruding.

Li must have heard him coming, for he boosted himself out and, after looking carefully in both directions, sauntered over to the wire.

Li was ageless, Edgerton thought, and still looked much the same as on the evening they had met in the Police Yamen of what was still called the German Concession in Tientsin. How long had it been? Eight, nine years? Li had been a corporal then, and had shown little enthusiasm for a mission with a strange American as his only assistant.

But now when they came face to face, Edgerton saw the lines beside the mouth and the wrinkles around the eyes. Most of them were new since their last meeting, and new also was a long scar which began in the hair over Li's right temple and disappeared under his chin. It looked as if it could have been very nearly fatal.

"You appear very prosperous," Li said, reaching across the wire to shake Edgerton's outstretched hand.

Edgerton patted his stomach. "Too prosperous. Too many papers and no adventures. How are you?"

"Surviving, John. Nothing lasts forever."

"I keep telling myself that," Edgerton said. "And now, what new thing is about to afflict us?"

"I'll tell you, but while I think of it, let me apologize for not warning you about Taylor and his license plates." Li paused, shrugging. "He's not in my precinct; by the time I heard of the matter, Wu already had his teeth in it."

"Don't worry. It gave me an opportunity to instruct Taylor in a few of the facts of life." Edgerton laughed at the memory. "Then I threw him out of the office."

[203]

Li looked amused. "You haven't changed, then?"

"Not too much, I hope."

"That makes me glad." Li's face turned serious. "I don't know what is about to happen, but some peculiar events have taken place already, involving your Russian, Sobolov."

Even in the midst of his surprise, Edgerton asked himself why everyone insisted that Sobolov was "his" Russian. Sobolov! It was the last name he expected to hear. Then he remembered the Russian's trip to the Yamen. "What's he done?" he asked, wondering bitterly if Sobolov was going to turn out to be less ingenuous than he seemed.

"That's just it: nothing that I know of. You knew that he was to report to my esteemed superior, Captain Wang?"

"Yes. Your other esteemed superior, Major Wu, called me about it. I thought it was something about his identity booklet."

Li frowned, then spat disgustedly onto the bricks. Listening to Li describe what had happened to Sobolov made Edgerton more confused than ever. The whole thing struck him as highly incongruous. That the Japanese and the police would indulge in such practices was believable enough. But that they would put on such a show for a man like Sobolov was ridiculous.

When Li came to the end, Edgerton could only stare at him. "Do you think I ought to ask him about it? It might be a simpler business than we think," he said.

Li shook his head politely. "I don't think that is a good idea just yet. But keep an eye on him for the present. I'll be checking further. You see, there is another aspect of all this that bothers me. It may be merely a coincidence, but I have learned to be suspicious of coincidences. Colonel Tanaka is somehow involved."

Edgerton felt his face stiffen with dismay and there crossed his mind the possibility that he had bitten off more than he could comfortably chew.

"Tanaka," Edgerton repeated, hiding his concern. "I met him once. Fat little man, head of the Military Police." His mind groped for the link which would draw everything together and make it clear to him.

"Yes," Li said, then hesitated. "It's supposed to be a Japanese secret," he went on slowly, "but Tanaka is slated to be chief Kempeitai man for the Peking district."

Cold fingers gripped Edgerton's heart. Anyone who had followed events in Japan over the past ten years knew of the Kempeitai and its domination by the worst elements in the War Office. It had become known as the thought police. He was strongly tempted to ask Li if he knew anything about Tamara's mother, but something held him back.

It hardly seemed likely that the Army would involve the Chinese police in such a matter. The investigation underway in Tamara's neighborhood for stolen goods, if it existed other than in local rumor, was probably just that. In any case, it seemed unlikely that so formidable an organization as the Kempeitai would concern itself with the injuries befalling drunken soldiers.

"Knowing that the Russian works for you, I thought you ought to know Tanaka's interested in him, and maybe in his job." Li took off his cap and ran a hand across his cropped scalp. "Well, now you know as much as I do."

"Thanks, my friend," Edgerton said, relieved to find at least a few of his problems simplifying themselves.

Li nodded. "Meanwhile, I will be investigating. Now, I must be getting back or Wang will be searching my desk." He touched a forefinger to the visor of his cap. *"T'sai chen."*

"T'sai-chen," Edgerton echoed, hoping that it really would be soon. He stood there watching until Li came to the gate tower and disappeared down a ramp toward Ch'ien Men Chieh.

Their relationship was a strange one, having grown upon the narrow foundation of the one escapade. It seemed compounded of such disparate ingredients as shared danger and excitement, and the curiosity between men of totally different cultures, who discover that in their humanity, or perhaps merely in their manliness, there are more things common to them both than they had guessed. On his own side, Edgerton felt an instinctive desire to come closer to this country in which he was destined to spend so many years on the business of his own nation. And then there was nostalgia. In spite of the war, life now seemed rather straitlaced. Nowadays, for an American vice-consul and a Chinese police corporal to rescue bodily and with firearms some hapless American would be unthinkable. Then, it had been merely an expedient unavoidable under the circumstances. *Mei-yu-fah-tzu.*

Standing there, Edgerton felt the tug of diverse impulses. But several things remained to be done if he were to get away that afternoon. And foremost among them was Tanaka's letter . . . Sobolov was surely finished with it by now. Li's extraordinary information made it imperative that the Tanaka business be understood at once. Edgerton started back to the Chancery, reluctantly directing his thoughts ahead to the tasks awaiting him.

He would speak to Smith first. Smith would be alone in the Chancery when he left for Tungchow, and ought to know that Procter was convalescing at home. And in the light of what Li had told him, it might be a good thing for Smith to undertake a discreet review of the

Legation's security measures. His fresh eye might very well detect mistakes which they could have all been blithely making. Security, Edgerton knew, was liable to neglect from him; it had always bored him. The Chancery could be wide open. Sobolov and Tanaka? He was unable to credit it.

There was the weekly summary to write up and encode. It was a dull chore. Before long he could turn the code books and all that mumbo jumbo over to someone else. The report went by Marine Corps radio to the American gunboat anchored in the river at Tientsin to be relayed to the big Navy transmitter at Cavite in the Philippines, thence to Washington. Coded traffic used to go by commercial cable, but the service had become too slow and too uncertain. Naturally the Japanese monitored all the frequencies just as they had copied all the messages sent to the telegraph office, but the diplomatic code was supposed to be a good one. The code books were changed at randomly spaced intervals according to complicated schedules emanating from the State Department. The people who knew about those things claimed the system was literally foolproof.

&&

Staring at the paper in his hand, Sobolov felt a pang of shame. Three hours spent and still not finished, the work filled with cross-outs and erasures. It would have to be recopied.

And from those three hours, only a hazy impression of the office's activity remained in his mind. Mr. Procter had come in early and departed almost immediately with Mr. Edgerton practically following him out the door. Some time later, an hour perhaps, Mr. Edgerton had returned, his face clouded and preoccupied. He had gone on down the hall to the small office occupied by Mr. Smith, but now he was back at his own desk. Sobolov could hear the rattle of his typewriter through the closed door. Mr. Edgerton almost never typed things himself unless he was working on a classified paper.

As soon as he was done typing, Mr. Edgerton would go upstairs to use the code books that were kept in the safe in the office of the absent Minister. He would be gone from his own office no more than thirty minutes.

If only Mr. Edgerton would be careless again . . . Sobolov clutched at the notion that his troubles would then be over. Puhalski and the Japanese would have what they wanted . . . was it not reasonable to expect them then to leave him alone? No, neither reasonable nor likely, his intelligence told him. The more they got, the greedier they would become. Sooner or later he'd be caught. If only he could postpone that inevitable moment until Anya were safely out of China . . . he would settle for that outcome without a quibble. His ruin would be hard on Maya but she was still young and tough. She would survive. But for the gentle and helpless Anya he would do anything. He would lie and cheat and steal and betray himself and his own honor. And he would betray Mr. Edgerton as well, for there was no way for Mr. Edgerton to avoid being involved in his disgrace.

The sound of Mr. Edgerton's typing ceased, and there was a long period of silence from his office. Sobolov waited rigidly, hardly breathing.

Twenty minutes later, Mr. Edgerton emerged with some papers in his hand and headed down the corridor toward the stairs. Sobolov could not avoid the irrelevant observation that Mr. Edgerton's shoes squeaked. Immobilized, he sat there and listened to the ascending footsteps. A door slammed overhead and the bell on Miss Kung's typewriter carriage chimed gaily. The moment had arrived.

Sobolov cleared his throat and picked up the translation. Whistling tunelessly, he ambled toward Mr. Edgerton's office. The rhythm of Miss Kung's tapping fingers continued without a falter.

The door stood open a few inches; Sobolov gingerly gave it a push. The distance to the desk seemed vast, and the floor precariously tilted. Sobolov's stomach churned. Summoning all his determination he crossed the soft expanse of carpet to consummate his betrayal.

The top of the desk was bare of papers, the correspondence baskets contained nothing of interest. Except for a crumpled cigarette package, the wastebasket was empty. With a trembling hand, Sobolov pulled open the drawers of the desk one by one and looked inside. There were no worksheets. Mr. Edgerton had not made the same mistake twice.

Numb, not knowing whether to be glad or sorry, Sobolov placed the translation on the blotter and tiptoed from the room. But instead of going back to his desk, he continued like a sleepwalker down the hall and into the washroom. He took off his coat and hung it up, then locked the door. Using the tank of the toilet to steady himself, he got carefully to his knees. Only when he was in position, did he permit himself to vomit into the bowl.

For several minutes after the last dry spasm he knelt there listening to the tank refill. The porcelain felt cold against his cheek. If only he could stay there and rest, out of the sight of everyone, until it was time to go home.

With infinite reluctance he got to his feet, put on his coat, dashed

[207]

water into his face, and returned to his desk. For fifteen minutes he sat there in a sort of trance, waiting passively for his mind to return to normal. He had not the foggiest notion what he was going to do.

Finally Mr. Edgerton returned to his office and closed the door.

Feeling as if he were being manipulated by exterior forces, Sobolov found himself on his feet and moving. What his purpose was, he could not really have said. All he knew was that he was going to see Mr. Edgerton. He tapped hesitantly on the door, opened it, and walked to the edge of the carpet.

Mr. Edgerton raised his eyes and looked at him strangely. His frown was deeper than usual and his brown eyes were cold and unfriendly. "What is it, Mr. Sobolov?" he asked in a precise and impersonal voice.

"I must talk to you." The words surprised Sobolov. They seemed to rise involuntarily from some inner source to echo briefly in the dried gourd that was his head, then issue mechanically from his mouth. "I am in terrible trouble," he said.

The room lurched sickeningly, and the flat surface of the green rug began to rise in front of him until it towered over his head like the front of an enormous wave, and the sound of an endless succession of combers marching toward him rumbled in his ears. Remembering that he couldn't swim, Sobolov fainted.

♣♣

Delicious odors rose from the tray which his orderly had just placed on the desk before him. Ordinarily Colonel Tanaka would not have approved of so large a midday meal, but on this day a small celebration was indicated. It was a splendid day, and Colonel Tanaka was very hungry.

One after another he uncovered the dishes and examined their contents, his mouth watering. He would have a good lunch, tidy up a few matters, and go right home. Puhalski had been instructed to have the woman there by two o'clock, and Tanaka wanted to take a bath and change into his best uniform. He paused for a moment, staring out of the window and pondering whether or not to wear his decorations. Women were impressed by things like that; he decided to wear them. The decision made him smile.

Ever since he had first seen the woman, he had experienced great difficulty in concentrating on his work. He would be in the midst of a telephone call or in conference with his subordinates when some portion of her anatomy would materialize in his thoughts and distract him in midsentence. It was the sort of thing which could become embarrassing; he owed it to the Emperor no less than to himself to keep his mind clear. Even so, he had considered all the ramifications with great care before making his decision. By a process of impeccable logic he had concluded that he ought at least to make the woman's acquaintance. She knew nothing of his plans for her husband and need never know. There was no bar to his being able to make, and to maintain, an excellent impression on her. She probably spoke Chinese and perhaps even a little English. Well, he spoke English and a little Chinese. They should get on famously. He would be the perfect officer and gentleman. They would have tea together and he would show her his house and his possessions. Perhaps she would accept a small gift from among them as a token of his good intentions. But such a gift might prove indiscreet. On the other hand, a sum of money, offered subtly so as not to offend, would do very nicely.

Colonel Tanaka smacked his lips and picked up his chopsticks. He was fortunate there was a good restaurant close by. One thing you had to say for the Chinese, they really knew how to cook.

Tanaka smiled around a mouthful of rice and shook his head. Poor Puhalski! He'd been very upset about the treatment given Sobolov at the Police Yamen. Of course that blunderer, Captain Wang, had gone farther than Tanaka intended. But there was no real harm done. Puhalski was afraid Sobolov was going to slip out of his own hands; he had reason to worry; as an amateur he knew nothing of the use of fear in controlling agents. In the end, Sobolov's experience at the Yamen had been salutary, as witness his present docility. Puhalski had a lot to learn.

His thoughts turned to the problem of a suitable, public punishment of the woman responsible for the unfortunate Seiko's injuries. So far the searches he'd instituted had proved unproductive. The character of the Special Unit was too Japanese; no Chinese would tell a S.U. man anything unless tortured into it. And there was no time for torture. The Chinese police had continued their own slow work until the evening before, when Tanaka had ordered them to desist. He had done this because the logical processes of his mind had brought him the information he sought.

Thinking about it now, Tanaka felt a glow of pride warm his blood. As he had confidently expected, a brilliant flash of intuition had indicated that the woman almost had to be either Edgerton's half-caste mistress or her mother. Acting upon this instinctive premise, Tanaka had taken the next logical step.

Among the personnel of S.U. was a Manchurian Japanese who could pass for Chinese. Sent into the Lius' neighborhood in the guise of a telephone repair man, he had engaged the woman who lived down-stairs from the Lius in conversation. The fact that the elder Liu woman had been mysteriously ill following the night of Seiko's mishap and had subsequently gone to visit relatives had been simple enough to discover. It fitted too perfectly to be ignored. Vague as it was, Seiko's description eliminated the half-caste as too young and too tall. Tana-ka's intuition stood confirmed.

The half-caste still occupied the flat, although at the time of the Manchurian's call, she had not yet returned from work. Just the same, the pattern of her movements had been easy enough to determine. Other pertinent information about her had already been entered in Edgerton's dossier.

In spite of his pride in this piece of work, Tanaka could not erase from his mind the suspicion that the despised Edgerton had tricked him . . . or had attempted to.

Tanaka was certain that by having the daughter followed he could locate the mother, but that would take time. Also, he was confident he could physically twist the information from her by either fright or force. He had decided he didn't want to go about it that way.

When the Manchurian had made his report, Tanaka came to the certain conclusion that not only did Edgerton know where the woman was, but that he had actually provided the hiding place for her, proba-bly somewhere in the Legation Quarter. It was ridiculous that such an anachronism remained inviolable more than a year after the surren-der of the city, but there it was. Tanaka would send his men into the Quarter only with the greatest reluctance. If one of them were caught, Minister Saito's wrath would be incandescent, and so would General Kawasaki's . . . with Itaki's hateful, balloonlike face smirking know-ingly from the sidelines, waiting.

But none of these risks would be necessary. Tanaka had considered the problem carefully and from every angle, and he had solved it. It would not even be necessary for Edgerton to tell him the location of the woman. He would arrange it so Edgerton would have no choice but to deliver her in person.

A sudden thought occurred to Tanaka. Shaking his head, he smiled at the irony of it. It would be Sobolov, of course, who would translate his reply to Edgerton's insulting memorandum. Although Tanaka could as easily have written in English, he had chosen Japanese out of reasons of pride.

Tanaka had worded the reply carefully, intending it to draw Edger-ton into a confrontation. From that splendid moment the evening before when he'd realized the beautiful simplicity of the lever he held against the American, Tanaka knew that he must personally witness its effect. Once he'd realized the inexorability of success, Tanaka had been suffused by a great calm. It was this calm which had prompted him to give Puhalski his instructions and freed Tanaka himself to enjoy this delightful sense of anticipation. Since Edgerton's response would determine the timing of his next move, Tanaka had the sensation of being on holiday.

The Japanese Legation had predicted that Edgerton would be due for reassignment within a year's time. It was a pity. Now that Tanaka knew he held the key to Edgerton's cooperation, he realized that he would miss him. Procter was too conventional; the likes of Yamaguchi could handle him.

Tanaka pulled thoughtfully at a plump earlobe before returning his undivided attention to his lunch.

♟♟

Opening his eyes, Sobolov wondered dizzily what was happening. Mr. Edgerton was peering apprehensively into his face, Miss Kung was next to him, with a glass of water in her hand, her cheeks wet with tears. Miss Kung tended to cry without much provocation. Sobolov wondered what it was this time. He turned his head cautiously and realized that he was flat on his back on the floor of Mr. Edgerton's office. How strange! Mr. Chiang was standing in the doorway, looking on with obvious disapproval. Then Sobolov remembered.

"Are you all right, Mr. Sobolov?"

Sobolov nodded, and the sore spot on the back of his head rubbed against the coarse nap of the rug. He winced and tried to sit up. He felt Mr. Edgerton's arm behind his shoulders. Miss Kung handed him the water and Sobolov gulped it down. Mr. Edgerton and Mr. Chiang helped him into the chair beside the desk. Sobolov leaned back. Vaguely he heard Mr. Edgerton dismiss the others and the sound of the door closing off the murmur of their curious voices.

Mr. Edgerton sat down and frowned at him with concern. "I think I'd better call the doctor from the Marine dispensary," he said.

"Oh, no, please!" It was somehow imperative that there should be no more fuss. "I'm all right now . . . just a dizzy spell."

Mr. Edgerton looked doubtful. "Well, if you say so," he said, and began gathering up the papers he had been looking at when Sobolov entered the room, including the translation. He slid them all into the center drawer of his desk. He leaned forward then, his elbows on the blotter and his chin on his fists, and stared intently into Sobolov's eyes.

[211]

"Now then, what is all this about some terrible trouble?" he asked, not unkindly.

Slowly, brokenly, with shame and resignation, Sobolov heard himself recite the story of Puhalski and the Japanese and the squeeze they had him in. The only change in Mr. Edgerton's expression was that his frown gradually grew deeper. When Sobolov came to the part about finding the worksheets of last week's report, Mr. Edgerton lowered his eyes and his face grew red.

Sobolov stopped then, and there was a long silence in the room. Mr. Edgerton covered his eyes with a hand and just sat there; he seemed hardly to be breathing. Finally he sighed loudly, gave his head a shake, and lighted a cigarette.

"Why didn't you tell me about burning the papers?" he asked.

"I didn't want to embarrass you, to make you lose face."

Mr. Edgerton gave a humorless laugh.

"And what about today? If you'd found my worksheets, would you have taken them?"

Sobolov wanted desperately to lie, but could not. "I don't know," he whispered.

Mr. Edgerton nodded. "Okay. Now tell me in detail everything you have reported to them so far."

He listened carefully while Sobolov spoke, and when Sobolov had finished he scratched his head thoughtfully, put his feet up on the corner of the desk, and stared at the portrait of Abraham Lincoln, frowning through the smoke from his cigarette.

To Sobolov the scene was totally unreal. He had never expected Mr. Edgerton to be so patient . . . he wasn't even angry.

Mr. Edgerton was probably trying to decide what to do with him. In his mind's eye, Sobolov could see a detachment of Marines marching over to lock him up until the Chinese police could be sent for. He dreaded the thought of going back to the Yamen and all that would inevitably follow . . . Captain Wang would be furious . . . but in a vague sort of way he was glad that at last it was all over. He wondered if Mr. Edgerton would let him send a message to Maya before they took him away. Poor Maya! She would certainly be angry. And Anya. Maya would just have to do her best to protect Anya, though how she was to manage that, Sobolov had no idea. The thought brought him to the verge of tears and made his head ache.

"Why didn't you come to me at once, when this business was first suggested to you?" Mr. Edgerton asked at last.

"I was afraid. They said they wouldn't let Anya go to America if I didn't do what I was told."

"Well, it's too bad you believed all that. It's one thing to make threats and quite another to put them into effect. If the U.S. Government is willing to grant a visa to a young girl, the Japanese are not likely to make an issue of it, not with all this as background." Mr. Edgerton gave an abrupt wave of his hand. "Don't worry about Anya; we can work all that out when the time comes."

Sobolov stared in disbelief; it didn't seem possible. "You mean Anya can still go to America?"

Mr. Edgerton looked puzzled. "Why, of course."

"But if I'm in prison . . ."

"Who said anything about prison. The Legation will see to it that no one imprisons its employees without cause. Don't worry about that either." He tapped his teeth thoughtfully with a pencil. "Just the same, they can make things very uncomfortable for you and your wife," Mr. Edgerton went on.

Uncomfortable was not the word Sobolov was thinking of. Even if the Americans brought no charges against him, things would be very difficult. He would have no job and Puhalski would be snapping at his heels, and right behind him would be the Japanese. They would want the money returned. Sobolov began to regret the hasty purchase of that hat.

"When they come back, I'll speak to the Sloanes about letting Anya stay with them, if you'd like. She'll be safe living in their house in case the Japanese try and get nasty. As for you and Mrs. Sobolov, I don't know. Maybe we can make some temporary arrangements here in the Legation Quarter. In any case we're not completely without influence. I can let it be known through some acquaintances in the Provisional Government that you are informally under American protection. I think they'll decide it's more discreet to leave you all alone. The Japanese seem to have a weakness for spontaneous incidents; when they know the facts beforehand, they're less inclined to hasty action." Mr. Edgerton gave him an encouraging nod, as if to say: well, that takes care of that.

Sobolov couldn't believe his ears. Caution told him to keep his mouth shut, but he couldn't suppress the turmoil of questions in his mind. "I . . . I don't understand," he stuttered finally.

Mr. Edgerton looked baffled.

"But my job?" Sobolov wailed in an agony of uncertainty. "Aren't you going to discharge me?"

Mr. Edgerton's laugh was wearily patient. "No, Mr. Sobolov, I'm not going to discharge you." He paused and frowned. "I suppose I ought to lecture you," he said, looking up with a slight smile, "but I

[213]

can't bring myself to do it. Besides, I'm inclined to doubt that any real harm has been done . . . to us. The information which you've given them is nonsense, really. They must have files bulging with that sort of trivia about every legation in Peking, and probably everywhere else. And nobody cares. My guess is that you were being tested, or perhaps they merely wanted you to incriminate yourself. As you pointed out, the moment you began, they had a hold over you." Mr. Edgerton shook his head. "No, the way I see it, you've proved your loyalty. Few people in your position would have burned those worksheets. I don't think you need to worry about your job. But you must understand that I'll have to discuss all this with Mr. Procter. I'm sure he'll see it my way, but in the end the decision will be his." Mr. Edgerton paused. He took out another cigarette and began tamping it against the table top. After inspecting it with care, he lighted it. "In the meantime, do you think you can stall them off for a few days? Put them off with excuses?" he asked. "For your own safety they mustn't know you've said anything to me, of course," Mr. Edgerton looked apologetic. "I'm a novice at this spy business, or I'd give you some useful suggestions."

Sobolov could only stare, incredulous at the words he was hearing. He nodded, his mouth working soundlessly.

Mr. Edgerton held up a hand. "No more for now." He looked at his wristwatch and groaned. "Look, it's after twelve. Why don't you put away whatever you were doing and go on home for the rest of the day. Take a rest. You've had a shock and frankly, you don't look well at all. I'll be out of the office this afternoon and so will Mr. Procter. I won't get a chance to talk to him until tomorrow. Just go home and don't worry. Don't talk about any of this to anyone, not even your wife. It'll only upset her. Tell her you became ill and were given the rest of the day off. If you see Puhalski, tell him you're making plans, describe all the difficulties, all the *theoretical* difficulties," he amended bitterly. "Tell him anything to justify a few days' delay. Can you do that?"

Sobolov nodded again.

"Good! Go along now; not a word to anyone and don't worry."

A man reprieved, Sobolov got unsteadily to his feet and stumbled from the room.

♨♨

She dropped the old ribbon into the wastebasket, then looked with distaste at her inky fingers. Hooking her little finger in the brass pull, Tamara opened the bottom drawer and got out a piece of tissue.

[214]

When she had wiped her fingers, she inserted another blank form in the typewriter and stared at it with bored resistance. She was little more than halfway through the members' accounts, and the remaining portion of the ledger looked depressingly thick. Monthly billing was a tedious chore. The whole process seemed nothing but a pointless treadmill, repetitive and futile. Did anyone really care about all those whiskeys and gins and tiffins and sandwiches served by the pool? Silly question. The manager of the Club did, and it was he who paid her wages.

She had hoped to complete the job by the end of the day. Now she knew she'd never manage it . . . she simply couldn't concentrate.

It seemed difficult now to believe that John's party—*her* party—had been only two nights before. It seemed an age past, though poignantly clear in her memory. There had been an unusual tenderness between them; never before had she been so certain of the depth of his feeling for her. Nor, she added bitterly, of his incapacity to act on that feeling. At the time, nevertheless, her awareness of his love had seemed more than enough to sustain her.

But with the brief time passing, the dream had faded. Already she was aware that she had moved farther from his mind, as if he were thinking more and more of America and his return there. Last night, when she'd come to the San Kwan Miao, after seeing her mother, he had seemed his old, eager, animal self, glad to see her and wanting to make love. Even though she hadn't really been in the mood, she would have responded quickly enough to the touch of his hands on her body and his lips. But he had cooled abruptly and hurried her out to the car as though suddenly pressed for time.

The flat had seemed lonely and desolate without her mother there, and stuffy from being closed up all day. Tamara had wanted him to stay with her, to sleep there—they could have spread a quilt on the bare wood floor—but instinct had told her not to ask. After muttering something vague about getting together the next night—which was tonight—he'd given her a perfunctory kiss and departed, ostensibly for the San Kwan Miao.

With her fingers resting on the keys, Tamara sat, deep in thought.

Beyond the open windows, a typical summer's noontime ambled forward, propelled by the heavy pressure of the sun. Around the edges of the pool, ladies lay on wicker chaises, turning brown, drinking gin-and-limes, and gossiping sleepily. Closer at hand, shaded by the *p'eng* which covered that side of the building, toddlers played and whimpered in the sandbox, while their *amahs* exchanged rumor and scandalous speculation regarding their employers. Only the older children, yelling and splashing in the pool, seemed to defy the sun; they and the men on the tennis courts, shouting their sportsmanlike phrases and reveling in their sweat. As background for it all was the *amahs'* interminable drone, broken occasionally by a derisive cackle.

Tamara had promised to call him that morning; she'd spoken to her mother, who was as well and as uncomplaining as could be expected. And Tamara herself had spent a passably comfortable night in spite of earlier nervousness. Early that morning, inquiring discreetly, she'd learned from neighbors that there had been no sign of police activity in the area. She knew John would be relieved by that news and had wanted to tell him—and yet she had resisted. She simply didn't want to hear his voice just then. She felt she couldn't trust herself.

There had been a party at the Procters' house Monday night, the night her mother was attacked. She'd heard the gossip . . . being wealthy, the Procters' social activities attracted great attention from the *amahs.* John had said he was there but hadn't mentioned any party. And Hal MacDonough too. On Tuesday at the San Kwan Miao, she'd sensed a thread of some recently shared experience between them. Well, that was all right; John could go where he wanted. And Franklin Procter was his boss, after all.

Franklin Procter wasn't the only member of that family to show an interest in her. In fact, it had been that same Monday when Mrs. Procter had come into the Club, with her empty smile and her bright eyes, not even trying to hide the fact that she knew all about the half-caste behind the counter. And something else, something Tamara had seen in the eyes of other foreign women. You're a pretty little thing, it said, and we know how you'd like to raise yourself by contact with our men; just don't try it. We're watching and won't allow it. They were afraid, these painted, raucous women, and well they might be. What man with any blood in his veins wouldn't want a change from one of those stringy, demanding bitches? Tamara had only contempt for them all. But this one's concern was not for her pale thoroughbred of a husband, but for John Edgerton. She had other plans for him, and now imagined them to be on the verge of fruition. Well, she needn't have worried about Tamara. Even were she to try to improve herself at the expense of some foreign lady, cautious, careful John Edgerton would hold the fort. Between the rules of his very proper Service and his own old secret wounds, he'd erected a very effective barrier around himself.

Tamara felt a hard fist of selfishness come to a knot somewhere deep inside her. She'd rather no one got him than see him go to that trim and tailored lady with the knowing blue eyes and the hungry mouth who had stood beside Pamela Procter while Tamara made out her guest card. Tamara had seen her type in the Club before, come to China for excitement and romance and another husband. In fact, that yellow head was at the pool this very moment, her smooth, pampered body, with its precious white skin, carelessly browning in the sun. It had not been an hour earlier when Mrs. Valerie Warner was called to the telephone . . . some excursion to Tungchow was still on, it appeared. It hadn't been necessary for Tamara to stoop to eavesdropping. The telephone was but ten feet away on a desk in the lobby. Whatever the excursion entailed, it was evident that Mrs. Valerie Warner very much wanted to go on it. It must be restful to worry only about play.

Tamara rebuked herself. She hated herself in these sour, complaining moods, when she became envious and suspicious . . . totally hateful. She must remember that she was herself, while they . . . well, they could be Martians for all she cared about their special circumstances. Before, just being herself had always been enough. She'd made her mistakes and experienced her small triumphs. In later years, loving John Edgerton might join the list of mistakes—there were times when she was certain it belonged there—but she hoped not. Although it was no triumph, it had had its exalted moments. Now she was determined merely to make the best of things. It was just that on this particular day the power of her enemies seemed particularly evident, not to mention the fragility of her own position.

Tamara looked around as though assessing the terrain on which she, the beleaguered native, fought off the foreign invaders. Beyond the counter that formed her corner into an "office" was the empty lobby. The old leather chairs seemed to sag a little in the rear, and the pages of a dog-eared magazine stirred under the languidly revolving ceiling fan. This was her bastion, with a small supply base back at her flat. Her mother, now beleaguered herself, was her force in reserve. Tamara had to smile wryly at the invention, remembering with relief that her mother was no longer really beleaguered.

She was turning back to the typewriter when the telephone shrilled. "Peking Club; good morning," she said crisply, impatient at the intrusion.

"Tamara? Hello, Tamara?"

In spite of her recent pessimism, her heart leaped to hear his voice. "Hello, John," she said, smiling delightedly into the instrument.

"How are you?" he asked, his voice warm and close, as though coming from the next room. "I was getting worried . . . why didn't you call?"

[217]

"I'm fine. I was waiting for a break . . . it's bill time, you know," she fibbed gladly, feeling her despondency begin to slip away. When she told him about her mother's growing impatience to return home, he dismissed the idea, unconvinced by the apparent inactivity of the police. There was a cautious note in his voice.

"Nothing's happened, has it?" she asked.

"No, no . . . there's just no point in being hasty. Your mother's okay there; let her stay a day or two longer."

"She'll only get grouchy."

"*Get* grouchy?"

Tamara laughed, abandoning all caution. "Look," she said. "I can shop on the way home. Why don't you let me fix you some supper? It will scandalize the landlord's wife, but who cares?"

The words made Tamara glad. They seemed to mark a casting away of all the dreary self-protective devices she'd been gathering around herself earlier on. That was no way to live.

Hearing the lengthening, solid silence on the wire, she felt a chilling stab of pain. By the time he spoke, the words had already become superfluous; she knew what they would be.

"That sounds wonderful, Tamara, but I can't," he said hurriedly. "I'm sorry."

He did sound sorry, a distant part of her mind told her. Oh, God! she thought then. Don't let him go on! She would have given anything not to have made the invitation.

"You see, Procter's laid up with some stomach upset," John explained seriously. "He was to have given a talk to some missionaries . . . there's been a new directive from Washington. Now I'm going to have to do it for him, and then he wants me to come by and tell him how it went. I'll be in Tungchow all afternoon and over at his place God knows how long." He paused, sighing with exasperation.

Through her very real tears, Tamara could see him embellish his statement with a helpless shake of the head. Tungchow. Fate was her enemy this day. Somehow she had always known John would be a clumsy liar. His nature was too blunderingly direct to sustain the pretense even of this simple charade. The fact that it must be at least half true—he could never have invented it all—made the pain of it all the more bitter. It wasn't only John, it was his wretched Service as well: intruding, interfering, demanding, succeeding. It always won; she never did, never could.

For several long moments Tamara let the silence linger. She felt powerless, speechless, her throat frozen and her head empty of words. And her heart empty also. Then, very gently, she hung up the phone.

[218]

It rang again almost at once.

"Yes," she said, knowing.

"Tamara? We were cut off." His voice was nervous with the stubborn effort to deny the obvious. "Can you hear me?"

Face it! she screamed silently, begging him not to prolong her agony. "Yes, I can hear you," she said.

"The damn phone service gets worse every day. Let's get together tomorrow night instead. Could you come for dinner . . . just the two of us?"

Tamara shook her head, half in anger, half in sympathy. He simply would not open his eyes and look. "No, John, I can't."

"Well," he said blankly, nonplussed. "Perhaps the day after."

"No, dear. Not the day after."

"You sound upset, angry . . . what's the matter?"

"Why should I be angry?" Tamara blurted, hating the weakness that let her voice break, hating the anger that robbed her of control. "You have work to do, so you must do it. For the rest, I simply cannot come."

"But I don't understand."

"But of course you do, John. This is all too bad for us; it can't be fixed. Look at the complications: Mr. Procter, the Legation, the foreigners, the . . . all the rest. It must come to an end sooner or later; let it be sooner, now, before something terrible happens, some scandal which will spoil everything for us both."

"But I still don't understand," he insisted, his voice intense with stubbornness.

"Of course you do, my dear; of course you do," Tamara whispered. This time when she hung up the phone, it did not ring again.

Nearby the fan throbbed dutifully, and the sounds from the pool and the tennis courts floated in through the open window like hot dry leaves, and the *amahs* murmured, making a faint, neutral wind. The typewriter keys blurred and wavered before her eyes. Oh, John, she thought, biting her lip. Oh, John . . .

"I say, is anything the matter?"

Startled, Tamara whirled in her chair, a faint gasp escaping her lips.

Looming over the counter was the beefy torso of the British military attaché. As usual, he wore his regimental necktie and a blue linen blazer with an ornate emblem on the breast pocket. His school or club, or something, she found herself thinking, her gaze fastening on it rather than on his round, poached eyes. His red face was puckered by a mixture of hesitation, curiosity, and, she supposed, daring. As usual, his mouth hung slightly open under a large moustache. Of her several clandestine pursuers in the Club, he was the most persistent. The only

[219]

thing recommending him was that, unlike the others, he was not married. It wasn't enough; she detested him as well.

Wishing fervently that he would go away, Tamara could only shake her head and dab at her eyes with her fingers. She felt humiliated to be seen by him like this.

"Oh, good!" he said, totally oblivious. He looked prudently in all directions before leaning closer. "I've been hoping," he began in a confidential whisper, his smile exposing long teeth, "you would relent, and let me take you somewhere for a cozy spot of dinner, some place of your choice? You know?"

♣♣

Something was wrong. It wasn't simply that Maya looked a mess, with her hair in a tangle. Nor was it that she was still in her kimono and broken-down slippers. He was no stranger to her in this state. It was the look in her eyes, or, more accurately, the absence of one. They were at that moment inspecting him blankly, incuriously, as though he were a stranger come to the wrong door. Most certainly there was no slightest sign of the hunger with which she usually greeted him.

"Well, Mayichka, aren't you going to invite me in?"

"Come in, then," she said indifferently, and went to sit at the kitchen table.

"There has been a change in schedule," Puhalski said, sitting down opposite her.

Maya shrugged. She fumbled in the deep sleeve of her kimono and came up with a bent cigarette. "I know nothing of any schedule."

Puhalski couldn't help laughing. "We shall see," he said confidently. He stared patiently at her averted face until, at last, her reluctant eyes returned to his. "Today you go to meet your new friend and protector," he told her quietly. "Make up your face and put on your best dress. We don't have much time, and the taxi is waiting."

Maya's eyes shifted to the study of the smoldering end of her cigarette. "I won't do it," she said in a low voice.

"Oh?" Puhalski said, elaborately casual. "May I be permitted to ask you for an explanation?"

"There is nothing to explain. I've changed my mind."

"You've changed your mind. Very interesting. Have you forgotten your promises to me?"

"No, but I'm going to break them."

"Why?"

[220]

Maya ground out her half-smoked cigarette. "I'm frightened, for one thing," she said.

"You are frightened?" Puhalski wanted to beat her face in with his bare fists . . . a luxury he could not yet afford. "But what about us, our plans, our future?"

She looked straight at him then, and he saw contempt and loathing in her eyes. "We have no future," she said. "What is this thing you have done to Andrei?"

"I?"

"At the Police Yamen. He told me everything." She leaned toward him across the table, her breasts surging forward under the loose kimono. "That was your doing," she accused.

"I had nothing whatsoever to do with it; I didn't even hear about it until this morning. It was a stupid blunder . . . a confusion of names or some such thing. I complained at once to the highest police authorities." He gave her an emphatic nod. "Those responsible are to be punished."

"I am not a child," Maya said coldly.

"But it is true!"

"You promised Andrei there was no danger in this thing you wanted him to do. He has a weak heart. One man has been killed already."

"A common criminal. Piffle."

"So you say. You could say Andrei was a common criminal next. They could kill him, too."

"It has nothing to do with what I say," Puhalski protested.

"That I know," she said sarcastically. "You are always boasting about your influence and your powerful friends, and then this happens." She snorted contemptuously and felt in her sleeve for another cigarette.

Puhalski made a point of lighting it for her. He gazed ardently into her eyes, then took her hand. It lay limply in his for several seconds, cold as a dead fish. Presently she drew it away and she stared off into an empty corner. Puhalski could see the tears in her eyes.

"You have used me badly," she whispered.

"No!" Puhalski cried passionately. "Everything I've told you has been the truth."

"The truth!" she sneered. "Look at us, for all of your schemes and promises. Andrei is in deep trouble, and you want to push me like a whore into the bed of your Japanese master."

Puhalski recaptured her hand. "That is not so, and it hurts me when you say things like that. What I want isn't the point. We're all helpless

[221]

before the power of the Japanese. We must help each other and sacrifice for each other. When you say these bitter things to me, you make me think that our love and the plans we've made together mean nothing to you." His voice vibrated soulfully.

Maya said nothing, but she left her hand where it was. "We can spare a little time," he said softly, stroking her palm. "Let's go into the bedroom."

She turned to look at him again; her expression a new one. She pulled her hand away and wiped it on the front of her kimono. "You are finished in my bedroom," she announced flatly.

Puhalski grinned at her. "Last time you were moaning like a cat . . . you couldn't get enough of it."

Her eyes dropped and her face flushed crimson. "You can't live without the cock I give you," he stated. "You love to have me fuck you; you've always loved it and you always will. You love me." He tried for her hand again, but she evaded him. "And I love you," he said.

She whirled on him then, staring squarely into his eyes. Her round chin jutted forward angrily. "You love no one, not even yourself," she informed him in icy tones. "I did love you once, but I was a trusting idiot then. I know you now. I am nothing to you and never was. I was only something for you to play with, to put your thing in, so you can pretend you are a man. But you are not a man. Andrei is a better man than you . . . in every way."

"You liked it well enough," ne said, curling his lip. She was making him angry.

"Maybe; maybe I did," she said, shrugging indifferently. "But you didn't, that's the point. You do it, but you don't really like it. A woman can tell about these things. It is just another one of your arguments to yourself, as though all you need is a hard-on to be a man. You only did it so you could use me."

What nonsense was the woman yammering now? he wondered, thinking about the time and the waiting taxi. "You live for my cock," he told her, leering confidently. "You want it now, and it is ready."

"No!" There was panic in her voice.

"Come into the bedroom and we shall see," he said.

"I am Andrei's wife."

Puhalski fell back into his chair, laughing silently. "And what were you the day before yesterday, his sister?"

"I was a fool the day before yesterday and all those other days." Maya was shouting now, and her eyes flashed angrily. "That is all finished. All I want from you is to be left alone. Leave us both alone."

"Shut up, you slut! You are a worse fool if you think you can disobey

[222]

me," he said harshly, finished with pretending. "So I am to believe that you are now transformed into a faithful wife?"

"I intend to be one,"

"Very commendable, I'm sure. And what do you intend to use for a husband?"

Maya stared, mouth drooping stupidly. "What do you mean?"

"How long do you expect your old fat Andrei to survive now that you've become so pure?"

"What does that have to do with Andrei? You said what happened to him was a mistake."

"Use your head! It's one thing to refuse me, and something else to refuse a Japanese officer." Puhalski shook his head, amazed at her impenetrable stupidity. "You and your precious Andrei . . . you are both blind, thickheaded donkeys." He smashed his fist down on the table. "This Japanese officer happens to be more powerful than most; he *must* be obeyed. Get that into your head. I work for him, Andrei now works for him, and you're just bloody well going to have to do as you're told."

"I refuse," Maya said, and he knew it was her last defiance.

"Andrei will die if you don't. They'll put a hose in his mouth and fill his fat gut with water until . . ."

"Stop!" she moaned. Her face collapsed and tears oozed from her squeezed eyes. She put her hands over her ears.

". . . it grows to twice its usual size and finally bursts."

Puhalski waited, drumming on the table with his fingers.

Several minutes passed. Maya's sobbing gradually subsided into sniffles. Somewhere in her sleeve she found a handkerchief, and when she had wiped her eyes and blown her nose, she sat staring into her lap, dumb and silent.

Puhalski took a deep breath. "Listen Maya: let's not fight with each other. It's too bad things are this way, but I can't help it. It's a mess, but it's not hopeless. It's all up to you, however," he said, pleased by the even reasonableness of his tone.

Her red eyes examined him dumbly. "Up to me?"

"Yes. It's up to you to save yourself and Andrei and Anya . . . and me, too, if that matters to you. You think I've lied and tried to use you. It's not so, and your suspicion hurts me. But my life's already full of pain . . . " Puhalski sighed stoically. "The point to remember is that this Japanese wants you, he's crazy about you. Play your cards right and in no time he'll be eating out of your hand like a pet dog."

Puhalski smiled, nodding encouragment. "It won't be so bad," he went on, sensing her softening will. "He's rich and will give you

[223]

presents, money. He's a high-ranking officer, a colonel, and he's very discreet. Andrei need never know about it, and you can put aside the money. All the time you'll know you're protecting Andrei's life—and Anya's. And then, when everything's over, you and Andrei can go back to your regular life together, if that's what you want. And I will go on my way," he added mournfully.

Maya shot him a suspicious glance at that and seemed about to speak. But she only rocked sorrowfully in her chair.

"But if you refuse, no one can help you. Andrei is in too deeply; the officer will blame him for your squeamishness and will be insulted. You know how sensitive they are about their honor. He'll put Andrei in prison. You'll be alone and defenseless . . . without money."

Puhalski took his time lighting a fresh cigarette. "I'll do what I can, because I care for you, but I'll be broke, too, and in disgrace. All that I've worked for will be gone. And . . ." He heaved an unhappy sigh and waited, letting the silence grow heavy with suspense. ". . . and before long Anya will be letting the soldiers fuck her for a couple of Chinese dollars."

Maya's collapse was total. Leaning forward with her face in her hands, a great moan of anguish escaped her.

Puhalski waited calmly, smoking and staring at the patterns etched into the crumbling plaster of the wall behind her. "It's all up to you, my dear Maya," he reminded her softly. "

She raised her head, her hands falling slowly into her lap.

Puhalski stood up. "Come, we've wasted too much time," he said very gently. "Show me what you're going to wear. I want you to look pretty."

Maya got laboriously to her feet and shuffled into the bedroom.

Puhalski crushed out his cigarette and leaned for a moment on the table. God, but he was tired! After today he was through with arguing with the stubborn bitch. Let Tanaka make his own arrangments in the future. The only thing that remained was to see that she looked halfway presentable. Running his fingers through his hair, Puhalski followed her into the familiar bedroom.

♟♟

The chicken sandwich Ch'en had made him sat on its plate like something made of papier mache, the corners of the bread turning up with the heat. Edgerton stared at it with aversion. Just behind it, the tall glass of Japanese beer sweated profusely, the golden liquid with its white head of foam suggesting only another unpotable liquid.

[224]

He lifted the sandwich halfway to his mouth, then put it down, his throat suddenly dry. He wouldn't think about Tamara just then, or the finality of what she'd said to him on the phone. He already had enough on his mind.

He got Tanaka's letter out of his jacket pocket. Reading it had seemed anticlimactic, coming on top of Sobolov's revelations, to say nothing of Tamara's inexplicable behavior.

His hand paused in midair. She'd hung up on him . . . twice, in fact. If the idea weren't so farfetched, he'd have sworn she must have known about the trip to Tungchow with Valerie. And even if she had known, there wasn't all that much to be upset about. She was nervous, he supposed. The attack on her mother, the hot, ovenlike days coming one after another . . . enough to set anyone's teeth on edge. Still, he hated to hear the sound of tears in her voice, especially knowing that he'd had something to do with putting them there. He'd call her again that evening, or go by and see her after he got back from Tungchow —after *they* got back—depending . . .

Frowning slightly, Edgerton unfolded the letter and smoothed out the creases. Rereading it gave him a twinge of embarrassment. By comparison, he was afraid his own letter must have sounded like so much bombast. He must learn to curb his tendency toward heavy sarcasm . . . no one seemed to appreciate it.

Tanaka's message was both complete and remarkably polite. Taking note of Mr. Edgerton's comments, he hastened to assure him that the protection of civilian life and property had high priority with the occupation authorities. He himself, as were all Japanese officers, was most anxious that the motives behind Japan's operations in China not be misunderstood or be distorted by rumor and anti-Japanese propaganda. As an official of a government long friendly with Japan, Mr. Edgerton would undoubtedly share this wish. If Mr. Edgerton could give him the details of any specific incidents he might have in mind, Colonel Tanaka would be happy to give them his personal attention. And so forth for several paragraphs.

Eminently sensible. Edgerton refolded the paper and put it away, smiling to himself. He couldn't fit this tiny glimpse of Tanaka's character into the physical presence he remembered so dimly. Tanaka's picture of himself was clearer: a foxy, inventive man ready and able to deal successfully with the barbarian. Did Tanaka really think, Edgerton wondered, that he would be so naïve as to reveal Madame Liu's name so the case could receive Tanaka's "personal attention"? Just the same, Edgerton felt a certain appreciation of the man. The tone of his reply had been so unexpected, so un-Japanese.

[225]

Acting on impulse, he'd asked Miss Kung to try and put him through to Tanaka. By some miracle of persuasion she'd managed it, and connected him to Tanaka's office. While waiting for the call to go through, Edgerton had reminded himself that there was little real doubt that this man was behind the intimidation of poor Sobolov for reasons which, if unrealistic, were still extremely serious.

Even now, recalling his own near calamity made Edgerton's guts writhe with humiliation and self-contempt, driving Tanaka and his letter temporarily from his thoughts.

How could he have ever been so careless, so stupid? In his twenty years as an F.S.O. he'd never blundered so badly. He cringed to think what would have happened if he'd repeated that fumble, and poor harried Sobolov had taken those worksheets to the Japanese. The only consolation was that there would have been no national disaster, the system being designed for just such an eventuality. The frequent changes of keys and code books and the assignment of different blocks of codes to different areas insured that a compromise of the system could be localized. Had Sobolov succeeded, the Japanese might have been able to read a few messages from Peking and Tientsin, but only for another week or so, until a new book went into effect. The various area codes used in China were as different from one another as they were from London's. But that wasn't really the point. Any fragment falling into Japanese hands was to be deplored; every stray leak made the system more vulnerable. None of which dealt with the personal consequences for him. He would have had to report it. To sit on a blunder of that magnitude would have been unthinkable. One result would be that decent posts would never again be offered him; poor old Edgerton; a nice fellow but can't be trusted with classified papers. He shuddered.

Edgerton stared blankly across the glaring courtyard. And Sobolov, that loyal old guy, covering up so he wouldn't lose face. He was reminded that he'd promised to get them some place to stay. He snorted humorlessly . . . La Garde would begin to think him some sort of nut. But he'd go along, at least this one more time. The year before Edgerton had been instrumental in getting a visa for his son to go to the States to study. La Garde had been effusive in his gratitude, but whether he could let Edgerton fill up his hotel. . . .

His thoughts veered back to his call to the Japanese officer. To Edgerton's surprise, Colonel Tanaka had been both formally polite and quite reasonable, suggesting that they get together—unofficially, of course—to discuss the substance of Mr. Edgerton's memo in detail. A time of eleven o'clock the next morning had been agreed upon.

[226]

Edgerton could remember hoping at the time that Procter would still be indisposed. With even a little luck, the whole Tanaka business would pass into history without Procter's ever learning of it.

As for Edgerton's regrettable sarcasms, they had evidently gone over the Colonel's head. Which was strange since he spoke excellent English, though with an odd and at the same time familiar accent. Edgerton found himself rather looking forward to the meeting. If nothing else came of it, at least Tanaka would leave convinced that he wasn't some newcomer to the scene, benignly unable to distinguish rumor and propaganda from fact. He'd been in Tientsin in 1932 and seen then how the Japanese conducted their "operations." Tanaka would be fully informed on that score.

Edgerton sighed and took a bite of sandwich. He would show Tanaka the face of perfect diplomacy. Although they would spar diligently for the record, and part with expressions of goodwill and the traditional friendship of the American and Japanese people, Tanaka would know he'd spoken to someone who knew the score. A valuable foundation might thus be laid for future unofficial meetings.

Edgerton paused in midthought, frowning. Angry as he'd been, writing to Tanaka was uncharacteristic of him. With the benefit of hindsight, he could see that it had been frustration pure and simple which had prompted him. Tamara had turned instinctively to him for help, and he had only the diplomat's solitary weapon: the note of protest. And what would come of it? Probably nothing. There would be no perceptible change in Japanese behavior. Madame Liu would still see him as a lecherous villain. And if his intuition were correct, Tamara saw him that way too . . . refusing to listen, hanging up on him in midsentence . . . how could she not?

A glance at his watch told him it was time to go. He still had to stop at the Socony yard on Hata Men Chieh and get gas.

Poor Procter. He had all Edgerton's sympathy, but his illness was still providing a release for others. This would have been no afternoon to spend in the Chancery.

As he picked up his jacket, he felt a vague sense of relief. It would be good for Tamara not to see him for a few days. He'd been monopolizing her; it wasn't fair . . . unwittingly leading her to hope for the impossible. A break would do them both good.

姦姦

Having a glass of beer had been a mistake; Sobolov knew that now. But he had been hot and thirsty and confused, and the idea of some-

[227]

thing cold and relaxing had been irresistible. He should have remembered his poor head for spirits. Now the malty fumes made him feel doped to the point of being half-asleep and more than a little queasy. And there was no sign yet of Puhalski.

Sobolov looked up at the young woman who was half-heartedly wiping at the tables with a damp rag. She looked familiar. She caught his glance and raised an insolent eyebrow. "Something else?" she asked.

Her voice was hoarse from too many cigarettes; her painted mouth smiled knowingly, combining with her eyes to suggest that she could supply anything he might want. Poor thing. He recognized her now: the second daughter of Zinoviev. He could remember her as a little girl, walking with her father and all decked out in hair ribbons. Old Zinoviev had died in 1936. It was just as well; he would die of shame and sadness to see her now.

"No, thank you," he said.

She tossed her head and sauntered away toward the bar, swinging her bottom at him contemptuously.

But for the two of them, the place was empty. The girl put a record on the phonograph and the room filled with the scratchy inanities of some dance. A fox-trot, he supposed . . . whatever those bizarre words were supposed to mean. As if to answer his unspoken question, the girl began langorously to dance. She knew he was watching, he was certain, for the movement of her hips became more exaggerated as the dance progressed, thrusting backward and forward in a way that embarrassed him . . . and excited him vaguely, making him think of Maya and the night before. And then he thought of Anya.

But he mustn't think of Anya; Anya was all right for the moment. He must think of Maya. And of Puhalski. The Zinoviev girl had told him that Puhalski was on an errand and would be back at any moment. What errand?

Why had Maya been with him and where were they going?

Sobolov shook his head miserably, cursing his own weakness. Coming home, the heat and the swaying of the rickshaw had been too much for him. Weak and unsteady after his collapse, he'd wanted nothing so much as to get quickly to bed, but he knew he'd be sick if he stayed in the rickshaw any longer. Almost home, he'd gotten down to walk the rest of the way, thinking a few minutes one way or the other wouldn't matter.

But they had mattered. He'd arrived at the corner of his *hu-tung* only just in time to see Maya and Puhalski go riding by in a taxi. Brief as his glimpse of her was, he'd seen that she was pale and worried and

[228]

was certain she had been crying. Puhalski wore his usual expression of smug indifference. The sight of them together had halted Sobolov in the middle of the sidewalk. Then a chance eddy in the noisy crowd had blocked him off from them; he could only wave helplessly and shout her name. In all that din, she hadn't heard him.

By the time he'd shoved his way to the edge of the sidewalk, the taxi had vanished. He'd been left standing there, confused and indecisive and in everyone's way. Finally it had occurred to him to come to the Café Volga and wait for Puhalski. He was still waiting.

Sobolov shifted in his chair in a sudden agony of impatience and distress. Where could they have been going? And Puhalski, always Puhalski! The man haunted him like some evil spectre. Puhalski dropping in for visits in the afternoon, to borrow a book or return a book; Puhalski stopping by in the evening for a glass of tea and a chat, a chat which inevitably became an argument. And Maya always taking Puhalski's side, losing her temper and blaming him because he wanted to be left alone. Whether Puhalski was there or not, she blamed him for their poverty. It wasn't fair. And now he had tried to do much more, tried to do something he knew was wrong and foolish . . . well, at least that was over. It was a good thing Mr. Edgerton had told him not to mention anything to her. Maya would be very cross when she found out; she always set such store by Puhalski's schemes. She admired Puhalski and there was always a certain look in her eye when Puhalski came around. . . .

The thought hung suspended in Sobolov's head . . . he had never let himself give that look a name. Maya and Puhalski. It was all suddenly, devastatingly clear to him. He had been a blind and trusting fool, and had gotten the fool's reward. The sweetness of last night's loving miracle turned to dust. What was to become of them?

He stared into the bottom of his empty glass, as though the answer were written on the foam which had congealed there. That morsel of Mr. Edgerton's optimism which had rubbed off on him began to disappear. It was easy for Mr. Edgerton to be optimistic; he was an American. Things were different for Americans. They might as well be living on another planet all their own.

He'd been a fool to think things could be made to work out . . . a fool at everything.

Slowly, reluctantly, he felt his eyes drawn to the bar. The Zinoviev girl was there at one end, polishing glasses and watching him. She had put on another record. Her eyes caught his boldly and she bumped her pelvis at him. Sobolov blushed and turned away, and the girl laughed.

[229]

Where are you, Maya? his heart called out. Come back . . . it doesn't matter.

♗♗

Again it was Valerie who opened the door for him. Her hand was out in welcome and her lips were smiling. When Edgarton took her hand, she pulled him forward and kissed him quickly, firmly, on the mouth. Although tempted to embrace her, he let her go. Time enough, he thought.

"You're very prompt," she said, her smile broadening but readable.

"It's good to see you, Valerie," he said. It *was* good. And she looked good in her white blouse and severe blue linen skirt, her golden hair ashine even in the dim cavern of the hallway. "Are Franklin and Pamela safely tucked into bed?"

"Yes, poor dears," she said. "Curtains drawn and everyone moving around on tiptoe. Will I need a jacket or sweater?"

"A light sweater, maybe . . . for the drive back."

"I'll just be a minute, then."

Edgerton watched her with appreciation . . . tanned shapely legs and a firm round bottom.

At Hata Men Chieh, they were held up by a funeral procession. Unable to see anything from the car and fast becoming an attraction in their own right, they got out and worked their way to the curb. It wasn't easy, and the tight press of the crowd plainly bothered Valerie.

The first of the procession had only just gone by. Directly in front of them a motley crowd of indifferent musicians shattered the air with thumping drums and wailing flutes, along with the clang of tuneless cymbals. They were dressed in dirty white gowns rented along with themselves for the occasion. A cluster of hired mourners straggled along behind, chattering disrespectfully among themselves.

Edgerton explained the symbolic largesse of the paper "cash" being thrown into the crowd and chased after by a horde of urchins. There was the usual multitude of paper figures: servants and animals, model houses and carts, and chests of household goods. They would all be burned at the graveside to accompany the departed spirit and comfort him in the afterworld.

By the time the coffin and the mourning family came into view, Valerie seemed more at ease. There was a large photograph draped in white leaning against the head of the heavy wooden coffin. From it an old man's face peered out apprehensively, as though somewhere out beyond the camera he had foreseen this moment.

[230]

A tiny woman with bound feet, filially supported by her two sons, tottered after the coffin. Valerie gasped when she saw the stumpy shapes of her deformed feet in their miniature slippers. "How awful!" she whispered, her face twisted with disgust.

Edgerton shrugged. It was an ugly thing. "It's not done much anymore," he said. "In twenty years there won't be a bound foot to be seen." He took her elbow and guided her back to the car through the rapidly thinning crowd.

"It's barbaric!" Valerie declared firmly.

Edgerton eased the car slowly into the stream of traffic, turned left and headed south toward the gate tower and the so-called Chinese City beyond.

The street was fairly crowded with a variety of vehicles ranging from ancient to modern and the inevitable daytime pedestrian traffic of any Chinese city. He had to give most of his attention to his driving. Through the back of his mind, however, vague disappointments wandered. Valerie was not enjoying herself. The freshness and easiness of her manner, so pleasantly obvious back at the house, was fast evaporating. In his simplemindedness, he'd imagined himself the knowing guide and Old China Hand showing her the sights while she, dazzled by the scope of his sinology, hung on his every word.

They continued for two long blocks, making only desultory conversation.

South of the Tartar wall, after they'd passed through the tunnel under the Hata Men gate tower, the street became even more crowded and the buildings more dilapidated. It was as though the ancient Tartar neglect of this, the city of mere Chinese, was being continued out of habit by the officials now in power. The dusty pavement was in bad repair, or no repair at all, and gaped with holes. Along the streetcar tracks great chunks of macadam had eroded away, exposing the high tracks dangerously.

As the scenery grew drearier, Valerie seemed to lose heart, sinking back into an unhappy silence. From the corner of his eye, Edgerton could see her brace herself against the bumps, loosening her grip on seat edge and window frame only long enough to brush futilely at the sifting dust which continually settled on her clothes. Hot and thirsty himself, Edgerton felt a dull resentment: irreversible forces of social and romantic disaster were gathering. Damn Procter and his bright ideas!

A weak hot wind stirred up small dusty whirlwinds. The clear sky of the morning had faded to the dull yellow of a commonplace summer's day. Edgerton yawned with resignation.

[231]

A horn blared raucously at his very elbow, snapping him roughly back to full awareness. A large Army truck was crowding dangerously, determined to pass whether there was room or not. Edgerton twisted the steering wheel to the left, toward the curb, and bore down on the brakes as hard as he dared. Clinging to her door, Valerie let out a little shriek.

A loud laugh and a string of Japanese curses came jeering out of the truck cab as it drew alongside, the truck driver deliberately risking a collision. Swearing under his breath, Edgerton fought to control the car as it bucked into the cart ruts along the edge of the road. With a contemptuous honk and a clash of gears the truck surged by them, only to cut sharply in front, missing the fender by inches.

Three soldiers stood in the back, sharing a bottle of beer and swaying to the motion of the truck like sailors on a rolling deck. Looking back and laughing, they saw Valerie and began pointing and elbowing one another. Clutching a companion for support, one of them grabbed at the fly of his baggy trousers, thrust his pelvis forward grotesquely, and jiggled his genitals at her. Slowly the truck drew away from them, losing itself in its own cloud of dust until it finally turned and went off toward the west.

Edgerton stifled his first reaction by telling himself that the vulgar, comical gesture should mean no more to him than a donkey's braying. Just the same, the fact that he felt no anger didn't mean that loosening a few of the soldier's teeth might not have been a pleasurable act. He eased the car back onto the crown of the road. "I'm sorry," was all he could think of to say.

Valerie was pale beneath her tan, her face drawn with disgust. "Never mind," she snapped, taking a deep breath. "It did scare me, though . . . the truck and that awful soldier. I know it's silly. He's just another Oriental, no better than an animal, really." She shuddered and her voice hardened. "I haven't been here long, but I ought to know by now what to expect of these people."

Her vehemence surprised him almost as much as her words. "Think of it as an ignorant man's salute to a pretty woman," he said, trying to speak lightly. "Something like whistling."

Valerie laughed unconvincingly and concentrated on brushing at her skirt. Oh, well, Edgerton thought, resigning himself to his driving.

Several blocks farther on the traffic began to thicken and was soon a packed mass barely able to inch along. Minutes passed and then they saw the barricade and the teeming road gangs at work behind it. A pair of policemen were there, blowing their whistles and shouting commands, trying to preserve some order in the midst of incipient

[232]

chaos. Bit by bit, they and the rest of the traffic were shunted and squeezed into a detour off to the left.

"Oh, how interesting!" Valerie said, perking up at the sight of the laboring coolies.

Edgerton divided his attention between the creeping traffic and the bustle of the road gang. The place was a swarm of activity. There must have been fifty men carrying earth and stone in baskets from two great piles of material. Their nearly naked bodies ran with sweat, and their backs bent tautly under the weight of the shoulder poles. Another fifty picked and shoveled at the old pavement and carried away the rubble. Where the new surface was already down, a huge stone roller was being hauled back and forth by a dozen men harnessed to it like mules. It seemed so massive that with one less man they could not have budged it. Leaning forward into his shoulder ropes, knuckles brushing the ground, each man was plainly working to the extreme limit of his strength.

The scene throbbed with chanting, the hot dry air pulsing with the mixed rhythms of the various groups. There was the fast marching chant of the carriers: *eh eh! aw aw! eh eh! aw aw! eh eh! aw aw!*; the slower cadence of the pickax men: *uh! uh! uh!*; and slowest of all, like a deep mass heartbeat, came the rollermen's explosive grunt: *huh!* step *huh!* step! *huh!* And through a hanging pall of dust the unforgiving sun poured down upon them all. They were lucky. When the weather was good, Chinese road gangs worked a twelve-hour day; when it was bad, they went hungry.

The sight of primitive manpower had never lost is repellant fascination for Edgerton. And he knew it never would, no matter how long he remained in China. The relegation of men to do the work of beasts was commonplace, but he could never get used to it. He kept trying to put himself in the place of the laborers, to imagine what had come to fill the void left by their vanished hopes. They must, once, have had hopes.

As they moved inch by inch toward the mouth of a *hu-tung*, the detour brought the car alongside a line of coolies, their baskets empty, moving back for another load. They were all lean, small men, ageless, stringy, veins and tendons standing out in stark relief. Their backs were bare, baked almost black by the sun, and their belts bristled with the bamboo tallies upon which their pay would be computed. Most plodded along stoically, heads down, here and there a man mopping at his face and chest with a bit of rag. As the stream of traffic veered away, one man caught Edgerton's eye. Smaller and even leaner than the rest, his head shaved until it gleamed, he seemed fairly to bounce

[233]

along, so great was the energy wound into his wiry muscles. Suddenly responding to something a companion said, the man threw back his head and laughed, and the laugh floated across the dusty road and over the heads of all the laboring coolies like music, clear and gay, light as the tinkling of bells. The sound moved Edgerton as if he'd felt the very earth move beneath the wheels. That was China . . . that man laughing! China! The name seemed suddenly to dazzle him, making his ears pound with the reverberations of millions of hauling, pulling, carrying, marching men—their feet all bare, all leathery—and all the people capable of incredible endurance. And of laughter. And in a year he would be gone from it.

"How incredibly primitive!" Valerie said.

A chance puff of air blew in through Edgerton's open window, carrying with its dust the smell of burning refuse, garlic, and boiled turnips, and a whiff of excrement from the jungle of buildings where their *hu-tung* was heading.

The way narrowed abruptly, the car's fenders almost brushing the walls on either side. Both behind them and ahead, the *hu-tung* was packed, crammed, clogged with humanity. Pedestrians, water carriers, barrows, bicycles, carts pulled by oxen and by mules, and one small old-fashioned Peking cart, like a miniature covered wagon meant for a donkey. Pulled by an old man and a boy, it carried a tiny lady so ancient she could have been the old man's mother. She peered at them curiously from eyes that were merely slits in her prunelike face. She was gumming greedily on slivers of dried persimmon.

As the *hu-tung* began to widen, the crowd flowed up around them, gaping in and laughing and pointing. Edgerton was thankful that Valerie understood no Chinese. She cranked her window shut and moved toward the middle of the seat.

"They gawk at us as if we were animals," she said, wrinkling her nose.

The car crept forward.

"We are animals to them; rare birds, anyway." Edgerton said. "Pink skins, round eyes, big ugly noses: I'm not surprised they stare."

"Well, I wish they wouldn't get so close. Don't they ever wash?"

Edgerton sighed. "When they can spare the water, they do. The road should open up soon; it'll get better then."

It didn't. The next bend brought them face to face with a heavy cart loaded with oil drums and pulled by a pair of oxen. The *hu-tung* was wide enough for the other carts to pass, but Edgerton could see with a glance that his car would never make it.

The yoke of oxen stood, shook their heads against the flies, and

[234]

regarded the car with their soft and patient eyes. The carter uttered an anguished *"ai-ya"!* and looked around helplessly for some way out of the impasse. There was none, except to back into the wider place through which he had just passed. Resigned to the workings of an indifferent fate, he began to goad his animals rearward. They did not much care for it and bellowed their protest plaintively. A chorus of mixed complaint and advice arose from the rest of the crowd, vexed at being delayed by this foreign equipage. The din grew steadily.

Valerie gave a quick frightened look around, then turned to Edgerton, her eyes pleading to be reassured.

"Don't worry," he said. "It's just a lot of good-natured noise."

What a day! he thought wryly. Valerie's skirt was streaked with drifts of dust, and under her arms faint beige crescents were forming on the white silk, certain to darken as time passed. Little remained of the golden shine in which she had set out so unsuspectingly, and Edgerton was sorry for her. To him it was merely a commonplace jaunt into the country, for all its inconveniences. To her it had become much more, a safari among strange people and beasts in a strange land, stinking, dirty, and unkempt.

The cart was finally maneuvered out of the way, and Edgerton was able to ease by with about an inch to spare. He gave the carter all the change he had: a handful of coppers and a wad of small bills, none worth more than a few cents. And, rather formally, he thanked the man for taking so much trouble.

The carter seemed as delighted with the thanks as with the money; he bowed and beamed fervently, displaying gums decimated of teeth.

"How much did you give him?" Valerie asked, not really caring.

"About sixty cents," he said, adding, "A day's pay."

"Ugh! What a wretched system."

The remark annoyed Edgerton unreasonably. He had no use for the system either, but he could imagine no practicable alternative. The people were desperately poor, and everything around them was poor as a result. There were mountains of taxes, misappropriated or squandered or stolen, so that practically nothing was left for municipal services. It meant no sewers, no water, no protection, no garbage removal, no honest civil servants. It was a vicious and unbreakable cycle, and it made for filth and stinks and dysentery and epidemics. It was a wonder any of them survived. The foreigner who could not turn his back once in a while and close his eyes and his nostrils, risked madness and despair.

Abruptly the row of buildings on their left ended, leaving the land to fall away gently into a long shallow bowl, checkered with neat farm

[235]

plots. Although the roadway widened, it became no smoother, but the air was noticeably cooler. The crops looked green and healthy, and hardly a plot was without someone, man or woman or child, hoeing or weeding or repairing the borders. On their right, what had been blank walls now gave way to a series of small open shops of every description and purpose. There was a continuous passing back and forth across the road.

Beyond the long swath of farmland, and perhaps half a mile away, was the southeast corner of the city wall surmounted by a shabby watchtower. The paint of its pillars and woodwork, once a bright red, had faded, and its roof sagged wearily on rotten beams.

Valerie sighed audibly. A glance showed her transformed, her eyes sparkling. "This is much nicer," she said, reaching over to touch him on the arm.

Ho hum, Edgerton thought, then chided himself for being dense and unsympathetic. The scene did have a certain bucolic charm. Softened by distance, the sight of farmers at their age-old tasks had a reassuring timelessness about it. Among the shops there were blacksmiths, coopers, carpenters, tinsmiths, basket weavers, bakers, bicycle mechanics. Approaching them was a knife and scissors grinder, his entire shop slung from the two ends of a shoulder pole. He was strumming and twanging at the steel tongs which were his advertisement. On their left, squatting among his boxes and using a homemade drill, a man prepared a broken china bowl to receive a row of metal staples and thus be useful for another year or two.

Almost every other house had a food shop as an adjunct to the family kitchen, and the air was alive with the odors of cooking.

A band of small boys attached themselves to the slowly moving car, and scampered along beside them, shouting and laughing and calling for cumshaw. Edgerton slowed abruptly, then had to stop and wait while an enormous sow ambled across in front of them, great dugs swinging, trailed by her squealing litter. Grubby fingers pulled at his sleeve and a grinning urchin with a snotty, dirty face tried to climb onto the running board. Gently but firmly Edgerton pushed him off and told him in the street vernacular to go home and help his father, to the delight and amazement of his companions.

As they moved on, the roadway began to swing to a slow arc to the right. Not far ahead Edgerton suddenly noticed a familiarly shaped cart, and he almost groaned aloud. Half-amused, half-worried, he wondered if they could get by it without Valerie's noticing. It was a high-wheeled mule cart, and lashed to the back of it was an immense wooden barrel banded with straps of braided bamboo. A bung the size of a man's leg sluiced its precious cargo into the buckets of a line of waiting farmers. Poor Valerie, Edgerton thought. "Hold your breath," he said, but it was too late. An overpowering effluvium filled the car, gagging them like some palpable liquid substance. Taken by surprise, Valerie gasped in horror.

Blessedly, the road ahead was momentarily clear. Edgerton stepped on the gas. "I didn't intend for your tour to be quite so graphic," he told her. He grinned hopefully, and was relieved to see her answering smile.

"When you show someone the sights of ancient Peking, you do a thorough job," she said bravely.

"We aim to please."

Bending further, the road plunged back into the crowded town. "We'll be out of all this soon and you can begin to enjoy yourself," he told her.

"Don't worry; I am enjoying it," she said. "I'm just not very intrepid."

"It takes some getting used to; don't be hard on yourself," he told her, relenting. And don't be such a cranky old bastard, he told himself. Give the woman a chance.

Soon he turned onto a secondary street, even shabbier and lumpier and noisier than Hata Men Chieh had been. As the massing traffic funnelled toward the dingy tower of Tso An Men, it swept them along with it.

They were checking travel papers at the gate, and pandemonium prevailed. A barbed wire barricade half blocked the road, and a horde of Chinese on foot, restless but intimidated, shuffled one by one past a bad-tempered Japanese noncom. Another sentry, with a bayoneted rifle as tall as he was slung across his back, spotted the diplomatic emblem on Edgerton's bumper, gave the interior of the car and the couple a glance of contemptuous boredom, and waved them around the crowd still waiting to have their documents inspected. The tunnel of the gateway was narrow and dark and had a fetid moistness about it that made even Edgerton feel claustrophobic. Then suddenly they were through, ejected into the sunlight.

A few small shops, a decrepit inn, and a combination garage and bicycle shop clustered untidily beside the road, as though clinging to the skirts of the gate tower for protection. Ahead, the road was lined with poplars and stretched away invitingly. There was a feeling of great openness to the green fields, and the air seemed clearer and fresher than before. They both sighed with relief, and Valerie gave him a smile of real pleasure.

[237]

Once they were on the open road, Edgerton looked at his watch. Their extra thirty minutes were used up, but the road would be clear now all the way to Tungchow, and they were still on time.

The road veered to the left and began paralleling the wall. In the high sunlight, the towers and buttresses loomed massively, the ravages of time and neglect too distant to be seen. On the right, the weed-filled course of the old Imperial Canal ran along beside them.

He was about to point it out to Valerie when, like a cannon shot, the right rear tire exploded.

A large oak stood incongruously in the line of poplars, and Edgerton let the car roll to an uneven stop in its more substantial shade. He set the handbrake and turned off the ignition. The engine chugged stubbornly for a few extra revolutions before it gasped and died, the way it often did when it was hot.

The whole heavy weight of the atmosphere settled down on them, its silence broken only by the muted sawing of innumerable cicadas.

Slowly the grip of his fingers on the wooden steering wheel relaxed and Edgerton permitted himself a sigh. "The fates have it in for us today," he said at last.

Valerie gave him a sympathetic smile. "So it would seem. Will it take long to fix, do you think?"

"A jiffy. I've had lots of practice."

"Well, you picked a nice spot for it."

"Yes, didn't I? These tours are planned down to the last detail." Out on the road, he took off his tie and rolled up his sleeves. He could imagine what his clothes were going to look like by the time he got the tire changed, but there was no help for that.

"Aren't we going to be late?" Valerie asked, getting down from the car.

"A little maybe, but not much. Anyway, our hosts are supposed to be a forgiving bunch."

"Well, I hope so. Franklin seemed to feel that this speech was a very important one."

"They've been contending with acts of God all their lives," he said carefully. "If they can bring themselves to absolve me, perhaps Franklin can too."

He rummaged for the wheel wrench and began to unbolt the spare.

"Look what you're doing to your clothes," Valerie said.

"What do you suggest?" he asked over his shoulder, suddenly annoyed.

"Just be careful. You don't want to show up looking a mess."

"God damn!" He threw the wrench onto the ground.

[238]

"Now what?" she asked crossly.

He had to face it: the whole thing was his own stupid fault. The acknowledgment made him blush angrily. "The spare's flat," he muttered.

"Oh, no!" she said.

Oh yes, Edgerton answered in his head. He went to the opposite side of the car, and leaned against the fender. He stared blindly toward the city, breathing deeply. If she said one more word about what Franklin was going to think, she'd regret it, he promised himself that. It was a humiliating oversight and he didn't feel like having his nose rubbed in it.

After a few moments, he went to get a cigarette off the front seat. When he rejoined Valerie, she was frowning down at the offending spare.

"What are you going to do?"

"Get it fixed. There was a shop back there by the gate."

"Can't you patch it?"

"Yes, but my pump is broken. I was going to get a new one but. . ." He tried to make his shrug nonchalant and failed. Keep your temper, he told himself.

"Are you going to roll it all the way back *there*?"

"What do you suggest? Carrier pigeons?"

"Don't yell at me!"

"I'm sorry, Valerie; but please stop giving me hell, will you?"

"But, how could . . . ?" She stopped and turned away. "Oh, I'm sorry, too, John. Everything seems to be going wrong." Her voice broke.

Stricken, Edgerton went to her and put an arm around her shoulders.

She shook it off half-heartedly. "You'll get my clothes all dirty," she sobbed.

Edgerton held her, shaking her gently. "Forget it," he said. "They're as dirty as they're likely to get."

She tried to glare at him. "Well, it's your fault."

"Piffle!" he said. "Absolutely not guilty."

Tears still streaming, she fought back the beginning of a smile. "What am I supposed to do while you're off with that tire?"

"Well, you can stay here if you like," he told her steadily, gesturing toward the car. "In splendid luxury."

"All by myself?" She got out a handkerchief and blew her nose.

"Or you can come with me," he said, grinning as though it were all a joke.

[239]

"It must be miles."

"One, at the most."

"It'll take hours."

"Thirty, forty minutes, for anyone under seventy." His smile was beginning to hurt.

She looked down at her dirty white pumps, their high heels spiking the dry yellow earth, "I can't go that far in these shoes."

Edgerton could only laugh. He spread his hands. "It's an impasse, then. You won't stay and you won't come along. I can only assure you that these are the sum of your choices, all that's available. Take your pick."

He left her standing while he threw the tools in the back of the car and found a rag to wipe his hands on.

"Well, come on then," she said to his back. He turned to find that she had already started back toward the gate, her purse swinging angrily from one hand and her heels wobbling. Her childishness both surprised and annoyed him. He got the spare tire and started off.

He made slow going of it at first. The tire was hard to manage, and it kept wanting to fall over against his leg. Once it escaped and rolled toward the ditch, and Edgerton had to run after it. But, little by little, he was getting the hang of it.

After a few minutes, Valerie gave a great sigh. "I want a cigarette," she said.

Oh, Christ! Edgerton thought, and felt his pocket with his free hand. "I left them in the car," he confessed unhappily. He would have liked one himself. "Don't you have any in your purse?"

"I'm not used to carrying cigarettes when a gentleman takes me out," she said, refusing to meet his eye.

"Well, let that be a lesson to you," he said, pushing on again.

Watching Valerie press stubbornly ahead, Edgerton was suddenly very sorry for her . . . for everything.

Their contretemps recalled a drive he'd taken with Tamara early in the spring. They had gone exploring down some side track, and he'd run his smoothest and thinnest tire over a thorn. He'd had no spare at all that time, having forgotten to get it back from the repair shop. Tamara had only laughed when he cursed himself, and quoted Confucius to him on the subject of serenity. While he had busied himself with tire irons and patches, she wandered over to a neighboring farmhouse. When she came back she had a pot of tea and a bowl of cold cabbage and noodles, and an escort of a dozen children. They all sang songs for him, challenged him with riddles and tongue twisters, and listened to Tamara tell the fairy stories she had learned from Russell *t'at t'ai.* When the tire was fixed, they had returned to the farmhouse for more tea with the farmer and his wife, to their mixed delight and confusion. They hadn't known what to make of the American who spoke Chinese and the Chinese woman who didn't look quite right. They never made it to the Summer Palace that day—and hadn't cared.

Edgerton stopped and leaned on the tire, staring up the long gentle slope toward the gate. That was the thing about Tamara: life around her always seemed to throb with a faint undercurrent of excitement; life was an adventure. The unpredicted might occur, but expedients were improvised and there was always gaiety and laughter. Or almost always. He thought glumly of their last phone conversation.

Three o'clock. Tamara would be at the Club for another two hours. He wondered if she were through her bills yet; she always hated bills. How hurt she had sounded, how hurt and angry. And who could blame her? Well, he was getting his just desserts, there could be little doubt about that. He looked down at his grimy hands, feeling the sweat running into his eyes, trickling down the small of his back. He'd precipitated that wounding, scarring scene and for *this*. . . he glanced bitterly at Valerie's retreating back, now several yards ahead.

But that wouldn't do, and Edgerton knew it wouldn't. It wasn't Valerie's fault for finding the rough edges of life in China too much for her, nor was it Tamara's for at least asserting her pride and trying, however belatedly, to guard herself. It was his, John Edgerton's, Foreign Service Officer Class Four—selfish, thoughtless, greedy, bound and determined to get his own self-indulgent way.

Glowering down at the tire, as though to shift all blame onto its black, neglected carcass, he started it rolling again.

Valerie was waiting in the thin shade of a poplar. "We'll never get to that meeting now, will we?" she asked as he drew even. She fell into step beside him.

Edgerton stole a precarious glance at his watch. It was nearly three. "I'm afraid not," he said.

"Won't Franklin be terribly disappointed?"

Annoyance prodded him briefly. "Won't he ever!" he said, making himself smile at her. "But Franklin's used to disappointment. Besides, I'll make amends by sending around an eloquent letter. His message will get through, never fear."

Valerie gestured up the road. "It looks like miles."

"Another ten minutes should do it. Buck up."

The packed earth under their feet came to an end not far from the gate. For the rest of the way, the road was paved with large flat bricks, leftovers from when the wall was built. He heard Valerie falter and

[241]

stumble beside him. "Oh, damn!" she said in a voice of total exasperation.

Poor Valerie. The heel of her left shoe was off, wedged in the crack between two bricks. She could only stare at it helplessly, the tears already streaking her dusty cheeks, one foot flat, the other still propped by its fragile spike.

"We're almost there," he offered. "Can you make it a little farther?"

She was so upset, she seemed actually to make a face at him before limping on ahead.

Edgerton picked up the abandoned heel and put it in his pocket. With something of an expert flourish, he got his tire rolling, and grinned to himself; he was beginning to feel slightly hysterical.

At the bicycle shop, a small but fascinated crowd of onlookers formed quickly. The bicycle mechanic assumed full responsibility for the tire, assuring Edgerton that it would be fixed in a few minutes . . . or perhaps half an hour. The crowd nodded wisely, repeating this judgment in a murmur. A stool was provided and Valerie sat down to take off her shoe. A small boy was sent running off with the two parts of it to a cobbler's in a nearby alley.

There was a tea shop next door, and there Edgerton and Valerie took refuge. Fortunately part of the public room was hidden from the road by a curtain of bamboo beads. With nothing left to look at, the crowd reluctantly dispersed.

The proprietor ceremoniously produced a pot of tea and a package of stale Chinese cigarettes. Once alone, they sipped their tea and smoked in silence for a while, letting the perspiration dry and cool them. Although screened off from the road, the side of the little room was open, giving them a pleasant view down the slope toward the farms and the old canal.

Finally Valerie turned to him. "You really are very nice. I'm sorry I was so bitchy about the tire."

Edgerton was touched. "Don't worry about it, please. My fault for being careless. I'm afraid I've ruined your day."

She shook her head but didn't answer. She stared out at the scene below them. "From here, it's all so nice and picturesque, but when you get up close . . ."

"It smells," he interrupted.

She laughed uncertainly. "Yes, I suppose that says it all."

Suddenly her face was in her hands, and she was crying bitterly, her shoulders shaken by deep sobs, her body stiff with the effort to make no noise.

Edgerton moved over to put his arm around her. Her distress

[242]

touched him deeply . . . and it excited him, too. He wanted to kiss her tears, to make love to her, to distract her, to distract them both from the day's blunders. But all he did was stroke her shoulder gently.

Valerie straightened and gave him a grateful, somewhat sheepish look.

"There, there," he said softly, as her sobs dwindled. "There, there." He was thinking about getting back to the San Kwan Miao. He'd make everything all right then.

҉ ҉

Deciding on the spur of the moment to walk the rest of the way, Puhalski paid off the rickshaw on Hata Men Chieh. The Café Volga would begin to fill with customers before long; he wanted a little time to himself. In the hour which had passed since delivering Maya to Tanaka's house, he had completely recovered his good humor.

Puhalski sighed luxuriously; he felt like skipping. It was an enormous relief to have that nuisance of a woman off his hands. And in that hour, he'd taken care of a number of profitable chores and straightened out a few erring associates, all of which would contribute in time to his growing savings. As he reviewed the past hour's activities and the cleverness with which he'd managed things, Puhalski began to feel like his old self. Another year like the last one and he'd be comfortably well off. The thought made even the trouble he'd been put to over the woman worth his while . . . the stupid cow. She'd been a pain in the ass right to the end, protesting and blubbering all the way to Tanaka's house.

Tanaka! Puhalski laughed silently as he turned into his *hu-tung*. What a picture: Tanaka resplendent in his white uniform, his paunch a dazzle of stars and medals . . . Puhalski had hardly been able to keep a straight face. He had to admit Maya had looked quite pretty in her new dress . . . he'd almost been proud of her. But what a job to get her there in a reasonable frame of mind. Well, at least the introductions had gone off smoothly and with dignity, and Maya's subdued manner could have passed for modesty. When Puhalski left them, Tanaka had been beaming and bowing as though a Princess of the Realm had come for tea. If only Maya did as she was told and kept her mouth shut, and made no girlish fuss about her virtue. Puhalski snorted. If Sobolov had sprouted a new set of horns every time his wife had opened up for another man, he'd look like a porcupine.

Taking the success of his other business as an omen, Puhalski decided things were going to work out all right. He was richer by over

[243]

seven hundred Chinese dollars, Maya was out of his hair for good, and Tanaka would have his hands full . . . too full for any harebrained scheming.

Puhalski turned jauntily into his café and stopped. He could feel a wave of rage rise in his throat, choking him. What in God's name did *he* want? Giving Natasha an inquiring glance, he got back a vacant shrug in return. Another cretin.

"Well, Andrei. This is a surprise," he said, trying to sound jovial. He pulled out a chair and sat down.

Sobolov was haggard and pale, and his skin hung loosely on his face. Puhalski noticed the empty glass and, looking more closely at Sobolov, wondered how many he'd had. He appeared befuddled, and his head seemed to wobble slightly on his neck. He'd aged ten years since morning, and he was wearing a ridiculous new hat. It rested on his fat ears like an inverted piss pot.

"Where . . ." Sobolov began hoarsely and had to stop and clear his throat. "Where is my wife?"

A peculiar edge in his voice made Puhalski tense instinctively. He gave an amiable shrug and raised his eyebrows. "Why, I'm sure I don't know, my dear fellow."

Sobolov gave his head a stubborn shake. "I saw you," he muttered. "In a taxi."

"Oh *then*," Puhalski said. "I happened to be driving through your *hu-tung* when she came out. Naturally I offered her a lift. I dropped her off near that new department store on Hata Men Chieh." He lighted a cigarette casually, certain that something was very wrong here. "Are you taking the afternoon off?"

Sobolov seemed to translate the question in his head. "Yes," he said finally. "The afternoon off."

"No trouble at the office?"

"No, no trouble. I fell ill and Mr. Edgerton sent me home."

"How nice of Mr. Edgerton. I hope it's nothing serious."

"I haven't felt well since yesterday."

"That's understandable. I'm very sorry about that rotten business." Puhalski smiled. "Those responsible are to be punished."

"Oh," Sobolov said dully.

"Yes. Now," Puhalski said, leaning forward, "have you been able to make any progress?"

"Progress?"

Puhalski wanted to kick his fat face for him. "Yes, progress. You recall, I hope, that little matter we discussed this morning."

"Oh," Sobolov said. He thought for a moment. "Yes, a little progress. But it's difficult."

[244]

"Right. Be careful, of course, but get a move on." Puhalski glanced at Natasha to see if she was minding her own business. She was. For the first time in years he felt nostalgic for the Army. Then you gave orders and they were obeyed. If not, you were punished. For imbeciles like Sobolov, there was always a hole to dig, a potato to peel, or a mine field to explore. They were an expendable rabble; lose one, you got another. There were thousands of them. He leaned back in his chair and crossed his legs comfortably under the table.

Sobolov was having trouble focusing his bleary eyes. Puhalski watched him with that semipatience reserved for the feebleminded.

"Where is my wife?" Sobolov repeated tonelessly.

Puhalski spread his hands. "But my dear fellow, I've already explained . . ."

The sharp edge of the table caught him just under the ribs, making him gasp with pain. Before he knew what was happening he was on his back on the damp floor with the table on top of him. Glass shattered noisily next to his head, and through the pounding of his pulse, Sobolov's voice came piping weakly, "I want my wife, you bastard."

Puhalski shook his head and his vision cleared. Sobolov loomed over him, his puny fists clenched in front of his chest. A cold fury gripped Puhalski. He hurled the table aside and scrambled to his feet. The miserable little shit had dared to attack him . . . him!

Sobolov came for him in a waddling charge, arms flailing like a girl's. Puhalski stiff-armed him in the head, feeling in the contact a pleasure that was almost sexual, sending Sobolov careening into the nearest table.

Natasha let out a terrified bleat.

"Shut up and lock the door!" he shouted over his shoulder.

She only moaned louder and cowered down behind the bar.

"Lock the door, you stupid cunt!"

More frightened of him than of anything else, she ran to obey.

Thank God, the place is empty, Puhalski thought. All he needed was for some busybody to see them and go for a policeman. Exhilarated now, he watched Sobolov disentangle himself from the chairs into which he had fallen, delighted with the chance of giving this putrid nuisance the trouncing he deserved.

Gulping for air, Sobolov came lumbering in again.

"Are you crazy, Andrei?" Puhalski asked him, catching him on the nose with the heel of his hand, feeling the cartilage give mushily under the impact. He sidestepped and let the fat man's momentum carry him on by. When Sobolov turned, the blood was already running freely down the front of his shirt and his usually pasty face was deeply

[245]

flushed. His breath came stertorously, bubbling the blood that had run into his mouth.

"Your're forcing me, old fellow," Puhalski informed him calmly. "I have no choice but to defend myself against this unprovoked attack."

"My wife," Sobolov gasped and came at him once again.

Calmly Puhalski waited. He ducked, easily avoiding Sobolov's first wild punch, stepped in close, and hit him precisely in the solar plexus.

The blow staggered Sobolov. He took two faltering steps, then bent double, hugging himself closely. His nearsighted eyes bugged out comically and his mouth was open as though caught in the middle of a yawn. He looked loose and strangely disjointed, a rag doll of a man. He still had his hat on, the silly ass.

Flexing his fingers, Puhalski stepped back and leaned an elbow on the bar. His hands were steady and he felt perfectly relaxed. He wasn't even breathing heavily.

As Sobolov started to straighten up, he stiffened suddenly, and his face went very pale, his eyes rolling slowly up into his head. A faint moan escaped from his throat, and for a long moment he seemed to balance awkwardly, as though suspended by a wire from the ceiling. The moment ended and Sobolov toppled sideways, his head striking the concrete with a thud.

Chilled suddenly, Puhalski hesitated, then walked over and nudged Sobolov apprehensively in the ribs. He didn't stir. Puhalski stared down, with each moment more aware of an inexorable catastrophe. He dropped quickly to one knee and placed his hand over Sobolov's heart. There was no beat, nor from his lungs the faintest whisper of breath.

Very slowly, Puhalski got to his feet. One punch in the stomach and the old fool was dead. How was anyone to have anticipated that? The stubborn and troublesome old bungler was a fucking nuisance right to the very end.

From the bar, Natasha emitted hysterical whinnies. In a fury, Puhalski whirled on her. "Shut up, you idiot!" he commanded. "And come over here. We have to get him into the back."

Natasha obeyed reluctantly but then couldn't bring herself to touch Sobolov. Puhalski slapped her hard on the side of the head, almost knocking her down. She was all right then. Together they managed to half-drag, half-carry the flaccid body back to the café's storeroom. Kicking aside a few cases of empty bottles, Puhalski made a little niche behind the door and into that they stuffed him. He went to get Sobolov's hat and tossed it in on top of the body, then pulled the door closed and snapped the padlock.

[246]

The therapy of his slap had worn away, leaving Natasha whimpering and wringing her hands, on the verge of a new storm of hysterics. Puhalski gave her a long and icy stare, wondering if he could trust her. For the moment he had no choice, but she needed bracing up.

"Listen to me, Natasha. This was an accident. One word about it to anyone, to *anyone*, and you are finished." He drew his finger across his Adam's apple. "Finished forever. Do you understand me?"

Natasha nodded stupidly, her mouth slack and her eyes blank with fear.

"Good. Don't forget it, and I won't forget you. I'll have him taken away later. In the meantime, straighten the place up, wash your face, and open the door. Our customers will soon be arriving. Get on with it." He slapped her encouragingly on the bottom.

There was nothing to do but call Tanaka. The Colonel was going to be very unhappy, but there was no help for that. Without Tanaka's help there was no safe way to dispose of the body. Besides, Tanaka was involved too deeply now do to anything but grumble.

Puhalski mopped his face and hands on the bar towel, then combed his hair carefully. He could thank God for one thing: this was the end of all that nonsense about code books, at least as far as he was concerned. No more of that madness.

Natasha swung the door open, flooding the dim room with sunlight. It must be four o'clock, Puhalski thought. Staranovitch was standing in the doorway waiting for his first drink of the day.

Pulling at his beard, the Russian strolled in. He put his hand on Natasha's shoulder and shook her gently, leering all the while at Puhalski. "A little slow in opening up, Serge," he said, letting his hand slide down to rub the girl in the small of the back. "Working on your accounts, I presume."

Natasha giggled.

Puhalski gave him a broad wink and reached for the telephone. "Come, Natasha. Put on a record for Count Boris. And pour his vodka, a double for keeping him waiting, on the house."

The record was just starting when the operator came on the line. Puhalski turned his back on the other two and gave her Tanaka's home number.

⚔⚔

Colonel Hideki Tanaka scratched his stomach meditatively and gave the telephone a morose look.

So Sobolov was dead. It was a bitter piece of news, bitter and in-

[247]

furiating. Weeks of planning, of hoping . . . so much had depended on Sobolov. Now it would all have to be done again.

Tanaka told himself to be philosophical. A man of his accomplishments and responsibilities and—it would be false modesty to deny it—his genius, was obliged to face adversity serenely, to weather the storms of fate and to begin anew. Tanaka smiled thinly, pleased with this picture of stoicism.

In the morning, the first item of business would be a careful screening of reliable interpreters. When the Americans began interviewing candidates to replace Sobolov—something they'd be doing quickly—Tanaka would have seen to it that the best qualified applicants were sympathetic to Japan's great work in Asia, and to his own programs. Since it would be some time before the new man could risk a start on his primary task, he would have to be willing and able to buckle down and do good work for the Americans. It had taken Sobolov six months; Tanaka sighed and lighted a cigarette. It was a long time to wait. But there were compensations, he reminded himself. The American was being deftly maneuvered into a box. Tanaka grinned, turning to stare blindly out of the window. In that particular game, fate had dealt him good cards, and he was playing them masterfully.

The reminder warmed Tanaka; his plan was as foolproof as it was simple. Had he not chosen intelligence work, he could have had a rewarding career in the diplomatic service. But the pleasant moment was all too fleeting.

There were times when memory wouldn't let him rest. Slowly his happiness faded as old and hated scenes resurrected themselves unbidden in his mind's eye . . . his father returning at sunset to the oven that was their iron-roofed shack, his spirit already breaking under the pressure of indentured labor in the pineapple fields, his body soon to follow . . . the cluster of hovels along a dusty road, far from the trade winds which cooled the coast for the American overseers and the rich tourists . . . his mother doing laundry for the foreman's large and dirty family and glad of the opportunity to eke out a few extra dollars of script to be spent in the plantation store . . . the sickly stink of rotting pineapples . . . the cockroaches the size of mice . . . the rats that roamed the fields and the villages in packs and gnawed the flesh of babies left unattended. . . .

Breathing slowly and deeply, Tanaka strove to restore his composure. He put a shaking hand over his eyes. Gradually the vision faded, and he felt himself grow calmer. The Americans would get what was coming to them . . . it had to be. All he wanted was a part in their destruction. He had earned it.

[248]

The Russian woman stirred, uttering a long and tremulous sigh.

Tanaka turned and studied her complacently. She lay on her back in the farthest part of the bed, as close to the wall as she could get. She was a timorous creature, Tanaka thought, his smile knowing, indulgent. It had required the exercise of all his powers to persuade her into his bedroom. Puhalski'd warned him she might pretend a certain shyness, but not such reluctance.

His inducement and her reluctance had limped along decorously at first, propelled incongruously by mixed bits of Chinese and English. If only she understood Japanese . . . but Puhalski had said she didn't and it was true. Tanaka had finally been driven to put his determination into almost threatening terms. Suddenly the woman had seemed to collapse, insisting only on undressing alone, with Tanaka donning his kimono in his dressing room . . . gross caricatures of newlyweds.

But Tanaka had felt supremely understanding, even a little amused at these embellishments. In his mood of anticipation, delay had only sweetened the prize. The woman was filled with latent passion to an extent never suspected by the conniving Russian. With their preliminary maneuvers, Tanaka became convinced that he was to be the man to bring to flower her deepest appetites. The thought had filled him with a sense of irresistible power.

And then, at the crucial, the climactic moment, the Russian scoundrel had made his depressing phone call.

Sighing at the memory, Tanaka watched the woman. Under his probing eyes the thin sheet revealed more than it covered, draping her full contours as if it were of the thinnest silk.

Tanaka's loins stirred demandingly, driving the dreamy smile from his face. He turned blindly, angrily, to fumble with his cigarettes. That deceitful bungler! Masquerading as a civilized man, he was nothing but a brutal Russian peasant with neither sense of balance nor restraint. Claiming self-defense . . . what utter, flimsy nonsense! Did Puhalski take him for a gullible idiot? Well, Puhalski was long overdue for a couple of lessons. He wanted help in disposing of the body, did he? He would get it . . . and perhaps something more besides.

Tanaka reached for the field telephone which connected him directly with his office and Captain Okamura. As he spun the crank, he gave his watch a glance. He would instruct Okamura to have a military police detachment meet him at Puhalski's café in twenty minutes. Clear the place for police inspection, block the *hu-tung* for ten minutes, bring a closed van to the back door . . . nothing could be simpler. It would be a scene no different from a dozen others taking place throughout the city every day.

[249]

The instrument crackled against his ear for an instant before Okamura's servile voice came over the wire. When his instructions regarding the deployment at Puhalski's cafe had been completed, Tanaka sat for a moment thinking, Okamura's adenoidal breathing whispering in his ear.

All very neat, but there was still Edgerton. Always Edgerton, everywhere Tanaka turned, that square, pale face seemed destined to appear, rising moonlike over all horizons. It was the time for decision. Now that he had the means to eclipse that hated presence, why delay further?

"And there's something else, Okamura," he began, dropping his voice slightly. A glance showed him the woman was dozing, her eyes closed, placid, resigned.

As Tanaka spoke, his mind pictured the execution of his orders, scene by scene. When he was done, it was as though the deed itself had been accomplished. The trap had been closed on Edgerton, and all in a matter of minutes. Tanaka hung up the phone, stubbed out his cigarette, and rubbed his hands together. Everything was under control. His brow clear again, his eyes relighting with excitement, Tanaka took off his kimono, folded it carefully, and laid it on the chair.

The Russian woman was awake now, eyeing him sidelong as he approached the bed. Tanaka drew himself up to his full height and observed her with calculated impassivity. She had much to learn, but he was a patient man and glad to teach her. She'd never cared much for her husband, Puhalski'd said . . . that was fortunate. Not only would there be no need for hysterics when she got the news, but, finding herself alone and defenseless in an indifferent world, she'd turn to him for protection. While they were still having tea together, he'd impressed her with the fact that he was a man of influence. There was probably now no reason for her to return home, at least not permanently. With discretion, she could be made to appear part of his household. Once she realized how vulnerable she was as the widow of a politically unreliable person, she'd be more than grateful for his generous offer of aid and shelter. Even the daughter could come along, provided she didn't whine and make a nuisance of herself . . . perhaps she could be trained to become a sort of maid.

Tanaka saw the future opening before him in delightful detail; the dull past, with its months of futile abstinence broken only by tawdry, unsatisfying episodes, faded. Everything was falling into place.

Standing there, arms folded and feet apart, Tanaka knew he must be an imposing figure. Now, with the woman's nearness causing him to respond splendidly, he felt like a lion. She, too, was magnificent, fittingly proportioned. His eyes caught hers and held them, seeing in them both fear and awe . . . and something else. She was a woman; like any other she craved only the domination of a strong, willful man.

Tanaka willed the woman's eyes to drop. As they moved down his body, reluctant yet fascinated, their impact was palpable, like the touch of tracing fingers. They widened when they came to his swelling manhood, and a moan escaped her. A moan of desire, Tanaka labeled it, his chest expanding as well.

For a moment he stood transcended, imagining herself a rampant bull, the very embodiment of Japan's irresistible power.

Slowly, unwillingly, he turned away; it was time to dress. It was Puhalski with his Caucasian arrogance and his insufferable blundering who was depriving Tanaka of his rightful enjoyments. Even if for only an hour or two, with Puhalski getting his come-uppance in the meantime, the enforced delay rankled bitterly.

Just the same, Tanaka reminded himself, his face brightening, when he did return, he'd be free until the next morning.

The sight of Puhalski across the table from him filled Tanaka with intense pleasure. Puhalski gave the impression of a nervous, uncertain man . . . as well he might; it was a good sign.

Except for Puhalski's wary greeting—to which Colonel Tanaka had not troubled to respond—nothing had been said for nearly a minute. The silence was getting to Puhalski.

Colonel Tanaka remained relaxed and supremely assured. Finally he said, "So, Puhalski. Tell me what happened."

Rather hesitantly, Puhalski began to speak. While the Russian talked, Tanaka smoked, letting his eyelids droop from time to time as though suffering from extreme boredom.

". . . but there was no pulse," Puhalski concluded, spreading his hands wide in a gesture of innocent helplessness.

"No pulse. Yes." Tanaka ruminated for a moment, then shook his head. "I am disappointed in you, Puhalski," he said sadly.

Puhalski bridled. "Surely I have the right to defend myself?"

"*Ah-so*, self-defense. A very good point. However, it's instructive to remember that Sobolov was a sedentary man in his late fifties with a heart ailment . . . or so you eloquently informed me when you complained about the coarse treatment he'd received at the Police Yamen. Recalling that, it might be said that you could have defended youself less forcefully. Hmmm, yes." Tanaka nodded his head, then shook it reprovingly. "You Westerners are always so clumsy. Either you do nothing, or you do too much." Sighing elaborately, Tanaka puffed

[251]

away at his cigarette. "The problem now concerns the selection of Sobolov's replacement."

"I've some ideas about that," Puhalski offered eagerly, obviously relieved to be moving on to this new subject. "There are several Russians, friends of mine, who . . ."

Tanaka cut him short with a weary wave of the hand. "Please, my dear Serge, please! I've had quite enough of Russians, if you'll forgive my saying so. No more Russians, thanks just the same."

Puhalski could not mask his chagrin. "Yes, of course. As you see fit, Colonel," he hastened to say. "But it'll be more difficult for me, working with someone I don't know."

"You, my dear fellow?" Tanaka raised his eyebrows in exaggerated surprise, wanting to laugh, "But you'll be having nothing to do with Sobolov's replacement."

Puhalski looked stunned. "But . . ." he gasped, a thin sheen of oily sweat breaking out across his brow.

"But nothing. You, my good fellow and former collaborator, are finished; completely and totally finished." Tanaka showed Puhalski his teeth, and gave him a happy nod.

The Russian's face hardened, and the lines in it grew deeper. "I demand an explanation," he said, a stubborn light in his eyes.

"You demand, do you? Listen to me, you lying bungler, you will demand nothing. You are a nobody, a guttersnipe, an insignificant pimp, and I'll tolerate no insolence from you." While he was talking, Tanaka's hand had drifted unobtrusively to his pistol holster and had undone the flap. Now he placed the pistol in his lap.

Puhalski was glaring at him angrily. Slowly an expression of utter contempt twisted the Russian's face. Suddenly unable to bear the sight of him, Tanaka cleared his throat, leaned abruptly across the table, and spat precisely into his face.

Puhalski's eyes closed and his contorted features turned crimson. As though petrified with outrage, he let the gob of phlegm and saliva slide slowly down his cheek to his chin, where it clung pendulously, then fell away. With infinite care, Puhalski took a handkerchief out of his pocket and wiped his face, and then his trousers. When he was done, he stared curiously into the handkerchief, folded it with trembling fingers, and put it away.

Puhalski wanted very badly to kill him, Tanaka was certain of that. The notion made him strangely happy; it was too late for Puhalski: he had been emasculated.

Tanaka raised a finger and shook it at the Russian. "In fact, Puhalski, you're not only finished, you're in serious trouble. Certain of your

[252]

activities have attracted official notice." Tanaka paused, letting Puhalski glare back balefully. "As Provost Marshal it is my duty to inform you of them." He raised a finger. "One: there are reports that prostitutes use your café as headquarters, and that you appropriate a percentage of their earnings." Puhalski's mouth started to open but Tanaka forestalled him with a wave." "All prostitutes must have municipal licenses and undergo a weekly medical inspection. As a brothel keeper you're responsible for seeing that these regulations are obeyed, but you've done nothing. As a matter of fact, you don't have a license for your own part in these activities. A double violation."

Puhalski sank back into his chair, his face long and watchful.

Tanaka added another finger to the first. "Two: there's considerable evidence that you deal in opium. Now, a great portion of Imperial Army effort in North China is directed toward eliminating this infamous traffic and rehabilitating the poor Chinese who have become its victims. This is a particularly serious matter."

The Russian's eyes were shrouded now, and he kept them directed at the table top.

"You have hurt me, Puhalski, and destroyed my plans with your clumsiness. I am a simple soldier . . ." Tanaka watched Puhalski's eyes darken with suspicion; under the table his feet shifted warily. Gratified, Tanaka continued, ". . . I'm tempted to prefer the appropriate charges against you, and let justice take its course." Tanaka allowed himself a thin smile, "But I have become a sentimentalist. Because of what I thought was a friendship between us . . ."

Puhalski seemed again about to speak; Tanaka quickly forestalled him. "No, don't interrupt! I want no further conversation with you, now or ever. You are free to go, but I warn you: no illegal or even questionable activities, or I will reopen your case. Who knows, by then even more evidence against you may have come to light. Now, get out before I change my mind!"

Tanaka glared at the table, listening to the scrape of the Russian's chair and the sound of his retreating footsteps with mixed feelings. At first, he'd intended to arrest Puhalski, make an example of him even at the risk of what the vindictive wretch might say. But driving down to the café, he'd seen that wouldn't be necessary, or even desirable. Puhalski in prison was a nobody; at large, hungry, ambitious, he could still be useful regardless of the hatred he might harbor. Puhalski was never the man to let a mere emotion interfere with a chance for profit. Smiling to himself, Tanaka reholstered his pistol. He turned to the sentry at the door. "Send in Sergeant Okubo," he ordered.

Sergeant Okubo stamped in, his hobnails clashing loudly on the

[253]

concrete floor, and crashed to attention next to Tanaka's chair. Tanaka looked up into his square brown face, then turned moodily away. He didn't like Okubo. He'd been invalided to the Military Police to recover from wounds and wore several combat decorations. It was Tanaka's opinion that combat experience was highly overrated, and that line commanders were far too free with medals. Besides, Okubo was coarse and cocky, and he always smelled of turnips.

"Come," he ordered, and strode across the empty room with Okubo clumping along behind. A narrow smelly passageway led to the rear of the place. To the right, a toilet gurgled ceaselessly. At the far end of the hall there was another door which opened onto a small service yard. A police van was waiting there already. To the left was the door to the storeroom.

Tanaka pointed to the padlock. "Break it open," he said.

Okubo drew his pistol and worked the slide, sending a round into the chamber, just as Tanaka had suspected he would.

Tanaka glared at him. "Not that way, you imbecile! Do you want to alarm the whole neighborhood?"

Hangdog, Okubo put the pistol away.

Tanaka sighed wearily. How they expected him to perform intricate police work with a rabble of stupid infantrymen, he'd never understand. "Kick it in," he told Okubo.

The sergeant stepped back, gauged the distance at a glance, and drove the bottom of his boot into the door. The frame splintered and the door flew inward.

"That's better," Tanaka said sarcastically.

The room was small and dim and crammed with broken chairs and tables, and with cases of bottles stacked almost to the ceiling. Puhalski was a pig about everything, it would seem. Some light came through a single dirty pane set high in the opposite wall. A pair of cracked black shoes, toes up, protruded into the room from behind the door.

Tanaka pushed the door aside and looked down at the shapeless body, his face expressionless. So this was Sobolov. It was strange to be seeing him now, for both the first and the last time, when so much had hinged on him.

In the gray light, the blood staining his face and clothes appeared a dark brown, like drying mud. Rather than a man, or the remains of one, he was just a lumpy bundle, a pile of dirty old clothes. There was nothing for Tanaka to do here. It was difficult to recall that the Russian woman was—had been—married to this mound of nothingness. He'd be very gentle when he told her what had happened.

"Dispose of him," he told the sergeant, speaking slowly, as though

[254]

instructing a child. "Put him in the van. Take him out to the city dump. Find a secluded part where no one can see you, and leave him there. The Chinese police can worry about how he got there . . . provided the dogs don't find him first." Tanaka paused, eyeing Okubo coldly. Ranking N.C.O.s tended to become insolent if given half a chance. Okubo's face remained impassive.

"Do you think you can manage that complicated task?" Tanaka asked him.

"Yes sir."

"Good; try not to bungle it. And no gossiping in the barracks."

Threading his way among Puhalski's battered tables, Tanaka felt a marvelous soaring elation. Despite disappointments enough to try a saint, he felt only a surging sense of power. For the first time in his life, he knew with certainty that all the reins were in his own two hands. There was an English saying about the tides in the lives of men . . . exhilarated, Tanaka could feel the tide lift beneath him.

♟♟

In the Gentlemen's Bar, a dice cup rattled vigorously, followed quickly by the rolling scatter of the dice. A great groan went up, punctuated by a solitary explosion of laughter, which quickly lapsed into a fit of strangled coughing.

Tamara looked back across the counter at the shuttered, empty office. Her desk was clear, her typewriter was covered, the light out.

"Did you hear the one about . . . ?" That would be Mr. Taylor with the piggy eyes. Another burst of laughter.

Reggie was in there with them. Not yet recovered from her rebuff, he'd looked at her with a hurt expression on the way in. But there had been others with him and he was too shy to speak; a blessing. Trailing the group—he was almost never late to these midafternoon summertime sessions—had been Mr. Taylor. To him she was that Chink girl . . . he didn't realize how clearly his voice carried from the bar. As usual, he'd favored her with a furtive leer, grinning wetly.

It was only a little after three, but her work was through for the day. She'd finished the monthly billing only minutes before and decided to go home early. She was going to miss her shower. Someone had evidently complained, for the day before, Wednesday, the manager had reminded her of the "Members Only" rule. He was a nice man . . . at least he'd had the decency to blush. Since there was nothing to stay for, she would go.

In a way she didn't want to leave. In a single day the little office had

[255]

changed from a dull place of boring work into a sort of sanctuary. Among the bills and ledgers, the comprador's invoices and memoranda from the manager, she had found distraction. It was a place where the pain of John Edgerton's rejection could be drowned in a river of trivia. She was too proud—*at last*, she added, gritting her teeth—to go back, and he was probably too angry to come to her. Besides, he had the other woman now, a nice safe Western woman, suitably white and properly documented. The all-to-ready tears began again, and she blinked them angrily away.

Snatching up her purse, she hurried across the empty lobby, her heels sounding spuriously resolute on the polished boards. To be seen blubbering by some member would be unbearable. She wanted to be outside, to throw herself quickly into the anonymity of the city. What if she were to see him with that new woman? She must start looking for another job without delay.

A small breeze stirred on Canal Street, and Tamara took a deep breath of it. It would seem even hotter outside the Legation Quarter, on the broad and relatively treeless streets of the Tartar City, and the streetcar on Hata Men Chieh would be a crowded oven.

Originally, she'd planned to drop in for a visit with her mother, perhaps even get a bath at the hotel before heading home. But now, with this unexpected time on her hands, she decided to shop for some of her mother's favorite dishes. If it weren't too late and the sentry permitted it, they'd go up on the wall for a picnic. There would be a breeze there, once the sun was lower in the sky, and a view of the city. Later it would be time enough to return to her hot and empty flat.

The only traffic going her way along Canal Street was an empty rickshaw. It was a new one, dazzling in the sunlight with its black lacquer and bright brass lamps. The seat covers had been freshly laundered, and even the brass tips of the pulling poles were polished. The rickshaw man was young and wiry and managed his vehicle easily. On impulse, welcoming the extravagance, she decided to do her shopping in style. Time enough later for economies.

At her wave, the puller headed in toward the curb. She told him the food shops she wanted to visit, all on Hata Men Chieh near the San P'ai-lou, and agreed at once to the fare he asked.

Although young, he was an experienced puller. He ran evenly, easily, with the poles lightly held so that the jogging rhythm of his gait was cushioned and his passenger comfortable. Tamara watched the traffic carefully, her toe working the button of the brass bell which was fastened under the footboards. It was expected of the passenger

[256]

thus to warn the traffic ahead, and save the puller from having to waste his breath shouting for a clear passage.

Ch'ang An Chieh was relatively clear of traffic. Like a horse that has been given his head, the puller stretched his stride. He was proud and strong, and not above showing off a little for his pretty passenger. Tamara knew this and was grateful for the flattery. She smiled slightly at the young man's back, thinking of what her mother would say to such unseemly notice taken of a mere coolie.

Her mother . . . Tamara shook her head, her smile fading slowly. Since that first night, her mother had said nothing more about what had happened, had simply refused to talk of it. Although Tamara had often considered the possibility that she herself might be raped, it never became real for her. Since the war, the act itself must have been repeated times without number; yet she could not accept it. Now, with the event striking into her closest family, she found herself obsessed with a morbid curiosity. What must it feel like, she wondered, to have the organs of love so misused? Thinking of John's lovemaking, she tried to imagine what such a brutal act might be like for a man and could not. She wished she had the nerve to ask her mother right out about it—woman to woman—but she hadn't dared.

To judge by her mother's manner, the event might never have occurred. Except for her breathless account at the beginning she simply refused to acknowledge it. In the end, it had only been the growing tension in the neighborhood which prevailed on her to be sensible. In spite of their attempted subtlety, it was quickly evident that both the Japanese and municipal authorities were conducting some sort of investigation. Although their moves seemed random, they were coming closer. Various rumors circulated, but the Liu women knew whom they were looking for. Finally her mother admitted she was being foolish not to accept John Edgerton's arrangements. And John . . . now by an effort of sheer will, Tamara attempted to push him from her mind.

And just as stubbornly, her thoughts clung to him, and she began to scold herself for being angry. It was pointless; what had happened was neither his fault, nor hers. The whole cruel and tender and heart-shattering affair had been doomed from the very start. She should never have loved him, never permitted herself even the small luxury of knowing him. She had always known it would lead nowhere, and certainly her mother had warned her. Circumstances were just against them; only a wishful thinker could have failed to see it. The world, confused and frightened by its own variety, just didn't work that way, their way. But why go over it? The thing for her, Tamara decided,

[257]

was to contrive a new role for herself, one that put no reliance upon love. Love ultimately meant pain. It was a fact she'd learned the hard way. But she was young and men found her attractive; from now on she would write the rules of the game herself . . . if she chose to play it at all. For the present she would work hard and help her mother and save her money . . . and look for a new job.

A battered taxi chugged abreast of them as though to pass. Then, for some reason, it dropped back, although the road was clear ahead and it could have easily gone by. It seemed to settle into place just to the rear of them, the sound of its old engine grumbling along, intruding and annoying and without sense.

Tamara tried to ignore it, but again it began to overtake them, this time crowding them dangerously. Tamara shot it an exasperated glance. The puller, slowing abruptly, veered warily to the left, toward the side of the road, as always crowded by the carriers and pushers and haulers to whom the sidewalk was forbidden. Asthmatically, the taxi forged ahead.

As it went by, Tamara tried to see the driver, but his companion on the front seat bulked too large. This one stared stonily ahead, incredibly oblivious. Was he blind, the idiot? Why didn't he warn the driver? He was a big man, and looked Korean. He wore a faded Army tunic and one ragged elbow rested on the door. The taxi passed so close, she could have reached out and touched him. His face was bloated and dirty, his once-cropped hair bristling untidily as though he had just gotten out of bed. His studied indifference sent a tremor of apprehension through her.

Over the years, with the spread of Japanese Army influence, there had come into North China a steady stream of Koreans. They came across South Manchuria in the wake of the soldiers and settled around the major garrisons. A new breed of camp follower, both male and female, they provided services of every sort. In Peking, they formed an exclusive underworld of their own, repaying the indifference of the occupying authorities with a willingness for specialized dirty work, of which the Japanese were reputed to require a good deal. Besides their own criminal activities, they were said to figure peripherally in assassinations, beatings, arsons, and other officially provoked reprisals. They were parasites, the utter dregs of a proud people, and were generally shunned.

Just ahead and to the right, the taxi slowed ominously, grinding along in low gear. Tamara's runner was slowing, too, his head moving from side to side, searching for some way out. The taxi swerved abruptly into their path and slid, brakes locked and tires squealing,

[258]

to a broadside stop in front of them. With a grunt of alarm, the young puller threw his weight back in the poles, fighting the momentum of the heavy rickshaw.

The big Korean piled out of the car, his broad face congested with excitement, and began to race toward them. Pausing, he clubbed the rickshaw man out of the way with his fist, knocking him over backward into the street. For a brief moment, Tamara gaped at him in confused panic. Then he turned, and she saw that his bloodshot eyes were on her, that he was coming for her. As his big hands reached out, she slashed at his face with the hard edge of her purse, feeling the metal frame connect solidly with flesh. The man gasped, spraying her face with spittle, but he didn't falter. Knocking her arm aside, he grasped her around the waist, his arms like steel ropes, his head pressed against her, crushing one of her breasts. Suddenly she was wrenched off her feet, able to do no more than squirm helplessly, and flail at the back of his head.

Muttering with fear and amazement, the crowd surged back a pace, staying clear of the Korean and his struggling burden. Shifting his hold on her, he groped for her wrist, found it and twisted it, pulling her arm sharply up behind her back. The pain made her scream, a long thin wail that seemed to come from somewhere else, and she felt herself go limp, unable to resist his awful strength. Her purse fell from her imprisoned hand striking the ground with a jingle of loose coins. Already the Korean was lurching toward the taxi, his breath wheezing loudly against her side. Tamara could see only a blurred mass of staring, uncommitted faces, with the rickshaw man's look of helpless outrage the only exception.

As the Korean bent to thrust her into the taxi, Tamara tried again to break away, and the man lost his balance. The two of them fell, half in and half out of the back door of the car. Tamara's head banged against the door post, stunning her, and the bulk of the Korean fell on her, driving the breath from her body.

As though from a great distance, she heard the incomprehensible shouts of the driver, and felt the Korean fumbling at her, trying for a grip on her clothing, and then she was being lifted and thrown bodily into the taxi. Dazed with pain and terror, she felt the seat give under her, tumbing her helplessly to the floor, her face grinding into the dusty carpet. There was the sound of the racing engine, the door slammed heavily, and then the car was lurching into violent motion, the tires squealing. A great noise roared in her ears, and the air was filled with exhaust fumes.

Tamara screamed again, but feebly, and then the man's hand was

[259]

quick to cover her mouth. It stank of rancid soy bean oil and Korean pickles. Reflexively, she sank her teeth into it with all the strength of her jaws.

Bellowing with pain, the Korean brought the rock-hard edge of his other fist down on the side of her head like a mallet, and a dazzling explosion of star-shot brilliance burst behind her eyes, only to dissolve at once into the deepest blackness.

᪣᪣

Canal Street was cool and shadowed as Edgerton turned onto it. Feeling he was already home, he breathed a sigh of relief. The old car chugged faithfully under his feet, the tires sound again and full of air.

He and Valerie had gotten back through the gate in the nick of time. So close was it, in fact, that the Japanese officer in charge of the sentry detail had been there himself, reviewing his men's final public ceremonies. Edgerton had seen, without bothering to tell Valerie, the officer's look of disappointment as they went by the check point. A few minutes later, and he could have pushed the gates closed in their faces, all diplomatic papers and emblems notwithstanding, thus forcing a wearying exchange of phone calls up and down the various chains of command. Finally, by nine o'clock perhaps, all the permissions would have been granted and all the forms filled out, and the gates would have opened to permit them to enter. Accompanied by many expressions of regret and much sucking of teeth, of course. Edgerton knew it was childish of him to get such pleasure from the imaginary frustration of a mere lieutenant of MPs, but he relished it nonetheless.

Although Valerie had been mostly silent since her brief outburst at the teahouse, he felt a particular closeness to her. She seemed to feel it as well, moving to sit closer to him in the car.

Considering the series of debacles which seemed to have been sent to try them both, she was really quite relaxed. When he'd suggested a swim and a drink before returning to the Procter house, her eyes had lighted up and her smile had been particularly warm.

Fatigue lifting from his shoulders, Edgerton turned into the narrow yard of the San Kwan Miao. He set the handbrake, turned off the ignition, and was halfway out of the car when he saw Madame Liu rise somewhat stiffly from the stone steps in front of his gate.

His mind went momentarily blank; then his body seemed to flood with a cold hard anger. The meddlesome old bag! Where had she come from? he wondered, feeling the helplessness of man pitted against great natural forces. As he got out, he was aware of Valerie's questioning look from the shadows of the car. Impassively he strode around to open the door for her.

She'd come from just across the street, Edgerton reminded himself bitterly. From precisely where he'd contrived to put her. The fates seemed determined to strew his path with obstacles today. Well, they could blow out his tires, but no grouchy old lady was going to poke his nose into his personal business; he didn't care whose mother she was.

As though hearing his cue, Ch'en appeared in the gate, his apologetic expression seeming to protest that he'd done all he could to dislodge the intruder.

Taking Valerie's elbow, Edgerton conducted her firmly toward the gate, determined to carry off the scene by the sheer massiveness of his refusal to be interfered with. Giving Valerie's arm a final encouraging squeeze, he bowed to Tamara's mother.

"Liu *t'ai t'ai*, permit me to present Wah *t'ai t'ai*, a visitor from America," he said in his best Mandarin.

To Valerie, he rephrased the introduction in English. Somewhat taken aback, both ladies bowed to one another. Turning then to Ch'en, he steered Valerie resolutely toward him. "Show Wah *t'ai t'ai* to my courtyard," he said.

Throughout these formalities, Edgerton could hear, over and above the roaring of his anger, a small voice telling him to be on his guard with this shrewd and stubborn lady.

It was then that it came back to him that it was she who had but days before suffered an experience which was fabled—in the West, at least—as being "worse than death." Outwardly, she seemed untouched by it. Her strong, handsome features remained unlined, impassive. Her back was as straight, her hair bun as tight and as perfect as ever. And her eyes as sharp and uncompromising.

Edgerton attempted a smile. "Won't you come inside," he asked her, indicating the open gate.

"No, thank you," she replied coldly. "I don't want to intrude."

"Not at all. We can go into the sitting room. Permit me to offer you some tea."

"I don't want your tea," she snapped, a faint flush suffusing her throat.

The rudeness was so direct that Edgerton recognized it as a measure of her distress, and forgot his anger. Still, he didn't feel like being pushed around. "Well, then," he said coolly, wondering why he should feel so uncomfortable. "What can I do for you?"

Madame Liu didn't answer at once, but looked at him for a long

[261]

moment, her face calm once more, all traces of her anger vanished. For Edgerton, the resemblance between mother and daughter had never been so strong: the firm chin, the mobile but controlled lips, the broad, serene forehead. Only the eyes were different . . . Tamara could never have assumed that look of unreachable austerity.

Madame Liu's expression eased perceptibly. "I am grateful for your help—I always have been—and now I have come to beg for more."

Edgerton nodded, acknowledging this unbending with a slight smile. "Anything I can do, you have but to ask."

"I am worried about my daughter," Madame Liu said.

Edgerton waited. Well, she's worried about you, he wanted to say. And I'm worried about the two of you, but what can anyone do for you, when you both struggle against every advice, every plan . . .?

"Has something happened?" he asked, suddenly apprehensive.

"I don't know," Madame Liu said, for the first time showing a hesitation, a vulnerability in her face. "I feel a strangeness in the air."

Good God! Edgerton thought, struggling to reconcile this vagary with the eminently practical woman who had spoken it. Then he remembered an indulgent remark of Tamara's about her mother's being something of a clairvoyant.

"What strangeness?" he felt compelled to ask, aware of a brief, momentary qualm of his own. He brushed it aside as nonsense.

"I don't know," she said. "She was to have come for a visit. I spoke to her by telephone earlier." Madame Liu paused and gave him a hard glance which told him she knew there'd been a quarrel between them and probably what it had been about. But when she didn't come, I telephoned the Club. They told me she had left early, more than two hours before."

"What time was that?"

"After five o'clock."

Edgerton glanced at his watch. It was seven; she'd been gone from the Club for four hours. "Did you call home?"

"The telephone is broken or taken away. Those people forget to pay the bill . . ." Madame Liu stopped, refusing to become distracted.

"Perhaps she merely decided to go home to rest a while." It sounded lame, the mere plucking of possibility from the air. But just the same, he argued silently, what could have gone wrong? The Chinese police activity had died down, and the investigation the Japanese were conducting on their own had ended the day before. Tamara had told him that. Maybe she had just wanted to be by herself for a while, away from her mother and her somber imagination as well as from him . . . away from everyone. She was probably walking in the park along the shore of Pei Hai and would show up any moment, or . . .

[262]

"Perhaps she has gone shopping and will be along later."

Madame Liu didn't think so. "She would have telephoned," she insisted.

Edgerton could feel a gathering exasperation but fought it down. He spread his hands. "I don't know what I can do," he said.

Her look said plainly enough that he wasn't very inventive then. "I thought perhaps you could go by the flat and see if she were there . . . she might be ill. Of course, I could go myself, if you're too busy." She was really angry now and blackmailing him; she knew he wouldn't let her go back there so soon.

Edgerton felt his face flush. "I can do that easily," he said stiffly, offended. And he would, too, but later, when he was ready to, when he had taken Valerie home. "But don't worry. I'm sure everything is all right." He paused, then added, "There may be a message waiting for you now at the hotel." The words sounded discourteous, and he regretted them at once.

Madame Liu's face hardened, and her eyes slid in the direction of Valerie's disappearance for an instant. Edgerton had the brief, dreadful certainty that she was going to light into him about Valerie and expend all the spleen she'd stored up against him.

But when she looked back, her face was blank, her eyes as noncommittal as two bits of black onyx. "Perhaps so," she said. "Thank you for your help." She bowed stiffly and turned away.

"Let me know if I can do anything," Edgerton said, meaning it, wanting to make some small amends.

But Madame Liu must not have heard him, for her slender, black-clad figure didn't falter as she marched out of the yard.

Edgerton watched even after she had disappeared into the street, a peculiar sense of desolation settling around him. He had managed the meeting badly, clumsily, and given offense for no purpose. Turning abruptly, he ran up the steps and into the San Kwan Miao. "God-damned woman!" he muttered as he slammed the gate.

Valerie was sitting in the shade of the back courtyard, fanning herself, a frosty glass at her elbow. "Sorry to leave you in the lurch like that," Edgerton said as he moved over to fix himself a drink. He couldn't remember ever needing one more.

"Who was that very severe lady?"

Although positive she'd guessed, Edgerton forgave her the subterfuge. It seemed like a time for complete candor between the two of them. "*That* was Tamara's mother," he said, giving her a short helpless shrug.

"Poor John," she said, laughing lightly. "You're having trouble with all your women today?"

"Only two of them, so far," he said, smiling, refusing to be needled.

"Touché," Valerie said, flushing. She took a cigarette out of the box on the table. "She reminded me a little of the Mother Superior of my convent school."

Edgerton raised his eyebrows in mock amazement. "I hadn't figured you for a convent veteran," he teased, letting a slight edge ride his words.

Valerie looked stung, but her glance was held defiant. "I wasn't a prize pupil, I guess. Although up until now, no one's complained."

Edgerton relented. "I won't be the first, certainly. Besides, I'm sure you were a very good little girl." He hoped this quip would end their sparring.

"Comparatively good," Valerie replied easily.

"And now?"

"A fallen woman."

Edgerton chuckled appreciatively. "How about falling in for a swim?"

"In one of your emergency suits?"

"One of them is bound to fit. Or you can do without. We have no rules here, no one to complain of indecent exposure . . . or any other kind of exposure."

"If someone came, I'd have to claim you enticed me."

"I'd take the rap for that, proudly."

Leaving her in the courtyard, Edgerton went to his bedroom and got a handful of suits off the top shelf of his closet. A couple were obviously too large, and he discarded them. One was Tamara's, the black wool suit she'd worn just the other evening. He stood quite still for a moment, looking down at it in the dim light, feeling the dry, soft material, remembering Tamara in it . . . how lovely she had looked, how close they had been that night. . . .

All the evidence to the contrary, he couldn't believe that they were finished with each other, that she wouldn't be coming over for other swims, other evenings. He refused to believe it, even to contemplate such a thing. They meant too much to each other for that to happen.

All right: she was angry with him, she'd read something into his sudden errand to Tungchow which wasn't there, and had taken offense. Well, that wasn't quite accurate. She'd read something that *was* there, but intuitively. She had no evidence.

But even so, Edgerton argued, shifting his ground, what did it all amount to after all? Valerie Warner was only a friend, and a very casual, recent friend, at that. She was good looking and sexy and, yes, he was attracted. But that was all it amounted to. Tamara had no cause

[264]

to break off with him so sharply, so cruelly, to hang up and refuse him any chance to explain. She'd even let her pique spill over into her relationship with her mother, missing their appointment and making her mother worry.

Edgerton put the suit back on the shelf, a little to one side of the others. It wasn't a guest suit, and never would be. A bitter sadness choked him, and he had to clear his throat. He gathered up a handful of suits and took them out to the courtyard.

"These aren't very fashionable, I'm afraid," he said, handing the lot over to Valerie. "But they'll keep you decent."

She grinned as she took them, but didn't say anything.

Having showed her into his bedroom, Edgerton went to change, then refreshed his drink generously and went to wait by the pool.

Sitting on the stubby diving board, he could feel the whiskey seeping into his blood, smoothing away the rough spots left by the day's misadventures, driving away Madame Liu and her nagging premonitions, clearing his mind of everything but Tamara. He shifted restlessly, impatiently, wanting to be left alone with Valerie, in spirit as in flesh. He'd been wrong about Tamara, had perhaps treated her insensitively. And he would make all that up to her; but not now.

Tamara's face appeared to him, as plain as if she'd been standing there in front of him. Her smile was the one she often wore when he was being stubborn, the same one she'd given him in the Western Hills when he'd begun railing against the busybodies and meddlers. Now it seemed to be saying that he could do whatever he chose, her only stipulation being that he decide himself what he wanted to do and then hold to the decision; make up his own mind about her rather than leaving it to her to prompt him.

Suddenly Edgerton found himself overwhelmed with confusion and regret, and a sullen resentment that she should be putting him through this agony. He put down his glass and dove into the water.

It was a miraculous relief. After tramping back and forth, and changing tires, and worrying about Sobolov, and arguing with Tamara and Valerie and Madame Liu, and with himself, the water felt like blessed oblivion closing over him, cool and soft and dark with algae. He let himself sink to the bottom and just rest there, his mind empty, all his nerve ends devoted solely to coolness and cleanness and refreshment.

When he came to the surface, Valerie Warner was standing just inside the moon gate, watching him, smiling secretly, wearing his white robe. The slanting rays of the sun threw the gate into shadow, leaving her blonde hair to stand out like a golden cap, the solitary

[265]

contrast to his recollection of Tamara. Even her posture was the same, and Edgerton felt a twinge of outrage, surprisingly intense. She was an interloper, this smooth, sophisticated white woman, with her worldliness and her passport and her suntan. She didn't belong here . . . another woman did.

What he ought to do, he saw quite clearly, was to end this charade as quickly and as painlessly as possible, take this strange but well-meaning woman home, and go and find Tamara, and discover what it was she thought she was doing to them all. But the moment endured no longer than the blinking of an eye.

Valerie's smile became self-conscious. "Don't look," she called. "Nothing fit, so I'm just wearing panties and bra."

Edgerton swallowed and took a deep breath. "Okay," he said, turning dutifully away, his heart pounding the blood up into his head, purging his brain.

There was a splash, and then a long sigh of luxury. "How marvelous," Valerie said. "You're a true gentleman; you can turn around now." She swam toward him slowly, her tanned body nearly lost in the dark water, marked only by the blur of her undergarments. They swam two laps side by side, reached for their drinks and carried them to where they could stand.

To Edgerton the water seemed to have suddenly taken on an incredible texture, a heaviness like tepid quicksilver. The dome of the sky seemed washed by the departing sun, leaving the walled garden, with its tiny pool, a dim cool grotto.

"Better?" Edgerton asked.

Valerie put down her glass. He could feel the water swirl against him as she turned.

"Much, much better. You could have been a doctor . . . or a magician."

Her face was suddenly very close, her skin dewed with water, her lips wet with icy whiskey. Edgerton could feel himself swell, responding to the invitation written so explicitly in her eyes. As his hand cupped the beginning curve of her hip, she surrendered to the buoyancy of the water, her legs floating upward, spreading to encompass him, climbing him sensuously like a pole. As her ankles crossed behind his back, she seemed to open herself to him, clasping his hips to her, her thinly covered crotch almost enclosing the insistent bulge of his erection. Dizzy with desire, Edgerton saw them for a moment as figures in a Pompeian fresco; then their lips met, and his tongue went into her mouth, and she was caressing it.

"Mmmmm," she murmured deep in her throat, her hips moving, her fingers tugging gently at the drawstring of his trunks.

[266]

The pealing signal of the telephone shrilled through the silence. At first, Edgerton refused to hear it even. Then, very reluctantly, he drew his mouth away. For a moment their bodies remained locked together, the source of a pattern of concentric ripples moving slowly across the pool.

"Oh, God, destroy that thing; strike it with lightning," Valerie whispered, clinging to him. Slowly she opened her eyes. "Can't you ignore it?"

Edgerton smiled, pulling her closer. "Ch'en will only answer it and come dutifully to call me."

"Wretched puritan," she said, smiling sleepily. "Did you train him to be so good? I'll never forgive you."

The ringing stopped, and they could hear Ch'en's querulous *"Wai! Ni nahr?"* coming from the dining room. By the time his white gowned figure appeared in the gateway, Edgerton and Valerie were a decorous three feet apart and sipping their drinks with every appearance of tranquility.

"Okay, Ch'en," Edgerton said, pulling himself onto the pool's edge. He stood for a moment, dripping, looking down into Valerie's up-turned face.

"My, my!" she said, admiringly.

"I won't be a minute," he said, nudging her hand with his toe. "Don't go away." Toweling himself, serenely confident that his slowly vanishing erection would spring back at a moment's notice, Edgerton picked up the extension phone in his bedroom.

"Yes," he said, running the towel through his hair.

"Mr. Edgerton?" A male voice came back in English, faint and distorted, elusively familiar.

"Yes, yes!" he shouted impatiently. "This is Edgerton speaking."

"Ah, Mr. Edgerton," the voice repeated, the connection becoming miraculously clear. "This is Colonel Tanaka of the Military Police."

"Yes, Colonel," Edgerton said, wondering what in hell he could possibly want at this hour.

"I hope I'm not disturbing you?"

Not much. "No, Colonel, no trouble at all."

Tanaka's voice sounded extremely jovial. Edgerton could imagine him beaming fatly at the phone. He wondered if Tanaka had been drinking. He had a sudden annoying picture of the little colonel, half-stewed on saki, calling up his new American friend for a chat.

"What is it?" Edgerton asked, his impatience thinly masked.

"Well, Mr. Edgerton, I have bad news. . . . I feel most embarrassed," Tanaka said, his voice dropping to a lower, suitably regretful tone. "You remember our appointment for tomorrow?"

[267]

"Yes, of course," Edgerton snapped, not even trying to hide his impatience.

"I am ashamed to tell you we must change the time."

"No problem, Colonel! Any time that's convenient for you."

"You are most cooperative," Tanaka said, his tone altering subtly. "I am sure we shall have a mutually rewarding relationship."

"Yes. Fine. But what *time*, Colonel?"

"Oh, I think tonight, Mr. Edgerton," Tanaka replied, his voice hard, his attitude suddenly reversed. "I regret to inconvenience you . . . come to my office in half an hour." The last words came over the wire with the unmistakable crackling sound of a military order.

"Nonsense!" Edgerton was suddenly furious with himself for being taken in by Tanaka's elaborate obsequiousness. He *must* be drunk, the arrogant little bastard. "Nothing we have to discuss is so urgent as all that. Besides, you're forgetting yourself, I think. I don't take orders from you."

"Nothing we had *planned* to discuss, Mr. Edgerton," Tanaka replied silkily. "This is a new matter . . . very important."

"Important to whom?"

"Why, to you, Mr. Edgerton . . . or so I would imagine."

"Then tell me what it is and stop wasting my time."

"Why, of course! Excuse me for being so slow. You see, it involves a certain Chinese national, one Tamara Liu." Tanaka's voice drew out the last name softly, holding it as though it were a musical note.

Edgerton's breath caught in his throat, and his knees began to tremble. He gripped the phone as though it were connected to some sort of lifeline. He had been led to the abyss and commanded to look down. He pulled up a chair and dropped into it.

"What about Tamara Liu?" he asked finally, the words threatening to strangle him.

"She is in custody," Tanaka announced importantly. "Charged with serious crimes against His Imperial Majesty's forces."

"In custody?" Edgerton repeated, feeling the beginnings of panic.

"All the facts have not yet been determined," Tanaka's voice interrupted. "I have done you the courtesy of informing you so that you may contribute to our investigation." Tanaka cleared his throat. "In half an hour, then. Good-by."

There was a click which must have been audible across the room. In the silence, Edgerton stood with the phone in his hand, the towel over his shoulder, gooseflesh forming across his back. His eyes stared at the blank wall over his bed, as though by some biblical magic, words would come to be written there, words to tell him what to do, to keep

[268]

him from making any mistakes. For if there was ever a time when he couldn't afford a mistake, Edgerton knew it was now.

In custody. The term was one of the most spurious of euphemisms. So bland and unspecific, it had the power to imply extremely ominous circumstances. It could mean a Chinese jail: brutal, filthy, infested with disease and vermin, the sort of place where people were literally lost, became mislaid, disappeared. Or it could mean the MP stockade. There would be a cell for women, and it might be cleaner but no safer, not for a young woman.

"*Wai!*" the operator demanded, her bored voice loud and unpleasant. "*Wai! Ni nabr?*"

Suddenly galvanized, Edgerton slammed the instrument back into its cradle. Flinging the towel aside, he hurried into the clothes he'd not so long ago discarded, his mind a jumble of possibilities. Tamara must have given his name, needing his help. He'd always told her to, if she got into any trouble.

Well, he was going to help. And he wasn't going to wait any half hour either. He wanted to know what Tanaka was up to, and he wanted to know now. It was incredible what he'd said: crimes against. . . .

Edgerton paused, one shoe still in his hand. That was it, of course, Tamara was being held for her mother's "crime." The investigations in their neighborhood had apparently not been as inept as he'd wishfully imagined.

He was almost across the courtyard when he remembered Valerie. He found her by the pool in a wicker chair, bundled into his robe and nearly lost in the gathering darkness. Her face brightened, then, seeing he was dressed, fell into dismay and confusion.

Edgerton felt a pang of remorse. To be leaving her was bad enough; to have forgotten her . . . thankfully she hadn't seen him hurrying away. "Valerie, I'm terribly sorry, but I have to go. It's an emergency. I'll have Ch'en call the Procters' house if you like. They can send the car or he can get you a taxi." He gestured helplessly.

Valerie tried to smile and failed. Her face went haggard for a moment, her age suddenly showing clearly. The glimpse was brief enough, but it imparted an extra vulnerability that touched Edgerton, deepening his regret. He didn't love her, but he liked her, and hated to see her so exposed.

She made a small gesture with one hand. "That's all right, John . . . if you must, you must," she said softly. "Is it about . . . her?"

Edgerton nodded quickly, anxious to be gone. "The Japanese have arrested her; I don't know yet what it's all about." He put his hand

[269]

on her shoulder and shook her gently. "I'll be talking to you."

Valerie's nod seemed to say she didn't think so, but Edgerton had already turned away and didn't see it.

♣♣

Suddenly it was dark in the shuttered room. Night had fallen. The intricacies of crumbling plaster and flaking paint were no longer there to distract her. For hours, the ceiling had offered her continents to trace, hidden faces, and the shapes of mythical beasts.

In the beginning, Tamara had dreaded the coming of darkness with its blindness and loss of diversion. But now that it was upon her, it wasn't so bad. Like the truly blind, she found her hearing sharpening. Now she was content to listen. Strange noises had been gradually increasing outside the house. They leaked through the shutters and permeated the paper-thin walls. Bit by bit, the air became filled with a muted mingling of sounds.

First there was music, the scratchy, mechanical sound of phonograph records. It started with one tune, a monotonous Japanese ballad, nasal and mawkish. It was an Army favorite and could be regularly heard blaring out of beer shops all across the city. After a time, another machine joined in dissonantly, playing a marching song. Then another came in with something else.

As the time passed, a muffled hubbub ebbed and flowed in the distance, growing steadily louder. It started as hoarse male voices jabbering in Japanese, excited, playful, with occasional shouts erupting. Then she began to hear women's voices joining in, cajoling, protesting, giggling, bursting from time to time into laughter. It was then that she began to understand her surroundings, knowing why those people were all there. There was more and more singing, sometimes accompanying the records, sometimes alone, both men and women. In her imagination she could feel the electric tension which filled the air, passionate, sensual, closer to rage than it was to the counterfeit love which was being bargained for all around her. Once a Chinese voice, some woman of the South, bitter with outrage, stormed into a string of gutter curses. Her complaint was silenced by a slap like a firecracker, with much laughter following.

In Tamara's mental picture of it, the neighborhood swarmed with drunken soldiers, free of all restraint, bent on doing as they pleased.

Contributing to her mounting feeling of helplessness was the fact that she had no idea of where she was, not even a vague notion of how long it had taken the taxi to drive here. She'd been hauled from the

[270]

car and rushed into the house. She'd seen the path, a few stunted trees, the blur of a nearby building, a decaying garden. . . .

Gingerly she shifted position, easing the tension on the cloth straps which bound her wrists to the bedstead. Under the thin mattress, the springs squeaked a protest. Stiffening cautiously, Tamara held her breath and listened.

Although she no longer felt the paralyzing terror she'd known when she'd regained consciousness in the taxi, she still didn't want to attract their attention unnecessarily.

Then, with the Korean's broad hand clamped on her neck, she had been certain that these total strangers intended to kill her. Now she was equally certain that they did not, but that only freed her mind to speculate on the other things which might be in store for her. The possibilities were few—and all unpleasant.

And yet, for all the abrupt brutality of her kidnapping, and the growing discomfort of her detention, there remained a persistent sense of unreality about it all.

From what little she'd been able to see, the house was old and mostly empty, but someone went to the trouble of looking after it.

In trying to analyze the situation, she considered the people involved. She had guessed the driver of the taxi to be Japanese, but she had never really seen him. No sooner was she out of the car than he had driven away. Already in the house when she arrived were a Japanese couple. It was soon clear that they were her actual custodians, with the Korean relegated to the position of servant. And they weren't man and wife—of that she was certain—nor lovers. No, definitely not. Although both wore rather nondescript Western-style clothes, they had the look of people more comfortable in uniform. The man was probably a senior sergeant, for he ordered the Korean and the woman about with the easy unarguable authority of long practice. And the woman had prison matron written all over her, with none of the femininity for which Japanese women were famous. On the contrary, burly and mannish, she strode around on muscular legs encased in brown stockings, her compact body leaning aggressively forward.

Just before dark the men had started a Mah-Jongg game. They were in a room just across the narrow hallway, and Tamara could hear every sound they made. And they were drinking, the clink of the glasses and the occasional gurgle of a bottle coming clearly through the thin walls. As time passed, the intensity of the men's voices rose and the sound of the tiles being slammed onto the table became louder. There were arguments now and then, but the Japanese man seemed to settle them quickly. Incongruous as they appeared together, they were obviously

[271]

familiars, and members of some organized group. The Police? The Army?

It was at this point that her speculations always ground to a halt. All this effort, this organization . . . for what? The audacity and timing of the act convinced her that they not only wanted her specifically, but that they also knew where to find her. It followed, then, that they represented some facet of Japanese authority. No one but agents of the Japanese could have been so indifferent to all those witnesses. But why? Who was she to attract all this attention? Could she have been picked by some ranking officer to be pressed into his personal service, to be a sort of slave? It sounded medieval, but so much about the Japanese did sound that way, with their swords and their elaborate samurai *bushido*. The opposite alternative was that she had been picked at random, a part of a general roundup of women for the Army's traveling brothels. Unarguably the women had to come from somewhere in the first place. And yet. . . .

She lay for a while inert, hardly breathing, her mind a blank, fatigue overcoming fear and forcing her to rest. The thought of John came back into her mind, and she allowed herself the luxury of imagining him in the process of rescuing her.

Through special sources of information, known only to the American Legation, he would discover where she was and how she came to be there. From that point she had a choice. It could be John, irresistible with outrage, confronting the Japanese Minister or even General Kawasaki himself, with the demand that she be released, or it could be John and Hal MacDonough leading a detachment of heavily armed Marines to her deliverance.

In a nearby house, a woman's laugh shrilled above the other sounds, rising until it disintegrated into a spasm of gluey coughing. While it lasted, the laugh had been aimed at her, in eloquent derision of her dreams.

An angry, despairing sob caught in her throat. Of course, John wasn't doing either of those fantastic things on her behalf, or any other things. He was doing nothing. Nothing but amuse himself. He didn't know what had happened to her, and he wouldn't know until some gossip told him she was no longer at the Club. And even then he might do nothing, assuming only that she had quit her job, perhaps even that she had done so in order to separate herself from him still further. And who could blame him for thinking that? The recollection of their last conversation brought fresh tears to her eyes.

Poor transparent John; he was no good at lies. Why had he at-

[272]

tempted such a weak one? Did he think no one knew anything unless he told them about it?

Perhaps he'd be at home now, reading, or listening to his old Victrola, and drinking too much, as she knew he sometimes did. Or at some party with his foreign friends, all of them enjoying the safety of that cozy cocoon of theirs, their little nest of inviolable privilege. She told herself it was petty of her to resent the better fortune of others, but it did no good.

In all probability, he was with that Warner woman. Tamara felt the acid of helpless hatred rise in her throat like bile. That bitch, she thought wretchedly, that scheming bitch! In a brief, flashing spasm of fury, she felt possessed of an indomitable strength. It was as though she could burst her bonds asunder, wrench the bed apart with her bare hands, and throw the pieces through the window. The moment passed, leaving her exhausted.

Once he got over his hurt feelings, John would come looking for her . . . she knew he would. He hadn't the meanness to hold a grudge. Nor had the Warner woman the power, for all her tanned whiteness, to wipe out all that they'd meant to each other. It simply couldn't be. And John would be able to do something—not the silly things she'd imagined—but something practical. But by then it might very well be too late. When the Japanese were through with her. . . .

And her mother, what agonies of worry she must be suffering! She always expected the worst; at last she was right. Her mother—suddenly the pieces fell into place. Tamara had to bite her tongue to keep from wailing into the night.

♟♟

Scowling sullenly, he listened to the sentry's voice. Finally losing patience, he shouted into the telephone, "Yes, yes, I know all that! Tell him to wait. I'll call you when I want him."

Tanaka hung up the phone in the middle of the sentry's nervous reply and threw himself angrily back in his chair.

So the moment had at last arrived: Edgerton had been summoned and was obediently about to appear. How long had he waited for this? Tanaka wondered sadly. And now it was ruined, spoiled for him by the insidious scheming of Colonel Itaki. The man was a devil.

As he contemplated what the Chief of Staff was doing to him, tears of rage and frustration gathered in Tanaka's eyes. It wasn't fair! Events had somehow misled him. The bitter loss of Sobolov had been softened

[273]

by his triumph over Puhalski. If the one was the nadir of his fortunes, the other could only be seen as the first step on the road back to power and influence. Puhalski's humbling had seemed an omen, a symbol of what his enemies could expect. He had anticipated that subsequent events would confirm it as such, and in the beginning they had.

He had returned home from the café to the welcome news that the Liu woman was safely in custody, her arrest having passed unnoticed except for a few passers-by. And the Russian woman had been there waiting, just as he had instructed. His pleasure postponed by Puhalski's blunder, he had been a bull. Tanaka felt a brief glow of pride, recalling the ironlike temper of his erection and its phenomenal persistence. Inspired by an unsuspected inventiveness, he'd ridden the woman through a dazzling series of positions . . . treacherous bungler though he was, Puhalski had not exaggerated the woman's charms. In the end, moaning with her own heat, the woman had been totally submissive. Next time . . . the thought of next time made Tanaka's loins stir and his hands tremble. The pity of it was that she was no longer there.

Tingling with impatience for a return engagement, he'd rushed to his office to arrange this dreamed-of confrontation with the American. Everything had been perfect: the American was at home, and had been successively impatient, astounded, frightened, and crushed into docility. Just the way Tanaka planned it And then Itaki had interfered. Edgerton had no sooner been given his instructions than the Chief of Staff had telephoned. Tanaka's exuberance had been drowned in the wash of that pompous lisping voice. He was actually calling from Tanaka's residence.

It developed that Itaki, having casually dropped in to discuss some routine matter, had been outraged by the "degrading circumstances" he'd uncovered there. There followed a long lecture on the necessity for discretion and reproachless behavior on the part of senior officers. To have to take this from Itaki, with his notorious parties and retinue of mincing hangers-on, had been galling. Almost as an afterthought, having no inkling of the effrontery of it, Itaki had casually remarked that he had ordered the Russian woman into a rickshaw and sent her home.

Recalling his helplessness in the face of this high-handed behavior, Tanaka could feel his heart pound with fury. One day soon, it would be Itaki who was vulnerable, with his perversions exposed to the contemptuous amusement of the entire officer corps, and his career threatened with disaster. Once established as chief of the Kempeitai, with the most intimate dossiers on every officer in the Kwangtung

Army in his possession, Tanaka would be impregnable. And Itaki's was the score he yearned most to settle. The former Chief of Staff could consider himself lucky if he ended up with a service battalion on the Siberian frontier.

Tanaka shook his head . . . that time was not yet. For the present it had been Tanaka's bitter fate to have to apologize for embarrassing the Chief of Staff—he'd found the woman "practically naked," he told Tanaka, his voice squeaking—and promise humbly to comport himself with circumspection in the future.

It was only after this prolonged torment that he was told why Itaki had gone there in the first place. He'd gone to inquire, on behalf of Minister Saito, as to the progress of disciplinary proceedings in the Tungchow Incident. To be reminded of that wretched business had been the final humiliation. Tanaka had wanted to tear the phone from its connections, to smash it to pieces, to destroy it utterly.

Tanaka sighed. It had been an unnerving day, and the future looked equally bleak. It was too soon to have the Russian woman brought back . . . it would be just like Itaki to have left a spy around, the sneaky pervert, hoping to catch him being insubordinate. It might be days, weeks, before he dared risk it. Meanwhile, he had only an empty house to return to.

Glumly, Tanaka stared at his desk. A thought struck him, and he brightened momentarily. There might be some neutral place unknown to Itaki, where the Russian woman could be taken, where the two of them could continue the business so delightfully begun that afternoon. He was surprised to realize that his feelings for her were almost tender. He'd have Okamura look into the business of housing in the morning.

It was eight-thirty. He had two hours respite, perhaps a little more. Itaki, ever intent on making himself as burdensome as possible, had insisted on a meeting at eleven, to "discuss developments." Itaki, the night owl, cared nothing for the convenience of others . . . he seldom arose before noon.

Tanaka's eyes shifted to the long sofa, wanting only to lie down and close his eyes. Upholstered in soft red leather, the couch looked inviting. His gaze moved to the other items in the room. Tanaka prided himself on having collected them wisely since being posted to China. The Ming vase was particularly good, and the screen, unfolded artistically across one corner, was more than a hundred years old. He knew that there was not in all the high command another office so tastefully furnished, not even General Kawasaki's. It had been his pride, and now he couldn't wait to leave it. It attested to Itaki's peculiar genius that his poisonous touch could work even through telephone wires.

Empty as his residence was, Tanaka preferred to go there. While Itaki had been there, so had the woman, and her essence would be the stronger; and there would be his robust memories to comfort him.

And now it was time to dispose of the American. He would toy with him a little, then send him away until another time. Tanaka had waited too long for his triumph to waste it on a moment already tainted by Colonel Itaki. He'd dictate his specific terms another time. The woman was safely in custody . . . let Edgerton stew a while. He could be predicted to bluster and protest and make ludicrous demands. They would avail him nothing. Nothing had changed . . . Edgerton was in a box, with every contingency accounted for.

With a sigh, Tanaka reached for the telephone.

$$\text{\clubsuit\clubsuit}$$

Although he stood a head taller than Tanaka, Edgerton found no comfort in the fact, nor any of the feeling of almost embarrassing physical dominance which his size sometimes gave him. Behind Tanaka's rotund exterior, he saw a man of determination and single-mindedness. There was no sign of the comical figure arrayed in decorations he'd been remembering.

Tanaka's plain khaki uniform, with its open white shirt, looked freshly laundered and made him uncomfortably aware of his own sweatstained clothes. He felt peculiarly disadvantaged. He should have taken the time to change. As it was, his haste had been for naught. He'd taken a wrong turning on the way, and had thus arrived almost exactly a half hour after Tanaka's call . . . just as instructed.

"You're very prompt, Mr. Edgerton," Tanaka said, nodding condescendingly. He rose grandly from behind the wide, cluttered desk, and held out a chubby hand.

Gritting his teeth, Edgerton hesitated over this pretense at normality, wanting to ignore the hand or to strike it aside. But he didn't dare. Odious as he indeed was, this man was his single link to Tamara, and he'd sworn to control himself, to be patient, to balance firmness with politeness, to ignore any insult. He reached across the desk and gave the soft fingers one brief shake, then sat down as Tanaka gestured to a chair.

Tanaka waited gravely, arms folded, his silence plainly calculated to achieve a psychological advantage. A tactic out of some police manual . . . Edgerton declined to be impressed. And he reminded

[276]

himself that while Tanaka was a ruthless trickster, he had all the frailties of an ordinary man.

"Well, what is this ridiculous business about Miss Liu?" he demanded at last.

Tanaka scowled. "It's not ridiculous," he said, shaking his head reprovingly. "Very serious . . . she's charged with grave crimes . . ."

"*What* crimes?" Edgerton insisted harshly, forgetting his promise to himself.

A faint pinkness tinged Tanaka's round face, and his mouth pursed angrily. But then, instead of retorting, he allowed himself a small secret smile. "Assault, to begin with. Aggravated assault upon a member of His Imperial Majesty's armed forces, one . . ." Picking up a document from the clutter of his desk, Tanaka made as if to check a name.

But Edgerton wasn't watching . . . his eyes were blind, and his thoughts were congealing into lumps. His stomach flooded with a bitter acid that rose in his throat like bile as he realized what he had done. It had simply never occurred to him that the Japanese police would even know that he and Tamara existed, much less the details of her situation and family. But given even a little of that knowledge, plus his gratuitous memo, and any simple country cop could have put two and two together. No wonder the search was stopped . . . he'd done their work for them.

That self-indulgent, grandiose gesture! How pleased he'd been, watching the words flow effortlessly from his pen, so eloquent, so righteous! Thanks to him, the Liu women never had a chance. No wonder Tanaka was smiling.

". . . a certain Senior Sergeant Toshi Seiko," Tanaka concluded smoothly.

"I suppose you have something purporting to be evidence," Edgerton said lamely.

Tanaka smirked. "Evidence is my business. The soldier will make an identification, of course. And there is your very welcome corroboration." He smiled brightly, nodding his head. "Oh, yes."

And if that weren't enough, you could always manufacture some, Edgerton thought bitterly, crushed by the sheer enormity of his blunder. He felt himself swept by rage. He could see clearly now that he'd succumbed to an unsuspected weakness: pure, unadulterated Caucasian conceit. He was the American *lao-yeh*, after all, with his prestige and diplomatic trappings. Who were these mere Japs to give *him* any trouble? Best to put the insolent buggers in their places!

And now what?

Tanaka dropped abruptly into his chair, making the casters grate painfully on the bare floor. Edgerton could only sit there and look at him, and as he looked, cast about in his mind for a way to approach the man, how to dissuade or divert him from whatever it was he had in mind. It was then that he saw the naked animosity in Tanaka's eyes. This wasn't the almost ritual dislike he was used to from the Japanese officers whom he might encounter on the street or coming and going from the Japanese Legation. This was hatred, deep and personal. There was no accounting for it . . . Tanaka hardly knew him.

Edgerton eyed him watchfully, sitting there in his chair like some evil deity: stolid, disdainful, and infinitely patient. There seemed to be no way to reach the man, no lever to be used against him. Edgerton felt a twinge of panic. It made him want to strike out blindly, to lunge across the desk and take that fat throat in his hands, to shake concessions from that hateful head the way a dog might shake the stuffing out of a rag doll. But, tormented by his impotence, he could only sit there and clench his fists not trusting himself to speak.

On the way to Tanaka's office, he'd probed his words and tone of voice for possible clues to his intentions. He got nowhere, except to guess that since Tanaka knew he had a friend of his in jail, he was disposed to attempt a bargain . . . but what? Edgerton hadn't a clue. Just the same, there was a germ of comfort in the thought, in the very fact of Tanaka's call. So long as he wanted something, Tamara wouldn't be purposely harmed.

So Edgerton had arrived expecting some preliminary maneuvering, a ritual avowal of Japan's benign purposes in China, and then down to business . . . but now it seemed there was to be no business, no bargaining.

And search though he might for some form of counter-pressure, Edgerton could come up with nothing better than the Tungchow affair. The Japanese Minister wanted very badly to have that matter disposed of once and for all, and the lingering reluctance of the Army to act was embarrassing him more every day . . . or so Yamaguchi hinted. Prodded astutely by Edgerton, the Minister could have Tanaka sweating blood in a matter of days. But waiting for days was out of the question. Hours were critical now . . . Tamara had been in their hands since three o'clock.

Sobolov. The name popped in his brain like a tiny bubble bursting. Could Tanaka possibly have further plans for that frightened little man? If so, it might explain his present reticence. Not knowing the cat was out of the bag, he'd be reluctant about making any embarrassing revelations. It was flimsy, but enough to give Edgerton a surge of

[278]

hope. Though intrigue was not his forte, he was ready to concoct whatever lies or promises or treachery that could effect Tamara's release. It was the moment for directness. "Come on, Tanaka, you want something from me. What is it? Maybe we can strike a bargain."

Tanaka was plainly taken aback, and Edgerton's hopes rose still further. The moment had been ripe; but, inexplicably, nothing came of it. "There can be no bargaining," Tanaka muttered, sounding as if he hardly cared one way or the other. "Crime must be punished."

Edgerton refused to believe it. "But she's committed no crime . . . you know that as well as I do."

Tanaka looked up, his eyes glinting. "The mother, the daughter . . . it doesn't really matter. The punishment is what's important; it must be prompt and severe. An example needs to be made."

At least the pretense was out of the way; Edgerton felt something like relief. "Japanese justice!" he said harshly, spitting the words. Tanaka's face darkened thickly, but he remained silent.

"Can't you see what this sort of heavy-handed behavior does to the reputation of your country?"

"Among foreigners?" Tanaka sneered. "No one cares what foreigners think."

"Many foreigners here represent governments with whom Japan does a lot of business."

"Yours, for instance?" Tanaka suggested slyly. "We don't worry . . . as long as there's a buck in it, you'll do business. It's the American way. The others are the same." Looking pleased with himself, he began fitting a cigarette into an ivory holder.

Nonplussed at hearing his own words handed back to him, Edgerton felt himself redden. As he became more aware of Tanaka's capricious nature, he began to despair of being able to reason with him. The man's mercurial temper, his personal bitterness, his unwillingness to face the issue between them, all worked against Tamara. And all the while, she was being held somewhere, in God knew what sort of humiliating, harmful circumstances . . . suddenly Edgerton found it too much for him. "But these women are innocent!" he cried. "I appeal to you in the name of simple humanity . . ."

Tanaka's humorless laugh brayed raucously. Then, suddenly he was very angry, and his open hand smashed down on his desk, scattering papers. "Humanity!" he shouted, the veins in his neck engorging. "You hypocrite, how dare you talk about humanity? You have murdered and robbed and enslaved from one side of Asia to the other for a hundred years!"

Edgerton stared back at him, his heart sinking. There was no reach-

[279]

ing this man. "Nonsense! We've murdered no one . . . you don't know what you're talking about," he replied, as much for the form of the thing as anything else.

"I'm talking about India," Tanaka began, fuming.

"I am an American; I have nothing to do with India."

"Look at the Philippines, then."

"They're scheduled for independence in only eight years."

"Only eight years!" Tanaka mimicked. "Now that they've been exploited for forty years and have become a liability . . . how splendid and humane of you!"

"What is the point of all this, Tanaka? Miss Liu . . ."

"The point is this, Edgerton: with your usual white man's arrogance you come out here thinking you can do anything you want. You preach this outlandish religion of yours, all sweetness and light and commandments . . . it's an insult to the intelligence of any civilized man . . . but all the time you are buying and squeezing and milking the people of their coppers, selling them things they've never needed. An American who couldn't get a job shoveling shit in his own home town can come out here and live in a house with plumbing for the first time in his life, and have four servants, and call himself 'reverend,' and proceed to get rich off the sweat and blood of Asians."

"You don't, I suppose!"

"God damn you, I *am* Asian! I belong here. What is happening here is between Asians, between the Chinese and ourselves. And believe me, the average Japanese has in his heart more sympathy and genuine goodwill toward the Chinese than a boatload of your pink-skinned, round-eyed lords and ladies. There wouldn't be a war if you'd let us settle things among ourselves."

Tanaka jumped to his feet and began angrily pacing behind his desk, his cigarette streaming smoke. There was nothing for Edgerton to do but let him rave on.

He did. "How dare you to lecture me about humanity, when you haven't the faintest idea what is happening in China, or what Japan is doing here!" He paused, glaring, his face gleaming with sweat. "We are fighting for the life of our nation, and yet no one bothers to take this into account, least of all you Americans. Our survival means nothing to you. Time and again, you've shown yourselves ready to sacrifice our interests."

He paced in silence for a few moments, then resumed in a calmer tone. "Sometimes I think you are a nation of preachers. You like nothing better than to sermonize, to instruct others on what is right and moral and humane . . . on what is *nice*. But I notice that in your own territory you do as you please, as in the case of those Filipinos on whom you are now about to bestow their freedom. The whole world knows how you slaughtered them by the thousands when they resisted you. What American raised his voice in behalf of 'simple humanity' then? Not a one."

Tanaka turned and stabbed at Edgerton with his cigarette. "That conquest was typical of you. Not needing those islands, you simply took them because you hankered to be a colonial power, like your English forebears. Now that they've become a burden, you talk about giving them independence, and brag about how democratic you are.

"Well, Japan doesn't operate in that slipshod, dishonest fashion. We act for national survival. We have a yearly population surplus of almost a million people . . . think of what that means in our tiny islands. Emigration is imperative for us; we have no choice.

"And there was Manchuria . . . an empty, bandit-ridden territory that was always beyond Chinese control, always governed by warlords and bandit chieftains for their own profit. We have been civilizing that land for decades. Every city, railroad, highway, factory there was built by us, or with our help. That place would be a wasteland without us, roaming with bandits and wild ponies. We have as much right to be there as you have to be in America. More, because we *have* to be there, and no amount of scolding is going to get us out. Until we were excluded by law, many of our people wanted to move to America. Although why anyone without a pink skin would want to go there, I can't imagine. There is no one in Asia who hasn't heard how the Japanese and Chinese who went there as indentured laborers were treated . . . worse even than the way you treat your Indians and Negroes, and the Mexicans you conquered."

Apparently distracted, Tanaka strode to the window and stared out at the deserted, night-shrouded parade ground. "We are an industrial nation, a trading nation," he said more quietly, his back to Edgerton. "We must have access to resources and markets. Almost our entire foreign investment is concentrated in Manchuria and China . . . it is our life's blood. And yet you want us to give all that up. What do you care? Your investment in China is tiny by comparison. Except for the greed of a few individuals, you don't need this trade. Why don't you go on with your exploitation of Canada and Mexico and Latin America, and leave us alone?"

"You're complaining about history," Edgerton said. "Besides, trade is one thing. You're engaged in armed conquest."

"That is because the Chinese have been encouraged by you to resist us, to be anti-Japanese in everything. That is the irony, for China to follow the advice of her worst exploiter. What would you do if we came over to Mexico and began interfering with your arrangements, lecturing and preaching and telling the Mexicans to resist you? Why, you would raise your hands in outraged horror . . . that would be against the Monroe Doctrine! But what do we have over here? Here it is the Open Door, everyone must have a share . . . equality for all, it's only fair, and so forth . . . all that rubbish you and the English so love to spout about. Think about that sometime.

"But you know something, Edgerton, we understand you people very well. We observe you carefully, and we listen to your speeches and read your papers, and we have discovered some things about you. It isn't really our trade that bothers you, or emigration to Manchuria. You care nothing about China, in spite of all your sentimental words. After all, France and England and Germany and Russia have plundered China at will, and you have been too polite even to mention the matter. But let Japan populate one barren acre of Manchuria, and you have the League of Nations sending English lords to investigate us and tell the world that we are uncivilized, and that other nations should boycott us. And why? *Because we are not white!*

"Why, in 1919, we couldn't even get our allies in the war against Germany—our gallant democratic allies—to declare that people could not be considered inferior on account of their race. Not even that! Can you believe it, Edgerton? Well, it's true."

Tanaka yanked out his chair and threw himself into it, his face streaming. Panting heavily, he glowered across the desk.

The silence lengthened uncomfortably. Edgerton wanted to break it, hoping that Tanaka's tirade might have drained him of passion to the point where he could be reasoned with, guided back into some useful discussion. But he hesitated, surmising that they'd never accomplish anything until the man got most of the venom out of his system.

Although some of what Tanaka said was valid enough, granting his narrow point of view, it rankled to have to sit through it all without chance for rebuttal. But that would have been futile; Tanaka's hatred had already hardened beyond the repair of mere debate.

When Tanaka resumed speaking, his voice was weary. "You Americans amaze me," he said, swiveling slowly, his thick fingers clasped across his paunch. "How can you expect a Japanese to listen seriously to your prattle of 'humanity'? You have obstructed us for years, moralizing about our behavior and holding us up to the ridicule of the world. You insult our culture and our history by excluding us, and you mock us with cartoons and jokes. You raise tariff barriers against our products—which you inconsistently claim to be inferior— but you expect

[282]

free entry everywhere for your own goods. You mistreat and humiliate our people living in your country, denying them the rights advertised by your so-called democracy. You denigrate everything we do, every effort we make to better ourselves, and you expect us to give up our pride and abandon our dreams for the sake of your approval."

This time Tanaka had spoken objectively, speculatively, almost sadly. But as his words emerged, he seemed gradually to shed his weariness as a snake might shed his skin. Now, resuming, Edgerton could hear a new note in his voice. "Open your eyes, Edgerton! We Japanese are marching now, and we are winning. And we are doing it in the name of all Asians. You remain here, you few Americans and other foreigners, only on our forebearance. When we are ready, you shall be driven out, and your power broken so thoroughly that you will never be of any consequence in Asia again. America's era in the East is finished; the Age of Japan is now beginning. You'll see. A few years from now, remember it was Tanaka who told you."

Repellent as Tanaka was, Edgerton found him strangely impressive at this moment. He had a dynamic force that went far beyond his mere physical presence. Filled with pride and arrogance and the bitter memory of old injuries, he seemed to personify the new Japan as it was emerging in the world. No longer could Japan be seen simply as that picturesque, miniature country, with its flower arrangements and tea ceremonies, and the almost excruciating politeness of its people. At that moment Tanaka *was* Japan . . . militant, vengeful, repulsing any interference with his free exercise of power. The thought of Tamara in his hands was terrifying.

Edgerton recalled watching a surfer in Hawaii. Dynamically balanced on his great slab of a board, the man had seemed as much a part of the wave as the foaming crest that raced to overtake him, and he'd envied the man the power he'd harnessed. But then he'd seen how precariously the man was related to the wave, how uncontrolled the power really was. The man would not be forgiven even one mistake. Nor would Japan. For all their bluster and posturing and military power, the Japanese were on a wave of their own; they would simply have to ride it out . . . or quit. Goaded by the extremists within it, the Japanese Army had been dreaming of the conquest of Asia for decades. Except where the blindness of American policy had inadvertently strengthened the militarists, the United States had done little to shape the course of events. Perhaps she couldn't have, in spite of what he'd said to Procter. Perhaps the forces of nationalism and population and wounded pride had been inexorable from the beginning. Groggy with worry and frustration, Edgerton's mind jogged. Hawaii:

[283]

the source of Tanaka's strange accent, of course . . . and very likely of much of his hatred, as well. A minuscule puzzle solved, leaving all other problems as intractable as ever.

His peroration had left Tanaka flushed with excitement, his eyes focused raptly on some distant vision. Then, as Edgerton watched, his expression clouded, and an angry frown creased his forehead.

"Since your victory seems inevitable," Edgerton said, sensing another lightning change of mood, "you can afford to be generous with the Liu women. Be magnanimous."

Tanaka grunted impatiently, as though he'd been jarred out of some unpleasant reverie. "The case of the Liu women is closed," he said coldly, getting to his feet. "Don't meddle in it further." He opened a drawer in his desk and began sweeping papers into it indiscriminately.

The ruthless announcement caught Edgerton unprepared and he started to his feet. "I refuse to be put off this way," he said, determined to revive the argument, to keep talking. "If I have to, I'll take the matter to your superiors . . . all the way to the top, if necessary."

Tanaka's laugh was indifferent. "Then take it, by all means. I assure you my superiors will support me. And now it's late, and I wish to go home." He pressed a button on his desk. "My orderly will show you out."

"But we can't leave things here," Edgerton protested.

"The case is closed, I said!" Tanaka slammed shut the drawer with a finality which was absolute.

Standing beside his car, Edgerton felt drenched with fatigue and dejection. Twice, he'd glimpsed success. At the very end, with Tanaka exalted by his visions, Edgerton had sensed that Tamara's release might be within his grasp. But then something, some vagary of Tanaka's mind, had destroyed the moment.

Edgerton's brain felt paralyzed, empty, deadened. Wearily he looked at his watch; it wasn't even nine.

And now, what's next? He'd have to see Minister Saito, of course, even if to do so sent Procter into convulsions. He'd put Tamara's case to Saito in the strongest terms, squeezing every last advantage out of his embarrassment over what the Japanese Legation was already calling the Tungchow Incident.

His mind drifting, Edgerton wondered at the fondness of the Japanese mind for that pretentious term. In 1932, it had been the Manchurian Incident, soon to be followed by the Shanghai Incident. In 1937, the Marco Polo Bridge Incident had begun the full-scale war against China . . . still known as the China Incident even after a year of heavy fighting. The previous December an American gunboat had been sunk by Japanese planes, making history as the Panay Incident. Now they had the Tungchow Incident . . . no event was too small to deserve the label. Well, if anything happened to Tamara, he'd see to it that Tanaka always remembered him as the instigator of the Peking Incident. But it would be too late then. The thought stabbed into his heart like an icicle.

Behind him the sentry stirred, the steel butt plate of his rifle grating harshly on the pavement.

The sound wrenched Edgerton back into reality. He would not let it become too late. Getting in to see Saito at this hour was going to be a problem. His staff was very protective. If he tried and failed, the attempt might only prejudice matters for the next day. Well, he'd have to chance that . . . the thought of simply leaving Tamara wherever she was could not be faced.

But where was she? His ignorance of that essential fact made him desperately fearful. It was as though by being able to visualize her in some specific place, he could be communicating with her in some way—by telepathy, perhaps—could be telling her that he was doing his best, that she wasn't forgotten, that it hadn't all been left in pieces by that phone call, and that he loved her and wouldn't rest until she was safe.

And more practically, until he knew where she was, he had really very little to take to Saito. He could imagine how it would go: after initial expressions of shock and disbelief, Saito or, more probably, Yamaguchi would call Tanaka. Tanaka would deny it all, insisting that nothing had happened, that Edgerton had misunderstood, that Tamara hadn't been arrested, or that she had only been questioned and then released. Where she had gone from there was anyone's guess . . . he could see the shoulders shrugging. Everyone would stand around smiling and denying and explaining, and Tamara would only become even more deeply hidden behind a screen of Japanese obfuscation. If he knew where Tamara was, he could simply go there and demand to see her. Once he'd seen her, or even just seen the place, his position would be strengthened. But Tamara's mother would inevitably become involved, and her irregular presence in the Legation Quarter revealed. LaGarde would be embarrassed, and might get fed up and simply ask her to leave the hotel. If Liu *t'ai t'ai* went home, Tanaka would have her: just what he'd wanted in the first place. And he'd still have Tamara. So long as something could be gained by holding her, Tanaka would hold her, no matter what he'd promised. Edgerton felt

[285]

overwhelmed. He was powerless . . . the whole business was simply too big for him alone.

As though a button had been pushed in some hitherto dormant mechanism of his brain, a name appeared in front of his eyes, and he felt a buoyant surge of relief. Flipping his half-smoked cigarette into the gutter, he climbed eagerly into his car.

Somewhere deep in the dark house a bell buzzed faintly. He waited but nothing happened. He pressed the button again, the sound coming back to him uncertainly, almost as though he might be feeling it in his fingertip instead of hearing it.

Edgerton shuffled his feet in an agony of impatience. He looked over his shoulder at the *hu-tung*. It was empty and lifeless, sombre in the feeble glow of a street light on the corner. Behind its brick wall, the small yard looked barren, neglected. It hardly seemed the place he remembered . . . Madeline had been an avid gardener.

He turned his back stubbornly, refusing to believe his trip was wasted, the house empty. Too much depended on Jimmy Chang for him not to be there.

Jabbing one last time at the bell button, he encountered an anonymous eye inspecting him through a peephole.

He was about to speak to it when the door opened and he recognized Chang Sun-cheh standing in the shadowed hallway. Strong fingers took him by the sleeve and pulled him through the narrow opening. What the hell? he thought as he stumbled over the threshold.

Edgerton turned to face the man he'd come to see, but Chang's back was to him and his eye again fixed to the peephole. Confused by these elaborate precautions, he waited awkwardly. After several seconds, Chang snapped shut the peephole and flicked on the light switch. For a moment Edgerton was dazzled by the flood of light.

Chang squinted at him. "Excuse the humbug . . . the Generalissimo has reportedly put a price on my head. Not a very large one, but I've been feeling nervous for a couple of days," he said, smiling rigidly, his eyes grave and guarded. "Well, this is a pleasant surprise," he added briskly, rubbing his hands together.

Edgerton had never seen anyone so obviously not glad to see him. Chang was in his shirtsleeves, and his short wide body bulked like a weightlifter's. His usually bland face was drawn and haggard, and tension had carved a deep frown between his eyebrows.

"Sorry to barge in like this, Jimmy, but I need your help," Edgerton said, gnawed by the growing pressure of anxiety. On top of everything else, this feebly pretended welcome was ominous.

Chang ran stubby fingers through his short stiff hair, his eyes shifting uncomfortably. "Glad to do anything I can," he said, muttering the conventional words absentmindedly. His gaze wandered to Edgerton's clothes and he tried to laugh. "You look like you've been in a fight," he said.

Distracted, Edgerton looked down at his filthy, knee-sprung trousers and scuffed shoes. The front of his shirt was splotched and damp. He'd left his jacket in the car.

"Had to change a tire," he said, feeling suddenly irritable at this time-consuming small talk. "Look, Jimmy, I really have to talk to you. It's important."

Chang nodded. "Sure, come in." He led the way down a narrow corridor and into the living room.

It had been over a year since Edgerton had been in their house. He recalled it as a warm and friendly place; now it was cold in spite of the heat—clammy.

Through wide double doors, Edgerton caught sight of Madeline Chang leaning over the dining room table. It was lighted brightly from above and strewn with piles of papers and notebooks. Heavy draperies had been drawn across the windows.

Madeline paused long enough to give him a guarded, empty smile. "Hello, John," was all she said, her voice cautious, as though she expected him to try to borrow money.

"Don't let me disturb you, Madeline," Edgerton mumbled. "I just want to talk to Jimmy for a minute."

Edgerton was dismayed by this cool welcome. He'd counted heavily on Jimmy's help . . . and on his concern too; yet, plainly, they had other things very much on their minds.

"No trouble," Madeline was telling him brightly. "We were just going over the household accounts . . . Jimmy hates it." She ended with a meaningless laugh. She turned out the light and carefully closed the folding doors behind her. The movement was a graceful one, and it drew the fabric of her Chinese summer gown close against her body. She seemed thinner than he remembered, and her face was even more finely drawn than it had seemed at the Procters' party. Before that it had been a year since he'd seen her . . . no, even longer ago than that. It had been before the occupation . . . he remembered it well.

"Won't you sit down?" she said, obviously intending to join them, although it must have been quite evident to her he wanted to see Jimmy alone. She was choosing to be dense. A sense of futility nagged

[287]

at him, a reminder of his helplessness. He fished in his pocket for a cigarette.

"How about a drink?" Jimmy asked perfunctorily.

Edgerton nearly refused, then changed his mind. A drink suddenly seemed a very excellent thing to have. "Thanks . . . whiskey and water, please; but make it light." He settled into an uncomfortable leather chair.

It was difficult to reconcile this nervous man with the one he'd chatted with so cordially at the party. Then he remembered that he had cause to be edgy about visitors. Kuomintang threats weren't idle ones, and their agents were reputed to pass continually back and forth across the Japanese lines. It was a depressing reminder . . . what were his problems compared to theirs?

Waiting, he glanced around the room. He would not have recognized it. He'd been here, drinking and talking and laughing, just before the battle at the Marco Polo Bridge. It had been a big party, with the phonograph playing and people dancing. And he remembered the furniture as being old and worn and comfortable, not this heavy leather stuff.

He'd danced with Madeline that night. It had been the occasion for a transient flirtation, the sort of thing which sometimes spontaneously overtakes old friends when they dance together after having a few too many drinks. It had lasted for perhaps five minutes.

To judge from Madeline's nervous hovering and the frown between her opaque eyes, she recalled no such intimacy, at least not with any warmth. Why doesn't she sit down? he wondered irritably, wishing Jimmy would hurry with the drinks. The leather of his chair was stiff and creaky, and smelled of tanning chemicals.

Jimmy gave him his drink finally, then he and Madeline sat together on a lumpy looking couch, side by side like a pair of judges.

"Cheers," Chang said unhappily, raising his glass a couple of inches. "What can we do for you?"

Were these his friends? Edgerton wondered, suddenly tongue-tied. "Well," he began with effort, his voice breaking. He cleared his throat, took a long swallow of his drink, and started again. "A friend of mine is in trouble," he said. "A Chinese girl. For reasons I can't quite figure out, she's been arrested by the Japanese . . . by Colonel Tanaka."

Jimmy Chang groaned aloud and put a hand over his lowered eyes. Madeline gave him a quick glance, then returned her cold face to Edgerton's. "Go on," Jimmy muttered.

"You see, her mother . . . . it's sort of complicated. . . ." Finally Edgerton got the story told. As he talked, his eyes shifted from one face

[288]

to the other, searching in vain for a flicker of expression on either one. "And now he's got her locked up someplace . . . God knows where," he finished lamely.

Chang stared for a long time into his drink. Finally he raised his eyes to Edgerton's. "And you want me to get her released, is that it?" he asked.

His flat, emotionless tone, devoid even of interest, told Edgerton that his effort had indeed been futile. "But Jimmy . . ." he began, refusing to believe the obvious.

"I can do nothing."

"But you're in the Interior Ministry, you run the police, you have influence with the Japanese. Pull some strings, offer bribes, lean on somebody . . . you know how to operate with these people."

Chang studied his shoes glumly. "I don't run the Japanese police." He looked up, frowning. "John, open your eyes! Don't you know what's been happening here? In this case, Buddha himself could return to help you and they'd only laugh at him. At me, they wouldn't even bother to laugh."

Edgerton felt chilled to the heart. It was true; Chang meant every word. He turned desperately to Madeline. Watchful as a suspicious cat, she stared back at him, her face frozen into blankness.

"But you must help us!"

Chang shook his head resignedly, as though forced to deal with the simpleminded. "Because Tanaka is one of the most powerful men in Peking. I refuse to become involved."

"But the girl's innocent."

"Innocent!" Chang repeated softly, shaking his head. He laughed quietly, the sound carrying a sort of patient sadness. "Where have you been, John? We're all in danger, my friend . . . even you. If I start interfering in these Japanese plots, they'll only give me the sack . . . or worse." Chang put down his drink and rubbed his face with both hands. "I'm not a part of this government because they like me, you know. I'm there because they need my brains and my experience and my honesty. Even at best, it's only temporary; they can get along without me. It's up to *me* to make this feeble arrangement last as long as possible. If the Japanese get fed up with the puppet government, hundreds of thousands of lives will be endangered. The Japanese haven't the patience to govern us—they don't care about us. Their solution for Chinese problems is to kill the people who create them. It's simpler that way. And it's logical; their main interest is conducting the war, not the maintenance of civic justice, or running the Water Department." Chang spread his hands eloquently.

[289]

"But I'm begging you!" Edgerton insisted mulishly.

Madeline's harsh laugh was like an explosion. "Now that's a refreshing sight," she said with heavy irony. "But worthless. It's much too late for begging, even from you. It's time for us Chinese to look after ourselves." She half-rose to her feet, her voice a shout. "You Americans have had your day in China, you bloodsuckers, you exploiters . . . !"

"Madeline!"

She glared at her husband defiantly for a moment, but fell silent.

Chang's face was impassive. "I'm sorry, John, truly. If I could help you and your friend, I would. I can't. What Madeline just said is unpleasant to hear, but essentially correct. We have to look after ourselves; not only us, the Changs, but all Chinese. I have too many responsibilities to take risks or squander my influence. Chinese will have died by the millions before this war is over, and countless lives will have been blighted forever. I may be able to save a few thousand of them. They're more important, those thousands, than one half-caste woman."

So even the Changs had known about Tamara. So much for his priggish maneuvering. How humiliated she must have felt! Sensible girl . . . she'd have known none of it was working. If he'd only used some of that energy protecting her instead of himself . . . .

He tried to tell himself that recriminations were futile, but he couldn't hold back the tide of guilt and remorse that was rising in his throat, threatening to choke him. She was out there somewhere in terrible peril, and his selfishness had helped to put her there.

Chang cleared his throat. "I know what you're thinking, John," he said, not unkindly. "But even that's of little importance anymore. Face it: here in China we all get raped, one way or another, sooner or later. My heart and my pride get raped every day by these bastards."

Getting restlessly to his feet, Chang went to stand near the bar cabinet. Although his expression was somber, there was tenderness in the look he gave his wife. "Even Madeline," he said, his eyes never leaving her face. "She had to go to Tientsin not long after the Japanese came. Things were quiet by then, and it seemed safe enough, but she happened to catch the fancy of some staff officers. She . . ." Chang swallowed hard and gave his head a shake, his lips clamped into a grim line.

It was all Edgerton could do to keep his eyes from shifting to Madeline's face. Coming as it had, the brutal statement of fact had been like a blow to the head. And yet, oddly, it was the controlled fury of Jimmy's reaction which was the more shocking. It made Edgerton wonder about himself. Had the victim the other night been Tamara

[290]

instead of her mother, could he have held himself so icily in check as that? In Jimmy's case, it could mean waiting for years before there'd be a chance of even the most rudimentary "justice"—to say nothing of the luxury of revenge. He had the feeling he could never be so reserved, so rational, so wise. No, he'd have gone off half-cocked, another Quixote heading for the windmills . . . doing Tamara no good and only making a fool of himself. To the undoubted amusement of the Japanese.

Well, perhaps. But Jimmy was a member of a patient race.

He had no such tradition behind him, nor was he faced with an accomplished fact. Since there was still time to act, he could do nothing else. But before he could renew his arguments, Jimmy was going on.

"You didn't know that, did you? Of course not. None of our foreign friends were told; it would only have embarrassed them." He snorted sarcastically, and his eyes went bleak. "And you can be sure I never hint of it to my masters. As a matter of fact, one of the officers is now a major on the general's staff. I've met him several times at conferences. Naturally we have no social contact, so he's unaware of our, uh, relationship." Chang grinned fiercely, Then for an instant, his iron control broke and his face flooded with blood. "*Mei-yu-fah-tze!*" he exclaimed, deeply pained by the admission.

Edgerton believed him. As far as Chang was concerned, quite literally, "there was no way." The interview was at an end.

Stunned and shaken, he got slowly to his feet. The incredible part was that it was all totally believable. Everyone had heard the stories, but no one wanted to acknowledge them as happening to a friend, much less to a lover or a wife. It all had to be happening to someone else, and very far away in any case.

He stared down into Madeline's beautiful haughty face. "I'm sorry; I didn't know," he mumbled, not really surprised when she turned away. "It just doesn't seem like the same old China anymore."

"It's not!" Chang said flatly. "Come; I'll let you out."

In a daze, Edgerton stumbled after him. Chang gave a quick look through the peephole, then opened the door. "Go now," he said. Then, in a softer voice, he added, "I'm sorry, John."

The door latch clicked solidly, positive as a vault's, closing him out. Entering the shadowed *hu-tung* was like wading into a strange river. He felt isolated suddenly, a wanderer in an indifferent country where once immunity and privilege had shielded him perfectly. Now these protections were evaporating like sweat in a cool wind. Hearing Tanaka's sentiments echo so smoothly from Madeline's lips seemed only to emphasize the inevitable.

[291]

But as long as a few of his elections remained, he would make them work for Tamara. The question was how.

Edgerton had no idea.

♞♞

The small apartment seemed strange without Andrei there. She couldn't remember having been there alone in the evening ever. In the other place, yes; but that was before Andrei's job with the Americans, when he still tutored and gave lessons at night. Now, he was always at home in the evening, reading or fussing with his papers. It was in the daytime she was used to having the place to herself . . . the daytime. . . .

Maya added an inch of vodka to the glass. Swirling it gently, she stared into it, admiring its clarity. It was like air, it was so clear, clearer than water, especially the water that came out of the pipes here.

It was early, barely nine o'clock and the building still pulsed with life. Toward the end of September, when the evenings began to cool, people would stay in their rooms and the place would quiet down. Now it seemed that no one in the building was asleep . . . how could they be with all that din?

People sat by every window, calling across to friends, waiting for a breath of air, or they crouched like monkeys on the fire escapes, chattering and drinking tea, or squatted in rows along the concrete steps at the entrance, watching the flow of people in the *hu-tung*. And above it all, the radios with their blaring music shattered the hot night. Maya swallowed some vodka, relishing the raw fire of it in her throat, then swallowed again. She hadn't been drunk for a long time and she was looking forward to it. Drunkenness brought not only waking oblivion, but led to a blessedly dreamless sleep. On the way, one floated through pleasant places where lights were soft and sounds were gentle, and the sharp corners of life were rounded.

Taking a cigarette from the pack before her, she overcame a momentary difficulty in bringing match and tobacco together, then inhaled deeply, pleasurably. They were American cigarettes—as different from the hay the Chinese smoked as vodka from cold tea. Reminded, she had another sip, then poured again, adding two inches to the glass.

The Japanese officer had given the cigarettes to her just before bustling off to his office. He'd made almost a ceremony of the presentation. He was an odd man. For all his flowery manners, he had a quick brutal temper. Remembering, Maya touched the bruise just above her ear. He'd only hit her once; luckily she'd been able to turn away, causing him to miss her eye.

At first she'd been terrified lest he turn out to be like those young Japanese officers at the Mukden garrison. Though it had happened before her marriage, Maya remembered every moment of that vividly. She and another girl had been hired to sing and tap dance at their club. The officers had expected more. . . .

Remembering them, even the tea and the cakes and Tanaka's laborious conversation had done little to reassure her. Although she had to admit that she'd been the one to make their talk laborious. His English was so much better than hers . . . she'd had to pad out many of her clumsy sentences with Chinese words just to finish them. When he'd asked her, right in the beginning, whether she spoke Japanese, some perverse instinct had led her to deny it. After she'd seen his temper, she regretted having lied, but was afraid to confess. Perhaps later she could pretend to learn. . . .

Maya smiled slightly, admitting to herself that it hadn't been at all as bad as she'd expected. Not fun, but not agony, either. Still, there was more to it than merely lying on her back and spreading her legs, as Serge had said, and thinking of something else. The man had been an acrobat, continually turning her and pulling her this way and that and climbing over her, seemingly intent on trying every imaginable position.

Maya giggled weakly, remembering his round glistening body, his gasping breath, the almost studious frown on his face as he concentrated on what he was doing. He approached the sex act the way a general would approach a battle; determined to leave nothing to chance. That was clever, she thought, and tried to laugh. The sound that came out was flat and mirthless.

Suddenly she was close to tears, her throat constricting with the pain of Serge's betrayal. He'd simply used her, because he wanted something from poor timid Andrei. And she'd known it, known it all along . . . God damn him! Knowing it, she'd still let him use her and humiliate her.

Where was Andrei? she wondered, looking blankly around the kitchen.

Poor Andrei . . . for two weeks he'd dithered about no letter from Anya. Now that there was one, he wasn't here to read it. Maya fingered the torn envelope with its round schoolgirl writing. The girl was having a good time, swimming and riding donkeys. And who wouldn't, living at the beach, eating American food, nothing to do but watch a couple of brats a few hours a day? Anya would manage them all right, with her firmness and precisely ordered mind. Anya liked everything neatly arranged in rows and piles, everything sorted and numbered . . . so prissy! Although dutifully addressed to both of

[293]

them, the letter was really for Andrei alone, from "Daddy's Little Girl."

They'd never gotten along; it was a relief to have her out from underfoot. And if Andrei's plans for the girl worked out, she might never live with them again . . . she'd be going to America with those people next month. Her papers were all arranged . . . the first of Andrei's pipe dreams ever to come true. That American at the Legation had made it happen. She'd never seen him, but she'd heard him praised so often there were times when she was ready to puke at the sound of his name. What American ever did anything for a Russian? They'd spend thousands, millions, to preach Christianity to a bunch of ignorant Chinamen, but never lift a hand for one of their own race. Even when they hired a Russian, it was at Chinese wages. But Andrei had been right about this American.

Soon Anya would be gone. Brushing away a tear, Maya stiffled a small sob, knowing in her heart she didn't really care. She'd been too young to have a baby and had never wanted it. If Andrei hadn't been such an ignorant fool . . . full of champagne, she'd left the precautions to him. The idiot had been a virgin; he didn't even know there were precautions. That was the end of her dancing career. Who knew what heights she might have reached without a baby and fat incompetent Andrei dragging her down?

Sniffling slightly, Maya felt in vain for a handkerchief. Getting unsteadily to her feet, she went to get one from the bedroom. It was cooler there, and for a moment she stood in the doorway, relishing the faint current of air. From across the darkened room, her reflection faced her from the surface of her dressing table mirror, the light from the kitchen silhouetting her body through the thin kimono. Not bad, she thought, smiling to herself and running her hands over her hips and down her thighs, not bad at all. Colonel Tanaka had literally gasped when he saw her undressed. Andrei had always said she was beautiful, and so had Serge in the beginning, and she was often aware of the eyes of other men.

A demanding series of knocks shook the door, and the knob twisted impatiently. Maya was alarmed, knowing it couldn't be Andrei . . . he'd never pound so forcefully, even if he'd lost his key, and she felt hesitant about opening for a stranger. Then she shrugged. No one would risk molesting her in this bee hive.

It was Serge Puhalski . . . she'd almost expected him. Debonair as always, he grinned his wolfish grin, blond hair hanging boyishly over one eye. In spite of all that had happened, she felt her pulse quicken and the blood rush to her face.

"Good . . . you're home," he said.

And where did you think I might be? she wanted to retort, suddenly angry.

"Well, aren't you going to ask me in?" he asked, hs head cocked disarmingly to one side.

"Come in then," Maya said, returning to her chair. She felt perfectly sober.

After hanging his hat and jacket behind the door, he watched her from across the table, seeming to tower taller than ever.

"Some refreshment, eh?" he said, eyeing her glass and the half-empty bottle. "How about me?"

"Help yourself," Maya replied, not stirring. She'd waited on him for the last time, she told herself.

He frowned, then shrugged and went to get his own glass. He sat down, poured, raised his glass to her mockingly, and drank. He eyed her for several seconds, his long face growing solemn. "I have bad news," he said.

Maya waited, saying nothing.

"Andrei is dead."

Maya felt the breath catch in her throat, threatening to choke her. She was cold suddenly, and she shivered, hugging herself. The poor gentleman, she thought, remembering for some peculiar reason his clumsy kisses of the other night, and the confusing, almost motherly emotion which had gripped her as she straddled him and guided him into her. Without warning, tears gushed from her eyes, and her throat became so dry she could not swallow. "What happened?" she whispered.

"I'm not sure. Someone told me he'd collapsed on the street . . . a heart attack. A city ambulance came for him, but he had already, ah, passed on. I've inquired where they took him, but there's been no information so far. You know how inefficient the Chinese are." He paused then, his face mournful, and reached out to take her hand. "I'm sorry," he said, squeezing her fingers.

Maya let her limp hand stay within his fingers, marveling at her lack of reaction to his touch. After today, she would have expected disgust, at least, but there was nothing.

"I'll take care of all the arrangements, if you'd like. We were good friends . . . it's the least I can do," Serge said sanctimoniously. "It's a sad moment, I know . . . even though you didn't love him."

The words shocked her, they were so cold, so unthinking. Pulling her hand away, she gulped some vodka, nearly choking on it. Then, staring down at the bare scrubbed surface of the table, she had to admit

[295]

he was right. She had never loved Andrei . . . not really. She'd only tolerated his bumbling helplessness as she had once tolerated his bumbling lovemaking. If it hadn't been for Anya swelling in her belly, she'd never have agreed to marry him. But she would miss him. He *was* a good man, better than the schemer sitting across from her.

"Yes," she said, distracted now by the certainty that Serge had lied to her about her husband, that the circumstances were quite different from those he'd described so glibly. Well, she'd find out the truth soon enough. Time then to face him with it, make him pay something for at least one of his lies.

Serge's face softened into a fond smile, and his hand found hers again. "Brave girl," he said. He paused, then added conversationally, "How did it go today?"

At first she didn't understand him. When she did, she almost laughed, tempted to give him a description: first we did this and then he put it here, and then I took it and. . . . "All right," she said, shrugging, watching him, remembering his pretended abhorrence at the thought of sharing her with another man.

"Good!" he exclaimed, nodding. "He's not such a bad fellow, is he? I told you it wouldn't be so terrible."

He waited, as though expecting some acknowledgment. Maya, feeling she'd become ten years wiser in the last ten hours, waited also, wondering what he was leading up to.

"You'll be going back tomorrow?"

"Perhaps," she said, doubting it. The enormous officer who had materialized so surprisingly right in the bedroom door, had threatened to punish her severely if she were ever seen there again. He was obviously a man of considerable authority, in spite of his mannerisms. She could only guess that he and Tanaka were engaged in some kind of feud, and that he had the upper hand—for the moment. But Tanaka had impressed her; she doubted he'd let the pansy call the tune for long.

She hadn't really thought much about going back or not going back. It was odd; she had automatically supposed that he would send for her when it was time. And that she would go. Of course, poor Andrei's safety was no longer a reason to oblige Tanaka. But he seemed to want her for herself, and she was in no position to take risks by offending him. Provided he developed no really brutal tastes, he might become quite tolerable. Already he'd been generous. While they were still play-acting over tea, he'd given her an unset diamond. She knew nothing about such things, but it was big and looked expensive. It was buried now in her talcum powder in the bedroom. It had occurred to

[296]

her to ask Puhalski about having it appraised—he knew all about that sort of thing—but now she decided not to. She'd had enough of Serge's kind of help. So long as her relationship with the Japanese required no more of her than it had so far, it could go on indefinitely as far as she was concerned. If she was to be alone, she might as well do the best she could for herself. So she was finally a whore, she thought suddenly, and was vaguely amused that the notion failed to shock her. She'd never been quite that before, not even in Mukden.

"Fortunately, I have some very good news as well," Serge said, giving her hand a final pat before reaching for one of her cigarettes.

Maya remained watchful. In spite of the vodka, her brain felt relatively clear.

"I've learned something that's going to get us out of this stinking country, and Andrei's American boss is going to arrange it for us," he said, nodding, proud of himself.

"I don't understand." She was confused, beginning to wonder whether she could have misjudged him after all.

Eagerly, Puhalski leaned across the table. "We are going to America," he said.

"Do you mean he'll give us that much money?"

"Not money . . . I've got enough money, or I can get it," Puhlaski said. "No, he'll pay with visas!"

"Visas?" Maya repeated, stupidly. It was a magic word. The common thread binding every refugee to every other one was an unquenchable desire for an American visa. "Can he do that?" she asked, suddenly skeptical, suspecting another Puhalski stunt.

"He's not supposed to, but he can."

"He has to get permission from Washington."

"Nonsense; they do it all right here in the Legation. I know what I'm talking about."

"Anya's visa had to come from Washington."

"That's because she's a child and traveling without her parents."

"Ah!" Maya murmured, convinced at last. America, she thought. Good God, going to America! After all that had happened, Serge was going to take her to America. Old feelings returned in a flood, choking her heart, memories of the days when she'd have done anything for him, when they were first lovers. She was ashamed of herself, she'd been unfair. Turning to him impulsively, wanting to embrace him, she met his calculating eyes. In their blue hardness, they were the eyes of a reptile, cold and devoid of feeling. She could read them at last, and knew the truth: Serge Puhalski would never take her anywhere, even if he could.

[297]

She made herself smile at him, then drank deeply. Now the vodka was working again, and she felt herself sliding back into that invulnerable state when only dreams are real.

"And what is this information?" she asked, hearing herself pronounce the words slowly, distinctly.

"Well, actually I have half of it," Serge said. "It's up to you to get the other half."

Up to you, Maya repeated in her mind. So much of what Puhalski wanted was "up to" someone else. "To me?"

"Yes, you'll have to get it out of Tanaka. I want you to go back to him tomorrow . . . this opportunity is perishable. We must hurry."

"I'm all mixed up," Maya said, suddenly wanting to cry, afraid she was going to be sick.

"Then listen while I explain," Serge said impatiently. "The Japs have arrested Edgerton's Chinese girl friend. He knows this, but he doesn't know where she is. And there's no way for him to find out . . . not even the regular Military Police know. Tanaka's keeping it a secret."

"Tanaka?" Maya moaned, more baffled than ever. "How can you know all this?"

Puhalski waved the question aside. "Don't worry, I know it. One of the MPs owes me some favors. The point is, Edgerton can't do a damn thing until he finds out where she is. And he has to do something because Tanaka has him over a barrel. If he does nothing, the Japs can leak the story and make him look like a heartless monster for turning his back on his sweetheart. If he tries to help her, he exposes himself as an exploiter of Chinese women . . . you can imagine how those American missionaries will like that. They'll skin him alive!" Puhalski laughed delightedly "Tanaka's had his own troubles lately; he'd like nothing better than to turn the spotlight on someone else. Either way it goes, he can do what he wants. He can leak the story, humiliate Edgerton, and then release the woman as a humanitarian gesture."

"It's all so complicated."

"No, it's simple. In any case, all you have to do is find out from him where the woman is."

Although Maya nodded, she wasn't really listening to him any longer. Through the confusion of his explanations, a line of memory had begun to lead her back to Tanaka's room. She couldn't be positive, but she had a feeling she already knew where the woman was.

She had been lying under a sheet on his bed, waiting for him. He'd just ordered her there, having struck her with his fist to emphasize his authority, and she was frightened. He was beginning to seem as bad

[298]

as the officers in Mukden after all. She was afraid of him, and was worrying that he would beat her and hurt her breasts, and that he would force her to suck him. And she remembered praying rather clumsily for God to help her, to make the time pass quickly and without pain, and to let her go home soon.

The telephone had rung as Tanaka was undressing, making him swear. Whatever the call concerned, Tanaka's part in it had consisted mainly of grunts, but it had prompted another call, this time on his Army telephone with its little crank. Listening with only half a mind, she'd been but dimly aware of a series of orders about trucks and patrolmen and so forth. What had attracted her full attention finally was a peculiar change in Tanaka's voice. The trucks he hadn't really cared about—they were military business—but this was something else, something close to his heart, something he'd been waiting for. Her instinct made her certain.

"Do you think you could do that?" Puhalski's voice broke into her thoughts.

"Uh . . . I guess so," she said, momentarily off guard.

Serge frowned at her suspiciously. "He didn't throw you out, did he?"

You're a real pimp, aren't you? she thought, relishing her detachment from him. She laughed lightly. "No he didn't throw me out . . . he's having a formal party tonight, I think. But he will send for me."

Serge seemed dubious. "Well, don't get him mad at you. You'll have to be careful, though, and not make him suspicious." He shook his head, "I don't know if you can do it."

"Don't worry so much, Serge; I can handle this man." She felt a rush of self-confidence. She could deal with both these men. "I'll encourage him to talk about himself, his most challenging cases, flatter him . . . you know."

"Fine," Serge said, nodding as though she were a prize pupil. "You'll do fine."

"What's the woman's name?"

"Liu," he said. "Tamara Liu."

"Tamara? Is she part Russian?" Maya asked, remembering.

"Half . . . her mother's a Chink."

"I'll do my best," Maya said, raising her glass. "To get out of China at last . . . it will be like going to heaven."

Serge nodded, molding his face into an eager, affectionate mask. He's such a rotten actor, she thought.

"Ah, Maya . . . I always said we'd go away together, didn't I?"

"Yes," she said, making herself smile. She could remember Tanaka

[299]

saying, "Pick up the Liu woman and take her to . . ." From that point on, her mind was now a blank. She had known where the place was, and had forgotten it.

Serge filled his glass, then drained half of it at a gulp. His eyes were unusually bright and the skin across his angular cheekbones was flushed. She realized suddenly that he was drunk. She'd never seen him this way. He was always so tightly controlled, letting nothing of himself be seen . . . nothing but his rages. Even making love, he was a machine, an automaton, and when he came, the event was marked only by a single grunt. She'd seen a picture once in a schoolbook, showing the tip of an iceberg. That was Serge: cold, hidden, the real man submerged.

She supposed that his elation over the prospect of leaving China had led him to unbend now and reveal himself so uncharacteristically. And that, too, was surprising. One of the reasons she'd always really known, deep in her heart, that Serge would never take her away, even when his promises were at their most eloquent, was that he had too many profitable irons in the fire to want to leave them. He seemed to know everyone in all the *yamens*, had influence with the Japanese and, compared to the other Russians, had unlimited amounts of money. Something must have happened.

To be able to see him at last so starkly made her feel pleasantly superior. She could look at him with objectivity now, not even hating him. What reproach she had was for herself, for her docility in letting him use her so crudely. All he'd ever been was a pimp, with his café full of girls. He'd merely added her to his list of whores. The thought occurred to her suddenly that he might have taken money from Tanaka, that the Japanese had paid for her. Half-amused, half-angry, she wondered what would happen if she were to ask him about it now, if she demanded her whore's share. Suddenly she remembered.

The District of Korean Whores. She could hear Tanaka's voice ordering the woman taken to the house at the end of the Wu-feng Hu-tung. The lane was notorious, leading as it did through one of the city's oldest red-light districts. By now, the designation was no longer really accurate, since the Koreans had moved to another part of the city, but the area remained a brothel district and the name had endured. Mr. Edgerton would know all about the Wu-feng Hu-tung, even if he were much too proper ever to have gone there as a customer. Serge was probably right. If the American loved the girl, and if it really were so easy, why wouldn't he issue a couple of visas under the counter in exchange for such good information? Maya wondered what it would be like to be loved by a man who would risk his career for you, and

[300]

then she remembered that Andrei had been that way; she ought to know already. The dear man . . . she felt the tears rise in her throat . . . and quickly amputated that train of thought. You're drunk! she scolded herself. And be sensible for once, she added. There was something make-believe in all this talk of visas. She had the feeling that there might not be a visa in her destiny. What was it Andrei was always telling her? Something about making the most of what one had, rather than complaining about what was missing. Anya was getting a visa. She was young and would make good use of it . . . perhaps it was enough.

She turned to speak to Serge, but he was already getting to his feet. He beamed down at her with calculated affection, weaving slightly. "We're nearly there, Maya. Do this right, and we'll be in the good old U.S.A. before you know it."

"I'll do it," she said. Looking up at him from behind her smile, she recognized a quality in him which was like steel . . . indestructible. His boast was believable, or part of it was. Someday Serge Puhalski would probably get to America, and with all his papers in order, too. But it would not be with her help, she promised herself that.

"Won't that be wonderful," she said, pushing back her chair. "Do you have to go?" she added coquettishly, mischievously, wondering how much she dared tease him. It was a risk; once started, he'd be difficult to stop . . . the idea of making love to him was repugnant.

"I'm afraid so," he said, hat already on the back of his head, coat dangling from one hand. "I have a business meeting."

It was true, then, she realized with a pang. He didn't want her anymore. Even loathing him as she did, she still needed him to want her, although she couldn't understand why.

"And I'm sorry about Andrei," he repeated.

"Poor Andrei," Maya said, suddenly deeply saddened. "He's better off perhaps . . . this wasn't the world for him."

Serge slipped an arm around her and pulled her close, pressing her breast against his side. As she submitted to his kiss, she was thinking that she'd have to make herself some strong tea and sober up. It would never do to make telephone calls when her speech was slurred with vodka. Andrei would never forgive her.

♟♟

As Edgerton replaced the phone on its cradle, he knew a moment of great relief, almost of rejuvenation. The soggy weight of despair was lifting from his spirit, and his brain was beginning to work again. He

[301]

stared out into the candle-lit courtyard at the figure of Ch'en, blurred by the mesh of the screen door, departing for his kitchen after setting out the snack Edgerton didn't want. But he wasn't seeing Ch'en or the courtyard; he was seeing the entrance of the Wu-feng Hu-tung as it had been the many times he'd driven past it, and wondering what it was like at the other end.

Nondescript and dreary by day, it became transformed at night, coming into earthy, frantic life. Garish and noisy, crowded with jostling Japanese soldiers, it was no place for a foreigner . . . or a woman like Tamara. But the other end was a mystery. As well as Edgerton could recall there was no way to get there except to start at the entrance on Hata Men Chieh and go on through. It was a dead end; Tanaka had chosen well.

And Sobolov was dead . . . the poor old fellow. It was hard to believe, but then everything that had happened this past week was hard to believe. The phone connection had been so bad, he hadn't known who she was at first, much less what it was she was trying to tell him. He was sure she'd been drinking, and the liquor had only thickened an already heavy accent. And how some friend could have overheard Tanaka in the act of giving his orders he had no idea, but he had no choice but to take her word for it. He felt a rush of gratitude for her having taken the trouble to call. She'd said something about appreciating the help he'd given her family. So Sobolov had praised him at home . . . even in death the poor man was doing him favors.

But how had *she* known to call him about Tamara? Feeling suddenly confused, Edgerton sat down and stared blindly across the room. Well, never mind that, he decided after a moment's fruitless thought. The thing to worry about was what to do next.

Blind impulse urged him to rush to the *hu-tung*, barge through the milling soldiers, bluff his way into the house—naturally he'd have no difficulty finding it when he got there—and whisk Tamara away to safety, all with the power of his irresistible will. Or with a magic carpet, whichever was handier. And his mind continually reached forward to the moment when Tamara would be free, instead of facing the realities which intervened. He knew he was going to have to move wisely, deliberately . . . he needed a plan. His only certainty was that he'd get but one chance to do what had to be done, and with that thought he restrained himself. He needed help. If he asked him, Mac-Donough would lend a hand, he was sure. He'd telephone him right away. Another thought occurred to him: his pistol. He was trying to remember where he'd put it when he heard the distant sound of the gate bell jangling, and felt a sharp twinge of annoyance. Whoever it was would have to be got rid of quickly.

He thought the pistol was somewhere in his chest of drawers. He dimly remembered having unpacked it and putting it there a couple of years before. Thinking of it reminded him of Li. . . .

MacDonough would be a good ally, but he had an idea Li would be a better one, more ingenious perhaps, and subtler. They would know at the Police Yamen where he lived. But he had better get moving. . . .

At the sound of a door closing, he went out into the courtyard to find Ch'en entering with another Chinese. The newcomer was tall and thin, and the gray of his long formal robe tended to make him disappear into the shadows. The man removed a rather shapeless felt hat and, giving a short bow, stepped forward into the lantern light.

Edgerton stared. It *was* Li. "I was just thinking of you," he said in English. Li's eyebrows lifted questioningly. Edgerton heard himself give a nervous laugh, then repeated his words in Chinese. He gestured toward the table. "Will you have something to eat, some tea?"

Li accepted the offer of tea. At Edgerton's nod, Ch'en hurried off to the kitchen and the policeman pulled up a wicker chair.

"I didn't recognize you in those clothes."

"Your Legation Quarter police don't like us to come here in uniform," Li said. "Besides, I was at home when I got the news, or rather, at the house of my betrothed."

"Ah," Edgerton said, wondering briefly why he'd never heard that before, and glad that Li intended to marry again. He found himself dazedly speculating on what the woman would be like, and had to shake his head to clear it. "Anyway, I'm glad you're here," he told the policeman. "I need your help. Tanaka has arrested a friend of mine, a Chinese woman."

Li leaned forward. "The Liu *hsiao-chieh?*" he asked quickly, plainly concerned.

Was it universal, then? Edgerton's mind demanded, protesting against fact. Was there anyone in Peking who didn't know about them?

He told Li briefly about his summons to Tanaka's office and about his futile visit to Chang Sun-cheh. "But I think my luck is changing," he added. "I've just learned that she's being held in a house at the far end of the Wu-feng Hu-tung."

"Mmmm," Li murmured unhappily, his frown deepening. His eyes seemed focused on some far corner of the courtyard. "There *is* an old house there, commandeered by the Army some months ago." He gave

[303]

Edgerton a sharp glance. "You know that *hu-tung* runs right through what used to be called the Korean red-light district?"

Edgerton nodded. "I know . . . not a good place for a foreigner, with all those Japanese soldiers . . ." He gestured impatiently. "There must be a back way."

"No quick one." Li gave him a sharp look. "And this is a time for haste. Tanaka won't use that house for long. The neighborhood is not secure . . . too many people and all those women gossiping." He thought for a moment. "The only other way in there is to go almost to the Chi Hua Men and then double back. And you would have to get through that warehouse district without being seen."

"I thought that company went out of business," Edgerton said, groping in his memory for a picture of the area.

"There are watchmen," Li said. "I might be able to arrange something with them, but not until tomorrow."

"No, that's out!" Edgerton said, getting to his feet and pacing the courtyard. He looked down at himself, at the white shirt and khaki trousers he'd put on after his shower. What does one wear on a rescue? he wondered, feeling very much out of his depth.

"You should wear a suit," Li said, as though reading his mind. "It's more dignified, seems more prosperous. Never be mistaken for a poor Russian. The Japanese can be impressed like everyone else, remember."

Edgerton snapped his fingers. "I meant to tell you . . . Andrei Sobolov is dead."

"That is what I came to tell you," Li said. "I tried to telephone . . . we found him a couple of hours ago."

Christ! The man knows everything! Edgerton thought, distracted for a moment and confused. "But I heard he had a heart attack."

"He did . . . like every dead man. Sobolov got his by being beaten in a fight. His body was thrown in the dump."

"The dump?" Wasn't death bad enough? Had this superfluous cruelty to be inflicted also? That harmless, well-meaning man . . . Edgerton felt sick. "Who would do a thing like that?"

Li's response was a snort. "Too many people, these days, but in this particular case, the Japanese. That is, they disposed of his body for someone else."

"Who *did* kill him? I take it you mean he was murdered."

"Yes; it was another Russian . . . a man called Puhalski." Li paused to smile with satisfaction. "I've been waiting to get my hands on him for years. This time I even have a witness."

Edgerton took comfort from Li's words, wondering if the man were connected with Sobolov's "plot." The thought made him shudder . . . it had been a close call.

He looked up to find Li getting to his feet. He couldn't be leaving? he thought, surprised and disappointed, then suddenly angry. Li was letting him down badly. He'd wanted to go over the situation with him, have him describe the area in detail, get his help in working out a plan. He couldn't just stroll over there, for Christ's sake!

Li was looking around the small courtyard, so homey and comfortable in the flickering light. "It's nice here," he said absentmindedly. He seemed to hesitate, and his thoughts were far away. Then he turned and gave Edgerton a quick smile. "I think it will be better if I go with you tonight," he said. "But we must hurry."

Edgerton was turning the car around when he saw Tamara's mother. She was crossing Canal Street from the side entrance of the hotel. Without possibility for doubt, she was heading for the San Kwan Miao. If she had thought ill of him before, what would she think now? For a fleeting instant Edgerton was tempted to pretend not to see her, to simply drive away.

"Just a minute," he said to Li, and set the emergency brake.

They met at the entrance to the yard. Her back was to the street light, and her face in a shadow in which her eyes glittered unreadably. "Tamara has been arrested," he told her quickly, ready to steady her with a hand if necessary. "I am going now to see what I can do."

Madame Liu stood like a rock. A deep sigh was her only concession to emotion. "I was afraid of that," she whispered.

"Perhaps I can get her released tonight," Edgerton said, seeing no reason to relate all the oppressive details. "In any case, tomorrow . . ."

"The Japanese, or the regular police?" Her voice was almost a whisper.

"The Japanese."

"Then how can you do anything?" she demanded, her voice suddenly harsh. Since you never did anything before, she might have added. Although Edgerton heard the unspoken rebuke, and it hurt him, he couldn't blame her for it.

"I can try," he said, wondering if this woman would ever understand him, or he, her. "Why don't you wait at my house. I'll know more when I come back; we can talk then."

Madame Liu looked at him steadily. "Is that foreign woman there?" she asked, her tone icy.

"No," Edgerton said, aware of the heat rising to his face. Something compelled him to add, "She means nothing to me, she was . . ." He put his finger to his temple and rotated it. ". . . I love your daughter only."

Madame Liu nodded then, her expression softening perceptibly. "I will wait at your house. Thank you."

After turning her over to Ch'en's hospitable care, Edgerton climbed into the car. "That was Liu *t'ai t'ai*," he told Li.

"I know the lady by sight," Li said.

Edgerton engaged the gears and drove out into Canal Street. "I'm not one of her favorites," he said.

Li laughed quietly. "Mothers of beautiful daughters are protective."

As he rounded the corner into Legation Street, Edgerton slowed to go over a traffic bump. In the momentary silence, Li spoke suddenly. "The Liu *hsiao-chieh* means a great deal to you?" he asked somewhat diffidently.

Letting the car coast for a moment, Edgerton looked over at him. "She is my betrothed."

"Aaah," said Li, very slowly, like a man at last coming upon the answer to an old riddle.

The sudden statement had surprised Edgerton himself. So explicit and unequivocal, the words brought him an unexpected measure of release, as might a long deferred confession.

They were out of the Legation Quarter and about midway across the glacis when Li spoke next. "Best to stop here," he said. "We must go on foot now."

Li paused with his hand on the door handle. "You must become an actor now. You are a European, a tourist, and I am your guide to places of fleshly delight. Although I urged against it, you insisted on seeing how Japan's fine soldiers amuse themselves. Make yourself live that role, and that is what you will look like." A smile came and went. "Or so the latest police manuals tell us. It can do no harm." Hesitating, Li looked away for a moment. "And now there's something else. I must speak honestly."

The broad glacis was silent and deserted, the polo stands a dark blot on the dusty, weed-patched earth. Behind them the Legation Quarter seemed already asleep, safe and decorous and tidy. Ahead, beyond the row of trees lining the bridle path, the old city throbbed with life . . . restless, dirty, jaded, but in her own way still beautiful. And in the middle of it all, not a half a mile away, was that garish clot of noise and light and flesh, the Wu-feng Hu-tung. Far away to the east, a long low bank of clouds lay along the horizon and flickered with summer lightning.

"You can say anything you wish to me," Edgerton said quietly.

Li took a deep breath. "Chang Sun-cheh would have helped you if he could, so don't be angry with him. Nor with me. I can approach this house with you, but if trouble develops . . . well, I can't repay what you did for me the way I'd like to."

He paused, and Edgerton wanted to interrupt. Was even Li unable to see that Tamara was worth some extra effort? Or did he, like Chang, hold her mixed blood against her? He wanted to protest.

But Li was going on. "We must be Chinese first these days, and friendship is a luxury. The Japanese aren't so bad now because they're winning. When they start losing, they will become enraged, and men like Major Wu will become terrified. Together they could destroy China. But they will be vulnerable . . . if a few of us are ready, it may be enough." Li peered at him expectantly in the starlight.

Resigned now, Edgerton nodded. It was all very logical, but no good to him. "No payment was ever necessary," he said, able to do no more than hope that if an emergency did arise, Li would relent and help him with it. Yet on a different level he was impressed. It was an awesome quality, that Chinese capacity to wait, to postpone. He had the feeling they could do it for generations if necessary, consciously biding their time. The Japanese were more Western . . . urgent, impatient, rash. He shrugged at Li. "Don't worry; I understand," he said, not really meaning it.

When the moment came to enter the *hu-tung*, Edgerton found it much more formidable than he remembered, and nearly lost heart. It was too bright a place, too Japanese. Every man there was a soldier, and every door opened into some kind of bar, with neon flashing and music blaring and garish banners hanging in the hot, muggy air.

To step off the sidewalk into the *hu-tung* would be to go out on a stage, and before an unfriendly, unbelieving audience. It was ridiculous. The Japanese would never let them through, and by the time they got themselves sorted out, they'd have wasted more time than if they'd gone around by the long way in the first place. But Li was ahead now, separated from him by the crowd, and they were there.

Almost holding his breath, Edgerton began to thread his way among the milling groups of soldiers, his eye fixed on Li's faded felt hat, now several yards ahead. He wanted to yell at him to slow down, but he felt too conspicuous already. Not really knowing what Li's "tourist" ought to look like, he made a feeble try and pasted what he hoped was a look of impersonal interest on his face. Pressing on, yard by yard,

[307]

he expected at any moment to be stopped. Nothing happened. It was working, and every step was bringing him closer to Tamara. He felt glimmerings of renewed hope.

But he wasn't liking it. There were stares and mutterings, and a feeling of animosity which was palpable. He'd been right: it was no place for a foreigner.

He badly wanted a cigarette. He was feeling for matches when a soldier staggered up and purposely blocked his path. Swaying, cap on the back of his head, his flushed young face said plainly that he thought he was a very funny fellow. Unsteadily but firmly, he reached forward and plucked the cigarette from between Edgerton's lips. There was nothing to do but grin and bear it, and provide himself with another. When he'd held a match for them both, he nodded affably and started around the man, anxious to move.

With a sort of dancing shuffle, the soldier shifted over to block his way again. Edgerton's original annoyance was at once overridden by apprehension, and he cast about for ways to escape this oaf without risking a fight or attracting any more attention. All he needed was for some of Tanaka's eager MPs to come along and stick their noses in.

But already several soldiers, sensing a developing amusement, were moving in for a closer look. And Li was nowhere to be seen. All Edgerton could do was hope he'd look around, take notice and come back.

Inspired by his growing audience, the soldier began to circle Edgerton slowly, grunting with amazement, and shaking his head, each move adding to the general laughter. Edgerton could smell the beer on him a yard away. And he knew he had to stand there, to remain studiously impassive. Sooner or later, in the manner of drunks everywhere, the man would tire of his game and move on to some new interest.

Wondering again about Li, Edgerton had to conclude he'd simply made himself scarce. Understandable, he supposed, although it gave him a pang of disappointment. He sympathized with Li's predicament, but he'd expected more staying power than this.

Beginning to feel a little desperate, Edgerton's eyes settled on two sergeants who had joined the crowd. Older men, and sober looking, they were observing things from one side with what appeared to be bored indulgence. He was wondering if appealing to them would do any good, and how to go about it, when a playful hand reached out of the crowd and yanked him roughly by the sleeve, making him shift his feet or lose his balance. He gritted his teeth, trying to remind himself that the soldiers meant no real harm, but knowing that the longer this idiocy went on, the greater the probability of trouble . . . and any trouble in these surroundings would mean the end of helping Tamara.

A hand touched him on the elbow, and Li was there, giving him a nod and an apologetic smile. He was moving, hat in hand, in the direction of the sergeants. Groggy with relief, Edgerton watched him, and the soldiers turned also; even the clown suspended his antics to see what was happening.

Bowing politely, Li commenced to address the two noncoms in fluent Japanese. And as the soldiers listened, their eyes went from Li to the sergeants to Edgerton, and back again, and they grew quite serious, and the ones in front moved back a pace. Finally one of the noncoms stopped Li in midsentence, and began to shout harshly at the clownish soldier, waving for him to move along. Anticipating some of the same, the other soldiers dispersed rapidly. All of a sudden it was over, and Li was bowing to Edgerton, gesturing for him to move ahead.

"What did you say to them?" Edgerton asked when they were clear.

"I said you were a German, a guest of the Provisional Government, and that I was your official guide." He coughed modestly. "I read somewhere that the Japanese Army feels great reverence for Germany."

Feeling reprieved, Edgerton could only shake his head admiringly. As they pressed on into the *hu-tung*, his spirits began to lift, releasing him from his blind preoccupation with the difficulties of the *hu-tung*, and let him become more aware of this bizarre environment into which he'd thrust himself.

The very air itself was permeated by a frantic, almost hysterical gaiety. Like some hypnotic gas, it charged the blood and compelled the spirits of the soldiers, as though some natural law required them to drink all the beer and mount all the women in the few hours remaining to them.

The narrow roadway was like a river, twisting its way along a canyon of cabarets and bars and brothels. To his passing glance there seemed to be little to distinguish them. They were raucous, blatant places, most of them, with strident music and tiny dance floors crowded with sweating soldiers and their women of the moment. And they all had rooms somewhere . . . at the back, or upstairs at the end of a rickety balcony, or in a row of cribs no bigger than piano crates running back into some smelly alley. There seemed to be a continual coming and going to the rooms, with much laughing and bragging, and arguments over prices and the quality of the services rendered.

[309]

Scenes passed across his vision like fragments of old dreams . . . jerky and staccato, and then gone: the door to a crib swinging open, revealing a man rather unsteadily doing up his buttons, the woman already squatting over her basin, cleaning up; then a young Chinese woman, offended by something in Li's look and swearing at him for it, and stabbing the air with her middle finger; and not fifty paces later a Russian woman doing the same to Edgerton, and for presumably the same reason; and a woman standing on a balcony, black hair braided demurely into pigtails, repaying Edgerton's chance look in her direction by opening her robe in casual invitation, letting him see her dark bush and a pair of full, pendulous breasts. Fragments of nightmares . . . he thought of Tamara in such a place, and he shuddered and hurried on through the throbbing confusion. Neon flickered everywhere, and the clamor spewed forth in ever increasing volume. Sweating faces, already flushed with alcohol, flamed eerily in the orange light, and the heat of summer was augmented by the heat of bodies and excitement. A musky aroma hung over everything, heavy, provocative, compelling . . . a mixture of sweat and perfume, of beer and urine, and the secret scent of women.

And although he tried to tell himself that Tamara was in no such plight as these women of the *hu-tung*, the gross, unpredictable figure of Tanaka loomed, raging, in the background of his mind. With Tanaka, anything was possible . . . the thought made him sick with fear for her. Once he actually started to run, and Li had to stop him.

Edgerton saw himself and Li as men apart, sharing nothing in common with the others, passing through the area almost without touching it. Yet no one interfered with them. Perhaps it was because they never loitered, or were careful not to stare, or even that the distractions of the place were too great for the presence of a mere foreigner to disturb. In any case, except for the contretemps at the entrance to the *hu-tung*, they might as well have been invisible. A few women noticed them, and a random soldier here and there, but no one else.

The paradox turned his mind to Li, and to what Li was really doing for him, and by extension, for Tamara. He wasn't only guiding him, and providing moral support, and making sure he made no mistakes, and acting as go-between, he was actually offering himself as a shield, for all of the reticence he'd expressed earlier when they had set out. If it came to trouble with the Japanese, Li would be the scapegoat. The realization gave him a shock of gratitude.

Suddenly a dark stretch lay ahead of them in the *hu-tung*. Not more than fifty yards long, it seemed to be an area given over to shops which were now shuttered for the night. Farther on was another cluster of

[310]

lights and another source of raucous sound. Even from this distance, it seemed smaller and shabbier. Halfway between the two enclaves, a single street lamp burned dimly. Seeing the apparently empty darkness as a sanctuary, Edgerton entered it with a feeling of relief.

It was to be momentary. Plunging toward them under the street lamp came a trio of soldiers. Arms around each other's shoulders, they staggered along, chanting loudly, tunelessly, weaving the full width of the *hu-tung*. At first they seemed to be the only others on that stretch of roadway, a trio of harmless drunks intent only on getting to the next beer hall. But then behind them, silhouetted in the neon, another trio materialized, not staggering but marching abreast. As they in their turn passed under the street lamp, Edgerton could see their arm bands and the long batons dangling from their belts. One of them also wore a pistol. They were Military Police. His gut tensing, Edgerton cursed under his breath.

The drunks tacked back across the *hu-tung*, their song rising with renewed vigor, and Edgerton looked into the dismal future. They were headed straight toward him now, and if they bothered him, as every instinct assured him they would, the MPs would inevitably interfere. Identification would be demanded, telephone calls would be made, and the whole crucial business of finding Tamara and getting her to safety would be delayed, complicated, obstructed . . . and Li would be in trouble.

But Li was no longer with him.

In their clumsy chorus line, the drunks approached inexorably, grinning and mumbling their song, seemingly oblivious to Edgerton in their path. He sidestepped, but fate—or the lead drunk's wily determination—intervened, and the soldier staggered, undoing Edgerton's evasion. Suddenly it was too late, and the man's shoulder caught him in the chest. Backed up by his two lumbering companions, the man was a juggernaut. Knocked breathless, Edgerton went stumbling backward. He crashed into the shuttered storefront behind him, lost his footing, and fell to the ground. The drunks, having used him for their carom, lurched off on the other tack, the *hu-tung* echoing with their laughter.

Sore, gasping, furious at his own helplessness, Edgerton got to his feet. Massaging his bruised chest and trying to catch his breath, he remembered the MPs. They hadn't forgotten him. They stood just down the road staring intently in his direction, their posture eloquent of suspicion. It only took a moment for the patrol leader to make up his mind. Hitching up his pistol, he began to stroll in Edgerton's direction, moving with that elaborately casual swagger sometimes af-

[311]

fected by armed men, whether gunslingers or samurai. Never had Edgerton wanted so badly to run for it, but there was quite literally nowhere to go.

An eruption of shouts and curses exploded above the general clamor, and Edgerton and the MPs turned as one to see what had happened.

All was confusion. Squinting against the glare, Edgerton tried to sort out the milling uniforms. And then he saw the drunken trio charge down upon the entrance of the nearest cabaret. A group of other soldiers waited for them there, apparently ready to drive them off a second time.

This was the most urgent duty, and the patrol leader shouted to his men. In a moment they were trotting toward the fray, unlimbering their nightsticks as they went.

Edgerton didn't hesitate. Trembling slightly, he hurried on, mopping at his face with his handkerchief, an imperative need for haste goading him relentlessly.

The *hu-tung* was beginning to seem endless, and the noisy patch of lights just ahead another morass of traps and pitfalls. And Li had probably gone for good . . . And the house, how would he know the house . . . To hell with all of that, Edgerton told himself, gritting his teeth. He'd just have to do his best when he got there. He'd passed the street light before something made him look over his shoulder, and he saw Li come running up behind him.

"Sorry," Li panted. "That MP corporal knows me . . . I almost didn't recognize him in time. He'd know at once I had no business in here. This is Japanese territory, and he has ambitions to be an officer."

Relieved, but still so anxious that his stomach hurt him, Edgerton could only nod.

Drab and dowdy and comparatively second-rate, the new collection of bars were suffering from neglect, the emptiness of the *hu-tung* further mocking their shabbiness. There weren't more than a dozen of them, and the music which they pumped out into the night had a tinny sound to it, unlikely to attract anyone. In one place a bare handful of soldiers loitered aimlessly, staring at a few women who stared back. The sole visible occupants of another bar were four Japanese women, deep in conversation at a table. Two Chinese girls crossed the *hu-tung*, eyeing them half-heartedly, as though too tired or too discouraged to really care anymore. A few paces beyond them, Li grunted to himself, then spat quietly into the dirt.

Suddenly the soldiers and the bars and the women, the lights and the noise, were all behind them. Lacking even a single street lamp, the way ahead was particularly dark and seemed ominous the way it sim-

[312]

ply disappeared into the heavy shadows. But against the glow of the city beyond, there were several long, low shapes: the warehouses. So they were getting very close.

On their right a row of shops seemed not only boarded up for the night but abandoned for good. Just opposite, the skeleton of a burned-out house stood against the sky, only one wall remaining and part of a chimney. Beyond it, like a starlit wasteland strewn with irregular lumpy shapes, was a slum area, a district of shacks and lean-tos, that Edgerton hadn't even known was there. A few lantern dots accentuated the inkiness of the rest of it. He wondered how far it might be across.

Li pulled his sleeve. "Stay out of there," he whispered, nodding toward the slum. "Even the police don't go in there at night." He pointed ahead into the shadows along the *hu-tung*. "Look."

Now Edgerton saw it, a brick bungalow, partly hidden by a row of small trees, and set in a yard that was overgrown with weeds and bushes. A partly finished stone wall guarded the front of the narrow lot, while a makeshift fence disappeared in the direction of the slum. In the back, a single curtained window glowed faintly.

"That can't be it," Edgerton said, his voice suddenly hoarse.

"It's the only Army house in this *hu-tung.*"

Staring at it, straining his eyes in the starlight, Edgerton felt his heartbeat quicken painfully, and his palms were suddenly clammy. "Well, I'll give it a try," he said, his words sounding braver than he felt. "And thanks . . ."

Li stopped him with a hand. "No, it's nothing," he said. He took Edgerton by the arm and pulled him into the shadows. "Now, listen: I'll wait until you get into the house, then I'm going over there . . ." he pointed vaguely toward the warehouses ". . . to arrange what I can. When you come out, go that way." He paused, his manner suddenly awkward. "And remember, if there are too many of them, run for it. Tanaka won't hurt the girl so long as he wants something from you. If this doesn't work, we'll think of something else."

Edgerton nodded, far from convinced. Too many of them, Li had said. Even one could be too many. And he had no such hope for Tanaka's rationality; after tonight, there wouldn't be anything else.

They shook hands silently. Li's long fingers were dry and strong, like claws.

Painfully conscious of the starlight, Edgerton crossed to the corner of the yard, and started in along the line of trees. And there were lights behind him as well, he remembered, moving more quickly, hardly breathing until he reached the shadows.

He squatted in the weeds for a moment, studying the house, eyes

[313]

straining. The persistent, mindless keening of nearby music plagued him, filling his ears when he was trying to listen for other things, stunning his brain with its racket. With a dull feeling of inevitability, he realized he'd forgotten his pistol . . . one more thing.

A shadow moved against the curtain. Crouching awkwardly, he hurried across the yard, parched weeds rustling against his legs. The curtain covered the window tightly. He held his head close to the glass and heard the measured sound of snoring. The shadow moved again, and someone coughed. So there were at least two of them . . . bad news.

The back yard was dotted with several small trees and litter for him to stumble over. He didn't like the look of it. And if anyone were sitting outside taking the air, that was where they'd be. On the other hand, the front of the house seemed bathed in starlight. He wiped his sweaty face on his sleeve and chose the light.

A large tree loomed in the side yard, and the ground was bare. The high, blank wall of a warehouse next door helped to thicken the shadows. Barely discernible against the side of the house were the outlines of two windows. He peered at them uncertainly. What if it were the wrong house? What if Sobolov's wife had been mistaken—she'd sounded drunk, after all—and Li had misled him as a consequence? It could be a Japanese Army house all right, but the wrong one. Suppose he got caught . . . what would happen to Tamara while *that* got sorted out? And what if it were the right house, and a guard was watching him from one of those black squares?

Edgerton suddenly felt very much alone—one man going up against an army. And probably the wrong man . . . neither experienced in this business, nor young enough for it. Nor brave enough. His mouth was dry and pasty, and his stomach felt like it had a hole in it. Futile musings: He was committed.

The first window was very dark. He could only guess that it, too, was curtained behind the dirty glass. The paint on the sill was peeling, and the hinges of the casement were caked with rust. He was afraid to try it, even behind the covering noise of music.

The next one, open an inch, challenged him. He hesitated, holding the edge of it in his fingers. Gently and with great misgivings, he began to pull. It opened with ghostly silence. Feeling wretchedly conspicuous, he stared vainly into the pitch-black room. This was the way in, he decided reluctantly; there was no point in looking further.

With his hands planted firmly on the sill, a short jump put him up. He stayed there for a moment, letting his rigid arms carry his full weight; then, working through the narrow opening, he got a knee under him. Leaning into the room, he was trying to get his foot in when he lost his balance and fell forward. His palms struck the floor with a force that jarred his elbows painfully. And made an awful noise, he was certain, although he himself had heard nothing. But maybe not; several long moments of listening brought no sign of any break in the silence.

Lucky, he thought, getting stiffly to his feet. As his eyes adjusted, he saw that he was in a small, square room, empty of furniture, with a closed door straight ahead. As he started cautiously toward it, a doorknob rattled somewhere, and there came a spate of determined footsteps. He'd been heard after all. Another door opened, very near this time, and he sensed rather than heard the presence of someone standing just beyond the thin partition, listening.

"You be quiet there!" The loud command startled him. The words were Chinese, but spoken with a hoarse Japanese accent. And the voice had an odd timbre, making it impossible for Edgerton to imagine the speaker. His hands felt empty and useless . . . he was an idiot to have come without any sort of weapon . . . even a stick. . . .

"Did you hear me?" the person insisted angrily.

"But I've done nothing."

Edgerton thought his heart would stop. The voice was clearly Tamara's as if she'd spoken with her lips against his ear. It was all he could do to keep from bursting from the room.

A band of light appeared suddenly under the door with the sound of heavy footsteps clumping past. Under its cover, he crossed carefully to the door and opened it a crack.

At the end of a narrow hallway, someone stood holding a flashlight. The light moved and Edgerton saw it was a woman. She was short with broad shoulders, and he could see the outline of powerful legs below her skirt.

"Don't argue!" she ordered in her odd, mannish voice. "Just do as you're told." She abruptly turned away, catching Edgerton by surprise. Certain he'd be seen if he moved, he could only stand there. But the woman was intent upon her own annoyance. Eyes on the floor, her fleshy face puckered with anger, she passed by. The door slammed behind her and the hall went dark.

Moving as quickly as he dared, Edgerton entered the hall. Although his thoughts were churning with excitement, he could still hear the cautionary voice warning that much remained to be done and much could still go wrong. His sudden arrival in Tamara's room brought a gasp of alarm from her.

"It's me," he whispered. "Where are you?"

[315]

Her sigh was long and eloquent. "Over here . . . I'm tied up."

Groping toward the sound, Edgerton struck his shin against the sharp edge of the bed frame and he hardly felt it. He let one palm rest briefly on her cheek, then knelt on the floor and began to work at the knotted ropes binding her wrists to the bedstead. He didn't speak until he had one hand loose. "Are you all right?" he asked, putting his lips close to her ear.

"I am now," she said, her breath caressing his cheek like a feather. Very quickly he kissed her, his own voice echoing in his mind. Betrothed, he'd said to Li not very long ago. He hadn't known the meaning of the word then.

He went back to work, all too conscious of the time slipping away. His fingers felt clumsy as sausages, and he swore silently and continuously at them and at the stubborn knots. Finally he finished, and Tamara could sit up. Holding his wrist, she tried to pull herself erect. Perhaps her legs were numb from being tied so long, or maybe she was simply exhausted, for her grip failed. Before he could catch her, she'd fallen back onto the bed, driving it into the wall with a noise that rang like a gong in Edgerton's ears.

Holding their breaths, the two of them listened to the approach of the woman's angry footsteps. Certain that she had come all the way, Edgerton was wondering what he'd do, when the sound stopped at the end of the hall. There was a long, inquisitive silence before she decided to go away.

Edgerton helped Tamara up and led her to the window, groping for it in almost total darkness. As he'd surmised, it was curtained, and he had to pull the heavy material aside in order to work at the latch. Stiff with disuse, it resisted stubbornly. He'd begun to twist at it with both hands when Tamara tugged at his sleeve. The woman was coming back.

Suddenly Edgerton wanted nothing so much as to get himself and Tamara out of that house immediately . . . the time for stratagems and concealments was at an end. Stepping back a pace, he kicked at the casement frame, and then again, and the old wood splintered away from the latch. As he wrenched it off its hinges, he could hear the rush of footsteps down the hall. "Hurry!" he urged, throwing the remains into the yard. He pushed Tamara forward. "Don't wait more than a minute. Just go east, away from the lights. Then go to the San Kwan Miao."

He'd already turned away when he spoke the last words and was lunging for the door. If he could get behind it, he might recover some shred of advantage. But he was only halfway there when it flew open

[316]

and he got the full power of the torch in his eyes. There was nothing to do but keep on going. He struck blindly at the light, hitting the heavy torch with his forearm and sending it spinning across the room. In the momentary flash, he saw the face of the woman, and her hand reaching out. His fist must already have been moving, for in the next instant he'd hit her squarely in the mouth.

Except for a girl he'd slapped for lying about him in the seventh grade, Edgerton had never hit a woman. He could feel the skin tear across his knuckles, and he heard some teeth break with a noise like twigs snapping. The sound sickened him. A groan escaped, and he realized it came from him.

The woman staggered backward through the door. Swaying groggily, she stood there for a moment, steadying herself with one hand against the jamb. The torch was somewhere beyond the bed, but its light illuminated her face anyway. Even as Edgerton watched, it became grotesque, with the lips swelling visibly. A foam of bloody saliva began to ooze from between them; it bubbled faintly as she breathed. But she wasn't finished. She was tough, this woman, and she looked very strong as she groped forward stubbornly. Edgerton knew he had to end it while he was still able—end it once and for all. Gritting his teeth, he stepped forward and drove his fist into the pad of flesh just beneath the point of her jaw. It was enough. The woman fell back against the wall of the hallway, leaned there for a second, then slid heavily to the floor.

Edgerton's hand felt as if it had been broken. Standing dazed in the abrupt silence, he looked down at the woman. Her skirt had ridden up her thighs, revealing a pair of pink, incongruously frilly bloomers.

But the silence was not to last. Edgerton had just bestirred himself to go for the torch, when a man's sleepy voice called questioningly from the opposite side of the house. Edgerton swore . . . he'd forgotten about the others. How many? he wondered as he doused the light. A chair crashed amid the pounding of heavy boots; a string of Japanese curses erupted.

A lantern's faint glow spilled into the hallway, showing him where the woman lay. Hefting the reassuringly heavy weight of the torch, he stepped over her and moved forward to meet the newcomer.

The man was moving fast when he came through the doorway, but clumsily, and Edgerton was able to kick his feet out from under him. He stumbled, and Edgerton clubbed him with the flashlight, driving him to his knees. He tried to get up but Edgerton hit him again, and he fell over on his side.

Edgerton felt like he'd been fighting for hours. He tried to turn on

[317]

the flashlight, but nothing happened. It was badly bent in the middle, and he was about to drop it when he remembered it was the only weapon he had. He and Tamara still had a long way to go . . . provided he could still find her out there in the night. He was heading for the window when a muffled groan and the sound of a shoe scraping on the bare floor intruded from the far room.

Dear Christ, not another one! Edgerton thought, nerves frayed to breaking. Deeply reluctant, he sidled to the doorway and peered in. On a table in the far corner of the room, a hurricane lamp smoked amid a welter of glasses and cigarette butts and Mah-Jongg tiles. On a nearby mattress, the figure of a man moved, groaning again, and an arm went out and knocked over a bottle. For a moment the silence seemed absolute. Then there came the deep gentle sound of snoring.

Edgerton found Tamara under the dark shadow of the tree, leaning against its trunk. He took her in his arms and held her for a long moment. "I told you to run for it," he said.

"I couldn't leave you."

He pulled back to look at her then. "I love you," he said.

"I know," Tamara replied huskily, trying to smile.

"Come then." Taking her hand, he led her around the end of the wall and into the shadows at the corner of the warehouse. There was a shallow ditch there, half-filled with rubbish, with a narrow plank for a bridge.

Pausing to reconnoiter, Edgerton was struck by the relative quiet, and saw that all but one of the nearby cabarets had closed, leaving only a single phonograph to play to the deserted *hu-tung.*

But back toward Hata Men Chieh, things still seemed to be going strong and bright. Although the light and sound of it were blurred by distance, in his imagination Edgerton could hear its clamor and see the crowds of soldiers. He thought wistfully how easy it would have been if all those places were closed, and the women asleep, and the soldiers gone back to their barracks . . . he and Tamara slipping along, unseen in the shadows . . . his automobile not much more than a mile away.

The long way around meant more delays—an alarm was bound to be raised soon, and then Tanaka's men would be swarming—but there was no choice. He was about to lead Tamara across the plank and into the empty *hu-tung,* when the music died in midpassage, and a man came out of the cabaret and began to put up shutters.

Edgerton took a deep breath and then exhaled slowly, telling himself to be glad of the rest. The air was soft in the stillness, and a gentle breeze was stirring, laden with the scent of excrement and garbage from the slum, but cooling, and bringing the promise of a better day tomorrow.

Looking down at Tamara he saw that her dress was torn, and several of her buttons were missing. "Did they hurt you?" he asked, sickened by the rush of possibilities into his mind.

She shook her head.

"Your shoes are missing," he said, too relieved to think.

She shrugged. "I lost them."

"Poor baby . . . it's a long way home."

"My feet are tough; it's in my blood," she said, grinning.

The bar's lights went out abruptly, and Edgerton heard the man clear his throat and spit. A door slammed. "Okay," he said. "Let's see how tough." He had wanted to sound confident, but the words came out heavily, a bad joke.

As they moved into the cul-de-sac at the end of the *hu-tung*, Edgerton thought of the uncertain miles that lay ahead of them, the warehouse yards, and the strange, distant streets where they'd be as conspicuous as Eskimos. God knew how long it would be before they could find rickshaws, and then there'd be half a city to traverse before they reached the sanctuary of the Legation Quarter. Tanaka's men would be out before they made it.

"Hurry!" he urged, tugging at her hand to make her run, hating to do it.

☖☖

Shifting his feet, Tanaka felt in his pocket for a cigarette. Hardly was it in his mouth before the orderly was rushing over with a match. He hurried away for an ashtray.

Puffing deeply, Tanaka glared after him through the smoke. Young and soft looking, with the round smooth face of a girl . . . serving in Itaki's entourage would never make a soldier of him . . . a whore, more likely.

On the wall to the right of the orderly's desk a large clock ticked loudly, the brass disk of its pendulum glinting with every swing. The room was bare and brightly lighted. The chair was very hard. Tanaka had arrived ten minutes early for his appointment. It was now a quarter past eleven, and there was still no sign of Itaki. The whole thing was typical of the man's arrogance, his indifference to others. Already fifteen minutes late in the middle of the night, and he didn't

[319]

even have the courtesy to telephone. The rudeness was deliberate . . . and worrisome. Itaki did nothing without a reason.

Tanaka felt as exhausted as if he'd been awake for days. He'd gone home for a rest but had been unable to sleep. The house, usually such a comfort to him, had seemed a prison, vast and empty. The absence of the Russian woman had been acutely felt . . . another thing he owed Itaki. The bedroom was so touched with her scent he couldn't bear to stay in it. He tried lying down on the couch in the drawing room, but sleep had eluded him there as well. No sooner would he drag his thoughts away from the woman, than they would fasten on his unsatisfactory and inconclusive interview with Edgerton. Those had been black moments and had brought him close to despair. He'd even wished he'd given in, had released the miserable half-caste and let Edgerton have her. Beset by pettiness and injustice on every side, why should it always be Tanaka who struggled against all odds? he had demanded of the darkness.

Thinking back on it now, Tanaka realized he'd passed through a critical juncture in his life. He'd been on the verge of putting aside the extra burdens he'd assumed for his Emperor's sake. He'd wanted to forget the Kempeitai and let someone else have the headaches, forget his plans for the American Legation. He'd been willing, even anxious, to go back to being merely Provost Marshal, plain Colonel Tanaka. In a year or so, when China was beaten, he'd retire to the little house he'd bought on the Inland Sea.

But his devotion to the destiny of Japan had been too strong to permit such self-indulgence. Pacing the dark room with determination, he'd worked to overcome his dejection by an exercise of pure will, to recapture the certainty of eventual success which had been so powerful that afternoon. And to a large extent he had succeeded.

Edgerton's humiliation, although temporarily postponed, remained as inevitable as the sunrise. As soon as Tanaka's final orders came by courier from Tokyo, he could begin laying the foundation for his Kempeitai organization. He would have a free hand then, and Itaki's disgrace would be only a matter of time.

There was a stir in the hallway, and the front door of the Headquarters Building closed with a crash. The orderly sprang to his feet and stood at rigid attention behind his desk.

The great man himself, Tanaka muttered disdainfully, rising at a more relaxed rate.

Colonel Itaki bustled into the anteroom, his specially tailored uniform resplendent with campaign ribbons, the gold cords of his Chief

[320]

of Staff's aiguilette looped over one shoulder. Overdressed fop, Tanaka thought. "Good evening, Colonel," he said.

"Ah, my dear Tanaka, so sorry to keep you waiting," Itaki burbled. "I was delayed at the General's dinner party." He picked up some papers from a basket on the orderly's desk and began to leaf through them rapidly.

Except for a reception to which every field grade officer in the command had been invited, Tanaka had never set foot inside the General's residence. He knew for a fact that other officers of lesser rank were in and out of the place continually. He was being slighted . . . Itaki's doing, he was certain.

Itaki's companion, a fat captain with hips like a woman's, coughed suggestively.

"Ah, Yamashita . . . forgive me," Itaki said, oozing charm. "Carry on, dear boy. See you in the morning."

"Thank you, sir," the captain simpered, giving the two Colonels a slovenly salute.

Itaki eyed his departing figure fondly. "A splendid young officer . . . great promise," he said.

Tanaka gave him a thin smile. "The Colonel sent for me," he prompted.

"Yes, Tanaka . . . quite so," Itaki gestured grandly. "Come in please."

Itaki's office was oddly Spartan, the furniture severely plain, barely one grade better than government issue. The desk was bare. A single filing cabinet and a small safe occupied one corner. Tanaka had the feeling that Itaki was seldom there, preferring to work out of his sumptuous residence, surrounded by his retinue of aides and ass-kissers. Tanaka shifted his feet on the thin carpet, impatience and worry eating into his guts. Why didn't the man get on with it!

Itaki took off his cap and mopped his shaved scalp with a large linen handkerchief. "It's terribly hot in here," he complained peevishly. His face brightened suddenly. "Let's not torture ourselves in this office. Didn't I see your splendid car outside? Come, invite me . . . we'll have a refreshing drive together."

"I'd be delighted, Colonel," Tanaka said, deeply suspicious of this unusual cordiality. Itaki had been quite abrupt on the telephone. Rude, actually, considering they were of equal rank and separated by only a few serial numbers.

Once in the car, however, Tanaka had to admit it had been a good idea. He rolled down the windows, then raised the glass separating

[321]

them from the driver. As the car moved off, they were washed in a cool breeze.

Itaki clucked admiringly, then cocked a jovial eye at him. "My, this is a comfortable automobile," he said.

"Thank you," Tanaka murmured cautiously.

"You're really most fortunate, my dear fellow," Itaki continued conversationally, "to be able to exercise your, um, private enterprise this way. A man in your position must have many opportunities to acquire small emoluments."

"Well, I don't know about that," Tanaka said, not liking the sound of things. If the Chief of Staff had somehow stumbled onto his opium deal with Puhalski, he could make it uncomfortable for him. But there was only one source for that information . . . Puhalski himself. The man must have run from the café to tattle to Itaki . . . the miserable, ungrateful weasel . . . after all Tanaka had done for him, literally raising him up from the gutter. He squirmed in anguish.

Itaki waved his fat hand. "Not that I could honestly blame you, my dear fellow. Mere survival is difficult on Army pay alone . . . how well I know it. We are called upon to sacrifice much in the Emperor's service." With a sigh, Itaki laid a hand over his heart. "I'm having a very difficult time. And working as I do under the—ha ha—benevolent eye of the General, I have none of your chances."

He knows about the opium, Tanaka concluded bitterly, wondering what use Itaki expected to make of the knowledge. The cruel irony was that Itaki took a generous squeeze from the proceeds of beer sold in the troops' canteens . . . it was paid to him by the brewery people directly, based on their gross receipts. And, as Chief of Staff, he had sole charge of the money collected in the Officers' clubs and brothels . . . or that fat-ass Yamashita did, which was the same thing. Tanaka had been trying to catch them with their hands in the cash box for over a year, but without success. Compared to that privileged thievery, a few packets of opium were nothing. The Army intended to give it away in any case.

Tanaka waited, but Itaki did not go on. Instead, he seemed to be dozing, the fat closing in around his eyes, his head nodding as the heavy car moved smoothly over the uneven pavement.

Tanaka sighed, trying to look at the bright side, trying to find one. The opium business was really a mere pecadillo, hardly the sort of thing to cause him anything more severe than temporary embarrassment. But the Sobolov fiasco was another matter. Had it worked, he would have been a hero. Failing, it could only disgrace him and make him the butt of the Army. He needed time to reorganize, to make

[322]

arrangements. If Puhalski talked about the one, he'd talk about the other when it suited him. He was going to have to do something about Puhalski.

Tanaka cursed himself bitterly. He could have done it all that afternoon; he'd been too lenient, too soft-hearted as always. He should have shot Puhalski and sent him to the dump with Sobolov . . . the pair of them belonged there.

"Minister Saito was at the General's party . . . he spoke to me again about the Tungchow Incident," Itaki said, turning suddenly to face Tanaka, his face puckered with annoyance like a huge prune. "I'm so tired of that subject; I insist you do something, Colonel."

"I'm relieving Okani of all duties," Tanaka said, deciding on the spur of the moment. "Captain Okamura is going down tomorrow to bring the men back under arrest. I intend to be the trial officer myself. Minister Saito will be more than pleased with the results, I promise you."

"You should have done that in the first place," Itaki said grudgingly. "It's been an embarrassing affair all around. Saito is anxious to get the Americans off his back."

"Yes, Colonel," Tanaka said, supressing an urge to defend himself.

Itaki got out an enormous cigar and began to prepare it for smoking, moistening it lovingly with his lips. Tanaka turned away, revolted. He reached for a cigarette of his own, but the packet was empty. The pungent aroma of expensive tobacco filled the car despite the open windows, aggravating Tanaka's need to smoke to the point of torture.

"Speaking of the Americans," Itaki began, "reminds me of an extraordinary story I heard today."

"What was that, Colonel?" Tanaka asked wearily. Itaki sounded very comfortable, too comfortable. It was plain he was enjoying himself and could go on indefinitely. At this rate, it would be daybreak before Tanaka got home.

"It involves an employee of the American Legation, a certain Russian named . . ." Itaki hesitated, one fat hand fluttering helplessly. ". . . Bosolov? You know him, if I understood correctly." Itaki leaned forward, his face bland, his eyes glinting watchfully, the cigar planted in the center of his face like a cannon.

Tanaka's stomach heaved, and saliva filled his mouth. Tensing the muscles of his throat, he waited through an eternity for the spasm to subside. The high collar of his dress tunic was choking him . . . why had he changed uniforms for this monster? "Bosolov?" he repeated. "No, I don't believe . . ."

"It's probably nothing," Itaki interrupted. "To be quite candid, I

[323]

got the information by telephone . . . the caller refused to identify himself. Anonymous tipsters are despicable, don't you agree? But one daren't ignore them." Beaming like a great bloated toad, Itaki reached over and patted Tanaka's knee. "It was a fantastic story . . . I knew you couldn't be involved. Forgive my mentioning it."

Sighing, Itaki sank back into the cushions, returning his full attention to his cigar. He smoked audibly, like a child sucking a piece of candy.

Tanaka was devastated. He would have liked to strangle Itaki with his bare hands. Of course, he was lying; he knew everything about Sobolov, including how to pronounce his name. From the sound of it, Itaki had no immediate plans for this information either. He would merely keep it; like the opium smuggling, it was money in the bank.

That his future was gravely threatened, Tanaka could see quite clearly. For the time being he would have to lie low and study the situation carefully. It was not the moment for ambitious moves. Even Puhalski was beyond his reach . . . if anything happened to that putrid ingrate now, he'd be blamed for it. Well, he'd get him eventually; the moment would be all the sweeter for having been postponed.

"By the way, Tanaka . . . wasn't that woman you were, uh, entertaining . . . wasn't that her name?"

Tanaka cleared his throat. "It could be . . . it's common enough, I suppose. Frankly, their names are so outlandish, I can't tell one from another. Besides this lady is a very casual acquaintance, I assure you . . . we don't trouble with names."

"Yes, hmmm," Itaki muttered, seeming to pause in deep thought before going on, "You know, Tanaka, I really am surprised." His tone was paternal, mildly amused. "That was really most indiscreet of you, having a foreign woman there like that. I'm a man of the world, after all, and a veteran soldier. I understand how things are, but in the middle of the day? Really! it's a good thing *I* found her, rather than someone who might be unfriendly to you."

"But, Colonel, that's my residence, my home!" Tanaka protested, goaded almost beyond endurance. "You . . . no one has the right . . . what happens there is my own private business."

"No, no, my dear fellow, I can't agree! You're a senior officer; you can have no private business. Anything which might bring your name into disrepute can only diminish your usefulness. To risk that is to cheat the Emperor. It's that simple." Itaki smirked sanctimoniously.

His heart aching with fury, Tanaka could only face his tormentor and acknowledge that he was helpless. The Chief of Staff was having a cruel joke at his expense. His pumpkin of a face wore a delighted smile . . . he wasn't even trying to hide his enjoyment. And Tanaka could do nothing, had no choice but to accept Itaki's rebuke as genuine; Itaki, whose perversions were a scandal throughout the command. Itaki would never see Siberia. . . .

If it was to be Tanaka's last act, he'd see Itaki drummed out of the Army, shorn of his rank and his medals, his aristocratic name disgraced forever. Until now the forebearance of General Kawasaki had protected Itaki, but once his crimes and unnatural proclivities were exposed with sufficient drama, General Tojo himself would be unable to save him.

But it would take patience, Tanaka reminded himself, stoic patience. For the present he would have to wait, sustaining himself against any insult with the certainty that before much longer he'd have Itaki where he wanted him.

"Yes, Colonel, I see what you mean," he said, wanting nothing so much as an end to this agony. He needed solitude and rest and an opportunity to collect his thoughts. He turned to Itaki. "The street becomes quite bumpy up ahead, Colonel," he said, his voice blandly deferential. "May I suggest we turn back?"

Itaki pretended to have been dozing. "Why of course, my dear fellow. Excellent idea . . . your wonderful machine has all but lulled me to sleep." He sighed heavily, fingering his lower lip. "That old command car of mine is a torture chamber." Itaki gave his head a sad shake. "A real torture chamber."

Tanaka's groan was nearly audible; he was to be dealt the ultimate humiliation. Simply to admit defeat wasn't enough. He would be made to grovel. His mouth was dry and his tongue felt swollen and useless. He cleared his throat weakly, not at all certain he'd be able to speak. "Well, Colonel Itaki," he began in a strained voice, "we're old comrades and have been loyal friends for many years." He was tempted to hark back to the happy days when they'd been cadets together at the Military College, but recalled in time how they used to snap wet towels at the naked Cadet Itaki, laughing as the welts appeared on his fat flesh and threatening him with the loss of his tiny penis if he didn't keep it covered. Itaki had probably not forgotten it . . . it would be like him to hold a grudge.

Tanaka took a deep breath. "Please permit me to present the car to you as my poor but sincere gift," he went on, tears of frustration welling into his eyes. "Traveling to out-of-the-way places the way I do, a smaller car will be more suitable. The motor pool will have something, I'm sure." So there it was: done. Tanaka choked back a sob.

A smile of delight creased Itaki's face, and his hands quivered ecstati-

[325]

cally. "How generous, my dear old friend! You can be sure I shall gratefully continue to report your activities to the General in the most flattering light." Itaki hummed happily for a moment, stroking the upholstery with both hands. "You must have my command car . . . it's the best one in the motor pool. I'll give the necessary instructions myself."

"The Colonel is too kind," Tanaka said.

"No trouble at all," Itaki said. "By the way, why not save us both some time . . . let me drop you off at your house. I'll send your driver back in the morning with my car. How does that sound?"

The man was without mercy, Tanaka realized, too sorely tried to protest. He was to be stripped of all dignity, left naked and humbled even in the eyes of his own driver. "If the Colonel wishes," he said meekly.

On the way back Itaki gabbled happily about the car and about a party he was planning for the following week to which Tanaka was, of course, cordially invited, and on and on . . . Tanaka could hardly bear to listen. He sat as though made of stone, unable to do more than mumble an appropriate monosyllable from time to time.

In front of his residence he got down, feeling like an old man. After instructing his driver, he turned and saluted the Chief of Staff.

Itaki's face appeared in the window like a moon. "By the way, my dear Tanaka, I almost forgot . . ." He eyed the stolid profile of the driver, then lowered his voice. "I'm afraid those special orders you were expecting will not be forthcoming after all. The Kempeitai are sending their own man out from Tokyo, and will set things up independent of the Army." Itaki's smile broadened perceptibly. "The General is furious, of course." Replacing the cigar stub in his mouth, Itaki touched the visor of his cap. "Goodnight, my dear Tanaka," he said.

Blinking and swallowing as bravely as he was able, Tanaka stood in the road and watched the twin tail lights blur and fade in a small cloud of dust, listening to the deep smooth purr of the engine recede into the distance.

As he turned wearily toward the house, he heard the telephone begin to ring. Would they never leave him alone? he wondered dejectedly.

☆☆

Unwilling to risk passing anywhere near the Wu-feng Hu-tung, Edgerton dismissed the taxi on Ch'ang An Chieh.

It was just after midnight. He couldn't believe so little time had passed . . . it seemed like hours since he'd started across that weedy yard. And when he'd pulled Tamara toward the end of the *hu-tung,* he'd thought the worst of it was just beginning. In his mind, long, unfamiliar reaches of the city had stretched ahead of them, with the unknowns of the warehouse yards to be negotiated first.

But Li, that most inestimable of friends, had paved the way. A sympathetic watchman had been there to lead them through as soon as they'd clambered over the wall, and a taxi was waiting in the street.

"How are those Chinese feet holding up?"

"They'll make it," Tamara said bravely, giving him her hand.

A thin moon rose from behind a low range of bulbous clouds, silhouetting the massive tower of Hata Men and laying a feeble silver wash of light on the empty glacis.

Suddenly able to see more clearly, Edgerton wondered about Tanaka, and whether he'd heard the news yet . . . and what he would do. But although he tugged a little harder at Tamara's hand, nothing seemed able to diminish the feeling of serenity which had been growing in him, a sense of things falling into place after a period of indecision, chaos, and confusion.

They'd said little to each other in the taxi. It hadn't seemed necessary. Exhausted by hours of fear and uncertainty and discomfort, Tamara had even dozed a little. With her head on his shoulder and his arm around her, riding in secure anonymity, Edgerton could have gone on indefinitely. There had been only one bad moment between them. She told him how afraid she was that he'd forgotten her, that he wouldn't miss her until too late. Bitterly ashamed of himself, he'd looked into her face for a long time, vowing silently never again to give her cause to doubt him. Loving someone, he had reminded himself uneasily, was going to require some thought and effort.

Lightning tore suddenly at the clouds, and a rumbling barrage of thunder rolled toward them like the firing of distant cannon . . . Cool air from somewhere touched him lightly, and he felt Tamara shiver. They had heard no thunder all summer . . . it made him wonder if what his nose detected could be the long unfamiliar scent of rain.

Briefly he thought of Sobolov and of his debt to the poor man. It seemed incredible that he should be dead. And grossly unfair . . . life had dealt meanly with him; he'd asked for little and received even less. All Edgerton could do now was make it up to the wife and child. If Mrs. Sobolov wanted to go to the States, too, it could probably be arranged; already he could hear Procter moaning about it.

"How are you doing, sweetheart?" Edgerton asked.

[327]

Tamara smiled at him, one hand sweeping back a heavy lock of hair. "Fine . . . I may never wear shoes again."

The lightning flashed again, nearer this time, and showed him the dark gleam of his car, waiting just beyond the empty polo field.

Edgerton turned sharply into the yard at the San Kwan Miao . . . too sharply. The car slewed to one side and a spray of gravel flew up from the rear wheels to scatter noisily against the wall. Suddenly euphoric, Edgerton laughed aloud.

They were halfway to the gate when it opened and Madame Liu appeared. She stood there for a moment, her eyes wide and unbelieving, the fingers of one hand pressed against her lips.

"Mama!" Tamara called, breaking away from Edgerton and running forward.

Instinctively Edgerton slowed his pace, wanting to leave them alone together. Beyond them, inside the gate, he could see Ch'en's figure hovering, a broad grin on his face.

For what seemed like minutes, the two women embraced in silence. Then, slowly, Madame Liu pushed her daughter aside and turned toward Edgerton. For what seemed an interminable time, she regarded him impassively.

Edgerton felt vaguely apprehensive, realizing that his resolution of his and Tamara's future hadn't really taken this disapproving, iron-willed lady into account. Recalling now her bitterness on their two previous encounters that day, he searched for some appropriate and conciliatory phrase, something which might begin to make an ally of her. His mind was blank. At a loss, he could only hold out his hand.

To his surprise, she took it in her two hands, holding it firmly in her cool thin fingers. Very slowly, she raised it to her lips and kissed the back of it. And then her eyes rose to meet his, and she smiled. There was a certain wryness in the set of her lips, the echo perhaps of the many things which would now remain unsaid between them, but there was affection and gratitude as well. It was her benediction.

His eyes misting unashamedly, Edgerton led the two women into the house. Ch'en approached tentatively, then fell back as though unwilling to intrude. Edgerton beamed at him benignly.

They were crossing the courtyard toward his bedroom when Edgerton became abruptly aware of Franklin Procter's white-clad figure standing beside a wicker chair, a bemused expression on his long face.

Christ, what now? he thought. "Well, Franklin," he said heartily, groping for words. "What a nice surprise!"

The platitude seemed only to perplex Procter the more, and Edgerton felt himself sliding toward the brink of hysterical laughter. "I'll just be a minute," he added weakly.

In his room, Tamara sank down on the edge of the bed, limp with fatigue. At his elbow, Liu *t'ai t'ai* cleared her throat impatiently, obviously anxious to get him out of the way so women's business could proceed without his unnecessary, not to say unseemly, presence.

Tamara looked down at herself. "I should have a bath," she said. "Maybe I can take one in the morning before I . . . ."

As she hesitated, suddenly doubtful, Edgerton could hear the unspoken questions about tomorrow, and the next day, and the day after that. . . .

Dismayed that he could have been so ambiguous, so equivocal, he sank to his knees before her and reached for her hands. "But, Tamara, you can do anything you want here . . . you're home now."

An unfathomable expression crossed her face, hinting at deep uncertainties. Through his eyes and his hands, Edgerton willed her to believe him. And finally Tamara sighed; slowly she smiled, her face lighting with relief. Very gently he kissed her. As he left the room, it occurred to him that he might at last have come home himself.

He found Procter impatiently pacing the courtyard, his expression one of mixed bewilderment and annoyance. Not even feeling guilty, Edgerton said, "Sorry to have kept you waiting, Franklin . . . should have at least offered you a drink. What'll you have?"

"Nothing, thanks," Procter replied frostily. He lowered himself into an arm chair and crossed his legs, his lips pursing disapprovingly.

Edgerton looked at him, feeling a certain contempt, "Well, then . . . to what do I owe . . .?" he began, grinning, spreading his hands.

Procter's face reddened and he straightened in his chair. "What am I doing here, you mean? When I got home from the British Legation dinner party an hour or so ago, Valerie tried to tell me . . . well, it was a most confusing story about Miss Liu being arrested. She seemed to think you were in some sort of danger. When I couldn't get anything out of your man on the telephone, I came over."

"Well, thanks, Franklin; that was good of you." Edgerton didn't know whether to be grateful to Valerie or not. "Tamara was arrested, but it's all been straightened out now."

"I'm happy to hear it," Procter said perfunctorily. He seemed only then to become aware of Edgerton's disheveled appearance. "From the look of you," he began disapprovingly, "you've gotten into a mess. As it will probably reflect on the Legation, perhaps you'd better explain."

Not caring whether it reflected on the Legation or not, Edgerton related briefly what he knew of events leading to Tanaka's phone call.

[329]

As he listened, Procter seemed to pale. "You agreed to meet this Tanaka *vis à vis?*" he asked incredulously. "That's most irregular!"

Edgerton felt his patience slipping. "Oh, come on, Franklin! Tamara was in danger. What was I supposed to do: wait until morning and go through channels? Cable Washington for permission to talk to him?"

"You might at least have informed me," Procter replied angrily. "I must say, I deplore your penchant for the unorthodox."

"There wasn't time; I did what I had to do."

Procter mulled that over unhappily. Then, sighing with something close to resignation, he said, "Well, I see Miss Liu is here now . . . is she all right?"

"Yes, thanks. All she needs is some rest."

"And the other lady . . .?"

"Her mother."

"The one who . . .?" Procter cleared his throat, his face pained. "I take it you obtained Miss Liu's release from this Tanaka?"

"In a manner of speaking."

"I don't like the sound of that, John. You're being evasive. For your own sake, I hope you haven't enmeshed the Legation in some wretched tangle. The Japanese are being difficult enough as it is."

"Don't worry about it. I may be a bit enmeshed, but I was acting privately."

"*You* can't act privately."

Edgerton sighed, but remained silent.

Procter pulled moodily at his nose. "I hope I don't get a rocket from Saito about your unconventional behavior."

"You won't, I promise." Edgerton said the words reluctantly. The fact was that he was just realizing that taking the whole mess to Saito had been unavoidable from the first. For the sake of the safety of the Liu women, if no one else, someone had to put a rein on Tanaka. If anyone knew how to accomplish that, it would be Saito. With Sobolov's mysterious death muddying the water, it became even more imperative. Saito would be glad enough to keep the coercion of Sobolov into "espionage" quiet. All Edgerton could do was hope his own fumbling forgetfulness wouldn't be exposed in the process. "I'm sure Saito will want to handle things discreetly," he added.

"Things? What things?" Procter sounded querulous. "Is there more you haven't told me?"

"Just a few details. Look, Franklin . . . I'm bushed. Can't it wait until morning?"

"It's morning already."

Edgerton had to laugh. "All the more reason to have a drink. I insist I need one, too," he said, going to the table where Ch'en had thoughtfully set out the ingredients.

When it came, Procter took the glass gratefully. "I wish I could share your apparent calm," he said. "To me, the whole business has the earmarks of ballooning into a very nasty incident. You're reckless, John. This predilection of yours for bizarre action, surfacing so soon after my assignment here, leaves me deeply concerned. You mustn't forget that *we* are the United States Government in this place."

The man's indefatigable, Edgerton thought. He held up a hand. "Please, Franklin, no more lectures! I'm sure I can explain everything to your satisfaction, but not tonight."

"And to the Minister's satisfaction? He's due back in a week, you know."

"I can try."

"Well . . ." Procter began, then let his voice trail off disconsolately. Turning his glass slowly in his hands, he looked around unhappily, almost visibly steeling himself for one last duty. Edgerton read his mind.

"If you're worried about how long Tamara will be staying, the answer is indefinitely."

Procter looked superior. "Don't be too sure . . . there are directives covering the situation. Perhaps you're forgetting that these are government quarters."

"Nobody'll complain if you don't."

"You're taking advantage of me," Procter said, injured. "It's most irregular."

In spite of his almost chronic impatience with him, Edgerton felt a rush of sympathy. As though somehow miraculously rejuvenated, he saw himself leaving the other man behind. Procter was too old, too cautious, too bound by antiquated conventions—unable to adapt.

"I intend to regularize things as soon as possible," Edgerton said, adding, not unkindly, "Don't worry."

Procter looked puzzled. "How do you propose to do that?"

"By marrying Tamara . . . if she'll have me."

A strangled gasp escaped from Procter's throat. Putting down his glass, he got out his handkerchief and mopped his forehead. "Oh, John!" he said, sounding stricken. "You really *are* in trouble!"

Edgerton grinned at him. "On the contrary, Franklin; I've never been in less trouble in my life," he replied, feeling the remains of tension and confusion fall away from him. Taking a large swallow of whiskey, he regarded his companion benignly.

[331]

Slouched in his chair, Procter was the picture of distress. "This will cause a dreadful flap back at the Department," he said sadly.

"Yes, I suppose it will. But console yourself: the Ship of State will hardly founder on account of it."

Procter wasn't amused. "You'll be finished in the China Service, I'm afraid," he said, a trace of doleful satisfaction in his voice.

Edgerton knew he didn't really mean it, that he was merely expressing an insistence that unorthodox behavior carry with it some built-in punishment. It was no more than a bit of harmless dogma: The Diplomat's Creed. It occurred to Edgerton that Procter might yet become understandable to him. He shrugged, pretending total indifference. "It may and it may not. Rules change as the times change, or so one hopes. Besides, maybe they'll make an exception for me, a reward for long years of devoted service and a generally unblemished record." Edgerton's grin broadened. "The Legal Section may, in its infinite wisdom, rule that Tamara is Russian rather than Chinese, thus obviating the question of future conflict of interest. I believe that the general rule provides that paternity determines in these cases." He chuckled in spite of himself. "The principle of *jus sanguinis,* I believe it's called."

Ever serious, Procter leaned forward in his chair. "Yes, that's right!" he said, clutching at this new straw. "I hadn't thought of that."

Ah, Franklin, Edgerton thought fondly, as he felt his own spirits lift. He hadn't thought of it before either. He'd been too concerned with the immediate problem to worry about long range implications. It *was* a straw, but the Department might just buy it.

With a sigh of considerable relief, Procter put his glass on the table and stood up. "Well, John . . . I guess I'll be getting along then," he said. Moving into the light, Procter fingered his bow tie, then coughed uneasily. "Please convey my respects and best wishes to Miss Liu." An agonized expression flitted across his face. "My congratulations to you both, of course. I hope you'll be very happy."

You hope, but you doubt, Edgerton said to himself, not at all disturbed. "Thank you, Franklin; I appreciate that."

"May I tell Pamela?"

"Of course. She'll understand . . . sooner or later."

Procter looked sad. "Valerie'll be very disappointed."

"I don't think so."

"Oh, really? Pamela thought you two . . . well . . ." Procter cleared his throat.

"Matchmakers are wishful thinkers. Valerie's very nice, but . . ." Edgerton stopped and shrugged. "I'll walk with you to the gate."

Valarie would understand far better than Pamela, he had a notion. And who cared anyway?

[332]

As he led the way toward the gate, Edgerton realized he was punchy with fatigue. The aftertastes of despair and self-recrimination still churned within him confusingly, mixing with his own uncertainties about the future.

Finished in the China Service, was he? Well, possibly. His light-hearted dismissal of that consequence of his miscegenation had been largely sham, legal technicalities to the contrary. The Foreign Service was capable of gargantuan stuffiness and, on that particular question, had a record of near-perfect intractability. Even if his arguments were accepted, it would be with deep reluctance. They wouldn't soon forgive him for pushing their precious rules out of shape and forcing sticky decisions on them.

But the sad thing, the thing Procter couldn't see, was that the issue was largely academic. The China Service, as they had known it, was on its last legs, and the China it had been devised to deal with was very nearly finished. No matter who won the war, China would never be the same. Jimmy Chang was right, and it hurt.

Edgerton didn't like to think about it. Buried deep inside him somewhere was the insistence that it was *his* China. No matter how that probably romantic notion might offend or amuse or annoy men like Chang or Li, or even Tanaka for that matter, what happened to China *was* his business. After nearly twenty years, he'd staked a claim and he was damned if he'd be run off it without a fight. Quaint heretic and boat-rocker that he might be, there was still useful work for him to do, even if it were only to find out what had happened and publicize the facts. But would anyone listen? Edgerton laughed in the darkness. If he made enough noise, they'd have to listen.

At the gate, Procter turned and shot him a quizzical look. "You've surprised me, John. I thought I knew you so well . . . earlier in the week when we were, ah . . ."

"Arguing," Edgerton supplied, easily.

Procter looked embarrassed. "Yes . . . but I had no inkling that you'd do *this*."

The emphasis made Edgerton chuckle. "Neither did I. I'm not quite the same man I was then."

"Can one change so in only a few days?"

"So it would seem."

Procter seemed to ponder that for a moment, then a rueful smile pulled down the corners of his mouth. "If that's so, I think I envy you," he said quietly.

Edgerton was surprised. As preoccupied as Procter was with his Legation's reputation, such perception was remarkable. Perhaps Procter would begin to understand him too. Made momentarily awkward, the two men stared at each other as though in the surprise at mutual recognition.

As the sound of Procter's car vanished into the quiet of Canal Street, Edgerton started back across the deeply shadowed courtyard.

A blaze of lightning burst around him, igniting the darkness. For the merest fraction of an instant, every minute detail of the courtyard was illuminated in the flat white light of a hundred moons. Then, seemingly overhead, the thunder exploded. Edgerton paused, listening to the blast of sound roll outward, reverberating across the restless city. For a moment, a vague terror gripped him, and a sense of futility. Circumventing a Tanaka as he had done—and was hoping Saito would do again—was the merest finger in the dike. Jimmy had been right once more: they were in danger, all of them, separated from disaster by little more than the whims of men like Colonel Tanaka. Edgerton had won one round, and he might win another. And after that . . .?

His spirits lifted . . . after that, there'd be yet another time to be met in its own way. It was enough.

Moving forward again, he felt compelled by an unfamiliar, driving instinct. It took him a moment to recognize it as man's primordial urge to gather together with his own and find shelter from the elements. The realization seemed to fill him with primitive strength. And he knew at last that Tamara was the wellspring of that strength . . . she was his own, his family, the hearthfire of his ancestors and the hope of his future and his sons.

As the storm heaved and rumbled across the sky, gathering itself for the mighty convulsion of its birth, a few great drops of rain began to fall, and Edgerton ran for the house.

[334]